STEAMFUNK!

EDITED BY

MILTON DAVIS

AND

BALOGUN

OJETADE

MVmedia, LLC
Fayetteville, Georgia

Cover art by Marcellus Shane Jackson

Cover Design by Uraeus

Editing and Layout/Design by Valjeanne Jeffers

Manufactured in the United States of America

ISBN 13: 978-0-9800842-5-2

ISBN 10: 0-9800842-5-3

First Edition

TABLE OF CONTENTS

STEAMFUNKATEERS, STAND UP!

I am a Steamfunkateer.

What is *that*, you ask?

A Steamfunkateer is a person who is actively involved in the Steamfunk Movement. If you are reading this book, then you are well on your way to achieving Steamfunkateer status and by the time you're done reading this anthology, I guarantee that you will be one with the funk.

The Steamfunk Movement is not a political party or interest group, nor is it a mass fad or trend. The Steamfunk Movement can be thought of as an organized, yet informal, social entity that is oriented toward the goal of cultural and historical awareness, enrichment and appreciation through Steamfunk—a philosophy or style of writing that combines the African and / or African American culture and approach to life with that of the steampunk philosophy and / or steampunk fiction.

Steamfunk was born when several authors of African descent who took a liking to—or, in the cases of a few, even loved—the literary and aesthetic aspects of Steampunk. These authors noticed that there was a deficit of stories by and about Black heroes and she-roes in the movement; and, as individuals.

They decided they would write Steampunk stories from a Black perspective. Some were also dissatisfied that most Steampunk ignored the "darker" aspects of the Victorian Era, such as colonialism, sexism, classism, racism and chattel slavery and wanted to write about those aspects in their expressions of Steampunk.

On a popular website, a discussion of Steampunk came up and the aforementioned authors agreed that they should put together an anthology. Author and publisher Milton Davis, who had published the definitive Sword & Soul anthology, *Griots: A Sword & Soul Anthology*, decided to bring thought into action and put out the call for submissions to the Steamfunk Anthology.

Author and Steampunk, Balogun Ojetade (yours truly) was brought in to work with Milton Davis as co-editor; and the campaign of raising the awareness of the Black expression of Steampunk, which we call Steam*funk*, began.

While many Steampunks choose to ignore the horrors wrought by colonialism—slavery, indentured service, sexism, classism—creating a world in which these things do not exist, or are sugar-coated so badly, the world might end up diabetic, we choose to look back at the world OUR ancestors and elders knew…the world we choose to express in Steamfunk; the world that provides a wealth of happenings, people and settings that make for great Steamfunk stories.

And to those who want to say "let sleeping dogs lie," or "let the past go," or some other insensitive nonsense: our MOTHERS sharecropped …our grandparents built the railroads…our great grandparents worked from "can't see morning" to "can't see night" for no pay. We grew up hearing the horror stories and the happy ones and they shaped and molded us, for better or worse. To *let go* is to let go of ourselves. Ain't gonna happen. Ever.

And now, without further ado, we proudly present for your reading pleasure…

The *Steamfunk!* Anthology!

—*Author Balogun Ojetade, 2013*

THE DELIVERY

MILTON DAVIS

"Wait—don't open your eyes yet! I'm undressed!"

Of course I opened my eyes, or should I say my employer opened my eyes for me. I watched unemotionally as she bounded across the cabin, her ample brown buttocks bouncing with each step. She grabbed her bed sheet and wrapped it tight around her body, but leaving it low enough to expose her cleavage. Her bosom was acceptable exposure. All else was to be hidden until her betrothal to my employer.

"I didn't see a thing!" Anthony Wainwright squawked through my vocal chambers.

It was a poor facsimile of his voice, but you get what you pay for. I've been equipped with far better vocal receptors but Anthony was a frugal man. Every aspect of this assignment suffered from his frugality. There was nothing about him that indicated he would make a suitable husband, but the woman staring into my faceplate didn't seem to care. She was in love, as was he, a situation that allowed for all types of shortcomings with both parties involved.

She caressed my faceplate lovingly as if the real man sat before her.

"I really don't mind if you did, my love," she purred. "Soon I will be yours."

"Yes, you will," he answered. "I can't wait to hold you in my arms."

"How has your trip been?" he asked.

A frown returned to her girlish face. "Terrible! This is the worst airship ever! The cabin is cramped and your doppelganger is too loud. It steams up the place, too."

"I'm sorry, precious," he squawked. "It will be over soon. Once you land in Terminus my men will meet you and the doppelganger will be on its way."

"I don't see why you sent this thing anyway," she pouted.

"It was necessary, sweet one, you know this," he said. "Be patient for two more days. I'll more than make up for it."

"I'll make sure you will," she replied.

"This is Bell Telegraph and Imaging Service. To continue communications please deposit one nickel."

"I must go, buttercup. I love you!"

She kissed my faceplate. "I love you too, Anthony!"

I watched her expression change as his face faded, a sad smile replace by a stony stare.

"What are you looking at," she growled. "Turn yourself off or something!" She dropped the bed sheet and stormed to her dresser, removing her undergarments and dressing. I sat silently, my engine chugging softly. She was quite beautiful indeed.

She brushed her hair as she hummed a joyful tune, one I did not recognize. After a moment she noticed my stare and snarled.

"Didn't I tell you to shut yourself off!" she screeched.

"I'm sorry, Miss Applegate, but that is not possible," I replied. "You filled my reservoir."

"Then go do something! I want to be alone!"

I stood and grabbed my wheel bag. "As you wish, Miss Applegate. When do you wish for me to return?"

"Never!"

"That's not possible, ma'am. I'm instructed to escort you to Mr. Wainwright. My contract states..."

"Just *go!*"

I nodded and exited the cabin. Miss Applegate was not my most difficult employer but she was surely the most volatile. Her emotional swings were epic and her commands usually made no sense. Still, I had a reputation to uphold. GWC Factories prided itself on the performance of its escorts and I was considered one of its best. I could not, would not, let Mr. Carver down.

I walked down the narrow passageway to the lift. I entered then pressed and held the button for the steam deck. The lift rose slowly. It was an inferior contraption, much slower than those at the Factory. I should have expected so. U.S. machinery was adequate but behind that of the United Kingdom, which in turn was far behind Freedonian ingenuity.

It was not a fair comparison, for neither country had access to the genius possessed but my creator, George Washington Carver. Freedonia was loath to share his talents, for many of his inventions gave our young nation a military advantage as well. There was some speculating that Freedonia was working on an army machines similar to me as well. This speculation was, of course, spurred by the Southerners. Who else would envision such a use of us?

The lift halted. I slipped open the door and stepped into the furnace room. Five soot-covered faces turned toward me; each one smiling. It was a much better reception than that of Miss Applegate.

"Okay boys, break is here!" Thaddeus Bridges, the shoveler-supervisor, clapped coal dust from his hands. He was a short man and shaped like an egg with arms.

"It's about time you got here, puppet man. We were about to come fetch you."

"Helping you is not my obligation, Mr. Bridges. This you well know."

"He knows," Percy Stiles said. Percy was a narrow man whose body did not reflect his strength or stamina. "We're glad for the help."

The other men said nothing. They grunted as they shoved past me, each one cutting angry glances. Southerners, no doubt. One smacked his shovel against my leg, a wasted gesture. Pain was not one of my attributes; though if he knew anything about my construction he could have ruptured a steam tube with a well place poke behind my knee.

I picked up a shovel and proceed to toss piles of coal into the furnace. Mr. Stiles joined me.

"Your help is not necessary," I said.

"You told me that before. It's not polite to leave all this work for one..."

"I am not a man, sir. There is no need for you to feel your words may offend me. They do not."

"Well, anyway..."

I worked throughout the night. Mr. Stiles kept pace for a few hours then retired with his friends, occasionally reappearing to fill my water and oil reservoirs. As the sun appeared over the horizon I relented, bidding the workers farewell and returning to the cabin. Miss Applegate was not only awake but fully dressed. She smiled at me, and did a pirouette.

"How do I look?"

"You look grand," I replied. She had forced herself into a yellow, spring dress that was obviously too small for her healthy frame. Her white gloves complemented her hat and her laced boots. She seemed eager to impress my employer.

"How long before we land?" she asked.

"Another hour at least, Miss Applegate," I replied. My timing wheel clicked. "Fifty-nine minutes to be exact."

She pouted, plopped onto her bed and I heard seams rip.

"This is taking too long!" she whined.

I stepped to the viewing port. New York City loomed in the distance, her towering skyline rising with every mile sailed. Dirigibles littered the sky like silvery clouds, drifting between columns of smoke and steam. Our destination was the Port Authority, the only area with platforms large enough to accommodate our craft.

"You can see the city if you like, Miss Applegate," I said. She scurried to the port and shoved me aside, her childlike exuberance reminding me of the children that visited the Institute with their parents.

Our dirigible landed minutes later. I followed Miss Applegate to the welcome pad, my wheel bag in my right hand, her luggage in my left. A small crowd of people waited and waved as we exited. As the other passengers and crew members met with friends and loved ones, we waited for Mr. Wainwright to appear. But the crowd dwindled until there was no one but Miss Applegate and I.

"I don't understand," Miss Applegate said. "He said he'd be here."

She looked at me, tears welling in her eyes. "Where is he?"

I checked my time wheel. He was definitely late. Thirty minutes late, to be exact.

"I have no idea, Miss Applegate," I replied.

Miss Applegate began to cry uncontrollably. I was perplexed. This had never happened before. Escorts were simple tasks requiring simple memory wheel configurations. My proprietor did his utmost to screen all potential clients, especially when involving international business.

Freedonians were not well liked in the U.S., especially among the Southern refugees who'd chose to flee the region rather than be subject to rule under the new government. Contractually I was not obligated to do anything further, but leaving Miss Applegate under such dire circumstances was unacceptable.

"Miss Applegate," I finally said, "due to the circumstances I think it would be best that we returned to Freedonia."

"No!" she screamed. "Anthony will be here! I know he will!"

"Do you have his telegraph code?" I asked.

A smile emerged on her face. "Yes, yes I do!"

"We should go to the platform station and communicate with him then," I said. "Maybe there is some reason for his delay."

We were proceeding to the office when a steam car sped onto the platform, heading in our direction. The vehicle pulled up to us and the door swung open. A large man stepped out, draped in a ragged suit and hat. The smile on his face seemed forced; his disdain for me was obvious.

"Miss Applegate," he said in a thick Southern drawl.

Miss Applegate's face brightened. "Yes?"

"My name is Beauregard Clinton. Anthony sent me to bring you to his home." He glared at me. "Your services are no longer needed."

Something was amiss. "Miss Applegate, please don't go with this man."

"It's alright," she said. "Thank you for your service. Your proprietor will receive the remainder of his payment as soon as I'm with

Anthony."

I took a step toward her. "Miss Applegate, I'm..."

Mr. Clinton shoved me away. "You heard the lady. Your services are no longer needed."

Miss Applegate stepped into the car. I reached out and grabbed Mr. Clinton's coat.

"Sir, I think we need to discuss this."

He turned toward me, a revolver in his hand.

"Let go of me, puppet nigger!"

He fired twice. The impact knocked me to the ground. The first bullet ricocheted off my breastplate and struck him in the shoulder. He yelped and fell back into the car. The second struck the steam vein controlling my right arm. The arm fell limp. I watched as they sped away.

Men were running toward me from the platform office while others chased the steam car waving their hands. The revolver extended from the window and more shots were fired, scattering the pursuers. The first man to reach me was Mr. Stiles.

"What the hell is going on, puppet man?" he asked.

"I don't know," I answered.

Others began to gather around me. I tried to stand but I was damaged. I was losing steam. Mr. Stiles noticed my situation and reacted quickly.

"Bring me a tool box!" he yelled. "And water!"

He took a handkerchief from his back pocket and secured my leak. "Is Miss Applegate in that car?" he asked.

"I'm afraid so, sir," I replied. "It's seems she's been abducted."

"I thought so. The police are on their way."

Mr. Stiles was very handy. He replaced my damaged vein quickly, filled my reservoir and added a few lumps of coal to my breast furnace. The police arrived as he replaced his tools. Both men wore light blue uniforms with firearms holstered at their sides. One looked at me with surprise, while the other with the red hair and billowing mustache smirked.

"By my mother's grave!" the black-haired one said.

The redheaded man frowned. "You never seen a puppet man before? Damn you Irish bumpkins."

He turned to Mr. Stiles. "What's going on here, flyboy? They say there was a shooting."

"Yes there was, officer," I said. The red-haired man looked astonished.

"You can *talk?*" he said.

"Yes," I answered. "I accompanied a Miss Applegate to your city to meet her future husband. He did not meet us at the appointed time. Instead two men pretending to represent him appeared and absconded with Miss Applegate."

The red-headed man scowled. "Damn Southern kidnappers! They'll hold her until her family pays a nice ransom for her."

"I can't allow that to happen," I said. "I will need your assistance."

"Not our jurisdiction," the black-haired policeman said. "This is international. You'll have to take it up with the Freedonian embassy."

The redheaded man had wandered to my bag and began poking it with his baton.

"Please sir, I would prefer you not do that."

His face took on a suspicious look. "Something to hide, maybe?"

I stood and walked to him. "No sir, this is my wheel bag."

He scratched his head. "Your what?"

I opened the bag and showed him the collection of still discs. "These are my command wheels. They tell me what to do."

"Well, anyway. We can't help you. You best be getting on to the embassy. Although I'll tell you, that won't help much either. We Americans ain't exactly on good terms with Freedonia."

"Thank you for your help, sirs," I said.

The policemen strolled away, the black-haired one glancing back with his eyebrows raised.

"I'm sorry they couldn't help," Mr. Stiles said. "I'm really sorry about Miss Applegate."

"Can you take me to a telegraph?" I asked him.

"Uh, sure I can," he said. "What's going on?"

"I need to make a call," I replied.

I followed Mr. Stiles into the platform office. A group of workers lounged about; apparently it was their break time. They eyed me curiously, though not as intensely as the 'Irish' policeman.

"Make room, fellas," Mr. Stiles said. "We need to use the telegraph."

The telegraph was in sorry shape, but it wasn't the device I needed. I went to it and disconnected the wires.

"Hey! What are you doing?" one of the office men shouted.

"I need these wires for a moment, sir," I replied. "I am in great need to communicate with my proprietor."

The man marched towards me. "You can't just come in here and..."

Mr. Stiles blocked his way. "Give it a rest, Harry. He's trying to rescue Miss Applegate."

"How's he going to do that?" The man called Harry scowled. "He's a puppet man."

I connected the wires to the terminals at the base of my neck.

Using my internal telegraph, I sent a message to the Factories. In moments I was connected directly to Mr. Carver.

"What seems to be the problem?" he asked

"Miss Applegate has been abducted," I answered. "The local authorities advise that I contact the Freedonian Embassy. I wished to consult with you, sir, before following through."

"You did the right thing," Mr. Carver answered. "We don't want to get the Embassy involved in such matters. It could affect our business. You'll have to find her yourself."

"I am not capable," I answered. "I don't have the proper wheels installed."

"You have your bag, don't you?"

"Yes I do, sir."

"Is there anyone nearby that is mechanically capable?"

"Yes there is, sir. Mr. Stiles."

"Good, allow me to speak with him."

I tapped Mr. Stiles on the shoulder. "Sir, my proprietor would like to speak with you."

Mr. Stiles' eyebrows rose. "Speak with me? How..."

He stumbled back when Mr. Carver's face appeared on my faceplate.

"Mr. Stiles?"

Mr. Stiles pulled up a chair and sat hard. "Mr. Carver?"

"Nice to make your acquaintance. I have a task for you if you're up to it. I am not asking for free service; you will be well compensated for your assistance."

The man called Howard looked over Stiles's shoulder. "Is that Mr. Carver? *The* George Washington Carver?"

"Be quiet!" Mr. Stiles snapped. "What is it you would like me to do, Mr. Carver?"

"I need you to make a few modifications on my man," he said. "It involves replacing his current wheels with a few in his bag. It's a lengthy task that takes delicate precision. Are you capable of such work, Mr. Stiles?"

"Yes I am, sir," Mr. Stiles answered confidently.

"I hope so. A woman's life hangs in the balance."

Mr. Stiles stood. "What do I do first?"

"Lay the escort on a flat surface," Mr. Carver instructed.

The only flat surface long enough to support me was the floor, so I laid there. Mr. Stiles slid my wheel bag to my side.

"That's good," Mr. Carver said. "Now let's begin."

Mr. Stiles was instructed to shut me down before performing the necessary modifications. When I resumed operation, I was immediately aware of my enhanced abilities. Mr. Stiles hovered over me, a worried look on his face.

"I did everything you told me to, Mr. Carver. He's still not waking up."

"You might have to go back inside," Mr. Carver answered through my voice box. "Something may be amiss."

"I am fine," I replied. Mr. Stile backed away with a smile as I sat up, then stood.

"How are you?" Mr. Carver asked.

"Better," I replied. I really was. I could feel things going on in my head that I'd never experienced before. Questions answering themselves, opinions forming, decisions being made. It was an exhilarating feeling. And that was the other new sensation. Feelings, or should I say, emotions.

"Thank you, Mr. Stiles," Mr. Carver said. "Escort, I believe you can handle the situation from this point?"

"Yes, sir," I replied. "I may need assistance later."

"Our resources are at your disposal."

Mr. Carver's image disappeared from my faceplate. I disconnected the telegraph wires and reconnected the telegraph.

"Mr. Stiles, if it is true that Southerners kidnapped Miss Applegate then our search area is greatly reduced. Is that true?"

"Yep. Most Southerners in the city live in the Dixieland borough. They pretty much have their way in there. But that's the problem. It's going to be hard getting in without being noticed."

"I understand. An escort and a Freedonian would stand out in an area that I assume is predominately white." Mr. Stiles nodded.

"Then we will have to find someone who will act in our stead," I concluded.

"I could ask Big Tom," Mr. Stiles said. "He's a Southerner but he's alright with black folks. I'm sure he'd take a look around for the right amount of gold."

"Where can we find Mr. Tom," I asked.

"In the Five Points district," Mr. Stiles replied.

"Then let us proceed, Mr. Stiles."

"Jimmy," he said.

"Pardon me?"

"Jimmy. My name is Jimmy Stiles."

He extended his hand. I'd never had a person wish to shake my hand. I extended mine and we shook hands; Mr. Stiles, I mean, Jimmy wincing. I eased my grip.

"I'll get us a car," Jimmy said. I watched him as he trotted away. I wasn't sure, but it seemed I had made a friend.

Jimmy returned driving a monstrosity of a steam car. The vehicle was clearly based on Victorian design. Freedonian steam cars were much smaller and efficient. Then again, the British did not have access to such a brilliant scientist as Mr. Carver.

The majority of the car was the engine which was situated at the rear. The riding compartment was large enough for two persons only. I was relieved that comfort was not a quality I required.

"Hop in!" Jimmy shouted over the engine noise.

We weaved our way through the dense New York City street traffic, our destination the Five Points district.

"What is this Five Points area?" I asked.

"They call it Five Points because five roads merge there," Jimmy shouted. "It's also a place where five different boroughs meet. Folks seem to be friendlier there. All sorts of people come to drink and dance and do whatever."

"Are you sure Mr. Big Tom will be there?"

Jimmy laughed. "It's just 'Big Tom,' and I'm sure he'll be there. He's the unofficial constable of Five Points. He's a fair-minded man and he's trusted. He's also big as a bull."

It didn't take us long to reach the district. Miraculously Jimmy found a place along the curb large enough for the car. Five Points teemed with people of all races and ethnicity; all mingling freely. It was a refreshing sight, one that reflected President's Douglass's vision of true equality.

Jimmy jumped out the car and waved me on. "Come on, let's go see Big Tom."

To say that I drew attention would be an understatement. Escorts are rare—even rarer in the U.S. since we are banned. I followed Jimmy to a large building occupying the corner of a wide thoroughfare. Music and laughter drifted through its, door as a constant stream of people entered and exited.

"Wait out here," Jimmy said. "I'll go in and get Big Tom."

A crowd gathered around me while I waited for Jimmy. The comments ranged from curious to insulting. Children ventured close to touch me and pull at me. Their parents scolded them and dragged them away. A sensation emerged and responded, forming a smile on my face plate. The expression seemed to disturb many of the onlookers and they hurried away.

Jimmy emerged from the building followed by the largest man I'd ever encountered. His eyes widened and he brushed Jimmy aside.

"You wasn't lying," he said in a thick drawl. "A goddamn escort."

"Big Tom?" I inquired.

The man stepped back. "And it talks, too!"

Jimmy stood beside Big Tom. "I told you. We need your help."

Tom folded his arms across his chest. "I ain't never helped a mechanical man before."

"You'll be paid for your services," I replied.

Big Tom scratched his cheek. "Well, there's a first time for everything. What to do I have to do?"

"A woman under my protection was kidnapped by..."

"Southerners," Big Tom finished. "They got a damn racket going with that kidnapping. They say they're raising money to fund an invasion of Freedonia."

"Really?" This was news to me. I blinked, activating my recording wheel.

"How could they do so?" I asked. "Wouldn't they need the permission of the U.S. government?"

Big Tom rolled his eyes. "Some blue blood got them all fired up. I say just let bygones be bygones. That President Douglass seems to be a fair-minded Negro. I'm sure he'd welcome them back, if they behaved. He never asked them to leave."

"That may be true, but I must focus on my current dilemma," I said. "It is important that I free Miss Applegate and return her home."

"Have they asked for a ransom?" Tom asked.

"Not that I'm aware." Another sensation emerged in my wheels. I later discovered it was called *worry*.

"Is there any other reason why Miss Applegate would be kidnapped?"

"Is she pretty?" Big Tom asked.

"Yes," Jimmy answered.

"Some blue blood might be looking for a new house slave," Tom said.

His words startled me. "House slave? Pardon me, but I thought slavery was illegal here."

"It is, but nobody cares what goes on in Dixie," Tom said. "If they don't ask for a ransom in a week that's her fate. Some blue blood will be paying that note."

"Then it is imperative that we rescue her as soon as possible," I said.

Big Tom nodded. "What she look like?"

I searched my image wheel and located Miss Applegate. I projected her image on my faceplate. Big Tom stepped back, his eyes wide. After a moment he leaned closer.

"She's a looker alright," he said. "Ain't no blue blood in Dixie gonna pass her up. We're gonna have to go get her."

"So how do we go about this, Big Tom?" I asked.

Tom rubbed his chin. "Y'all meet me back here tonight. I need to get a few things squared away. Eight o'clock, okay?"

"We'll be here," Jimmy replied.

Big Tom went back into the building.

"Could we stay here?" I asked.

Jimmy frowned. "No we can't. That's a brothel. Big Tom is a good man but he works in some bad places. We'll go to Piney Grove Baptist Church. It's just down the road. Folks there are Freedonians."

"Are you a church going man?" I asked,

Jimmy smiled. "When I need to be."

I followed Jimmy to Piney Grove Baptist. The church was almost empty. A few of the parishioners were cleaning the pews and sweeping the floor. A tall, thin man with skin as black as coal greeted us. His fading gray hair circled his head like a halo, and a pair of bifocals rested on the bridge of his wide nose. He smiled at both of us as if we were frequent visitors.

"Welcome, back, Jimmy," he said in a melodious voice. "It's been a while."

"Hey, Reverend Jones. I've been working mighty hard these past few months. This here is an escort from Atlanta. I'm helping him out for a spell, and I was hoping we could stay with you till nightfall. I got some business with Big Tom later."

Reverend Jones frowned. "Any business with Big Tom is bad business," he said.

"Sho' is," Jimmy replied. "This escort's proprietor was likely kidnapped by Southerners. We're going into Dixie to find her."

The Reverend's eyes became deep, his eyebrows bunched together. "Damned heathens! We should have wiped them off the face of God's good earth when we had the chance."

I was shocked by the Reverend's bitter tone. "Harsh words coming from a man of God."

The Reverend's eyes brightened. "A talking escort! Excellent!"

He stepped closer to me. "May I?"

"Of course."

The Reverend began to inspect me, paying close attention to my chest area.

"Aahhh, I see the steam is circulated to activate vocal reeds," he commented. "This is very delicate work. I bet you're a Carver escort."

"That I am. I'm surprised at your knowledge."

"I'm an engineering major from Morehouse," the reverend replied. "We built a few mechanicals, but nothing as elaborate as you. I wouldn't admit it then, but Tuskegee has a better department solely because of Mr. Carver."

He extended his arm towards the rear of the church.

"You're welcomed to stay as long as you like. Mrs. Jones is cooking dinner as we speak, and I'm sure you could use some oil and water."

"Thank you, sir," I replied.

"I'm assuming they'll be some other things you'll be needing if you're going into Dixie."

Jimmy's face turned serious. "Yes sir, we will."

"I'll make the arrangements."

It was then I learned that the Reverend was more than just a man of God. He was a Freedonian agent: a man assigned to keep tabs on the U.S. in general, but Dixie in particular. He reported directly to Vice President Tubman, as did all Freedonian agents.

Miss Tubman was a very religious woman, and she insisted that all her agents be the same. They were faithful and fearless, and one of the main reasons Freedonia has been able to maintain her freedom for so long.

Darkness was upon us sooner than any of us expected. We were resting in the church sanctuary when Big Tom came in.

"Hey, Reverend," he boomed. "I'm here to pick up a few strays."

The reverend was polite, but not friendly. "Tom."

If Big Tom was offended, he didn't show it.

"Come on, you two. It's time we went to work."

Jimmy tipped his hat to the reverend. "Thank you, sir"

"God bless you," he said. He looked at me and smiled. "And you, too."

We followed Big Tom outside.

"I swear that man hates my guts," he commented.

"Ain't nothing personal," Jimmy said. "He hates all Southerners. He's a veteran."

Big Tom shrugged. "We best be getting on, then."

"Wait gentlemen," I interrupted. "We have a problem."

"Me."

Big Tom grinned. "Already thought of that. Follow me."

We followed Big Tom down the gas-lit crowded streets to a narrow alley shrouded in darkness.

"I'd have a problem bringing both of you into Dixie, truth be told," Big Tom explained.

"Jimmy, you're dressed too good for anybody's taste inside. And you—" he looked at me— "are just *you.*"

He disappeared into the alleyway and returned with a horse and buggy. He reached in the back and took out a bundle of clothes.

"Put this on," he told Jimmy. "Escort, you climb into the back. Jimmy's my property now, and you're cargo."

I was immediately concerned. "This is a simple ruse. Are you sure it will work?"

"Sometimes simple is better," Big Tom replied. "Besides, I have a certain reputation inside. Nobody will look too hard. We can also use the wagon to sneak out Miss Applegate; if we find her."

I climbed into the wagon and slipped under the heavy canvas. My vision blocked, I became motionless as the wagon rocked back and forth to our destination.

Once I was under the blanket we set off. The wagon rocked as we rode to Dixie. There was little conversation between Jimmy and Big Tom, but what little I heard conveyed to me that Jimmy was nervous. He probably was not born a slave like President Douglass, and many older Freedonians. So he did not know what to expect when we entered the borough. I searched my memory wheels and experienced a new emotion, as I reviewed the images and words: *disgust.*

The wagon stopped.

"We're here," Big Tom announced.

The canvas lifted, revealing Dixie. The borough was not unlike most I had seen thus far: rows of brownstones bordering paved streets, illuminated by gaslight posts. The streets were more orderly, the abundance of plant life a noticeable and pleasant different to the stark appearance of the other streets.

The reason for such neatness appeared moments later. An old man, his skin brown like Jimmy's, pushed a trash wagon down the sidewalk, searching for trash. The man looked at Big Tom with an expression similar to those I observed on my memory wheel.

"Good evening, Mr. Tom," he said.

Tom nodded. "Moses. Are they at the parlor?"

"Yes suh, Mr. Tom."

"Good, I got somebody I want them to meet."

Tom came to the wagon.

"Escort, you stay in the wagon until I come for you. Jimmy, you come with me."

Jimmy seemed skeptical. "What exactly are we going to do?"

"These are the Sons of Dixie," he explained. "If anybody has your Miss Applegate it's them. I'm not on the best of terms with them, but tonight that's going to change. At least for a little while."

"Wait just a goddamn minute!" Jimmy exclaimed. "You ain't planning on giving them me, are you?"

"It's part of the plan, Jimmy. Just play along until we find out where Miss Applegate is."

I sat up with in the wagon. I was beginning to feel the same doubt as Jimmy.

"I'm not sure about this," Jimmy said.

Big Tom revealed a revolver, pointing it at Jimmy's head.

"How about now?" he said with a grin.

I climbed from the wagon bed. "Big Tom. This was not our arrangement," I protested.

Tom looked at me and laughed. "So what are you going to do? We know all about you escorts. You're designed to obey and serve. Damn Freedonian niggers got smart enough to make their own slaves."

This new emotion was called *anger*. I reacted before I thought — my left arm shooting out. I snatched the revolver from Big Tom's hand then struck his head with my right hand. I heard a loud crack and he fell to the street. Jimmy immediately knelt by his side.

"I'll be damned! You killed him!"

"Did I?" I knelt beside Jimmy and looked.

"We're in a world of trouble!" Jimmy whispered.

"Y'all come on," someone said.

I looked up to the face of the man named Moses.

"Sir?"

"I said come on. Help me clean up this trash and then I'll show y'all where them Sons of Dixie is."

"Allow me," I replied.

I picked up Big Tom's body and placed it in the wagon bed. Jimmy seemed too upset to help and Moses, despite his eagerness, was obviously too old to handle someone the size of Tom. The elder man came up to the side of the wagon and spat on Tom before pulling the canvas over him.

"I knows where dat girl is," Moses said. "Dey been makin' a big fuss over her."

Jimmy seemed to shake his fear. "They ain't done nothing to her, have they?"

Moses shook his head. "Bless the Lord, not yet. But we ain't got much time. Dey gonna sell her to an Englishman. He's gonna pay big money for her, then take her overseas."

I was curious about Moses's motives after Big Tom's betrayal. "How do you have so much information?"

"We ain't folks," he said. "They say anything around us like we

don't understand."

"So why are you helping us?"

Moses eyes went wide. "You hafta axe? I show y'all to the girl and you take me with y'all. That's the deal."

Moses led the wagon into the alleyway. "We don't have much time. The Sons is meeting a couple of blocks down in the Haney House. I can take you there, but once y'all get there you on your own."

As we crept down the empty street my wheels spun furiously. With Big Tom, I had an idea how we would free Miss Applegate. Without him, I had no clue. I would have to talk to Mr. Carver at some point. But how or where I did not know. A man and woman exited a brownstone ahead of us. Moses shooed us into the nearest alley.

"How y'all doing?" he said cheerily.

The couple looked at him with disdain. "Where you supposed to be, boy?" the man said.

"I'm cleaning the street, suh," Moses said. "Just being friendly, that's all."

They walked past Moses and the alley. Moses watched them for a moment then signaled us.

"Come on, now."

We turned the corner to a street full of horses, carriages and steam cars. The porch lamps indicated which building The Sons occupied.

"They in there," Moses said.

"Is there a telegraph inside?" I asked.

"Yes...suh," Moses said. It seemed at that moment he actually noticed me. He did well hiding his shock.

"I'll go in alone," I said. "The oddity of my appearance and my durability should allow me to overcome them. Once I secure Miss Applegate, I'll contact Mr. Carver and he will give me further instructions."

Jimmy looked at me crossly. "You actually think that's going to work?"

"Do you have a better suggestion?" I asked.

"Well...no, no I don't, but I'm going with you."

It was then that Jimmy revealed Big Tom's revolver. "Let's do this," he said.

"Please stand back," I urged Jimmy. "I must increase my steam consumption. This will make me rather hot."

Jimmy stepped away. I reached behind my back and adjusted my flow button. I began to emit a low chugging sound. Moses eyes widened and he backed into the darkness.

"God Bless y'all," he whispered.

"Thank You, Moses," I said.

I ran toward the door then bounded up the steps. I smashed through the front door of the home, wood and splinters flying into the formally dressed men standing nearby. I swung my head about as I ran through the room seeking Miss Applegate.

I discovered her sitting properly before the fireplace, her lovely brown face doused with fear. A short plump man dressed in a British officer's uniform stood by her, a proud look on his face. Southerners sat around them on ornate couches, smoking cigars and pipes. Everyone looked at me wide eyed as I charged into their midst, then shoved the officer into the fireplace.

"Escort!" Miss Applegate squealed.

I looked to her and nodded. "Miss Applegate."

The British officer leaped from the fireplace in flames. The others rushed to him as their cohorts converged on me. A gunshot stopped them.

"Everybody on the floor!" Jimmy shouted. He stood at the door, the gun raised.

The Southerners finally had a threat they could recognize. One of the younger men started toward Jimmy. Jimmy lowered the gun and shot him in the arm.

"I said everybody on the floor!"

The men quickly lay on the floor, their heads rose as they glared at Jimmy.

"Come on y'all! Let's get out of here!"

"Not yet," I said. "I have to make a call."

"We don't have time for no telegraph!" Jimmy exclaimed.

"How do you expect we'll escape?" I replied.

Jimmy looked at the prone men on the floor, each of them staring back with malevolent intent. He swept the floor with his gun as he walked to me and Miss Applegate.

"I got five bullets left in this gun," he revealed. "I can't' kill all of y'all, but I can kill five of y'all. When you decide which five are gonna die, start standing."

He stood between Miss Applegate and me. "So what's the plan?"

"If there's a telegraph in here like Moses said..."

One of the gentlemen looked up. "Moses? The street sweeper? I'm going to have that nig..."

Jimmy pressed the gun barrel against his head. "You volunteering?" he sneered.

The man dropped his head.

Jimmy's eyes widened. "Since you're talking, tell us where the telegraph is."

The man lifted his head again. "Find it yourself!"

"I know where it is!" Miss Applegate offered. "They used it to contact Colonel Wainwright!"

The British military man moaned at the mention of his name.

"It's upstairs."

I looked at Jimmy with worry, reluctant to leave him alone.

"Y'all gone ahead. These fellas don't feel like dying yet."

I turned to Miss Applegate. She looked at Jimmy with a slight grin and a gleam in her eyes.

"Miss Applegate?"

Her head snapped my way. "Yes, right. Follow me."

Miss Applegate led me up the stairs to a sitting room. The telegraph rested on a table near the wall.

"I will need your assistance," I said to her. I disconnected the wires and had Miss Applegate attach the wires to my contacts. In moments Mr. Carver's face appeared on my faceplate.

"Ah, Miss Applegate! I see my escort has located you. I believe you are safe now?"

"No, sir," I replied. "We are in a home used as a meeting place for militant Southerners. I'm sure we'll need some assistance to leave."

Mr. Washington rubbed his chin. "I'll contact the ambassador. I think we may have a few Dragonflies close enough to reach you in a few minutes. Take Miss Applegate to the roof and wait."

Mr. Carver's words were interrupted by gunfire then rapid footfalls.

"Miss Applegate! Escort!" Jimmy shouted.

"I believe we'll need those Dragonflies soon than later, Mr. Carver," I said.

"I'll do what I can," Mr. Carver replied. "You do what you must."

His words sparked a strange sensation in me: one which I later learned is called *duty*.

"I will, sir."

I disconnected myself then led Miss Applegate into the hallway. Jimmy was at the top of the stairs. He fired two shots then looked at us.

"That's the last of the bullets," he said.

I went back into the sitting room. There was a large couch in the corner. I lifted it over my head and returned.

"Jimmy, please take Miss Applegate to the roof. Mr. Carver is sending a Dragonfly to rescue you."

Jimmy and I exchanged places.

"We're coming to get you, boy!" someone shouted. "You and that damn mechanical man!"

I waited until the Southerners began their ascent before throwing the couch down the stairs. I turned to get more furniture and saw Jimmy and Miss Applegate still standing in the hallway.

"Please, you must hurry," I said. "The Dragonfly will be here soon."

"What about you?" Jimmy asked.

"I will do my best to delay these men. Hopefully the Dragonfly will arrive soon for you."

I saw Miss Applegate's eyes glisten. "But what about you?"

"Do not worry about me," I replied. "I am a machine. I can be repaired. You cannot. Now go."

Jimmy and Miss Applegate reluctantly climbed the stairs to the roof. I rapidly grabbed furniture and piled it onto the stairs below. The Southerners cursed and fired their guns at me, but I continued until the stairwell was completely blocked. I then followed my companions to the roof.

A cool wind blew across the rooftops. Miss Applegate stood shivering, Jimmy holding his arms around her to provide her warmth. We could hear the Southerners clamoring with the furniture. The pile would hold them for a while but not forever. I scanned the horizon, shifting my energies to my vision lenses. After a few minutes I spotted a faint light in the distance.

"The Dragonfly is coming," I said. The craft appeared over us minutes later, its cyclo-propellers buzzing in the night. The bottom hatch opened and a rope ladder fell to the roof.

"My word!" Miss Applegate exclaimed. "You don't expect me to climb that thing, do you? You could see up my dress!"

"Ma'am, if you don't get up that rope those Southerners are going to get to see more than that," Jimmy said. "I think they're done being nice."

Miss Applegate hopped on the rope and climbed as fast as her daintiness allowed. Jimmy stepped on the rope then hesitated.

"Ain't no need for you to sacrifice yourself now, escort. You come on up after I'm clear."

"Of course," I said.

Gunfire erupted again. I looked to my right: the Southerners had climbed to the roof of the adjacent building and were firing on the Dragonfly. The Dragonfly tail gunner strafed the roof with his Gatling, and the men scattered.

"Come on!" Jimmy shouted at me.

"No, sir," I replied. "I must secure Miss Applegate's safe return."

I ran across the roof then jumped. My momentum carried me to the next roof. By the time the Southerners returned I was among them, striking at them as rapidly as I could. The Dragonfly rose higher then streaked away into the darkness.

Its timing was fortuitous. My motions were slowing and the Southerners gathered closer about me. It was obvious that my water reserves were depleted. I froze to a stop. The first men to me were burned when they touched me. The others threw blankets about me then lifted me over their heads.

As my last reserves were drained they threw me over the roof edge.

§§§

"Hello, escort."

My vision cleared and I stared into Mr. Carver's kind face. I looked about and discovered I was in the escort repair room of the university. I was sitting; my lower legs were being worked on by two apprentices, there dexterous hands weaving flow tubes around my pipes.

"It's good to have you back," he said.

"How are Miss Applegate and Jimmy?" I asked.

"They're both fine. Miss Applegate's father demanded the delivery fee be returned, of course, which I obliged. I believe Miss Applegate had found a match despite our failure."

"Who?" I asked.

"Your friend, Jimmy. He's been by her side since they returned to Atlanta. They make quite a couple."

It was good to know that they were safe. My wheels switched to other concerns.

"There was someone else, a man named Moses. He was instrumental in finding Miss Applegate."

"Moses is fine, too," Mr. Carver answered. "He used the ruckus you caused to slip out of Dixie and go to our embassy. By daybreak Dixie was swarming with Federal troops searching every house. The people the Southerners were holding as servants were our people: Freedonians. They came back on dirigibles and are in the process of resettlement."

It was good to know our efforts saved more than just Miss Applegate.

"How long have I been under repair?"

Mr. Carver scratched his chin. "About a month, I believe."

His answer surprised me.

"Sir, I am an escort. I believe it would have been an easier effort to build a new escort."

Mr. Carver looked thoughtful. "All things being the same that would be true. But all things are not the same. You're unique, escort. The way you process information is more human-like that any of the other machines. It's like you have your own personality. That was something I wasn't expecting. Besides, you're a hero."

"So what does this mean?" I asked.

Mr. Carver sat beside me. "Well, it means you won't be doing any more escorting. I think your skill would be better served as my lab assistant."

"I am honored, sir. What is it you wish me to do?"

"Ah, good question!" Mr. Carver jumped from his seat and scurried from the room. He returned with his fist closed. He stood before me and opened his hand.

"Do you know what this is?" he asked.

"Yes. It's a peanut."

"It's more than just that," he said. "Much more. This tiny seed is a miracle waiting to be revealed. You'll help me find all its secrets."

I was not excited about Mr. Carver's new endeavor, but I would do as he asked. He was a great man; surely what he saw in this seed was beyond my imagining.

After all, I was a machine. I always did as I was told. But I was beginning to think there was more beyond my duties. Maybe this project would show me exactly what that was.

"You'll need a name," Mr. Carver said.

"A name, sir?"

"Yes, a name. I can't keep calling you escort. You're my assistant now."

I thought for a moment, my wheels moving so rapidly they buzzed.

"Frederick," I finally said. "Frederick George."

Mr. Carver laughed. "Frederick George it is!"

I smiled. It was good to have a name.

Whatever the future held for me, I knew it would be more than I could imagine.

TOUGH NIGHT IN TOMMYVILLE

MELVIN CARTER

Rude awoke just as the wings of the *hopper* were stilled and folded back onto its upper fuselage. The landing had been perfect. Rude looked out the window and the night scene of activity. Overall-wearing ground crewmen were hurrying about outside—some going over the hopper for signs of any stress.

Others were rolling from the underground storage bins fuel lines. And there were those who'd begun unloading the heavier baggage and cargo from the hold of the hopper. All of the machinery was destined for Thomasville: a medium-sized city along the west bank of the Lanyard River, in the territory of Benedict.

Rude stretched his long arms and yawned audibly. The flight wasn't crowded; just a few soldiers in dress uniforms, a young missionary husband and wife duet, and some civilians who lived in or about the Thomasville area. They began to get up from their seats, stretch as he had done, and collect their carry-on luggage.

Rude reached under his seat for his black leather satchel bag. After a customary look inside, he unstrapped himself from his seat, stood up, threw his coat over one arm, put on his derby, and walked down the aisle of the hopper. The only passenger still seated was his "podnuh" of close to twenty years: the shaven-headed, barrel-chested, sun-darkened brown skinned, Philip Boatwright. Otherwise known to all as "Boatwright."

Rude switched his satchel to his left hand and flicked the ear of the still sleeping Boatwright.

After a moment of brushing away the annoying "insect," Boatwright opened his eyes, to see the smiling Rude.

"Say hey, Long Man! I take it this be the place?"

Rude "Long Man" Manners, was an eye-blink, fast gunman for hire and freelance bodyguard. He waited for his friend to gather himself, and made room for an attractive stewardess to pass. Then he asked her to give his compliments to the pilots...and whether or not this was a stopover for her.

"Any luck?" Boatwright asked.

"Nope," Rude said with a shrug.

"Her name is Brenda. You ought to find a way to bottle that charm, so I don't have to spend so much!"

"The first two bottles be free, Boatwright," Rude said. "The rest be at a special discount."

They walked down the ramp, laughing, but at the same time warily. The ground crew was watching them closely. They had been hired by a boss going by the name of 'Rip' Tatum, all expenses paid, plus $1800 walking around money in coins and bills. Tatum's ex-wife Gracie, and a river wolf and bushwhacker named Daddy Green, were making some serious nuisances of themselves.

According to Tatum's wire, there had been fifteen killings and a welter of both air and river hijackings. The regulars didn't care. No citizens had been harmed and their supplies for their upcountry forts and outposts were coming through. Out here on the frontier that was how things played out. Tatum wanted to keep them neutral. But if it came to an out and out push, he had no intentions of going out quietly.

"Let's take a stroll and see if this place has a passable diner," Rude said after a while, as the pair neared the terminal.

The fumes of the machines, fuel and workshops lessened as they stepped onto the sidewalk leading into the three-story, glass windowed building. The lights of the terminal were in contrast to the starlit sky above them. The ground-bounded lights of Thomasville were to the north: forming their own constellation.

Rude smiled, having read that particular line in a book in one client's personal library. It was Boatwright who spoke on noticing the two younger men at the terminal entrance. By their open display of holstered guns, it was apparent they were strikers. But whose?

One had the acne-scarred look of a delinquent. His heftier of build friend had the look of one who stabbed his grandmother for the last biscuit. The leaner delinquent brought a *type* out of his shirt pocket and the pair looked at it.

"Some welcoming committee, Long Man. I was kind of hoping for a marching band and a speech by the mayor."

"There's still time. They're probably in town setting up."

"Uh-huh!" a frowning Boatwright said. "That's what got me worried—being set-up."

Rude grinned, and then turned to look back upon the welcoming committee.

§§§

Thomasville had been founded one hundred and twenty-seven years back, and named after an eastern entrepreneur: Benjamin Thomas. Mr. Thomas and his public relation departments, both in-house and hired, had webbed a myth that portrayed him as a frontier-born, bear and buffalo wrestling hellion, who became both a guide and

later a scout for General "Ham Fist" Hammond and his elite Eleventh
Lancers. An all-around American Hero. The reality was that he had
only been west of the Lanyard and into the North West Territories
twice.

His only true adventure had been an upriver journey to get
trading rights with the Chippewa-Sioux. His second, was as an older
and wealthier man, dedicating a statue, to "Corny" Cornelius Opopo: a
real frontiersman among whose accomplishments were, he had
prevented one—who'd grown so fed up with Mr. Thomas's whining on
the expedition—from splitting his fat skull.

Over the decades the bronze statue became that of the 5'6"
potbellied businessman, rather than the 6'2" West-Man. Thomasville
had become an important trade hub by that time. Not even the tornado
of '67, the occupation by regional separatists in '73, or the subsequent
pitched battle in the Regulars counteroffensive had slowed its growth.

Nor had, fifteen years after that, the force of Tallyrandists from
New France, who in pursuit of the former governor of West Burgundy
—the cruel and unbelievably corrupt monarchist, Sieur Montaigne—
plundered and burnt Thomasville to ashes: leaving Montaigne's head
on the barrel of a rifle. Each time the town was rebuilt. New colonists
from the East and downriver came to settle in a region that had become
noted as rich soil farming country.

But because of the lingering effects of particularism, the
territory hadn't become a part of the Union. Despite the growing
numbers of citizens, and the presence of a large garrison, a succession
of opportunistic or just plain stupid politicians wanted to keep it
separate. And so too, did the outlaws: bandits, gamblers and smugglers.
Many of them were renegades from the established areas of the country

held by firmly rooted crime bosses. These scoundrels now had a wide open territory to make their own.

Such a man was Stanford "Rip" Tatum. He had parlayed a pool table, a green-felt card table, and three Ohio River Valley whores, into dominance of the shadowy Tommyville; or as he, and many others of both sides of the law, called "Thomasville." His first place was directly on the river. Any recalcitrant customer either wound up swimming or face down in the Big Muddy.

From there, Rip went into the barge/hauling business with an aggressive Rasta Carib, Royston Drowerd. From one they grew to a squadron of seven, and gained a four year contract with the Regulars. When Tommyville got an Aethernaught Terminal, there were soon three cargo ships in their own hangar— plus a smaller passenger liner.

Then Rip met the voluptuous, green eyed Grace Baptise-Neely from downriver Cameron City. It was P-whipped at first sight. Grace, after half-year of exquisite poise and manners, won over the legitimate part of Tommyville society. She made their women jealous and began making her own deals and taking up with lovers from all ranks.

Roys, one of the first, made the mistake of telling her that he wanted no more to do with the shadier enterprises. He was talking drunkenly of wanting to be bought out. His body was found, twenty-five miles out of town, in a shallow grave with six bullets in him. This blew the love haze finally from Rip's eyes. He sent Grace away with just what she had on that morning in their bedroom. The two strikers she'd had kill Royston were soon found too. But not whole.

§§§

Two years later Grace came back, accompanied by one of the Bayard District of Cameron City notorious stars: Lloyd "Daddy" Green. Lloyd was a smiling, 6'2", 314 pound, red-bone, black soul evil indulger. He led a pack of hijackers and thieves preying on both river and air traffic. Because he had contributed to the campaign chests of certain local politicians, he hadn't tested the durability of any rope in the public square. But an upheaval of reformers suddenly blew through Cameron City as suddenly as a hurricanes.

The jail cells and gallows began doing a brisk business, three of the previous administrations contributed to the well-being of the carrion birds. The idea of moving to relatively wide open country and possessing the enticing Grace had Daddy Green in a smiling mood again.

In the front of the terminal a line of carriages, both horse drawn and horseless, waited for customers. The lanky adolescent waved to a horse-drawn one which resembled one of the frontier stagecoaches. Rude suspected it might be armor plated.

The driver was a sun-painted Caucasian, proudly wearing a fringed and beaded jacket of one of the Nations, further west of where Rude and Boatwright were posted. He wore an upturned brim charro hat and a wiry nest of a red beard. The leaner striker went around the front pair of the six horse team, patting their noses, and climbed up beside the driver. Then he reached down and pulled up, a drum-fed, Hiram Bolt Thrower, pumping a round into the firing chamber.

"I ain't giving that one a tip. He didn't open the door for us," Rude said climbing into the coach.

"Now now, Long Man. You're expecting weasels to act like poodles," Boatwright said in an exaggerated aristo's tone of voice.

Once they were inside the well upholstered coach, they opened their satchels and pulled out their .45 automatics, slammed a magazine into the heel and put it into their flapless shoulder rigs. After a moment, walking ahead of the luggage cart jockey, was the more personable (if one who looked like a grandmother-killer could be considered personable) of the welcoming strikers who looked in the coach.

"You gents want your suitcases inside with you?"

"That's alright," Boatwright answered.

There were sliding, engraved metal plates that shut the windows. Also two inside lamps set on a low light.

"I almost feel presidential, don't you Long Man?" Boatwright said sliding shut the window where he sat.

"I'm thinking of my speech right now. Should I be a humble man of the people, or a lofty wordsmith?"

"Man of the people, some of your words might go over their heads. I know they do mine."

"Aw, Boatwright! You just being anti-intellectual."

"I ain't got nothing against Im-Piscopalians! That girl in Silver Springs was Im-Piscopalian. Some of my best friends... "

"Said you were the last to leave a party and the first one to start a fight over someone else's woman."

"That sir, is a slander! I was drawn into the melees, an innocent bystander, by the pleading eyes of the offended young ladies."

"That woman in Pittsboro wasn't so young. "

"Yeah, but her husband woke my ass up rather rudely!"

The two laughed as the sound of the loading of the trunk came to them. Then the burlier striker who gave his name as Dellums, got in the coach.

He pulled a silver flask from the inside of his bright colored vest. "It's local juice. Somewhere near the whiskey family."

He unscrewed the cap which served as a drinking cup, and poured what look like a citrus shot into it.

"May I?" asked Boatwright.

Dellums grinned, and some of the hardcore bravo faded from his features as he did. That changed to puzzlement, when Boatwright reached into his vest pocket and pulled out a rectangular card. He tore a strip from it and dipped it into the cup. After a few seconds immersion, he then held it up in the light of the lamp. That which had been wet, showed a faded green.

"Goddamn! It's alcohol and it's drinkable, but I don't know what sane person would want to!"

To show what side of the line he was, Boatwright knocked back the cup in a single gulp.

"EEyah! That'll burn off a hemorrhoid! Hey, Long Man, remember when we were posted to Fort Millard and were drinking Old Dirty Sock? Meet its cousin, Real Filthy Drawers! Don't be shy now youngster! Top it off!"

Dellums did. Boatwright screwed up his face, and then handed the empty cup to Rude. After Rude downed his sample he thought the name Boatwright gave it was too gentile.

There came a violent lurch, and then three shots rang out.

"Bushwhackers!" shouted the voice of the driver. A blast of a Hiram and the coach jumped into a full out run. The horses were strong but it was no telling how long they could pull this armored-up coach. There were bullet hits on the back of the coach. The Hiram boomed three more times.

Rude jumped to the front inside of the coach, and began banging on the roof of it. The coach slowed, and then Rude and Boatwright jumped out the doors. Rude rolled and came up in a kneeling firing position, both hands about his automatic. His pistol spoke at the onrushing horsemen.

A rider was sent backward out his saddle. Boatwright fired and another rider threw up his arms and fell from his saddle, to bounce along the road to wind up a twisted heap.

Rude fired and another was dropped to fall into the brush that lined the road. There was sporadic return fire from the now fleeing bushwhackers.

"You okay Boatwright?"

"These hicks done got me dirtied up! But I'm okay! You alright?"

"So much for my speech!"

"Let's see who these bastards were."

They looked over the three bodies. Collarless pullover shirts, gold hooped earrings, corduroy pants tucked into high top lace up laborers boots, was what they wore in common.

Boatwright voiced his opinion: "River Trash!"

"Yeah, must been sent to scoop us up by that sonofabitch Green," Rude said.

"I'm surprised they knew how to get on a horse, let alone ride one. If they had downed the lead horses, things would have been kind of hectic around this camp," Boatwright said before turning swiftly at the sounds of footsteps coming from behind them.

It was the two strikers. The full moon's radiance softened Dellums features some more; even making the Hiram bearing, pimply-faced man seem more presentable.

Boatwright in a more jovial manner indicated the bodies. "The welcoming committee. Anybody y'all know?"

After a moment of going over them, Dellums said, "They was Green's dawgs!"

"I dropped two of 'em on the run up to heah," the Hiram carrier said in a soft voice that seemed surprising coming from him.

"I had told Mr. Boatwright," Rude' said walking back to the coach, "that we'd be met by a marching band."

Dellums didn't know whether to take that seriously.

§§§

"Nulty's dead?"

"Is them two strikers dead?"

"They's the ones who chopped down Nulty and the others, Breen! If we hadn't of got in the wind the rest of us been stretched out beside 'em!" Tappan one of the surviving bushwhackers said angrily.

He was the younger brother and first cousin to Elmo Tappan and Petey "Pitiless" Pitney: two of Daddy Green's meanest old timers.

This gravel for brains Millard relied on that. Offa Breen would have killed him for being a mess up, if it hadn't been for that. That's what that gator souled Grace was probably going to do to him anyway. Dad had wanted to buy the strikers or buy them off. Grace wanted them dead.

She had wrapped the ambitious Breen around her honey-colored little finger. Whispering in his ear as she ground against his erection, how much Dad would appreciate if one of the Chickamauga

Breens had got the deed done.

§§§

The stage made a loop along the unpaved Old Road to avoid
any possible back up ambushes. Soon they came up on homesteads
standing alone. They neared Tommyville, moving into outskirts of the
town proper. Wood-frame houses gave way to brick buildings. The
cross-streets seemed to be as well kept as the main avenue. Two of
them even had a line of lampposts just as the main avenue did, on
either side of the street.

"That must have been some type of code you banged out to old
Kelly the driver," Dellums asked eagerly, with the look of a rookie
appreciating being let in on the conversation of veterans.

"He looked like he been on the frontier for a few days,"
Boatwright said.

"Garrison troops who pulled route duty detail out there,
worked out a code with the drivers—especially on them troublesome
roads. Got to lure in some bushwhackers and renegades who'd thought
had an easy swoop in."

Rude yawned, but nodded his head in agreement. "Put paid to
quite a few outlaws thinking they had struck it rich, right Boatwright?"

"The poor dumb bastards," Boatwright agreed.

The coach pulled up to one establishment on the main avenue.
Some well-played Hi–Di–Ho music came from inside, as well as three
happy customers singing the chorus off-key. The only thing that threw
off the relaxed atmosphere was three armed strikers in the front. One
was armed with what looked like a sawed off shotgun.

"Food any good here, Dellums?"

The food was good; and the waitress who served them made a pleasant eye-dessert to Rude and Boatwright. Rude paid and left a ten for the warm atmosphere. This earned him a beaming smile when she noticed.

They were shown to their rooms upstairs by a plump woman of mixed race, causing Boatwright to tip his bowler and wink. She chuckled and closed the door.

"Thinking on settling down, Boatwright?"

"I ain't been everywhere yet, but I can slowdown to take a better look."

§§§

Grace Baptiste pictured Daddy Green with a loop of his guts around his neck, swinging from a street lamp. It helped, since the man was now kissing her fervently. When he pulled back a line of spittle was upon her chin.

"Aw now Baby! You gone and took all my lipstick off," she said in her best genteel manner.

"That ain't all I like to take off! C'mere Woman!"

"Uh-uh! You got things to be thinking about."

He huffed and stomped over to the bar, pouring a large glass full of bourbon, and then drinking from the bottle.

Oh good shit, Grace thought frowned inwardly. *This lummox is gonna work himself up to do something real stupid, and I might have to kill his ass!*

She wore her purring, baby girl face as she came up behind

him. *If horns sprouted from his bald oblong head, he and the Minotaur could pass for brothers.* Grace picked up the glass and pretended to sip from it.

"How's the plan lookin' sugah?" She stroked his knife slashed cheek with a fingertip.

"They's should be pullin' up on 'em now," Daddy said. "They's wearing the uniforms of that outfit that was here a month ago... C'mon woman! It's been a week since we did it!"

"Time for celebration be when Tatum hears that last drumroll before the trapdoor opens. But just to keep you interested..." she began unbuttoning his pants.

Daddy Green was almost in tears.

§§§

The two citizens approached the one building on the street which had a lamppost near it. It was a partially whole one; the back part had been broken out by a thrown bottle. With hesitant steps, the two entered the smoky and funky dive.

One long, crowded bar with a cracked mirror behind it, hid four full card tables, a roulette wheel and two pool tables, an empty stand for the now on break musicians, a staircase, and a seated, bored looking guard with a shotgun in his lap.

Rude walked up to the guard. "You serious about your job?"

"What da hell you talkin' bout? Ya'd betta git out ma face!"

Rude drew his gun and blasted the man backwards from his seat. The crowd was hushed, then started screaming when Dellums shot a river rat brandishing an Illinois Tickler, and coming up behind Rude.

The pair raced up the stairs—shoving men and some females over the railing which soon collapsed.

Shots were fired at them. Those who did, soon fell dead or wounded from the return fire. Those hit by Rude were dead. A half-dressed man stepped out a door on the second floor a pistol in hand. Rude sent him back into the room and on the unmade bed. His straw-headed whore crouched in the corner screaming loudly.

He quickly slammed another clip into his .45. Dellums was reloading his .38. Four were firing from behind the bar. Rude could see them reflected in the mirror. He made a gesture for Dellums to race across the floor. Dellums gulped, and then took off firing as he did. The bartender popped up only to be slammed backwards into the shelf of cheap drinks.

The second man clutched the bar with both hands, attempting to bring himself fully erect. Death, brought on by the bullet hole in his left upper chest ended the river rat's attempt. The third crouched shivering in fear, splashed with blood and alcohol. The fourth lay outside the dive's swinging doors, a bullet in the back.

Grace made it down the backstairs just to run into the stock of Boatwright's short barreled carbine. Daddy Green stood silhouetted in the door at the top of the stairs, attempting to pull up his pants up over his knees with one hand, the other covering his deflating erection. Boatwright shook his head, and then called up pointing his carbine.

The pimply faced Hiram gunner was grinning broadly. "Gotdamn, fool! Pretend you got some class, pull up yo' pants and come down here and pick this heifer up."

§§§

Offa Breen was wearing the uniform of a Second Lieutenant in the 334th Artillery, when he showed his papers to the recruiting sergeant at the riverside depot.

"Your papers seem to be in order, but I be gotdamned if you are—sonofabitch!"

The last thing Offa saw, was the muzzle of the cannon that flashed a blinding light and blew off the back of his head. Millard Tappan, who was driving, screamed as the spray of blood, brains and skull spewed over his face. It was cut short by the rifle bullet that slammed him against the seat, to slump out the driver side window.

The false artillerymen began jumping from the three trucks, to run into the fire being put out by the forewarned guards. A corporal named Dills had spotted them from a side street blocks back. He had been sent on an ale run, and raced off as if a Tallyrandist cuirassier was bearing down on him.

The bushwhackers wore the parade ground uniforms of the 334th, not their work clothes. And they still used horses and mules to bring up their guns. The river rats began to give way to the accurate firing of the seven guards, who were behind cover.

Seeing too many of their own either still or writhing in pain on the street, they fell away from the trucks; only to be blasted by a volley from the recently landed half company of infantry from the outpost across the river.

"Fix bay-yunets! Work time!"

With that, the riflemen charged after the even more hastily disintegrating river rats. The officer in command and his trumpeter marched to where a wounded Sergeant. Brasse was being bandaged above his left knee, by Corporal Dill.

"What's this mess about Sam?"

"Hell if I know Mordecai! These sonsofbitches wanted to be dumbass traitors."

A young rifleman came up with two prisoners that he could equal in size— if he stood on someone his size's shoulders.

Corporal Dill began cracking his knuckles. Lieutenant Mordecai Evans pictured them on a gallows.

Rip Tatum stood when Grace entered the room; and then walked over to wear she stood to take both her hands in his. Daddy Green growled, but was beaten into unconsciousness by the butts and stocks of Rude and Boatwright's weapons.

"Baby, if you had waited another year I'd of taken you back," Rip said squeezing her hands between his, then kissing the palms of them.

"Really?"

"Baby didn't you see?"

Grace thought a moment then looked Rip directly in the eyes. "Yes, yes you would have. What can I do to make this all up to you sugah?"

" Die beyatch!" Rip drove his knife into Grace's side. She fell forward into his arms wide eyed, but smiling. Rip kissed her lips. She stroked his cheek.

"You were my real man all along. "

"You didn't believe me!" Rip shouted with tears rolling down his cheeks.

"Oh, I do now," she half whispered. And then she strolled

away into Death's embrace.

§§§

There were hangings all the next day, while Rude and Boatwright slept, Rude sharing his bed with the waitress named Paula. A small funeral was held with Rip Tatum following behind an undertaker's horse drawn glass-sided wagon. Inside was a fine wood coffin of simple design. Daddy Green wasn't found.

When Lieutenant Evans came into the office of one of Tommyville's councilors, Stanford Tatum, he found him in the company of Rude and Boatwright.

"Look a here! Look a here! They made Mordy an effin Prince," said an applauding Boatwright, putting his glass of real whiskey down and standing up.

Rude although still sitting, was clapping too. "So you and Old Grumpy Hamilton's daughter hitched now?"

The former "working man" Sergeant Mordecai Evans looked on his former comrades with a twisted look of surprise, happiness, and wonder.

Rude rose and taking Mordecai by the arm, turned to Rip. "Excuse us Mr. Tatum. We are glad for the business. But we must talk over old times with a soldier friend, until our flight back east. Take care now."

MEN IN BLACK

P. DJELI CLARK

Tall, green stalks slapped at Laurence as he ran. He might have been one of the smallest eleven-year-old boys in town, but it didn't matter if he held a strap of schoolbooks or no. He could run like the wind.

"Rabbit! You slow down!"

Laurence laughed, catching sight of Big Walter crashing through the field behind him. The boy was older by just a few months, but had the body of a small man. Mrs. Carver, the seamstress, whispered Walter was the son of some traveling peddler Walter's mother had grown sweet on.

When Walter's father heard this he'd stormed down to Mrs. Carver's house, telling her to keep her mouth out of his family's affairs, or he'd fill it with a rock so big she'd never be able to open it again. Mrs. Carver was so angry she threatened to set her husband on him. But Mr. Carver only laughed— even offering to help find the rock. For about a year thereafter, children left the biggest rocks they could find at her door before knocking and running away.

"Stop running so fast! I ain't no hare like you!"

Laurence slowed to a stop, fixing the bigger boy with an annoyed glare. "It's Rabbit. Y'all gonna call me a name, keep to just one."

Walter bent over, hands on his knees and gasping for air. "Rabbit, hare, ain't no difference. Both got big ears and run like the devil after 'em."

Laurence ignored him, turning to push apart some tall stalks. They were on a slight rise overlooking a town of wooden buildings and dirt roads where people milled about, laughing and carousing.

Reaching into his pocket, he pulled out a makeshift telescope he'd fashioned himself—from a bit of stovepipe and his grandmother's lenses. His father had been furious. But his grandmother always liked his inventions, and claimed she didn't much feel the need for the spectacles anyhow.

"You and your strange contraptions," Walter murmured.

Everyone thought Laurence was strange, the way he devoured stories about fantastic machines that might one day travel in the air, deep beneath the sea or even to the moon. He'd sit dreaming about such things for hours, and tried his hand at inventing whenever he could, just like the characters from his favorite novels.

"What you seeing through that thing?" Walter asked.

"People," Laurence replied. "Only close up."

There was a moment of quiet.

"I ain't never been to Whitewood," Walter murmured.

"It's just another town," Laurence replied. Walter was quiet a moment longer, gazing with him.

"Them sure is a whole lot of white folks," he said finally.

Laurence nodded. He certainly couldn't argue with that.

Whitewood was near all white, except for the few colored folk on its outskirts who eked out a living. His father often said with disgust that they lived like slaves. He didn't mean real slaves of course; that had ended almost forty years ago.

But they weren't like the Negroes in Blackwood, who had their own general store, school, and blacksmith—even a colored doctor.

Blackwood had grown larger than its neighbor, which was relatively poor. White folks knew it, and hated it. So they took their frustrations out on the remaining colored people in their town who worked for them, too poor to live in Blackwood.

Every now and again there was news of one running afoul of local whites. And people would talk in hushed tones about a lynching.

Those were the rumors Laurence heard swirling around Blackwood for a few days now. Some colored man near Whitewood had tried to force himself on a white girl. He'd been arrested, but already news circulated there'd be a hanging. Laurence had even seen a scrap of paper detailing it—complete with time of day and directions.

He didn't understand why if they knew they were going to hang this colored man, they put him in jail and pretended there was going to be a trial. He heard his father tell his mother, it had something to do with whites playing at being fair.

The thought that somebody who looked like him was going to be murdered so nearby consumed Laurence. Yet no one in Blackwood openly talked about it, as if the colored man was already dead. At dinner the previous day, he couldn't hold it any more. He brought it up. He even suggested that maybe Negro men from Blackwood could go with guns and protect that colored man, or get him out of jail.

He had thought himself quite clever. But his mother's fair-skinned face went ashen. She grabbed him, scaring him half to death and screaming he should never think about anything like that. His grandmother remained quiet. And his younger sister scowled, calling him stupid under her breath. His father, as usual, was an impassive mountain.

As Laurence lay in bed that night, he wrestled with his family's reaction. His parents taught him that he could be anything. They made sure he went to school, rather than haul ice for his father's business or work the farms of neighbors. Like many citizens of Blackwood, they were proud of all they had accomplished. Yet before these whites, they cowered. He hated that. And he hated knowing they would just let this colored man die.

So this morning when he awoke, he'd made up his mind. He was going to see this lynching. He'd skip school and probably get a switching if he was caught. But he didn't care. He was going to witness this terror that so frightened everyone around him.

"We won't see him good from here," he said, putting away the telescope. "We'll have to go down there: into town."

As expected, Walter balked. "You crazier than a rabid dog! Ain't no colored men in they right mind gonna be down there!"

Laurence knew Walter had only accompanied him on a dare; that didn't lend itself to any further courage. "We ain't men," he reminded his friend. "Just two boys. They won't pay us no mind."

Walter shook his head defiantly. "You out your mind like senile ol' Augustus Washington who think he Abe Lincoln! And I'd be crazier to follow!"

Laurence shrugged, pretending not to care. "Fine then. I'll just go on my own, iff'n you scared."

Walter stiffened. "I ain't scared none! Just got more sense than God gave a goat is all! What if them white folks set on us?"

"They won't," Laurence assured, although he knew no such thing. "We ain't done nothing."

The bigger boy muttered worriedly, contemplating doing what moments ago he'd swore against.

"Alright then," Walter said finally. "But we—"

Laurence never let him finish, taking off down the slope. Walter quickly followed. Half running and tumbling at times, the two reached the bottom, dusted themselves off and walked cautiously into town.

The crowd was larger than they Laurence had thought. And it was noisy. Children their age ran about, playing or chewing messily on watermelons. Men smoked cigars and laughed raucously while women in bonnets bantered away. If not for the thick rope dangling ominously from the dogwood tree in the middle of the crowd, it might be mistaken for a carnival.

"I don't like this none," Walter whispered, one eye on the crowd and one on the ground.

"Just don't look at nobody," Laurence whispered back. "Once we get to the front, we'll sit low on the floor."

"Why come you want to be so close? We could stay back some at least!"

Laurence didn't answer. He couldn't really say. It was just something he wanted to do. And when he had a notion, it was hard to shake.

"I heard bout this other hanging," Walter whispered. "This colored man was there, watching. And when he told them white folks they was wrong, know what they did?"

Laurence said nothing. Walter had a habit of asking questions he planned on answering.

"I'll tell you what," the boy said right on cue. "They hung him right there too—just for speaking his mind!"

Laurence tried to keep his composure while Walter buzzed on.

As brave as he tried to be, he had to admit he was nervous. There wasn't one other colored face here. He thought at least some of the man's family would have come out. But this crowd was as white as a cold day in December. He'd almost reached his breaking point, when a cry went up.

"They bringing him out now!"

A roar like a great beast surged through the crowd and they clapped in glee. Somewhere a fiddler struck up a playful tune.

"Well ain't that the darndest thing you ever seen?" someone said. "Two little pickneys creepin' through all of us like mice!"

Laurence looked up to find a man pointing directly at them. Several others turned to look with surprise. At first they said nothing. Then there came a flurry of questions.

"Where you boys from?"

"Dressed so fine."

"Them boys from Blackwood."

"Blackwood, with all them uppity niggers?"

"Thinkin' they betta than other niggers."

"Thinkin' they betta than the best white man!"

"Well what you boys doing here?" the first man asked. Each of his eyes was a different color, while his long matted beard was bright red. Laurence didn't answer. Walter looked ready to faint or cry.

"You come to see the hanging?" the man pressed. "Speak up now! Ain't you been taught how to answer a white man?"

Laurence finally found the courage to nod. There were cackles from the crowd.

"They come to see them a big one get hung."

"Push them through to the front!"

"Let them get a good look!"

Laurence felt arms grabbing and pushing them forward. It was frightening as the crowd hollered and urged them on. In moments they were up front, a few people pointing and laughing at them in surprise.

And it seemed they'd arrived just in time. A horse-drawn cart approached. As it drew closer, Laurence made out a bound figure with a black bag over his head sitting between men with rifles. The crowd began to yell.

"Take his mask off!"

"Let that black devil see a white man before he get to heaven!"

"Ain't no niggers in heaven nor hell! They end up where the hogs go!"

There was great laughter. And the black bag was lifted. Laurence gaped. For some reason he'd pictured in his mind a giant of a man, who stared down and frightened his captors. But instead there was just a smooth-faced boy, just on the brink of manhood. And from his eyes, he was frightened out of his wits.

"Please!" he pleaded, tears streaming his face. "I ain't done nobody no harm! I'm a good Christian, just like all of you! I praise the lord every day!"

"Pray all you want boy," a man spat. "But you gonna get this here rope today." Even as he spoke, the noose from the tree was lowered, a dangling promise of death. The young man screamed, trying to resist being dragged to his doom. But the crowd responded to his cries for mercy with curses and jeers.

"I want to go home!" Walter whimpered. "I want to go home *now!*"

Laurence turned to stare at the big boy. Walter was terrified.

And he had to admit, he was scared now too. The crowd had taken on a crazed look, eager for blood like pigs for slop.

As they fitted the rope around the young man's head, his eyes found Laurence and Walter. There was no contentment at seeing them. Not even bewilderment. There was simply a blank gaze, the only thing that could accompany such hopelessness. Laurence had to fight not to look away from his trembling face. The two stared at each other, as if nothing else existed.

A whooping cheer erupted as the man was abruptly hoisted up by his neck. Laurence watched in horror as his body jerked and dangled, his bound hands twisting to get free. A spray of spittle burst from his lips, as he sputtered for air. Laurence gritted his teeth, praying the man would die soon so they could flee from this place and these mad people.

A sudden rumbling jerked him from his thoughts. A blast of wind followed, buffeting them like a storm. Laurence pulled his eyes from the dying man to look. What he saw sent his jaw slack.

For a moment the air in the distance rippled unnaturally, like water. And then, out of seeming nothingness, there appeared a colored man.

Laurence blinked several times to make sure he wasn't imagining things. But no, there was a colored man. Tall and dressed in a dark suit with a top hat, he seemed completely out of place. But it was the figures behind him that gave everyone pause.

They were men, giant men, all clad in black. Each stood taller than even the biggest man Laurence had ever seen—and near three times as wide. Their faces and bodies were hidden behind great black robes with hoods. He counted seven in all, still as statues and ominously silent.

The strange colored man who led them pointed a black cane with a rounded silver head at the figure dangling from the tree. Immediately one of the giants lumbered forward, his footsteps a churning heavy sound of whirrs and clicks that reminded Laurence of a locomotive.

He lifted a massive arm, and from within his sleeve a light whistled like a bullet through the air. It struck the rope that held the man, cutting it clean. He fell to the ground, gasping and choking, but still alive.

"This man will not die here today," the strange colored man said loudly. "Not by your hands."

Laurence listened, stunned. He'd never heard anybody talk like that to white folks.

"Who the hell you think you is?" someone in the crowd growled. He stalked forward, several men behind him, all holding rifles.

"Who I am is unimportant," the stranger replied. "But you would be wise to heed my words." If he was the least bit frightened, he did not show it. The hulking figures in black behind him remained silent.

The mob leader said something like a curse, leveling his rifle.

But before he could shoot, one of the robed giants quickly stepped forward. He yanked the rifle from the startled mob leader, and snapped it in two like a twig. He reached for the smaller man, hoisting him aloft by his overalls before pitching him away. Laurence watched the man scream as he flew like a stone, clear over a building and from view.

Pandemonium broke out after that. Most in the crowd fled. A few stopped to shoot at the black-robed giant. They might as well have thrown grains of rice. He stalked forward, the bullets ripping through his clothing but bouncing off him easily.

He made quick work of the mob, tossing them about like dolls. Lifting his arm, he sent another shot of the odd light from his sleeve. When it struck a would-be attacker the man turned bright as the sun, before burning away like paper: leaving nothing but ashes. That was enough for the rest. They turned as one and scurried away in terror.

Laurence stared out at the dirt streets of Whitewood, now deserted, save for them and the mysterious new arrivals. He walked over to the young Negro man who lay on the ground, putting fingers to the rope about his neck. It felt thick in his hands as he loosened and pulled it free. The two said nothing to each other, sitting in stunned silence, until Walter ran up to them pointing frantically.

"They coming! They coming!"

Laurence looked up to find the giants clad in black walking in their direction, their pounding steps reverberating in the emptied streets. They were led by the strange colored man, who strolled confidently with his cane. Walter pulled on Laurence, begging to leave. But he stood his ground, wanting desperately to meet this stranger.

The colored man stopped before them, looking down. Laurence met his gaze and the two stared at each other. He wasn't old; probably near in age to his father. He was tall too, not bulky but broad and with big wide hands.

He wore a close-cut beard, and his set face gave off a powerful countenance. Yet it was his eyes that were most striking: determined, unwavering. It was hard for Laurence to keep his composure under such a glare. But his steadfastness was rewarded with a sudden smile.

"Laurence Johns," the stranger intoned with a deep voice.

Laurence's eyes widened. This man knew his name! Yet they'd never met before—he was certain. Someone like this, you didn't forget.

"Your mother wouldn't be too happy if she knew you were kneeling there dirtying those pants," he went on. "Best get up now." He offered a gloved hand, winking as if at some private joke. Laurence accepted his help, coming to his feet.

"And don't look so frightened Walter," he continued. "I'm a friend."

Walter looked ready to faint at hearing his name. But the man put a steadying hand on their shoulders.

"It's alright," he assured, as they trembled beneath his grip. "You don't have to be afraid. I'm here to make the fear go away, forever."

§§§

Laurence sat playing with the shining object between his fingers. It was a nickel, or at least it had once been: a Liberty Head five-cent piece of nickel and copper celebrating the year 1900.

It was a birthday present from his mother. He'd taken this one and placed it on a railroad track, wanting to see what would happen; and ended up retrieving a flattened wafer of metal. It had been one of his first experiments. He searched over its surface for any vestiges of the prior artwork. It was amazing how a brief moment of destruction could erase all that someone had probably labored so hard to create.

"Stop fidgeting!"

Laurence glanced up to his older sister. She scowled before turning away. He scowled back, stuffing the nickel into his pockets. He wasn't fidgeting, just bored. It'd been hours now they'd sat in this church, listening to people talk. It was already turning dark and he feared they might be here all night.

He and Walter had run all the way back from Whitewood. They'd only made it to the home of Elias Whittaker, a colored blacksmith whose house sat on the outskirts of Blackwood. He stopped them, asking where they were racing to—"like the devil was nipping at their heels." The two blurted out everything in a rush, before collapsing in exhaustion.

The blacksmith collected them, giving them water and then packing them into this wagon.

Moments later they were telling everyone in Blackwood. At first many scoffed. Big Walter's father even threatened him with a whipping. But Mrs. Carver, the seamstress, came running down the road—her long skirts hiked high.

Breathless, she began repeating a story almost identical to theirs, related from some of her poorer kinfolk near Whitewood. There were still skeptics but Mr. Carver, for once, backed up his wife's claims. That changed matters considerably.

Within the next few hours more reports trickled in. By afternoon church bells rang, announcing an emergency meeting. Now all the colored citizenry of Blackwood were gathered, eager to discuss these bewildering developments and what it might mean for their small settlement.

§§§

Laurence looked up to where his father stood behind the pulpit.
Reverend Johns was a big man—taller than most everyone in
Blackwood, with a barrel chest and fists like hams. People told
Laurence that despite his small size he'd grow up the same way.
Reverend Johns was a successful businessman, mayor and spiritual
leader of Blackwood. Expectations for Laurence were no less
ambitious.

From his position of power the reverend listened to the excited
crowd. Right now Paul Weldon spoke, the young colored schoolteacher
who'd moved from up North. With his honed speech, fine looks and
well-tailored clothes, Laurence had heard many men snidely remark he
was a "dandy," whatever that was. Women named him much the same,
but with admiring eyes. His sister especially giggled like a fool
whenever Weldon as much as tipped his hat.

"I'm not sure I understand," he was saying. "No one here can
name this stranger. But he can name our children? Perhaps he's lived
here before?"

"No colored folk like that from round here," Bernard
Pickerson, the postmaster, put in with his gravelly voice. "Colored folk
in these parts know betta than to rile up that lot down in Whitewood."
Murmurs of assent rose from the crowd.

"And what bout these men in black—these giants?" the
shopkeeper Dabby Mason asked, a round man with a demeanor as
relaxed as his drawl. It was joked Mason could catch on fire, and still
casually pump a bucket of water to put himself out. "What you
reckon's to be made of them?"

Weldon laughed. "Come now man. Do you really believe such

fanciful tales? Told by two shaken up little boys?"

"Two shook up lil' boys is a fancy tale Mr. Weldon," Dabby retorted, unflappable as always. "But we done heard the same from some of the finest colored citizenry in Blackwood. Ain't no fancy tale no more."

"And who are their sources?" Weldon scoffed. "Poor Negroes who live around Whitewood? How much more reliable are they than children—superstitious and easy to fool? No fault of their own, mind you. They're kept quite ignorant."

There were some uncomfortable murmurs. Most in Blackwood held the same views, but it was considered rude to actually voice them, especially given that more than a few were kin. A hush came as someone else rose. Laurence saw it was his mother, her gaze fully on the schoolteacher.

"Mr. Weldon," she stated crisply. "One of those shaken up boys is my son, whom I have raised to tell the truth before God and the world. I do not know the ways of the colored men of New England. But in Blackwood, gentlemen strive to uphold the virtue and morality of colored mothers."

The normally haughty schoolteacher shrank back under the eyes of Blackwood's most prominent lady. Muttering an apology he promptly seated himself, a wounded look on his face.

"Then what we gonna do?" someone asked. It was Mrs. Glover, the widower. Her husband, the saloon owner, had died in a bizarre accident involving a hatchet—sometime after he was found consorting with the local schoolmistress.

Laurence didn't know the particulars, but shortly thereafter the schoolmistress hastily departed Blackwood and Mrs. Glover took over the saloon. A large painting of her dead husband remained hanging in the establishment, which she personally polished each day.

"I asked what we gonna do?" she sounded again, hands on her stout hips. "Don't know bout the rest of you, but don't much like some stranger speaking for me and Blackwood."

"How you reckon he doing that?" the postmaster asked.

Mrs. Glover gave him a rueful look. "That lot up in Whitewood might be stupid, but it don't take the sense God gave a chicken to know they gonna think that stranger is one of us. Think blame ain't coming our way? Sure as thunder come after lightenin' it gonna be so."

The crowd grew loud and Laurence could sense their fear.

"We need to make sure they know it weren't us," someone ventured.

There were quick affirmations, a sea of unanimity rare for this assembly.

"Perhaps we could draft a letter!" the schoolmaster put in, recapturing some of his self-esteem. "A declaration signed by the best citizens of Blackwood, disavowing any ties to this stranger! I would be happy to compose it!"

More approval came as many seized upon the idea, a way out of the tangled crisis deposited on their doorsteps. Paul Weldon began taking names for a letter committee. The animal doctor, Mr. Blackmon, offered himself up as an ambassador of goodwill, having cared for livestock in Whitewood. Carpenters even volunteered their services to help rebuild any damaged structures. The women's organization talked about collecting monies for surviving family of slain members of the mob.

Laurence listened in stunned silence. Just hours ago the people of Whitewood had attempted to kill a man—a man who looked just like all of them. He'd been there. He'd *seen* them, celebrating murder. And these were the people that were now to receive their sympathies?

"But he saved that man!" he found himself shouting.

Shocked eyes turned to Laurence. His sister gave him a look that could split rocks. Gazing up, he found his father glowering from behind the pulpit. What had made him blurt out such a thing, he could not say. But he felt he had to speak.

"The stranger saved that man," Laurence went on, trying not to stammer. "I saw it. They was going to hang him. Weren't for the stranger and those giants, that man would be dead now."

A hush descended on the assembly. Laurence looked up to his mother and was surprised to find not anger, but sadness. The other faces about him were now much the same. Some turned away when he looked to them, wincing. It was in the midst of this lull that a new voice rose up. All eyes turned to the pulpit where his father now stood, towering and speaking in deep tones.

"I was here for the foundation of this church," he recalled fondly. "Back then Blackwood was just growing. Didn't have much of nothing. Dabby Mason used to sell goods out his home. My wife was teaching lessons out the back of ours. Bernard Pickerson was hauling our mail all the way from Whitewood. And ol' Will Blackmon used to complain wasn't nothing here to help cure, but a few sick mules that needed to be put out they misery." There were some laughs at this, amid the nervous fear that still filled the room.

"Now look how much we got. Own our homes. Our own stores. Our own school. Got our own everything. Some of us got so much, we could hire some of them broke down whites in Whitewood—

if they'd take the work!" There was more laughter at this, as the crowd grew at ease.

"Ain't no other place like what we got here for miles. Ain't no other place like this in the state. Probably no place like this in the whole country." Nods of approval and murmurs of assent sounded from the crowd, held in sway by this appeal to their ego. "Yes we done come a long way Blackwood, by hard work, strength, prayers, and the grace of God."

"But you know what done sustained us even more? You know what keeps us growing, and prospering and surviving? It's more than sweat, more than our hands, more than our prayers." Reverend Johns leaned forward, capturing his audience with his gaze. "It's our wisdom."

"And I don't just mean figuring. Or book learning or any of that fanciness. I mean what my daddy taught me, and what all of us know bout the way of the world. We done sustained and survived here in Blackwood, because we been blessed with the wisdom to know white folk." Shouts of approval came now.

"We know how to smile for them! We know how to bend for them! We know how to make them feel at comfort! And 'cause of that, they leave us be! That comes from our wisdom! Because we know what's important! Our homes! Our families! What we done built here!" Reverend Johns lifted a wagging finger, as if scolding a child. "The fool colored man lifts up his head, and loses it for a moment of pride! The wise colored man bows his head, but lives to keep it!"

Actual applause came now, and Laurence felt himself shrink into his seat. Reverend Johns let it all crash upon him, before lifting his arms to call for calm.

"Now then," he said in the quieted hall. "Let us use that wisdom to protect what we got here; instead of ruining it with foolish pride. Blackwood done weathered many storms. We'll do the same again."

There were nods of consent and a seeming relief, as if those words alone had brought comfort that this crisis could be handled, and would pass like any other.

"Not every storm can be weathered," a new voice said. "Some might sweep you away."

Every head turned at the unexpected interruption. Eyes went wide and jaws hung. But Laurence only smiled.

Standing at the back of the church was the stranger.

Impeccably dressed with cane in hand, he strode forward in that same imperious manner that made him so outlandish and yet fascinating. No one spoke, dumbfounded at his presence. He gave Laurence a knowing wink before stopping at the pulpit.

"Forgive my intrusion," he said, removing his top hat with a gloved hand. "But I thought it only right I attend a meeting held in my honor."

His slight joke was lost upon the reverend. He looked the stranger up and down as if taking his measure, before speaking. "You the man stirred up all this trouble." It was more accusation than question.

"I'm the man who saved another from the hands of murderers."

"Up to the Lord to figure who live and who die," the reverend said.

"Then perhaps I am an instrument of the Lord then."

Reverend Johns opened his mouth but didn't speak, seeming

momentarily stunned. The assembled crowd gasped as one at the stranger's brazen speech.

"Don't know who you are," the reverend pronounced strongly, having regained his voice. "Don't much care. But this is Blackwood. And we don't get mixed up in outside affairs."

"Vernon," the stranger said. "My name is Dr. Julius Vernon. And I haven't come here Reverend, to cause you or the good people of Blackwood trouble. I've come to save you."

"Save us?" someone ventured. It was the schoolteacher, Weldon. "From what?"

Dr. Vernon turned to the crowd. "The Negro boy that was going to die today in Whitewood, his name is Clay Macon—who made the mistake of having a tryst with a white farmer's daughter. His murder was only going to be the beginning."

"Rumor would spread that Macon was related to affluent Negroes in Blackwood, who colluded in the alleged rape. A white mob intended to march on Blackwood by nightfall, demanding Macon's accomplices be turned over. Words would be exchanged, leading to a shootout. The whites flee but return in hours, with hundreds. In three days of violence they kill every inhabitant of Blackwood, and burn it to the ground."

It was not only Laurence who sat stunned now. The entire assembly had gone deathly still.

"I don't understand," Paul Weldon said, breaking the silence. "How can you know these things?"

Dr. Vernon fixed the schoolteacher with stern eyes.

"Because where I come from, it's already happened."

He extended a set of folded brown sheets he held beneath one arm to the school teacher. A newspaper. People surged forward to read. Laurence managed to get a glance of the headline as they did:

NEGRO TOWN BURNED SCORES SLAIN

There were photos. It was Blackwood, but barely recognizable. Dabbey Mason's shop lay gutted and smoldering. So too was Mrs. Glover's saloon. And there were bodies.

One was chained to a tree, a charred mass so badly burned it was no longer identifiable. The naked form of the animal doctor, Mr. Blackmon, was unmistakable however: eyes bulging in death. So too were the remains of Mrs. Carver and her husband, hanging from a nearby bridge. There were more. All dead.

"What is this?" Paul Weldon stammered. He looked near faint, all of his usual pomp reduced to nothing. He pointed to a photo with a mutilated body tied to a pole. It was the schoolteacher himself, still wearing his fine clothes, pages from torn books plastered to his body. A group of white men posed and grinned behind him, jostling for position about their human trophy.

"A postcard," Dr. Vernon replied grimly. "It will become quite popular, a lesson for agitators who stir up local Negroes with education."

"Where do you come from?" Laurence looked up to find it was his mother who spoke, her voice trembling, but demanding. "Where do these horrible images come from?"

Dr. Vernon looked at her and seemed to waver before answering. "I come from tomorrow Mrs. Johns. Many, many tomorrows."

There was silence. Laurence knew none of them could understand. But he had soared in his thoughts where they didn't dare. He had just read a book like this. The story was about a man, an inventor, who built a fabulous machine and traveled through....

"Time," he said aloud, startling those around him. Dr. Vernon met his gaze, a hint of something in his eye that looked almost like pride.

"Time," Dr. Vernon nodded, sharing a knowing smile. He returned his gaze to the stupefied crowd. "It is not where I am from, but *when*. And I come from the future, to save this town from a terrible fate."

There was a lengthy stretch of silence as the church congregants gaped in confusion.

"What fool talk is this?" Reverend Johns boomed, breaking the quiet. He scowled at the man that dared enter his sanctum and cause such unrest. "This town got serious times coming, trouble done by your own hand. Now you come in here with this? Fanciful stories? Nonsense?"

Dr. Vernon snatched the paper from the schoolteacher, opening it wide for all to see.

"Does this seem nonsense to you?"

Laurence stared up at the photo on the page. It was this very church, the heart of Blackwood—with nothing but its smoldering frame remaining. Many gasped. A few cried out. But Reverend Johns remained stoic.

"We all seen magic tricks, Dr. Vernon," he declared. "Flim-flam men. Snake oil. Circus pranks. I even seen a dog-faced boy one good time!" There were a few timid laughs. "Slick talkin' ain't new to

Blackwood. Only new thing would be when we start believing it!"

There were some shouts from the congregation now, desperate to believe in the practical over the fantastic. Even Laurence's earlier enthusiasm faltered. He glanced at the newspaper. Could it all really be a hoax?

"Come to think of it," Schoolteacher Weldon said, "I'm not so sure this likeness truly favors me." He managed a slight laugh that, if not convincing, at least conveyed a challenge.

"And if all this supposed to pass like you say," Mrs. Glover put in, "how you reckon you gonna stop it? Come all the way here by yourself?" She sniffed. "Might well just stay put where you was."

Dr. Vernon smiled slightly, lifting his cane to palm the rounded silver head.

There was a loud sound, like a set of steel anvils dropping onto the ground. It came from outside. Reverend Johns had commanded that his church be built "high as heaven," like European cathedrals with carved spires that reached to the sky.

Blackwood's spiritual and communal center had none of that magnificence, and was made of wood rather than stone. But it did have vaulted ceilings. Yet when the monstrous figure stepped through the tall doors and came to full height, it made the structure look no bigger than some crude thatched cabin.

It was a giant. One of the same he had seen earlier. In his long black robes and confined in this small space, he looked even larger than before. It would have taken several men just to match his breadth, and none could ever equal his height. He stood silent and unmoving, face hidden beneath his cowl.

For Laurence there was a twinge of vindication. But no one

here was in awe. They were terrified. When someone dared shriek, panic erupted. People rose from their seats, stumbling over themselves to get away. A few braver men picked up chairs as weapons. Mrs. Glover pulled out a stashed away revolver from her skirts.

"No! Please! Stop!" Dr. Vernon cried. "There's no need to be afraid! I can explain!"

"Explain?" Mrs. Glover asked heatedly. "Explain this monster you done conjured up?"

Dr. Vernon managed a slight laugh despite the mood. "It's not a monster." He walked down the aisle to the giant who yet stood as still as a statue. "It is a gift. My gift—to the people of Blackwood."

He grabbed hold of the black cloth and pulled, sliding it off the hulking form it covered, revealing a wondrous sight.

Laurence gaped. It was a man. Or at least it was the shape of a man, only much larger and made of metal—a patchwork of gears and pipes that looked like some contraption wrought by an engineering god. It had a head, a mere oval thing, but no face to speak of. Long arms were attached to a barrel chest, and its legs ended in booted feet.

"Sweet *Jesus!*" Mrs. Glover exclaimed. "If that ain't no monster, what you call it?"

"A machine," Dr. Vernon replied, "like any engine or steamship, but built in the image of man."

"Is it alive?" Dabby Mason stammered.

"No. Not like you and me." Dr. Vernon reached up to the broad chest. There were the sounds of shifting gears and a vast area opened. Inside was a large square copper colored object. Laurence wondered if that was the machine-man's heart.

"A battery," Dr. Vernon said. "Like the ones that power

telegraphs—only much more powerful."

The gathered crowd listened as the man explained his fantastic creation. Mrs. Glover even took cautious steps forward, using the tip of her gun to touch the giant. A red circular light flashed to life in the center of its oval head, swiveling towards her.

And then, most unexpectedly, it spoke. *"Designate: Glover, Elizabeth S."* The voice of the giant was deep and muffled, as if it fought its way from within the iron frame. *"Wife of Zachary J. Glover: Deceased. Citizen: Blackwood."*

"That thing can talk!" Mrs. Glover exclaimed, backing away. "And it know me!"

Dr. Vernon nodded eagerly. "It knows all of you. Point that gun at it all you want Mrs. Glover. Curse at it. Shoot it. Beat upon it with your fists. No matter. It won't attack you. It won't try to protect itself. Because its only purpose is to safeguard this town."

There was silence. More than a few faces now stared at the iron giant with a contemplative look, even if pensive. Mrs. Glover let her revolver fall to her side, daring to place a hand on the machine-man's iron skin, her eyes widening like a child's at whatever she felt beneath.

"How many of these contraptions you said there is?" she asked.

Dr. Vernon smiled. "Seven. All waiting right outside."

"And these...machine-men," the schoolteacher, Weldon asked. "They can stop this mob?"

Dr. Vernon laughed. "Don't you all see?" he asked. "Today Clay Macon should have been murdered. But he wasn't. The white mob should have been here hours ago. But they never came. The destruction of Blackwood was stopped, by them." He pointed to the machine-men.

"Blackwood was born out of a dream, that colored folks could have something of our own. That dream is safe now. And if you accept what I have to offer, I can take that dream to heights you haven't dared imagine."

He let his eyes roam the crowd, stopping on Laurence with a brief smile, as if the two of them were conspirators in some great plot.

Then, squarely meeting the inquisitive and eager gazes of all gathered, Laurence's old grandmother began to speak. Every face lit up in response.

"I remember when de freedom come," she said. "Me and another woman done some shoutin' and hollerin.' Yes Lawd, we did. We tore up some corn down in de field and danced all over Masta's cotton patch. He threaten he lash on us with de rawhide quirt. But we ain't paid him none. We was free. He wasn't our Masta no mo.'"

Laurence sat listening to her. She could spend hours recounting what it had been like in slavery. Sometimes the stories were harrowing. But tonight she spoke of when freedom came, of how her Master wept openly at losing his valued property, and of how the freed slaves danced and frolicked for days. Perhaps because tonight they had a new member in the audience, he was rapt as he listened to her tale.

§§§

It was his mother's idea to invite Dr. Vernon to stay with them, at least for the night. The man protested, insisting that someone's barn would do. But Mrs. Johns would hear nothing of it, demanding he get a home-cooked meal and a night's rest. In the end it was the machine-men that slept in a barn, while their maker was offered a warm bed.

Reverend Johns had surprisingly agreed. Laurence thought it was his father's way of watching the man. Even as they sat to a late dinner, the Reverend kept a cool gaze on his houseguest, as if trying to figure out a puzzle. Dr. Vernon, too engrossed in devouring his food, didn't seem to notice.

"My goodness," Mrs. Johns exclaimed. "Do they not feed you in this…tomorrow…you come from?"

The man took pause, looking abashed. "I'm sorry. My manners are usually much more refined. It's just…I haven't eaten or slept appropriately in days—so eager to embark on my work."

"A mother always knows," Mrs. Johns nodded, sipping from her own glass. "So Dr. Vernon, you know so much about us, but we little of you. Do you have a family of your own?"

Dr. Vernon shook his head. "No ma'am. Haven't had time for marriage or family."

"That's unfortunate," Mrs. Johns replied. "If you plan on staying on in Blackwood, you'll find more than a few colored women here who'd make you a fine wife." Dr. Vernon looked taken off guard, managing a sheepish smile. His mother kept up her gaze, one he seemed unwilling to meet.

Laurence sighed impatiently. None of this interested him in the least. Here they had a man who'd traveled through time and built machine-men, and they were talking about women who might grow sweet on him?

He had so many questions! How did this time machine work? Could the machine-men think? What was the future like? And mostly, he wanted to know more about the magnificent offer Dr. Vernon had made to the town—which was likely being discussed around all the other dinner tables in Blackwood.

Dr. Vernon proposed an ambitious plan. If they would have him, he and his machine-men would stay in Blackwood. The man claimed the iron giants were equipped with the knowledge of construction, of making wondrous inventions that would change their lives.

These goods could be patented and sold, bringing in great wealth that could be invested. In time Blackwood could rival big cities like New York or Paris. They'd be a beacon for colored folks throughout the country and the world over. The stunned crowd had agreed to meet up the next day, to debate and vote on the issue after a night's rest. It was hard to believe, however, that any of them could possibly be getting any sleep.

"Why Blackwood?" Reverend John's question cut through Laurence's thoughts and the casual banter. "All the places you could go? Why here?"

Dr. Vernon hesitated, looking across the table." I suppose I have an attachment. From the history books, I mean. I thought building a foundation on a righted wrong was best."

"And that's what you think you done?" Reverend Johns asked. "Righted a wrong?"

Dr. Vernon frowned. "Of course. What else would you call it?"

"Maybe… meddling in God's affairs," the Reverend replied.

They gaped at the leader of Blackwood in surprise— no one more so than Dr. Vernon.

"You think God intended for your town to be burned down? Its entire people killed?" he asked incredulously.

"Wouldn't even known it was to happen, if you hadn't come,"

the reverend said. "But if it's what come to pass in your time, who's to say we meant to change it? God lets floods wash away people and homes. He lets locusts eat crops and sets the earth to shaking. He let us get dragged from Africa to this land as slaves, then set us free like the Jews from Egypt. And we suffer, yes. But for His greater plans, which we can't glimpse."

Dr. Vernon sat stupefied, before laughing ruefully and shaking his head.

"I'm sorry Reverend, but if that's the way your God works, I can't condone Him."

There was a deep silence after those words, and those who sat at the table went still.

"Don't know how you was raised," Reverend Johns said sternly, his strong preacher's voice coming out. "But in my house, the Lord is shown respect."

"And I don't mean disrespect," Dr. Vernon countered. "I don't know if there's a God or not. But I know by some means I've been gifted this power of change. Maybe in that way I'm doing His work—or correcting His mistakes."

Laurence held his breath. He had never heard any colored man talk like that. He certainly had never seen anyone talk like that to his father. Dr. Vernon was going to end up sleeping in the barn with his machine-men, or run out of town on a rail. But instead, surprisingly, the reverend only laughed.

"Man look on himself and thinks he's something. Betta than God even, with his tools and inventions. Now he done figured a way to go back and undo God's will as he please. But man ain't God. He's just a child, playing at things he don't know." He fixed their guest with a penetrating gaze. "Don't care how much you try, can't change what meant to be."

Dr. Vernon didn't respond. But the silence that hovered between the two men, seemed greater in depth than distance.

§§§

Laurence stood dressed in his nightshirt, preparing for bed and wondering how he could be expected to sleep. Slipping into the hallway, he peered over the staircase at Dr. Vernon. Still dressed in a pants and vest, the man sat staring at something in his hand.

"Might as well come down if you want a good look."

Laurence ran at the invitation. He could now see the man played with the round silver ball that had been attached to his cane. Examining it closer, he could see finely cut grooves all along its surface.

Dr. Vernon smiled. "Curious aren't you? Well, it's a control device." He palmed the ball and it peeled apart, like the petals of a flower. Within were a host of things—lights, dials and miniature cogs that turned like a ticking clock. He handed it over to Laurence. "I use it to control my machine-men. In here, is everything you ever need to know about them—how they work, how they were built."

"How you do it?" Laurence asked in fascination, staring at the device. "Travel through time I mean?"

"That's a bit difficult to explain," Dr. Vernon replied.

Laurence stiffened. "You thinkin' I'm too young to understand?"

Dr. Vernon laughed. "Not at all. I know how smart you are. It would just take some time."

"Does everyone travel in time where you come from? And have machine-men?

Dr. Vernon shook his head. "Just in stories. My inventions are unique, even in my day."

"Never met no famous colored inventor before," Laurence said.

"There are many things you still have to see." Dr. Vernon gave him a wistful look, as a spark of excitement lit up his face. "Laurence, I thought I'd never see you again. Now here we are, together. I have so many things to show you, to teach you. What is going to be set down in Blackwood, I'm doing for in great part because of you. We're going to change the world. We're going to change everything."

Laurence said nothing, confused at what all of this could possibly mean. Before any of those questions could be answered a voice thundered down from above.

"What you doin' down here boy?"

Laurence jumped to his feet. Reverend Johns stood at the head of the stairs. His eyes went from man to son, frowning for a brief instant as if something tugged at his mind.

"The boy just awakened and found me down here," Dr. Vernon quickly said. "I kept him up talking I'm afraid."

"Well he need to get to bed," the reverend ordered.

Laurence muttered a hasty, "Yes sir," handing Dr. Vernon back his device before bounding back up the stairs.

Glancing one last look at their houseguest, he found his way to his bed and laid down, mind swirling with more thoughts than he could handle.

§§§

Sleep came, but it was fitful. Laurence's dreams were filled with Blackwood burning, maniacal whites dancing in the flames. He awoke with a start and might have gone back to sleep, had his eyes not caught something odd outside.

A flash of light came from the barn—where the machine-men were housed. It lit up the small structure, like someone had released a bolt of lightning within. It flashed twice more, and his ears detected a sound—like a blacksmith hammering.

For the second time this strange night Laurence slipped out of bed. Downstairs, Dr. Vernon slept wrapped in blankets, oblivious to the goings-on outside. Walking to the door, Laurence pushed it open and was greeted by the muggy summer night. He had only reached halfway to the barn, when the door to the structure suddenly opened and a man stepped out.

Laurence froze. It was dark, and neither of them carried lamps. But he needed no illumination to identify the man. Reverend John's large body and strong features spoke for themselves. He was fully dressed in pants and shirt, all dark, even down to his shoes. In a gloved hand he held a long thick hammer, the kind used to break up rocks.

"Boy what you doing out here," he demanded roughly. The reverend was not above being surprised, but it never lasted long.

"Thought I saw something—in the barn...."

His father scowled. "You ain't seen nothing. You understand?"

Laurence stood lost in confusion. What was going on?

"Reverend!"

The call came from down the road. Someone was running

towards them. Laurence made out the form of Haley Johnson, the butcher's son. He ran like the wind, looking scared out his wits.

"Boy, why you out here this time of night?" the reverend asked.

Haley stopped before them, gasping for air. "My Pa! Say you gotta come! Come to the church! News from Whitewood! A mob marching! Say they gonna kill all the colored folk!"

Laurence's blood went cold. Was this a nightmare? Was he still dreaming?

"How you know this?" Reverend Johns asked dubiously.

"Some poor colored folk from Whitewood brought warning!" the boy answered. "Say the blacksmith, Mr. Whittaker, already dead! White folk shot him up, and strung up the body!"

Laurence felt a pang of horror and sorrow. Poor Elias Whittaker. If mourning crossed Reverend John's mind he didn't show it. Instead he drew himself up, as if shaking out of slumber. Grabbing onto both boys, he began barking orders.

"Tell your Pappy to get up to the church!" he told Haley. "Tell him start ringin the bell! Get everybody up! Go!" The boy nodded, sprinting into the night. The Reverend turned quickly back to the house, dragging Laurence behind. "Get your sister and mama and grandmammy up. Quick now!"

Laurence was practically pushed through the door. He bounded up the stairs, driven by fear and his father's urgency. Below, Dr. Vernon came awake, peering about and sensing the tension.

"What's happening?"

"Mob coming," Reverend Johns said curtly. "Up from Whitewood."

"What? But that's impossible!"

"A man already dead. More blood gonna be spilt before this night out." The accusing tone in his voice was hard to miss.

"But I stopped them!" Dr. Vernon said, scrambling to his feet. "This shouldn't be happening! I changed things!"

"You scared a few white folk!" the reverend growled. "You think that all it take? Always more of them out there! Always anotha one to lead anotha mob! All you did was slow down what God done set in place! What gonna be, will be!"

"No!" Dr. Vernon shouted. He stumbled about, searching for his clothing. "Not again! It's not going to happen again! We can protect ourselves this time!" He gazed out to the barn.

Reverend Johns only frowned, his jaw going tight. Glancing up, he caught sight of Laurence who stood transfixed at the top of the stairway.

"Boy I told you to go! Don't make me put a switch to you now!"

That was all Laurence needed hear. He bounded up the stairs, in short time reaching his mother and sister and grandmother. In a whirlwind he somehow managed to get out of his nightshirt and into some clothes. He was still lacing on shoes when his mother grabbed him and ushered him downstairs where his father waited. They were out of the house quickly, heading for the church. It was the wail that caught his attention. It came from the barn.

Dr. Vernon!

Somehow Laurence managed to wrest free of his mother's grasp, running towards the barn. Not even the shouts of his father dissuaded him.

Reaching it, he flung the door open and gaped in shock at what he saw.

Dr. Vernon was on his knees, his face filled with anguish. The machine-men were present as well. But something was wrong. Their chest cavities were open. And the hearts that sustained them—what Dr. Vernon had called batteries—were damaged. Gears too had been broken, and all along their bodies they leaked black fluid like blood.

"Laurence!"

Reverend John's massive frame filled up the doorway like an angry mountain. For a brief moment the eyes of father and son connected, and each knew what the other was thinking. There was no confession in the older man's eyes, no shame or fear of recrimination. Between them there was no sense of equity, and thus no need for explanations. But for Laurence, the world he knew came crashing down.

A distant sound like thunder broke through the night. Gun shots. Then screams.

"It's beginning," Dr. Vernon whispered. "Just like before...."

"Come on boy!" his father demanded, grabbing him. He turned to Dr. Vernon. "You can come or stay here, suit yourself!"

Laurence was pulled from the barn, catching only a parting glimpse of Dr. Vernon staring at his sabotaged inventions in grief. He was spun about, to see his sister and mother and grandmother. He had been so lost in his own thoughts he hadn't noticed their screaming. Then again, it seemed by now everyone was doing so. Fires burned everywhere. Men on horseback rode about with rifles. They shot at anything that moved, hurling curses and promising death.

"Move boy! *Move!*"

Laurence ran at his father's urging, following his family. All around him screams of people fleeing and dying filled the night.

Then he saw it. His father's church, the heart and soul of Blackwood.—ablaze. Flames poured out of its shattered windows, licking a blackening roof and sending up smoke into the night. Many fell to their knees at the seeing it, lost in despair.

Only Reverend Johns remained standing, an unbendable tree in a raging storm. "God's will," he murmured.

A gunshot broke his words, so close it made Laurence jump. He looked to his father, his gaze going down, to where crimson rapidly spread across that strong chest. In shock, he watched as the towering figure fell.

His mother screamed, running to her husband. His sister cried, held by his grandmother. There were more gunshots, so close Laurence could feel their heat on his skin. And the cries of his family ceased. He watched wordlessly as the murderer rode up on a dark horse, his rifle taking aim.

There was a loud crack.

Laurence blinked in surprise as the man tumbled from his horse, landing with a thud onto the ground. Behind him was Dr. Vernon, his father's hammer in his hands. He came over, gazing at the fallen bodies about Laurence and stifling a sob.

"Have to get you out of here," he said. "I failed them...but I won't fail you. You have to come with me Laurence. You have to come now."

Laurence shook his head. "I have to stay here...get momma and my sister and grandmomma Johns to the church. That's what Pa told me..." Some part of him knew he didn't make sense, but the words kept coming.

"No boy," a voice said weakly. "Can't stay here."

It was Reverend Johns. The leader of Blackwood lay in a pool of blood, some stubborn bit of him clinging to life. Laurence fell down, willing him to get up, to be the strong mountain he always was, to sweep them up in his arms and make them all safe.

"Pa," he trembled. "I ain't leaving you!"

Reverend Johns reached up with a feeble hand. "I'm dead already boy. You have to go…with him." He shifted his gaze to Dr. Vernon. "You. Couldn't see it at first. But now… so clear. Take him… take him where it's safe. That's how it was meant to be, wasn't it?"

Laurence looked between the two men, who shared knowing looks he couldn't decipher. There was a final release of breath from the reverend, and then a chilling stillness. Dr. Vernon knelt beside him, bending down to close his father's open eyes.

"We have to go," he whispered.

Laurence nodded, tears welling up and running down his face. With a final look at his slain family he rose. Dr. Vernon grabbed him and they ran. At times Laurence barely felt his feet touch the ground, trying his best to shut out the terrible scenes all around him. It took a moment to realize they were heading back to his house—the barn. Reaching it, they pulled open the door, only to find it occupied.

Three white men stood inside with rifles and a lantern, staring in awe at the immobile and ruined machine-men. They spun about at the opening door, rifles aimed. Laurence heard Dr. Vernon shout, shielding him with his body as gunshots rang. Then he went down.

Laurence watched in shock as the man fell back against him, sending them tumbling down together. For some reason, he'd thought

Dr. Vernon beyond such things as mere bullets. But now he could see this mysterious stranger was just a man, nothing more than that and no less mortal.

Lying there, he could see the three white men advancing, murder dancing in their eyes. Panic gripped him. What was he to do? He was just a boy. How could he fight people so much bigger? In his despair, his eyes spied something on Dr. Vernon, just inside the man's vest. The silver ball.

Laurence quickly pulled it out. Not knowing how to use it, his fingers danced across the thing, pressing here and there, hoping and praying something would happen. Then, to his surprise, the contraption unfolded, breaking and spreading apart. A piercing red light erupted to compete with the lone lantern in the dark space. And a familiar voice filled the silence.

"Designate: Johns, Laurence. Citizen: Blackwood."

Laurence looked up to find one of the machine-men come alive. *"Help me!"* he cried.

The three white men by now had turned about, stunned to see one of the metal beings speak. That red baleful eye swung about to regard them.

"Designates: Unknown. Detection: Weaponry. Intent: Hostile. Action taken: Threat nullification."

The machine-man lifted an arm and there was a bright flash. Laurence shielded his eyes, watching as the three white men burned away where they stood. When the light died, smoke and gray ash filled the air.

"Threat nullified," the machine-man confirmed. It turned to its creator. *"Designate: Vernon, Julius. Life signs: Critical."* The

machine-man lifted a leg to walk forward then stopped. *"Battery cells: Compromised. Power levels: Critical. Shut down procedure: Initiated."* The red light slowly faded as the iron giant went immobile once more.

"No!" Laurence shouted. "Don't go! I need your help!"

"They don't have enough power…." a voice said hoarsely.

Laurence looked down at Dr. Vernon. The man was still alive, but barely. He struggled to help him sit, leaning him against a wooden post. Blood soaked his white shirt, seeping from wounds beneath.

"I'm sorry," he rasped. "I failed you. Too arrogant. Should have been more careful."

"You gonna be fine," Laurence trembled.

Dr. Vernon shook his head. "No. I won't. But you'll live. And that's enough. Perhaps, that's how it's supposed to be." He met Laurence's gaze. "I'm sorry I kept things from you. It would have been too much. But now…." He paused, struggling to breathe. "When Blackwood was destroyed there was one survivor. One lone figure that escaped the massacre. You Laurence. It was you."

"Laurence Johns was the only living witness to what happened at Blackwood. He was smuggled out of the county, by a sympathetic white family in Whitewood of all places, and sent up North. Fearing reprisal, he took a new name, fashioned from a writer who sparked his imagination. He grew up in Negro orphanages, and wasn't supposed to amount to anything. But he beat those odds. He taught himself. He learned. He traveled the world. He became an inventor. And he never stopped dreaming."

Dr. Vernon reached into his pocket, pulling something out and opening his palm. Laurence stared down at the impossible, reaching into his own pants pocket, feeling for something that he always carried, that even in his haste tonight, he had managed to stash away. Opening his own palm, he showed the flattened nickel and compared it to the one the man held. They were identical.

"The only survivor of Blackwood," Dr. Vernon said. "Come back to save this town, to save us. I wanted you to have a better life." A painful look crossed his face. "I'm sorry I couldn't give you…give us…that. But still, I won't let it be like before."

He beckoned for the silver ball and Laurence quickly handed it over, his mind swimming. He studied the man's face—his face. He thought of his father's final words. Somehow at the end, he had known. A loud hum made him turn about. The machine-men miraculously come to life.

"They back!" he cried eagerly. "We can save the town!"

Dr. Vernon shook his head gravely, extinguishing the brief flicker of hope.

"No. Not enough power for that. Just enough, if they link up, for something else."

At his words there was a loud roar. And as Laurence watched thunderstruck, a rippling began to form in the air while a strong gale picked up. It looked as if a hole was appearing, right in the middle of nothing. He remembered seeing such a thing only once before, when this mysterious man and his giant men clad in black first appeared.

"It is a doorway through time!" Dr. Vernon cried out above the din that now shook the barn. "It will take the machine-men to where I came from—and you with them!"

Laurence's eyes rounded. "You not coming with me?"

Dr. Vernon looked to him with sadness. "I wouldn't survive the trip. Not like this. And I don't know what would happen, if the two of us, one in the same, were to make that journey. I won't risk it. I won't risk you."

Laurence began to protest but the man stopped him short.

"No! I planned for this possibility! There's a place set for you! You'll have a home, the finances you need, schooling! You won't be alone!" He took Laurence's hand. "My laboratory is waiting for you, if you would have it. My inventions—our dreams—all there waiting for you to pick up! I'm giving it to you! If you live, I live, we live! Our dreams live!"

He fell back wearily. "There's nothing else for us here, Rabbit. Go. Live. Dream."

Depressing something on the device he thrust it back at Laurence, using the last of his strength to push the boy towards the machine-men and the gaping hole behind them.

"Goodbye and Godspeed!" he called out. "May you have better fortune, than I!"

Laurence tried to catch hold of something as he fell towards the hole. A powerful rumbling sounded, and the world looked as if it were collapsing on itself. There was a terrible wrenching in the pit of his stomach as darkness swiftly enclosed him and the machine-men. Then in a suffocating rush they were yanked away, gone.

§§§

Chimezie hit the sand hard. He glared up at his captor, the one who had shackled him in iron that bit into his flesh like teeth. There was no pity in that face, as ebon as his own, or in the faces of his companions. By their markings and peculiar tongue he guessed they'd come from further north— invaders on horses, with iron spears and those sticks that made thunder, spitting smoke and sharp metal that cut through flesh like locusts ate through wild grass. Men had fallen at Chimezie's side before they could even raise their weapons. Somehow he had not.

Those that survived had been set on a march, their captors beating them mercilessly. They had finally arrived here, at the coast, by a sea of which he had heard but never set eyes upon. Who knew there could be so much water? And that was not all.

There were men, different from Chimezie's captors or any he'd ever seen. Their skins were pinkish, like meat that had not been fully cooked and their faces were covered in matted hair. From all the clothing they wore, they must have been cold even in the midday sun.

Chimezie had heard tales of these pink men, who heaved their hulking ships across the sea from faraway lands. Some said they once came for ivory, cloths or gold. But now they only came for people. And those they took away, never returned.

Whole villages had been carried off—for whom were bartered weapons, fine cloths and strong drink. Some of his captors haggled and drank heartily from their ill-gotten goods, stumbling in their drunkenness. Others however watched the pink men carefully—as if suspecting their ever-hungry partners would clamp them in chains if given the chance.

Chimezie gazed around in desperation. Most of those held captive were unrecognizable. Many muttered in tongues he couldn't even place. And more than a few held vacant stares or trembled and wept. No, they would be no help. What he needed were others like him, who held the fires of vengeance behind their eyes—the ones that could reach up and murder when given the chance. Then he would know there was hope.

His thoughts were broken by rumbling. The ground shook. He gazed up, confused, for there was no thunder in the sky. Then he saw a truly spectacular sight. The air about him rippled, as if it were water disturbed by a rock. Then out of nothingness, something appeared.

They looked like men, impossibly tall with massive chests and skin that glistened like iron. He counted three at first. Then there were over ten. Still more appeared. Some stood on the beach, or hovered over the waters.

There were no faces upon their rounded heads, only a bright fiery eye that glared out at captives and captors alike. Then one of the giant men lifted an arm. Light as bright as the sun flew from a hollow space where his hand should have stood, striking the hulking ships upon the sea and setting them ablaze.

The pink men cried out as their vessels sank into the waters, some of them lifting their fire sticks. The giants retaliated, burning many away where they stood. Those native to this land were not so foolish. As one they turned and ran, seeking the safety of the forest. The pink men who remained followed. A few ran to the sea, throwing themselves into the waters as if they could swim back to their far off homes.

Chimezie sat, gaping. The smell of smoke and scorched earth filled the air. The giant men remained motionless and silent while the bound captives on the beach wailed, wondering what into what new tumult they'd been thrown. Chimezie's eyes however, were set on a lone figure that walked the beach in his direction.

It was a man. He wore clothing much like the pink men, but his skin was dark. He moved between the iron giants unmolested and came to stand right before Chimezie, staring down. He said something in a foreign tongue and one of the giants stepped forward.

What looked like fine strings of light erupted from the giant's hand, striking the shackles at Chimezie's wrists and ankles which immediately fell away. Released from his bonds Chimezie stared at the giant and his master, wondering from where such beings could come.

"Do not be afraid," the man said.

Chimezie's eyes rounded. The man spoke his tongue, though it bore a certain strangeness—as if it were not his own.

"Who are you?" he managed.

The man smiled. "My name is Laurence. But you can simply call me Anyi."

Anyi. It was a word from his people. It meant: *friend.*

"And that is who I am," the man said, as if knowing his thoughts. He extended a hand, helping Chimezie up. "You don't have to be afraid. I'm here to help. To stop all of this from ever happening. If you accept what I have to offer, we can make a world together, one you haven't even begun to imagine. I'll tell you how…."

Chimezie listened as the man spoke. Others had gathered about them, recently freed and listening intently. He didn't understand everything that was said. But the parts he did grasp made his eyes go wide and set his heart beating faster. He didn't think anything would ever be the same, ever again.

MUD HOLES AND MISSISSIPPI MULES

MALON EDWARDS

I should have known it wasn't going to be a good day when Vim Jackson finished his yo' mama jokes at half past ten in the morning.

He was on his sixth shot of whisky when he slurred to no one in particular, "Yo mama so fat, li'l boys follow her 'round screamin,' 'Oh, the humanity!'"

Usually, Vim Jackson went strong and drunk with his jokes routine, and Sam Hill's whiskey, until two in the afternoon. That's when the coal-blackened miners off the first shift came in for their first drink of the day.

But on that day the Bald Head Man walked into the Collier's Folly at a quarter to eleven, it was as quiet as a whorehouse on Sunday morning because Vim Jackson was passed out on the table in a puddle of his own sick.

Me and Aeshna was at our usual table in the back corner having a beer so watery it might as well been piss. Wouldn't be surprised if you'd told me Sam Hill pissed in it himself to make it go further. Sure as hell tasted like it.

Anyway, when the Bald Head Man walked into the bar, he came straight over to me and Aeshna like he knew who we were. I'd never seen him in my life. Neither had Aeshna. And I should know. We've been together since Old Heck was a pup.

"Been looking for you," the Bald Head Man said, his dark brown eyes on me.

"Is that right?" I asked, setting my mouth hard.

"That's right. For quite some time."

Now, between you, me and the fence post, people don't come up in the Collier's Folly looking for me. They come for Aeshna. She can look at a person with those compound dragonfly eyes of hers and weigh their soul.

Yeah, you heard me. My sweet thing got these compound eyes and insect mouth-parts from a flesh doctor who spliced human and dragonfly genes to make her. We're two peas of a different pod, me and her. It's why I love her.

But back to what I was telling you. If Aeshna don't like what she sees when she looks at a warm body, well, let's just say what happens next ain't pretty.

And these fools who come see her know that. But what really trips me out is how they pay for that sort of thing. Good hard-earned scratch, too. It don't make sense to me. You'd think in these days and times the last thing someone wants to know is if they going to hell or not. Especially considering Aeshna can send them there at a moment's notice.

But I'm getting ahead of myself.

Like I was saying, the Bald Head Man eyed me up and down, and then said in a calm, clear, but quiet voice: "I come for some dirt."

I nearly shit myself. But I played it off.

"Do I know you?" I asked him, narrowing my eyes. My steam clock heart was ticking like nobody's business.

"No. But I know you."

I glanced at Aeshna, trying to pull the Bald Head Man's eyes to her gaze and her eternal judgment. Of all the people to mess with, he should have known better than to mess with me. My sweet thing Aeshna don't play. But the Bald Head Man wasn't as stupid as he looked. He wouldn't fall for my little trick. So I decided to get siddity on him.

"Get out of here, little boy," I said, waving him away like he was some poo-putt mudlark's child. "You ain't got coin enough for us."

The Bald Head Man chuckled, and then nodded. "You're right, I don't. But the Hanged Man does."

Chile, I couldn't tell you the last time I nearly shit myself twice in one day, but I almost did right then and there. And with good reason.

The Hanged Man don't play. In these days and times, he's the Head Negro in Charge. If your steam is clean and plentiful, it's because of him. And if ain't, it's because he don't want it to be.

They say the Hanged Man lives in the Old Sears Tower, in what used to be downtown Chicago, and he has his people on every single floor. They also say the Hanged Man wants to bring this barren, desolate, dusty land back from brink of the end of the world—so he can rule it with an iron fist. Or hanging upside down from the ceiling blindfolded.

Either way, if you ask me, ain't good for us little people trying to make a living out here.

It was as plain as the nose on my face that man wanted to be more than some steam baron who gets his jollies by hanging like a bat. It was also apparent to me that the Hanged Man wanted to rule this worthless city that was once Chicago with help from the dirt in my chest. The only dirt that will grow anything at all in this godforsaken place.

But I decided to play the role, anyway.

"I don't know what you're talking about," I told the Bald Head Man. My steam clock was still going a mile a minute, and my smut—that's the boiler in my belly for you gutter-minded people—was working overtime, too.

The Bald Head Man smirked at me. "Your name is Petal McQueen. You're fif—"

"You better stop right there," I said, cutting my eyes hard at him, "if you know what's good for you." The Bald Head Man just grinned. "Ain't nothing funny nor respectful about revealing a lady's age."

He wiped that grin off his face, but fast. "My apologies," the Bald Head Man said, and then continued. "You were born in Vicksburg, Mississippi, but you moved to the South Side of Chicago and Jeffery Manor when you were seven years old. When you were nine years old, you were stricken with polio.

"The disease ravaged every organ in your chest and torso, especially your heart. Your mother, Willie Mae, took you to a steam surgeon, who just happened to specialize in metallurgy and glasswork. She didn't think you would live. But you did, and then some.

"Not only do you now have a steam clock heart, but for some reason only the devil himself knows, that steam surgeon also fitted you with a compost boiler. Every three weeks, that one-of-a-kind smut of yours fills your wonderful chest with pristine, fertile dirt you sell on the down low to the poor and starving so they can eat the bounty their vegetable and fruit gardens produce."

It pisses me off when people think they know you when they really don't. And it pisses me off even more when those people who try to tell you about yourself are right.

The Bald Head Man leaned forward and reached for the neck buckle around my high-collared, double-breasted Vivienne Westwood pea coat. I grabbed his hand, quick as a snake, and twisted. His eyes widened at my strength.

"You might think I'm as old as dirt and black pepper, but that don't mean I'm slow and weak." The Bald Head Man tried to take his hand back, but I wouldn't let him. I wrenched it even harder, and he gasped a bit. "Why don't you just set here for a while so we can talk like grown folks do, young buck?"

The Bald Head Man nodded, but I looked at Aeshna to make sure she was ready in case he had one of those gear guns on springs up that long-sleeved Galvin overcoat of his.

Now, I didn't tell the Bald Head Man this, but I don't mind telling you: all that stuff he said about me is true. I'm a Delta Child. Polio nearly killed me. I am fifty-something years old, but black don't crack, so I don't look a day over thirty. And I have more dirt and worms in my chest cavity than my mama Willie Mae does, and she been dead going on forty years.

You open up my pea coat and it's all there, plain as day. There's even a glass panel that swings out, for easy access. And in case you're wondering at my shape; my tits are made of glass and swing out, too. So do the nipples.

But that don't mean some chap I don't know can walk up to my table, unbuckle my pea coat, and get all touchy-feely. That's how hands get broken.

I relaxed my grip on the Bald Head Man, but I didn't turn him loose. "What do you want?"

"It's not what I want. It's what he wants."

"What does he want?"

"You. Your dirt. In his stable."

"I ain't no animal."

"He didn't say you were."

"What if I say 'no?'"

"No one says 'no' to the Hanged Man."

"Looks like I'm the first, then."

The Bald Head Man tried his best to make his face give me an I-could-whoop-you-like-you-stole-a-Mississippi-mule look mixed with an I-will-stomp-a-mud-hole-in-your-ass glare.

But it didn't work. It takes more than the side eye from some baby-faced, no-good chap to intimidate Petal McQueen. 'Sides, if anybody was stomping mud holes in asses, it was me.

The Bald Head Man realized that, and brought his other hand from beneath the table. That was the moment he forfeited his life.

Just like I thought, he had a gear gun up his sleeve, but Aeshna was on him. She backhanded it away faster than quick gets the news, all without upsetting the table. Aeshna's speed surprised the Bald Head Man so much, that he couldn't help but look at her open-mouthed and slack-jawed. That meeting of their eyes was all she needed to appraise his soul.

And it wasn't a good appraisal.

Aeshna's labium thrust out from beneath her mandibles and latched onto the Bald Head Man's face. He screamed like a little boy as she devoured his soul, sucking it out of him like a straw. His beautiful brown skin greyed. His face shriveled and puckered. And only then his screams stopped.

Mouth still open in shock, the Bald Head Man fell to the sawdust-covered floor, a pulpy hole where his eyes and nose used to be. Ain't nary one of the half dozen coal miners around us say a word. They'd seen it all before—out of the corner of the one eye that didn't take in Aeshna, that is.

I nodded to my sweet thing, and we stood to go. I might not care for the Hanged Man, but I wasn't stupid. He would just send more of his bald head men who died like little boys.

Since I was the one on side -eye display as we walked to the entrance, I patted my thin and shiny 360 waves to make sure nary a one was out of place. Willie Mae didn't raise no fool, and she certainly didn't raise no nappy-headed fool.

But before we walked out the Collier's Folly, me and Aeshna paused in the doorway and looked around. We'd worked out of that bar for years. Last thing we should be doing was running away from our office, our place of business, with our tail between our legs.

So we didn't.

I looked at Aeshna. She nodded, took my hand in hers, and we walked right back to our table and sat down.

And that's where we're sitting right now.

Waiting for the Hanged Man.

Waiting to appraise his soul.

A WILL OF IRON

RAY DEAN

In the years after a war that had never quite been civil, there were small men that wanted to be big; and then there was the genuine article. John Henry was a man who was more than physically big: where he walked people watched him and when he spoke people listened.

That was no small feat in the valleys of Talcott, West Virginia where men were thin and short beside the stands of tall trees, and soft and insubstantial next to the rocks they were hired to move.

The C & O Railroad had track to build and, like any company with an eye on more than survival, they wanted to do the job and do it fast. They hired men and set them to work, urging them forward, ever onward, laying track for the line.

Songs would rise, shimmy up the tree trunks and shake the leaves above. Songs that gave the men a pace, a stint to follow, and kept them all on the line. And there, in the middle—in the middle of it all—was the big hammer of John Henry: the one they called *The Steel Drivin' Man.*

John Henry, must have seemed as big as one of those trees for the men around him certainly looked up to him, listened for his call. They watched the wide swinging arc of his hammer and they struggled to keep time.

Stories, there were stories, of that Steel Drivin' Man. The stories traveled up and down the Appalachian Mountains and far and wide like a Western tide. The stories grew in size as they traveled, but everyone swore they were true and soon the name of John Henry was as big as Bunyan and his Blue.

That's why that morning, that cold and shivery morning, they heard a braying sound. A man rode up that mountain pass a team of donkeys pulling his wagon up the long and winding road. A man with a pert straw hat flicked the reins of his wagon and drew all eyes to him as he entered the C & O Camp. The bang of hammer on stone slowed down, the songs stopped one voice at a time, and eyes turned toward the curious site stopping work all through the camp.

The Boss wasn't a man with a lot of patience. The boss wasn't a man that took many breaks. The boss didn't like anything that slowed down the work.

He pushed his way through the lumbering workers and stopped the rig with a look. "State your business, sir," the boss said gruffly.

Pushing his hat back with a finger crooked under the brim he gave the boss a measuring look. "I'm here about your business, sir. I'm here to make you a very happy man—a very happy man indeed. If you'll just give me a few minutes of your time to explain."

The Boss wasn't a man to let much distract from the job. Holidays had slipped by with little notice. And if someone had thought to ask for time away, they never did it a second time. The Company, he'd explained, was the only thing to think about until the line was done.

Now, as he looked about the site and saw the wide-eyed curiosity of his crew, he stopped. "You men can get started on your meals...Make it quick, mister."

Food drew the men away, lining up with their plates and mugs in hand they watched the unfolding scene.

With a smile, the man set the brake of his wagon and stepped down into the dirt. He brushed the dust of the road from his fine woolen coat. "I am a purveyor of fine goods, gentlemen. But rather than cart around dry goods and pickles I've come to fill another need."

He looked about, measuring each and every person in a glance. Much as a doctor might look a body over to determine a sickness, this man had a practiced eye for need; and in the hunched-backed bodies of some of the men he saw an opportunity. "I hear tell of a deadline you men are working towards... punching a tunnel through a mountain can't be easy work."

The men laughed amongst themselves as they shoveled rice and beans into their mouths.

"Boss says we do all right." Caleb, one of the men on John Henry's crew, piped up.

The salesman held up a finger. "Sure, sure... good enough, but to what cost? You men get your pay, but the wear and tear on your bodies must be a dear cost." Reaching out a hand, the salesman unhooked the rope that held his merchandise in place. "If you men are serious about reaching your goals," he yanked on a corner of the cloth covering the freight-bed of his wagon and let it fall, fluttering and flapping to the ground.

Some of the men stood, plates in their hands, to stare at the metal monster sitting up proud in the bed of the wagon. Sitting up and staring them down from its perch on high.

"This," the man insisted with a flourish of his hand, "is going to save your strength and save," he pointed at the boss, "you money. Gentleman, this is a steam drill." He drew out the last words, sounding each syllable out as though he relished the feel of it within his mouth. When he was sure that he had everyone's attention he stepped up on one of the back wheels and he pointed out the various features of the machine. He knew by the time he'd finished extolling its virtues, the Boss would be on board.

He was wrong. The Boss stood watching him, arms folded over his narrow chest and fraying blue woolen coat. "Just how fast did you say it was?"

The boast was loud, echoing against the rock wall of the mountain. "Three... maybe four times as fast as any man." Raucous laughter scraped at his confidence, lifting his chin and hardening the line of his jaw. "What am I missing?"

Caleb slapped a hand on John Henry's shoulder, barely interrupting the steady scrape of the big man's spoon against his metal plate. "Well, John Henry here ain't no regular man; and, if I'd money to bet, I'd say he'd beat your machine on his own."

Perhaps it was the huff of air from the salesman's lips or the wild cheers from the men, but the Boss gave a nod toward his best man. "What do you say, John Henry? You up for a race?"

The big man turned his head. "Can I finish my meal first?"

"It's only fair," answered the Boss before the salesman could object, "If the machine is as fast as you say it is, you shouldn't worry."

Shrugging off the words, the salesman stepped up to the long wooden table and looked into the metal plate that sat in front of John Henry, wrinkling his nose at the modest fare that the workers were quickly tucking away.

"At least my machine doesn't require beans for fuel," he explained. "It can work for hours and hours and needs no break. A simple twist of a valve lets go of any excess heat. And," he added, pride in his voice, "if it needs fuel it doesn't have to stop, a shovel or two of coke and it's good to go." His laugh was lost in the sudden hush of the world around him.

John Henry had set aside his plate of beans and turned sideways on the bench. "A machine may not eat like we do, yet you feed its fire. We drink water to cool our thirst and you quench its furnace at the end of the day."

Caleb nodded and others joined in. "A machine," John Henry continued as he stood, nearly blocking the salesman from the light of the afternoon sun, "has no pride in its work, no heart. It doesn't want anything— it only answers orders that it's given." A low murmur ran through the men as they tightened into a group.

John stepped over the bench and picked up his hammer, turning the simple tool over and over in his work roughened hands. "I'll show you what a man can do against your engine, sir." He gave the salesman a smile. "I think you'll be surprised."

As the big man walked through the crowd of workers, each of them called out encouragement and hands clapped down on his broad shoulders.

The salesman leaned closer to the Boss, his voice soft. "You don't think he'll be too embarrassed when the machine beats him into the ground, hmm?"

"What about you?" The softly spoken words were tinged with mirth.

The salesman leaned back, confusion marking his features. "What do you—?"

"How will you feel when my man beats your machine?" With

that, the Boss walked off after his men, trailing them to the mountain.

§§§

By the time the salesman had found a way to lower the machine to the ground, clearing its path of rocks and debris he found John Henry leaning up against the mountain: his eyes half-closed and a smile on his lips. His friends didn't help the mood, chuckling amongst themselves.

Jerking open the furnace door, the salesman held tightly onto his temper. "One last chance, son. Back out now and there's nothing to feel bad about; no one needs to hear about it." He gave the metal belly of the engine a pat and smiled, regaining his confidence. "Remember, this here is a steam engine: the best thing you can buy."

Caleb gave the man a grin and set his hand on John's shoulder. "This here's my friend. And he's the best thing you can't buy." A rousing cry roared into treetops.

Digging through his pockets the salesman brought out a box of matches and opened it. Reaching into the box he seemed to drop a few matches into the dirt.

"What've you got there?" the Boss wondered.

Lifting the box, the salesman said it simply. "Have to start the furnace with fire."

The Boss shook his head. "Not now you don't." He looked at John Henry. "When he starts... your machine starts."

The salesman pressed his lips together in frustration. "But I have to warm up the engine."

"Not my concern, really." The Boss gave the man a big grin.

"You said it would beat my man. You never said you'd get to have extra time."

"Fine!" The man bit out the word. "No matter what 'delays' you try to impose on me, you'll see... you'll see that the machine will win."

The men cleared the area about the two competitors and John Henry flexed the muscles through his shoulders and his back. He was a man used to hard work; but he was a man who knew how to take care of himself. He sized up his competition with its wide girth, pistons shining with the sun's light and the box of coke sitting on the back of the platform. It looked solid, well made, and ugly as hell.

"Don't you worry none," Caleb whispered in his ear, "you'll beat it."

John Henry nodded. He would win, he had to. If that machine could beat him, what would that mean for their jobs? How long would it be before they brought in a score of those machines and sent them off down the road.

The Boss stepped up between the two and gave his man a nod. "You know what to do, John Henry."

"Yes, sir." He hefted his hammer in his hand, letting it fall with a solid smack of the handle into his free hand. "I know."

Raising his hand high in the air, he looked to the salesman. "Ready? Well, go!"

The salesman nearly dropped his box of matches in his haste to pick out one. He ignored the laughter that mingled with the cheers for John Henry, as the big man swung his hammer in a high arc and hit the rock with such force that the air around them rang with the sound of it. Shaken, the salesman bent to his own task stoking the fires within the

furnace and feeding it with a shovelful of fuel he waited: his foot
tapping a rapid counter tempo to the building crescendo of John
Henry's heavy driving swings.

The men around them called out to the big man, giving him
their support while he worked. But when the hiss of steam and a shrill
whistle of escaping air threatened to drown out their cheers, John
Henry felt a little bit of heat in his lungs ready to escape. And so in
time to his next swing he opened his mouth: and a rally call was heard
through the angry hiss of the machine.

Stilling for a moment, the men smiled amongst themselves, and
answered John Henry back with their own voices. The men of the C &
O crew had their songs that kept the work moving through the heat and
monotony of the days. They had their songs and John Henry's voice
called them to it. His voice didn't bark out any orders, didn't call for
their help. No, this song was new. It was a call of drive and
determination.

The salesman set his machine to work, punching holes into the
rock nearly a foot behind the man raising his voice in song. His own
words of frustration were lost in the ringing answer of the men. They
progressed on and on, the questioning voice of John Henry ringing in
the salesman's ears asking questions that he had no answers for.

"What is steam but water burnin' up?" John Henry smiled as
his hammer slammed into the rock. "I got sweat a burnin' from my
skin."

The machine surged forward and pressed on just past the man.
The men turned to their friend, urgent pleas in their eyes.

"What need I for oil or grease?" He kept his eyes on the
growing channel of space, cleared by his hammer in the face of the

rock. "I have two eyes to see what's comin' up right in front of me." Adjusting his swing he knocked out a chunk of rock that would have interrupted his swing otherwise—that might have sent a stone flying back at his face. He smiled as he moved, using his own judgment to guide him.

A few feet away, further into the rock, the machine found itself in the same vein. Pistons labored heavily, pushing ever onward; but the new rock lay out before it was its own stumbling block.

The machine dug in, determined to follow orders, and found no relief to the strange situation. Its back wheels rose up, as the front pushed down beneath the weight of rock and its own impotence. The bit continued to twist and turn in the rock, leaning the body of the machine to the side as though it was hoping for a glimpse at its opponent.

John Henry was gaining steadily, his skill pushing him forward, as his feet stepped around fallen chunks of stone and the air punctuated with calls from the outside that waded through the thick dusty air.

He offered one look back over his shoulder at the Boss and the salesman standing at the mouth of the tunnel. "Might as well take that machine apart, Mister. If you melt it down we can use it for ties on the rail."

The cheers pummeled the rock with sound.

As the challenge wore on and the hours passed, the sunlight available in the tunnel barely covered the ground at his feet. John Henry saw the flickers of light and knew the lanterns were lit. The air about him was thick and weighed heavily on his shoulders. He heard the machine laboring behind him, the ground had been cleared and the machine was now flat on all four wheels as it drove into the cave walls.

"I must be gettin' close," called John Henry over his shoulder. He'd been keeping track of his progress by the pacing of his feet.

His boot from heel to toe was just over a foot and he knew he was close to the end. Here, deep into the cave of his own creation the air was tight and thick with dust and, even as he opened his mouth to sing, he felt the pressure on his body as though the air around him had become a physical weight upon his soul.

Like the bellows in the smithy, he pulled air into his lungs and fought to continue. He moved forward the arc of his hammer slowing, shrinking, more and more with each strike.

There's another thing, thought John Henry as the cheers of his friends muffled slightly in his ears, *a man can decide when to stop... when he should stop. The machine goes and goes until someone else flips the switch, tells it to stop, tells it to rest.*

The pain he felt radiating to every possible part of his body was one he could have saved himself. Losing the bet would have been one decision to make. But now as he set down his hammer, the handle sliding free of his numbing fingers, he realized this winning would be this last.

"John Henry?" Caleb's voice pulled at him, trying to turn his head.

Hands grabbed at him, trying to keep him up on his feet. His bulk was too much for their backs, but not their hearts. They collapsed with him on the ground, laying him out gently to ease his pain. The salesman stood by his machine, listening to the shuddering hiss of the engine as the boilers blew off their remaining steam. He watched their down-turned expressions lengthening with the shadows of oncoming night.

The Boss made his way between the men, kneeling down beside the big man laid out in the cooling evening shadows. Pressing his fingers to John Henry's neck he waited, and wondered, and finally shook himself. "One of you best fetch Polly here."

A few men at the edge of the group pushed to their feet and ran off down the road, hands reaching up to hold onto their hats. The salesman felt a knot tighten deep inside his chest. John Henry had beat the machine. Gone further than the machine. He'd pitted himself and his knowledge against iron and steam and had won, just once. He'd never repeat the win.

There was no one else like him left in the world and, like it or not, things had changed right before his eyes. He wasn't sure it was for the better.

The crew didn't have to wait long. Polly was suddenly among them, stepping through the crowd to be near John Henry. She knelt down in the cool earth and pressed kisses to his face. "Caleb? Fetch me his hammer."

There was a shuffle of movement and the hammer was found amidst their gathered crowd. They handed it over to her and she took it in both hands, her shoulders bending with its weight. She leaned closer to him. "Open your hand, John Henry," her whispered words were full of love and pain, "go ahead now, open it."

She watched as his fingers twitched and began to open...a slow, hesitant, painful movement before she laid the handle of his hammer across his palm.

"My hammer." The words escaped his lips and men bowed their heads under their weight. "Jus' like my Papa said." A gasp of air came from his lips...and then all was still and silent save for the soft mournful cries of Polly over the still form of John Henry.

THE PATH OF THE IRONCLAD BISON

PENELOPE FLYNN

Zahara hung back beside the brick Mercantile building, just off the curb of the cobble-stoned street in Baltimore. That's where Porter suggested she should stand while he negotiated.

She didn't draw too much attention dressed in her work pants and shirt covered by her blue work jacket. Her hair was pulled up on the top of her head and stuffed inside her stovepipe hat which was oversized and pulled down tight around her temples. Porter was dressed the same but where she looked awkward and disheveled, Porter who stood six feet three inches tall (nearly seven inches taller than she), appeared tidy and commanding.

Porter consulted his pocket watch and briefly glanced in her direction, as the wagon master continued to gesture and scratch his head. Finally the two men shook hands evidencing the positive conclusion to their dealings.

She remained where she had been directed to stand until Porter gave her the "all clear" sign. She walked quickly and met him in the center of the street, and then together they headed east.

"Well... are we set?" She asked anxiously as she kept pace with his longer strides.

"So it would seem," Porter smiled, his pearly teeth displayed in an uncharacteristic grin, "but we don't have much time. They're leaving for points west, tomorrow."

"Tomorrow?!" Zahara asked not able to hide her surprise, and allowing her voice to modulate higher than what she intended.

"If we don't make the wagon train tomorrow, we'll have to wait until next month. And with us both out of work and nothing firm on the horizon, I don't see us making it another month."

She knew he was right. Although they both squirreled their money away judiciously the dearth of meaningful labor had whittled their funds down to near nothing.

They quickly strode the street toward the boarding house that Porter had come to call "home" since he left the Cross Continental Airship Line a year earlier, and which Zahara had called home for the past two months. Cross Continental had been the third employer to hire Zahara after the War. It was the best job she'd ever had. That's where she met Porter... in the engineering section.

Engineering in the Airship industry included both in-flight and ground crew positions. The engineers did all repair and maintenance and even corrected design flaws. But the best thing about engineering at the dawn of the industry, was that it didn't matter whether you were male or female or any color of the rainbow.

Lives and livelihoods depended on the proficiency of the engineering staff. So, the Airship lines always made it a point to recruit the best. Porter Dreyton was the best engineer in the city...maybe even in the country.

Zahara had been a dirigible pilot at the end of the War Between the States. The transport company she worked for had a contract with the Army of the Republic to move supplies behind enemy lines. The quiet Airships dodged in and out of the clouds at night, making deliveries of food, arms and medicine to the troops where no one had been able to break through before.

It was dangerous harrowing work, but it paid well. She acquired a small apartment in Maryland, decent food, well-made clothing and a bit of schooling. She moved to Baltimore permanently after the war because there was so much talk that there would be equality across the board. Skin color or sex would no longer determine an individual's destiny. Those were heady times.

For a while it appeared that the newly remitted nation would live up to its creed and for a few years it actually did. Employment, housing, education all seemed to be meted out based upon merit. Work was plentiful. Her ability to do minor repairs on the dirigibles was enough to get her onto a work crew for any of the newly created Airship companies. And, because of her flight credentials, she was highly sought after to routinely pilot the large Airships pre and post launch to insure their integrity.

If she wasn't the best at what she did when she started her career, she certainly became the best after working with Porter Dreyton.

It was widely known that Porter Dreyton had studied at the Benjamin Banneker Institute, and graduated at the top of his class. It was rumored that even as a student he had worked on very top secret missions for the Army of the Republic. Every now and then someone would try to get him to discuss his past, and although the War ended nearly ten years prior he refused to confirm or deny anything. He didn't like talking about himself.

Even so, Zahara counted herself lucky to have been selected for his crew. He ran a tight ship and accepted no excuses and everyone benefited. Cross Continental became the most flown Airship Line in the Republic, the first Airship Line to fly the golden triangle between

Baltimore, New York and Chicago, and they were the first to introduce service to the west. But with no funds for an Airship ticket and no company loyalty to former employees from Cross Continental, Zahara and Porter had to find more economic means of transportation to make their way westward.

"How much is the wagon master charging?" Zahara asked as they continued down the street.

"He's charging less than half of what it costs to take the train to Chicago," Porter replied.

"So he'll take us all the way to San Francisco?"

"That's what he said. Once we get to San Francisco everything will pick up. The Airship industry is just starting out there and they'll need good engineers."

The two continued down the road more slowly, and then Zahara asked, "Porter, don't you ever wish you'd stayed on at Cross Continental? Don't you think maybe you shouldn't have quit…because of the rest of us?"

Porter stopped in the middle of the street, looked her in the eye and said, "No one could have predicted the thousands of unskilled laborers that flooded into Baltimore these past few years, Harry. Cross Continental, like all the other Airship Lines, saw an opportunity to cut costs by replacing skilled engineers with people whose only previous jobs had been plowing, lifting and hauling."

"Maybe you should have just let them replace us. I'm sure you could have taught anyone to do what our crew did," Zahara said.

"Your crew would have been impossible to replace. It's one thing to train a couple of new workers. But even I didn't have the skill to replace an entire crew of skilled engineers with field and dock workers in the time they were demanding. I had to leave. I didn't have a choice. It would have been a disaster."

You mean it *was* a disaster," Zahara said quietly.

Porter's face clouded with anger. "Thirty-three people dead on the ground and in the air. It was the worst launch disaster in history and all completely avoidable. *The Integrity* was a fine ship with no design flaws. That crash resulted from the inexperience of the engineering crew. Were those lives worth the few extra dollars they saved by employing laborers incapable of performing the work? How could anyone with ethics and morals be part of that?"

Zahara nodded in accord. Porter was exacting when it came to issues of safety and *The Integrity* disaster reinforced his belief that Baltimore had become more concerned with commerce than safe, reliable transportation. It was then that he decided a change of scenery was required.

Both New York and Chicago were already stocked with skilled engineers but San Francisco, all the way across the country and just starting its Airship Lines was desperate for skilled engineers. There was plenty of work. All one had to do was get there.

It was purely Porter's largesse that had her dressed in men's clothing and sneaking into Kelly's Gentleman's Boarding House. She had just lost her apartment and was literally down to her last dollar, and considering taking dangerous work with shady characters when Porter caught up with her.

The original plan was that she would stay a few days until she found suitable lodging. But after a week of the two of them being able to eat and sleep in the same quarters without getting in each other's way, they decided that it made more sense for them to pool their resources and stick it out at the boarding house as long as they could.

Porter entered first and Zahara entered immediately behind him. They were lucky he had a room on the first floor near the rear entrance. They didn't have to interact with too many people and could generally come and go without observation.

They quietly slipped into the small room stocked with a wash stand, two beds, a small table and two chairs. Each of them had two bags sitting against the wall containing all their earthly belongings.

"We can only afford one bag each," he said, "You need to sell everything else or give it away."

"But I've sold and given away almost everything I own… everything I've worked for since I've been here," she moaned.

"It's alright, Harry. Once we get to San Francisco and start working you'll be able to buy all new things," he said with optimistic finality.

There was no point in arguing. She sat down and began to divide her personal items into what she could keep and what she had to leave behind.

"And we have to do a money count," he added.

She hated the money count. At the end of every week the two of them would sit at the table emptying their wallets and all their pockets scrounging for every penny, dividing up the funds and determining how they would be spent in the coming week.

Once the determination as to how the funds would be spent was made, it was immutable. For the past six weeks they had been living on the bare minimum, socking away everything else to have enough to make the journey.

"One hundred twenty-five dollars each to pay the wagon

master," he said. "How much do we have left?"

"Twenty-two dollars and forty-three cents," she said.

"Not nearly enough," he said biting his lip.

"I'll sell my dresses. They're worth a lot. If we're careful, that should be enough to get us food and lodging in San Francisco for a few weeks while we get work lined up."

"I think I have a few items that might sell—a few tools. We'll start out early in the morning, sell what we can then meet back here at two o'clock. The wagon train rendezvous point is near the Mercantile building. We have to be there by three o'clock. So..." he said, glancing at his pocket-watch, "We should head out to the market, now and pick up some food...beans, rice, corn, some jerky...the basics to last us the thirty days to Chicago."

They immediately set out to market and purchased things they needed for the trip. Even though they spent a little more than they had estimated, the items were things they knew would be necessary on the trail or that would make the journey more bearable...new canteens, a hunting rifle, blankets, crackers and jam, and eating utensils.

By the time they got back to the boarding house all they had time to do was repack and prepare for bed.

"These bags are going to weigh a ton," she said as they carried the load of supplies into the boarding house.

"It won't matter," he said, "Once we get to the wagon train everything will be packed away in our compartment. We won't have to lift it again until we get to San Francisco."

The moment Porter slipped the key into the lock and turned it she knew something was wrong. His brow was knit. He quickly pressed his index finger to his lips and she immediately fell silent focusing on the door.

Porter pushed the door open slowly, but before she could see anything clearly, he rushed through and pounced. The man who was crouched on the other side of the door rifling through their bags was taken completely by surprise. Next to the man on the floor was a large sack which he was filling with various items from Porter's packed bag.

In that moment, everything appeared to slow down. Before the man could move, Porter was on him slugging and grappling. The man was as tall as Porter, not as well-built. He was wiry and his long arms gave him an advantage when he pulled a knife from his jacket pocket and began to swing wildly.

Zahara's bags were farthest away and with Porter and the thief crashing and maneuvering back and forth across the floor, there was no opportunity to grab the handy wrench she always kept at the bottom of her bag. But this proved unnecessary, as Porter subdued the thief then slammed him against the wall, pulling his arm behind him in an arm-lock.

"Harry, go get the authorities," Porter called to her.

"Wait! Wait, mister I can explain!" the man cried, "I work for Kelly! I work for the boarding house."

Suddenly the situation became clear.

Both Zahara and Porter knew that one had to be careful with boarding houses. Many were reputable but when you were down to your last coins and couldn't be picky, you had to be vigilant. Most places charged by the day. But if you had been there a few months they'd get used to your money.

If they got wind that you were pulling up stakes and moving on, you might come back to your room with all your personal belongings gone, and a long bill: equal to a week's rent left in their place with a Notice, alleging that you had made damages to the facility. Any truthful man would swear were they were there the day before you moved in—and probably five years earlier besides. But, you didn't have much choice. Unless you paid their inflated fines, you'd never see your belongings again.

"I was just doing my job! I was sent to get a deposit!" the man cried.

"Mrs. Kelly already has her security deposit. She won't be getting a dime more. And what's this?" Porter growled as the man's jacket opened up, displaying Porter's journal hanging precipitously from an interior pocket. Without warning Porter grabbed the man by his throat and began to throttle him.

Porter's placid demeanor evaporated and a homicidal rage twisted his features. Zahara was shocked and momentarily paralyzed as the man's face turned red and his eyes began to bug out of his head.

"Porter!" She yelled then dashed over to where he stood with his hands wrapped around the man's throat. "Porter, let go! Let go!" She shouted as she beat on his forearms. "You're killing him!" she cried.

It took a full five seconds before Porter let go. His hands shook as he stumbled back away from the thief who slumped to the ground.

"Are you all right, Porter? Are you all right?" She asked as she led him to the bed where he dropped down, now shaking all over.

"My journal...those are my private thoughts. He had no right —!"

"No, no... Of course he didn't," she said, as she patted his back trying to calm him; then immediately flew to where the thief lay on the ground recovering. She rifled through his pockets finding Porter's journal as well as his cigar case and shaving brush.

"You clean this mess up!" She hissed at the man as he sat up stunned and fearful. He immediately rose to his knees and began repacking the stolen items into Porter's bag.

"I think I got everything," she said evenly, "You should check your bag before we let him leave."

But Porter was still shaken whispering, "I didn't mean to…it's just my private thoughts. He had no right."

Zahara monitored the thief. When he was done, she pulled the bag over to Porter for inspection asking: "Is everything there?"

"I think so," he sighed, as he completed his review.

She motioned for the man to leave and he took off without another word. Zahara began packing away the newly purchased items for their journey.

Several minutes passed before Porter spoke. "I didn't mean to frighten you."

"You didn't frighten me, but I can't say the same for Kelly's thief!" She laughed.

Porter flashed a faint smile and then said: "I don't talk much about my problems or my past. I prefer to write things down, then review them. It helps me gain perspective. Sometimes I might write something I don't mean or that I might be sorry for later. But since what I write isn't for anyone else's eyes, I permit myself the luxury of writing what I feel at the time."

"You don't have to explain anything to me. It was yours and he shouldn't have put his hands on it. You had every right to do whatever you thought was necessary to convey your displeasure."

Porter smiled and heaved a sigh of relief. "It is late. We should be getting ready for bed."

Zahara threw herself onto one of the beds, while Porter took his place in front of the washstand. He looked in the mirror and shook his head. He hadn't shaved in weeks, but still hadn't grown a full beard. He used a pair of scissors to trim his mustache and his sparse facial hair.

From habit Zahara turned to face the wall, so that Porter could complete his bathing in peace. When he was done instead of going to bed, he sat at the table by lamplight writing in his journal, a ritual he engaged in every evening. It passed the time and captured his focus while she undressed and bathed. Some evenings if he completed his writing early, they would engage in conversation. But that night, after all the excitement, she was exhausted and fell asleep to the sound of Porter's measured lettering.

The next morning Porter's watch sang out its alarm before daybreak. They rose purposefully, ate some of the soda crackers and jam they had purchased for their trip then headed out at dawn to sell what they could.

Zahara walked from one end of town to the other. She was sure Porter wouldn't approve. He just wanted her to get the items sold for whatever they could recover the quickest, but she was intent on getting the best price. It took her until midday to try and sell her small cache of jewelry and figurines. She was hoping to at least recover enough that she might be able to hold on to one of her dresses.

But what she was being offered for the jewelry and figurines was substantially less than what she had hoped; and though some vendors showed interest in her work clothes, she knew she would need them immediately after she arrived in San Francisco and they would cost her ten times more than what she could get for them in Baltimore.

It was after one o'clock when she arrived at the dress shop. The beautifully made gowns she carried had been purchased the previous year. They were still in style and looked brand new. She had worn two of them at the lavish parties that Cross Continental gave for their employees for New Year's and the company anniversary.

She never got the wear the third dress. She had been let go before New Year's. The proprietress gasped at the beauty and workmanship, then became very officious saying, "These *are* yours, correct? I mean you *did* purchase them?"

Sahara's eyes narrowed slightly and she quirked her brow a bit. Three years ago she would have thought nothing of the woman's comment. Three years earlier, Baltimore was still living the dream of an egalitarian society. If a shopkeeper made a comment like that it would have simply been to verify ownership. But now with jobs scarce, food becoming pricier and prosperity quickly fading into memory, those old biases began to rear their ugly heads.

She and Porter had learned to ignore the signs reading: "blacks and women need not apply," and turned their attention to working for employers who knew and appreciated their caliber of work. But again, with more and more unskilled labor flooding the city, it was impossible to get anything steady.

The first time there was a complaint whether it was about the amount of pay, the timing of receipt of pay or working conditions it didn't matter. The first comment would earn an engineer his or her walking papers. Zahara had learned how to look the other way out of necessity, but Porter refused. He was a principled man. He believed in the promises of the War of the Republic and every day that he watched those ideals slip away in Baltimore was like a slow death. Baltimore was killing him and the wagon train to San Francisco held out the possibility of a new beginning.

Maybe that was why Zahara, who on any other day would have stripped the gowns from the woman's hands and stormed out the door, instead smiled politely and said: "Of course," then pulled out the receipts for the three gowns establishing their price and provenance as Henri Michel originals. Henri Michel was the most prominent dressmaker in Baltimore at the time.

"Well, these were made last year!" The proprietress said with a huff, "I don't know how my patrons would feel about wearing a gown made last year."

Zahara knew exactly how they would feel. They would feel exhilaration at the prospect of wearing a Henri Michel original even if it was *five* years out of date. The dresses were bustled with expensive embroidery and lace. The one she had not yet worn was still at the pinnacle of fashion.

She had paid twenty-five dollars for each gown, an exorbitant sum. But back in the heyday, when Engineers were paid as skilled laborers and where she was paid bonuses for her piloting skills it seemed a drop in the bucket. Now in her time of financial need she was almost embarrassed that she had spent her money on something so frivolous.

"Ten dollars each," the woman said.

"But this one hasn't even been worn," Zahara said pointing at the new gown.

"That's what you say. How do I know it's true? Ten dollars each is the best I can do."

Zahara knew she could do better. Henri's name was becoming more well-known each day and continued to draw the best prices. The three gowns would easily sell for exactly what she purchased them for and the proprietress knew it. But Zahara had no time to haggle. It was getting close to one-thirty and she still had to cross back to the boarding house to meet Porter.

"Ten dollars each? Fine," Zahara said then watched the proprietress hurriedly scoop the money from the register and thrust it into her hand. It was so much less than what she wanted, but Porter was counting on her and she would not disappoint him.

When she left the dress shop she felt like crying, but she knew it wouldn't help her situation so she mentally began to tally how the extra funds would meet their financial needs. As she made her way toward the boarding house, she made a stop at the Pawn and Consignment shop to see if she could get any more for her jewelry than the fifteen dollars she had been offered.

Otherwise she'd just as soon keep it. She would explain to Porter. He would understand. She could eventually try to sell it in Chicago or San Francisco, if necessary. She hurried into the pawn shop with not too much time to spare before she had to meet Porter.

After haggling with the pawnbroker, she left feeling unhappy but not as taken advantage of as she felt leaving the dress shop. As she stepped out onto the sidewalk she saw Porter walking out of the Curiosity Shop. She waved. He waved back and met her half way down the street.

"All right. I successfully sold the last of the things I purchased in Baltimore that made me feel like a successful member of society," Zahara said half-jokingly.

"It will all be worth it," Porter said.

"I have no doubt," Zahara said with a heavy sigh.

She looked down. Porter was still carrying both their packed bags. When they left that morning they knew they would not be welcomed at the boarding house again and if anything was left behind Mrs. Kelly would not make the mistake of sending one unarmed man, again.

"I was able to get thirty dollars for the dresses," she said, as they walked down the street toward the rendezvous point.

"You did well. No one was interested in my tools for anywhere near what it would cost to replace them, but I got twenty three dollars for my watch," he said.

"Your *watch?*" Zahara cried as she stopped in her tracks, "But everyone knows that it was special to you—an award from the Institute! You shouldn't have sold it, Porter!"

"How could I ask you to sell everything you've worked so hard for and not be willing to do the same? When we get to San Francisco and get back into the industry, I'll buy a new watch...an even better one."

There was really nothing more to say. But for the first time Zahara understood how truly committed Porter was to their journey, and how much he sincerely believed that they were going to a better life.

§§§

When they arrived at the appointed place, the wagon train was already lined up for departure. The twenty-three individual compartments, as they called them, were all connected to each other; and ultimately all connected to the Iron bull steam tractor, that would move the entire train of wagons from Baltimore to Chicago and then from Chicago to points west.

A young man with a stack of papers walked down the long line of people assembled there: calling out names. Dozens of people carried individual bags, while just as many others carried what looked like entire households. Eight horses and six oxen were also yoked to the rear of the train.

"Disembarking in Chicago?" He asked each person; then, based on their response, he would direct them toward the front of the train or toward the back of the train.

When the young man reached Zahara and Porter he took their money, and directed them toward the back of the train saying: "All travelers going past Chicago please move to the rear compartments!"

When all the travelers who were headed past Chicago, aggregated at the rear of the train, the young man cleared his voice and began to speak loudly:

THIS IS A PUBLIC ANNOUNCEMENT: THE IRON BULL TRACTOR COMPANY IS A TRANSPORT COMPANY AUTHORIZED TO TRANSPORT PEOPLE, CHATTEL AND PERSONALTY. IRON BULL TRACTOR COMPANY IS NOT A SECURITY FIRM. BEYOND CHICAGO, PASSENGERS TRAVEL AT THEIR OWN RISK. FROM CHICAGO TO OUR FINAL STOP IN SAN FRANCISCO

THE STEAM WAGON TRAIN TRAVELS NEAR THE
INDIAN TERRITORIES. THERE HAVE BEEN REPORTS
OF RECENT ATTACKS BY THE IRONCLAD BISON AND
OTHER HOSTILES NEAR THE INDIAN TERRITORIES.
YOU ARE RESPONSIBLE FOR YOUR OWN SECURITY
AND ARE REQUIRED TO REMAIN NEAR THE WAGONS
UNLESS INSTRUCTED BY THE WAGON MASTER TO
DO OTHERWISE. THERE WILL BE NO REFUNDS ONCE
THE WAGON TRAIN LEAVES CHICAGO.

There was momentary uneasiness on the faces of the potential
passengers, but no one left. Each passenger continued the walk down
the docking area, looking for their designated compartments which
were actually old stock covered wagons but with gypsy caravan type
doors attached.

As they made their way through the dozens of people milling
about trying to locate their compartments and those loading their
goods, Zahara and Porter finally arrived at their compartment. It was
the wagon third from the rear, and easily one-third the size of the large
ones. It could realistically only house four people without baggage and
barely two comfortably with the few bags and supplies they were
transporting.

The wagon had seen better days but it was structurally sound
and appeared water tight. Porter pulled up onto the buckboard then
gave it the once over.

"We should probably sweep it out before we load up," he said
wrinkling his nose.

"Sweep it out? You mean dump it in the Chesapeake for a

month! This thing smells foul...like sweaty feet and body odors and filthiness! It makes the Engineering floor at Cross Continental seem like a perfume factory by comparison!" she cried.

Porter laughed saying, "Calm down, Harry. You'll survive."

"No I won't! This stench will *kill* me before we even leave Baltimore!"

"How about this," he said taking a dollar from his pocket, "You run over to the General Store and buy a bag of charcoal."

Zahara didn't want to spend money unnecessarily but she grabbed the dollar faster than she had ever moved in her life and said: "Bless you Porter! I could kiss you!"

She ran to the store and purchased the largest bag of charcoal she could carry, two bandanas and a scrub brush. Porter didn't have to be told. He tied the bandana over his face and she did likewise as they immediately went to work crushing the charcoal down to powder. When it was fine enough they sprinkled a heavy layer over all the wooden surfaces of the compartment.

Zahara used the brush to spread the charcoal evenly and made sure it got into all the cracks and crevices, and then she squeezed onto the buckboard with Porter and their two over-stuffed bags.

"By the time we get to our first stop the charcoal should have soaked up some of that smell," Porter said.

"I hope so," Zahara replied, "Otherwise I'll be sleeping out here on the buckboard."

Porter laughed again, "I always took you for a country girl Harry... farming, tending the goats, pigs and chickens."

"I'll have you know that I come from a town...a small town, but a town nonetheless. I have never slopped a hog or wrangled a chicken before in my life!" Zahara said with a huff.

"Well then, small town girl, you are going to be in for an experience," Porter smiled.

"Some experience," she smiled, "you know a top of the line airship could do this entire trip in two days."

"But we couldn't afford the price of one Airship ticket...much less two. A month from now we would still be sitting here in Baltimore at Kelly's Boarding House waiting for an opportunity. This way we take our destinies in our own hands."

"All Aboard!" the wagon master shouted. All the people who were milling about near the wagons either jumped on board or stood away from the connected compartments. Dozens of people stood by the first fifteen or so compartments smiling, crying, waving, well-wishing.

"Waaagoooons Ho!" The Wagon Master shouted. Then the wagons groaned as the Iron Steam Bull's engine lurched forward. For a moment it appeared that they would all be stranded there. Then little by little the wheels on the wagons began to turn...slowly at first, and gradually picking up speed. In a few minutes time, the wagon train was moving along at a steady pace.

Although she'd flown airships in the war, and at work, this experience was new. As she watched the streets of Baltimore fade behind them, Zahara decided that she wouldn't complain about the accommodations, or the food or the smell. She would accept it. She would accept all those things as the fair price she had to pay for a new and better life.

§§§

It was a beautiful sunny day. They had left South Bend, Indiana their last scheduled stop before great city of Chicago. The crispness of fall spiced the air. Porter and Zahara sat on the buckboard of the wagon twenty-eight days after leaving Baltimore. She watched the scenery roll by while Porter scribbled furiously in his journal. The weather had been good and the wagon master indicated that they were making an average of twenty-five miles a day.

Zahara wanted to scream. What started out as an adventure, atop her mind, had become an absolute nightmare. She'd fantasized that the steam wagon train was going to be a family-like atmosphere where everyone worked together; a place where neighbors would share with each other to help one another along the way. She couldn't have been more wrong. The individuals and families on the train were greedy, petty, self-interested pigs who would just as soon steal from you as look at you.

Theft was rampant. At least three times when they encamped near watering holes to refill the Iron Bull's steam engine and to water the livestock, she and Porter had caught other passengers rummaging through their compartment; then swearing that they were confused and had mistakenly stepped into the wrong wagon.

Twice Porter had to physically reprimand someone who was attempting to make off with their rifle and Porter's tools. Four times men had been caught trying to force themselves on women and there had been two attempted shootings—one where someone had actually been injured.

It certainly didn't help that she couldn't stand the sight of the wagon master. It wasn't his looks...not really. She had dealt with more than her share of the portly red-faced denizen of Baltimore who were the essence of the milk of human kindness…salt of the earth people. And it wasn't the fact that he was a southerner. She had dealt with more than her share of southerners during and after the war—some good, some bad. But this wagon master was up to no good.

He tried to hide his accent. She wasn't certain that anyone else noticed it. He tried to speak as if he was from Boston, clearly affecting his accent—at least to her. He was straight out of the Georgia hills. In the newly-remitted Republic where there was supposed to be equality for all, there was no reason to hide where he came from—unless he was an outlaw.

She told Porter what she suspected, but he explained it by saying: "A lot of southerners feel shame for their position in the War and want to disassociate themselves. Wouldn't you disassociate yourself from that if you could?"

"Well, I have to admit that, if I had been one of those low life slaves who protected their masters during the Raids of the Republic, I would have been ashamed to show my face in polite society after the war. I think I would definitely have left tried to start a new life." That's what she said to Porter, but she still didn't trust the wagon master.

There were the looks that she and Porter got too. She still dressed and comported herself as a male, especially seeing how vulnerable women on the trail could be. Although he called her "Harry" and didn't treat her with the genteelness that was conferred on the women of the camp, Porter couldn't help making certain that she was generally within shouting distance. His concern resulted in raised eyebrows more than a few times.

Some of the more nosy individuals would try to elicit

information from her, asking if Porter was her brother. She would calmly reply that Porter was her friend, and had been her boss and that they were looking for work in San Francisco. She would *never* say that they were skilled laborers. Once two brothers, who were carpenters, indicated what they did for a living they couldn't keep thieves out of their wagon.

Malachi Johnson, the so-called minister and his pinch-faced wife who claimed to be looking to build a church in San Francisco commented, good-naturedly of course, that the two of them should make themselves more available to the young women of the camp; and that it was *unnatural* for two attractive men like themselves to stay so much on their own. The sidelong glances, and smug countenances, though ignored by Porter, irritated her to the point of wanting to knock their expressions off their faces.

She didn't really care about their stupidity or their rumors. She had no intention of getting to know those gossip-mongers. But she did care about how their actions affected Porter. He was a good man. A few snide comments and rumors didn't concern her.

But it was no secret that someone being termed "unnatural," had been used to condone violence and other mischief against too many people to count. *In Toto*, life on the trail had to be the closest thing to hell that she could imagine on earth.

Be that as it may, she didn't want to spoil things. She didn't want to ruin the journey for Porter but all her instincts were screaming at her to get off in Chicago. She was no longer concerned with being an Airship pilot or an engineer. She would take any job anywhere just to get away from that wagon train.

"What's on your mind, Harry?" Porter asked not even looking

up from his journal.

"Nothing," she said.

"You've been sitting here all morning and not saying a word. Even when the wagon master said that we'll most likely arrive in Chicago tomorrow, you didn't seem excited."

"I'm fine. I guess I'm just tired…and bored."

Porter stopped writing. He looked over at her and said, "We forgot to bring something to occupy your time. I've been writing in my journal, but you don't have anything to do."

"I've got lots to do. I pick berries when we make camp. I string them and dry them. I help gather wood to burn the furnace for the Iron Bull. I help to transport water and help with the engines. I set traps for small game, and I kill and dress the game…"

"That's not what I meant, Harry. Of course we all have chores, but we also need to do something enjoyable to pass the time."

"I haven't had a spare minute of time to 'pass' since I was let go from Cross Continental," she said.

"So before you left Cross Continental, what did you like to do?"

"Well…" she said, sitting up slowly and smiling recalling her wonderful life in Baltimore, "I used to go to plays…I liked dancing," she said. "I would go to museums and eat at restaurants with very nice gentlemen."

"Certainly," Porter said, "But we cannot do many of those things here on the prairie. Is there anything else?"

"I used to read a lot."

"Perfect! When we get to Chicago we'll get you some books. I'm sure you're going to need them during the portion of the journey from Chicago to San Francisco. It's more than twice as long as this leg."

"Hmm...I'll consider that," she said.

"I know this hasn't been the great adventure I suggested it would be," Porter said as he closed his journal. "I wasn't trying to mislead you, Harry."

"I know you weren't," she said. "It's just that I expected something different. You read the news stories about the pioneers and how they all got together and functioned as one big family. That hasn't happened here."

"Maybe it's because the group is so big," Porter said, "Once we get to Chicago and the larger part of the group is gone, the rest of us might become more close-knit."

"That is a very big ' maybe' Porter," she said.

Porter looked out on the prairie and asked, "You're thinking about getting off in Chicago, aren't you?"

Zahara was going to deny it but she hadn't been in the habit of lying to Porter and didn't intend to start.

"I've been thinking about it," She said.

"I thought so," he said still looking out at the prairie. "This steam wagon train is twice as fast as the ox drawn wagons, and don't need the rest that the animals do. This trip used to take more than forty days. Now we do it in twenty-three."

"The steam train does the same distance in two days and an Airship makes the trip in a day and a half," Zahara said. "We've been out here for a month, and still have nearly three months more on the trail before we reach San Francisco. Frankly, I prefer to take my chances in Chicago. I'm sure I can find work. I'll let the wagon master know that I'm going to disembark and that you will continue on to San Francisco."

"You intend to stay in Chicago alone?" Porter asked.

"Well, I should be refunded the amount I paid for the portion of the trip from Chicago to San Francisco. Surely that should be enough to get me started," she replied.

"Do you really feel that strongly about it?" Porter asked.

"I do," she replied.

"All right, then. When we get to Chicago we'll tell the wagon master that we're going to disembark. Even if we receive a pro rata share of our ticket price back, minus their fee, it will still be tight living. But if we're careful it's possible to earn enough to be on our way to San Francisco in month or so."

"I didn't mean you had to stop with me. You should continue on to San Francisco. That's your dream!"

"It used to be your dream too, Harry," he said then nodded slowly. "Maybe you're right. If we stopped and took some jobs in Chicago for a while we could afford the train the rest of the way."

Right then, she didn't care who was watching. She threw her arms around Porter and kissed him on the cheek. "You won't be sorry for this, Porter. I'll work from sunup to sundown to earn what we need to get to San Francisco. "

Porter laughed as she peppered his cheek with more kisses, and then sat back on the buck board: thrilled at the prospect of life off the trail and in the great city of Chicago.

§§§

"I'm sorry. I don't believe I understood you correctly," Porter said to the wagon master, as they stood at the embarking point at the Chicago station.

"You heard me….No refunds," the wagon master said scowling, his portly face turning red.

"That's not what you said in Baltimore, sir," Porter said slowly grinding the words out, attempting to keep his rising anger under control.

"When we fill these trains going west, we don't have the luxury to give money back to people who can't adjust to life on the trail," he said cutting his eyes at Zahara, "We need every penny we collected to make this journey work for everyone. The rest of these people are counting on your money as well as their own to pay their way across the prairie," he railed.

"Well what if just one of us stays?" Zahara interjected. "He can go on and I'll stay in Chicago. Just give me back *my* share."

"You can stay in Chicago by yourself or you can both stay in Chicago for all I care, but no one is getting a refund," the wagon master said then turned and left.

"I knew that man was a crook. I just had no idea how much of a crook," Zahara bristled.

"Harry, I am so sorry. He told me that we could disembark at any time," Porter groaned in frustration.

"The man is a crook. There is nothing you or I can do about it," Zahara sighed, resigned.

"You were right about him, Harry. I should never have trusted him," Porter said.

Zahara hated when Porter was dejected. It didn't happen too

often, but when it did she felt as if the earth was going to open up and swallow them whole. Porter had become her rock and when he felt misgivings or self-doubt the world became a frightening place. But this time she wasn't going to let it frighten her. The wagon master had stolen their money. But he wasn't going to rob Porter of his peace of mind, as well.

So, she patted Porter's shoulder genially and said through a forced smile, "Well, we don't have too much time here in Chicago. So maybe we should have lunch and buy those books you've been talking about."

Porter, however, wasn't smiling. His eyes were narrowed and set. He reached into his pocket and handed Zahara a list and a handful of bills, "I don't mean to send you into the city alone, but I think I better stay here and watch the wagon," he said.

Zahara nodded in agreement, stuffed the bills into her pocket and took account of the list. It included food, camping supplies, a few comfort items and twenty books.

He smiled. "Buy the books, first Harry...okay?"

She smiled back and rushed down the platform into the city.

Chicago was a city in the process of being rebuilt from a terrible fire. But it was still beautiful and energetic. She hated that she couldn't share the experience with Porter. But she maintained her focus and went from store to store grabbing everything on the list. By the time she arrived at the steam wagon train embarking point, the sun was beginning to set.

The train, which was originally twenty-three cars long, was now only seven cars long with the Iron bull attached at the front. They were now the fifth car.

"I heard the wagon master say that we're leaving at daybreak," Porter said still sitting on the buckboard where she saw him last.

"You shouldn't let this upset you so much," she said. "We've dealt with people like this before. Remember," she said modulating her voice into her best Porter Dreyton imitation: 'It'll all be worth it when we get to San Francisco.' "

He couldn't help but laugh. They both began packing away the items she secured from her shopping, then sat in their compartment and ate steak and potatoes, and drank a bottle of wine that she'd managed to eke out of the budget he provided her.

"You better enjoy this," she said. "It's probably the last decent meal we'll have between here and San Francisco."

"You'd be surprised the kind of good eats you can get on the prairie," he laughed.

"Like what?" she scoffed.

"There's deer, wild turkey, prairie chickens, squirrel, and quail."

"Really?" she asked.

"Buffalo still roam the range and there are rabbits—"

"Rabbits?" she cried, "Why not just eat rats?"

"Rats? Oh, no! A lot of people think that rabbit tastes like chicken."

"I am not *ever* going to eat that," she said turning up her nose.

"You say that now…but when you're out there on the range with no other food in sight—that rabbit is going to look awfully good!"

The two of them laughed and talked until long after dark. They fell asleep accepting of the fact that they had at least seventy-five more days on the trail until their next decent meal in San Francisco.

§§§

All right, so it hadn't been so bad. Thirty days on the trail and it was just as Porter predicted. The decrease in wagons and parties on the trail brought them all closer together.

Even the judgmental minister and his wife would join in the evening songs played by the large Hungarian family, as the tractor bearing the seven wagons and now four horse and two oxen, chugged its way across the prairie. With their numbers diminished, hunting was easier and there were no reported thefts.

When they stopped to camp out under the stars Porter, in his rich and rolling voice, would read to the grouped travelers by moonlight from one of the many books they bought with them from Chicago.

This wasn't to say that everything was rosy. Some days in the distance they would see smoke rising. The wagon master indicated that they were probably isolated wildfires on the plain. But she saw how Porter bit his lip and began sitting with his rifle on the buckboard.

"What's wrong?" she finally asked after the appearance of the fifth smokestack.

"I'm not certain but I believe those might be smoke signals," he said.

"Smoke signals?" She asked.

"I have heard that the natives will send up smoke signals when they believe an enemy is approaching."

"Where did you hear that?" She asked.

"I don't recall. I just *heard* it," he responded with an air of curtness that let her know that the conversation was over.

But, as they traveled west the distant wildfires continued. Sometimes a week would pass and there would be nothing; but then off in the distance the trails of smoke rising up into the air would begin again.

After weeks and weeks spent on the trail they stopped and encamped nearly one hundred miles outside of Alliance, Nebraska. As the travelers sat for dinner around the campfire, the wagon master stood to address them. "It looks like I'm going to need to scout ahead a bit. We're nearing a hostile area on the border of the Indian territories.

"Sir, haven't we been in their country for the past four hundred miles?" Porter asked.

"Well yes, technically we have been in Indian country but there have been some recent reports of hostile activity further west," the wagon master said, "I just want to make sure the way is clear. You know there wouldn't be such a problem if it wasn't for the Sioux and their damned Ironclad Bison," the wagon master said.

"What is an ironclad bison?" One of the Norris girls asked.

"Well, back during the war, the Army of the Republic wanted to make a deal with some of the Indians to keep the Confederate Army from encroaching into the prairie. They approached the civilized tribes, but they weren't interested. However, the Sioux up north, they made a deal—quick."

"Their warriors would come down from the north and keep the Confederates and their Indian scouts from any moving any further north through the country's interior. They managed to keep every tribe hostile to the Republic off the entire prairie."

"The Sioux would never have enough warriors to cover all that ground," one of the carpenters said.

"Well that's where the real deal was struck. That's how the Sioux got the Ironclad Bison. In order to help them cover that ground, the Republic built the Bison. It's an airship capable of carrying nearly one hundred warriors all armed to the teeth."

"So, it didn't matter how many guns the soldiers on the ground had. They could never compete with a hail of arrows and bullets singing down from that flying bison. 'Death from above,' is what they called it. And that's what might be waiting for us as we move west," the wagon master said.

"I've never heard any instance where the Sioux have attacked any travelers or settlements since before the war." Porter said.

"Well they have," the wagon master said, "I think at least five wagon trains have been massacred by them since after the war, using that Ironclad Bison. Maybe it's not important news in Baltimore, but it *is* important for those of us who have to travel these prairies for a living."

Porter didn't respond but Zahara recognized the look in his eye. He was unconvinced. When he caught her looking in his direction, he walked off to join the remainder of the men who comprised the hunting party. Unlike the smaller game that Zahara and the carpenters set traps for Porter, the Minister, Mr. Norris and the Hungarian salesman were the men in the group who had experience hunting big game.

With the seasons changing they figured it was a good idea to see if there was anything they might be able to take down and bring back. The four men saddled up the horses took their rifles and headed south. Once they were on their way, Zahara and the carpenters and the rest of the Hungarians, who were on snares duty, began the process of walking out over several miles throughout the day checking the snares they'd set the previous evening to see if they caught anything and then went about the task of setting new ones.

From thirty snares set they yielded four quail and a turkey. They brought back the little they had recovered and hoped that the other men had come back with larger game. With the sun still up and nothing to do for another hour until they planned to go back out and check the snares again, Zahara decided to take this unexpected moment to herself, to read.

Porter had included several different types of books on the list. He focused a bit on adventure books but also had the complete works of William Shakespeare. He had her purchase the complete works of Charles Dickens and Edgar Allen Poe (which Porter planned to read to the children if they were still on the trail by Halloween).

In her own spare time she was reading Jane Austen. Of course she would never admit it to Porter, since she'd turned up her nose calling it romantic drivel, when he included it on the list. So she was happy that he was nowhere near camp when she snuck back onto the wagon to read a few chapters before they were called out to work again.

When she settled into her favorite reading spot and leaned back so that the sun could stream over her shoulder, Porter's journal tumbled off the back of the buckboard where he left it and onto the wagon floor.

Porter...put your things away. I am not your maid, she sighed to herself shaking her head.

As she lifted the journal to stow it back on the seat the pages fell open. Instantly she forgot about Jane Austen, or the snares or Porter. The journal he wrote in religiously didn't appear to be filled with the personal thoughts and dreams of the enigmatic Porter Dreyton.

Instead it was filled, page after page with drawings...machines the likes of which DaVinci and Benjamin Banneker himself would have been envious. But these weren't simply drawings. They were designs with specs and modifications. There had to be nine different Airship designs, steam boats, heating and cooling units, vehicles designed to traverse all types of terrain.

It was rumored that Porter was a genius. Now she knew it to be true. Each design carried with it a set of notes describing its inspiration and his intentions for its use. The vignettes were compelling, thought-provoking and sometimes whimsical. The romantic in her was enthralled with his lyric prose. The engineer in her was fascinated with the design and proposed methods of manufacture. She ate up page after page of the journal with time almost standing still.

"Hey, Harry I've been calling you for the past five minutes!" Porter's voice broke her concentration.

For a moment she was paralyzed. Porter had never told her that she couldn't read his journal and alternately he never told her that she could. *How long has he been standing there?*

"Ah, see! I told you. Jane Austen *is* entertaining," he smiled.

Jane Austen, she thought, and then looked down.

There in her hands was the journal, framed within the pages of the Jane Austen compendium. He hadn't seen it. From the angle where he stood all he saw was the cover of the Austen book.

"Well come on. Come see what we brought down!" he said.

"I'll be out in a minute," she replied.

"No one cares about your book, Harry. Just bring it with you," Porter said excitedly.

"All right, all right I'm on my way she said as she closed the Jane Austen book around the journal and stuffed it into her jacket pocket.

Zahara climbed out of the wagon and instantly beheld the spectacle. The hunting party had successfully brought down what must have been a ten point buck.

"This meat is going to take us a long way over the next month," Mr. Norris beamed as his wife and daughters examined the animal.

"Well, I'm no Indian, but I am very sure I can figure out something to do with the skins," Mrs. Norris said.

As they all clamored around the deer, one of the Hungarians shouted, "Look! It's the Iron Bull!"

And just as he indicated, off in the distance, the thin trail of the steam engine's smokestack puffed across the sky. Everyone watched and waited anxiously as the engine finally came into view, rolled up to the camp then backed up to its place in front of the first wagon.

The wagon master had a somber expression as he hopped down from the engine.

"Well everyone, it's about what I thought. By all indications the reports were true. There appear to be hostiles along the trail ahead."

A loud gasp rose from the group of travelers. Comments like: "What are we going to do? Are we safe here? Do we need to turn back?" were voiced.

But the wagon master waved his arms above his head, as if to wipe the concern from the air around them, and called out: "Be calm everyone, be calm! There's nothing to worry about. This is not a problem. We just have to travel a bit north to get around the troubled area, and then come back down."

"How much longer will that take?" Dr. Roxbury, of Dr. Roxbury's Fine Medicines and Concoctions, asked.

"No more than two additional days I would think," the wagon master replied.

"But what about the natives to the north?" Porter asked." What about the Sioux?

"We never had any trouble with them this far out," the wagon master replied in a clipped tone. "Now, I know this is a bit of bad news but it's only a few days. We'll still get to San Francisco faster than... a jack rabbit!" He shouted then threw back a cover on the floor of the Iron bull revealing ten fat rabbits.

Everyone began to applaud.

"One of the ranchers up the road a piece kindly offered these to you all. He says that trapping gets kind of slim this time of year and you probably could use them."

The women of the train headed by the minister's wife eagerly snatched up the rabbits and began the process of skinning them.

For the first time Zahara was happy to have drawn snares duty. The sight of them skinning and dressing the rabbits was more than her stomach could bear. Even after the rabbits began to roast and the aroma that was a lot like baked chicken encircled the campsite, she could not shake the image of them being served up a steaming hot plate of roasted rats.

The sun descended and the night rolled over them. As stars filled the horizon the campers sang and danced and enjoyed their rabbit along with some of Dr. Roxbury's "tonic," Zahara simply spooned beans onto her plate.

"Hey there, now! The wagon master cried as she passed him, "This rabbit was a gift! Everyone should have some!"

"No thank you," she said. "I don't eat rabbit."

"Nonsense! Just try it. It tastes like chicken," the wagon master said. He slapped a large portion of rabbit onto her plate.

"Thank you," she said, as she walked stiffly past him then dropped down onto a log near the campfire beside Porter.

"Aha, so I see you finally decided to try the rabbit," Porter smiled with a mischievous twinkle in his eye.

"No, I didn't decide to try the rabbit," she hissed, "that bossy wagon master just dumped it on my plate."

"Well now that you have some, you might as well taste it. It's good," he goaded.

"If you like it so much, you can have it," she said, deftly scraping the rabbit onto Porter's plate."

"I thought you were adventurous, Harry," he smiled.

"I am with other things but with this, no thank you. But if anyone deserves an extra helping of these prairie rats Porter, it would be you," she laughed.

Granted she didn't want the rabbit, but even if she did she would have gladly given it to Porter. He always had a positive outlook. He kept her focused on their long-term goals and he had become her dearest friend. Maybe that's the reason she felt so awful about the journal.

She could feel along with the Jane Austen book filling her inside jacket pocket: an indictment, a reminder of her terrible breach of his privacy. When Mrs. Kelly's thief in Baltimore put his hands on it, Porter made it clear how he felt. She'd even egged him on in his anger

— justified it even, saying that he had every right to display his displeasure in whatever manner he saw fit. She didn't want to think about how he would react, and tried to put the incident out of her mind. For a few hours she managed to do just that.

The relief of getting a feast that they didn't have to scare up themselves gave them so much more free time that evening that everyone was in a celebratory mood. Music played and songs were sung. There was even a little dancing. Doc Roxbury's great elixir machine (or as she and Porter called it: "His portable steam powered still") was working at full tilt.

All the adults, even the minister and his wife downed more than their share of Doc Roxbury's tonic. Even a few of the children snuck a swig here and there. "Good for improving the moods," the Doc would say as he handed out cup after cup to the travelers.

As far as moods were concerned, Porter really needed it. Since the crossing from Chicago, Porter had become more circumspect. Many of the days they spent camping out with the remainder of the travelers, he would be watchful and didn't engage in any of their activities beyond what was necessary to bring in food and other supplies.

That night, to see him interacting with everyone telling jokes and singing songs was a cheerful reminder of how their lives had been and what they could be when they reached San Francisco. However, if he discovered that she had read his journal without his permission she wasn't sure if he would ever trust her again.

She had tried a few times to break away from the festivities and sneak back to the wagons, but each time she was held up by one thing or another. The easiest thing to do was simply to confess, to let Porter know what she had done, beg his forgiveness then work for however long it took to regain his trust.

But she was never one to do things the easy way. What she decided to do was to wait until long after nightfall, after Porter was asleep, sneak back to the wagon and put the journal back where she found it, and pretend the incident never happened. Once she determined her course of action all she had to do was to wait.

Of course she failed to take into consideration all the revelry and merrymaking and the storytelling and singing. When she laid out her bedroll across the campfire from Porter and watched while he and some of the other men sang what had to be fifty choruses of some old drinking song...Zahara gave up. She was exhausted and her eyelids felt like lead.

How long can they possibly go on? She thought to herself as she watched them finish a verse then repeat the song's chorus for what seemed like the sixty-sixth time.

Finally, she had to admit defeat. As her eyes closed she told herself that she would wake after a few hours when it was dark and quiet. Then she would slip back into the wagon and put the journal back where she found it.

She drifted off to sleep to the sounds of the men's laughter and their singing the sixty-seventh chorus of the song.

§§§

Zahara woke with a start. She raised her head and peered around the campfire. All was quiet. The fire was smoldering and the light was dim. Porter and the two carpenters lay on the opposite side of the fire exactly where they were when she last saw them, before she fell asleep. Mr. and Mrs. Norris were huddled together not far from her feet and their two daughters slept not too far away from them.

She didn't see the salesman at first, but then realized that he was leaned against the far side of the rock near her head. Doc Roxbury and the Minister and his wife were near the Hungarians. The wagon master however was not where she last saw him. In fact, the wagon master, the iron bull…all seven wagons, the horses, the oxen, all their belongings…were gone.

"Porter! Porter!" She yelled forgetting to modulate her voice as she scrambled across to where he lay sleeping. "Porter! Porter! Wake up!" she shouted as she shook him.

But try as she might she couldn't rouse him. She suffered the same result when she tried to wake the carpenters and the Norris clan. When she shook the Hungarians, they woke but were groggy and achy. Two of them immediately began to vomit. She left off trying to wake the travelers and tried to follow the path left by the wagons and horses.

But in the darkness she could only track the wagons so far before it became too dangerous to be out on the prairie alone. She made her way back to camp where all the travelers were waking and experiencing the same symptoms as the Hungarians.

It was a long three hours or so before anyone could stop vomiting long enough to speak. Everyone who dragged themselves up moaned complaining of headaches and nausea.

"Too much of Doc Roxbury's tonic," one of the carpenters groaned as he dragged himself up.

"What should we do, now?" The other carpenter asked.

"I guess we should wait for the wagon master to come back,"

Mrs. Norris sighed, as she sat down near her daughters who were still experiencing dry heaves.

"He probably left to find water for the Iron Bull and the horses. The wagons are a lot lighter when we aren't in them and easier for the Iron Bull to pull," one of the Hungarians said.

"Yes, yes. That must be what happened," was the chorus that went up from the group.

"Of course because that would also explain why some of the canteens are missing. He probably had to use the water to run the Iron Bull, and took them to refill," the first carpenter said.

Zahara saw the expressions on the faces of some of the other travelers. The anxiety was evident. Quietly, without fanfare she buttoned her jacket shielding the filled canteen she wore underneath.

"Look we're all getting very excited over what is probably nothing," Mr. Norris said, "Let's just break camp, maybe pick some more of these berries and set some snares. By the time the wagon master gets back, we'll have a bushel of berries, some fresh rabbits and we will all have something to laugh about."

The crowd of travelers nodded in agreement as they slowly dispersed, but Zahara wasn't fooled. She knew they were watching... waiting for her to let her guard down. With Porter still incapacitated she was on her own. She already knew they were thieves. If the wagon master lived down to her expectations, soon they would be desperate thieves.

§§§

In spite of the situation, the travelers appeared optimistic.

Moving slowly, stopping now and then for the errant case of heaves or a hurried trip to the small grove of trees several yards away where their makeshift latrine was located, the group broke down into parties in order to manage as much of their usual daily activities as they could.

Everyone shared supplies, but Zahara noticed that no one was sharing water. The Norris group continued to reiterate how certain they were that the wagon master was probably refueling the steam engines. The others all agreed, though the choruses were becoming less audible and less enthusiastic.

When the sun rose on the third day after the wagon master disappeared in the night, everyone was tense. There was no more interaction. Even the fake laughter and halfhearted singing were gone. Two search parties had been out and back in each direction over the past two days looking for water. There was none. Even their rifles were gone...taken in the night. They had no means of hunting food and no means of defending themselves.

The horror that had been clear to Zahara since the beginning was starting to dawn on the rest of the travelers. They didn't want to believe it, but they were beginning to wonder whether the wagon master had chosen that particular spot, intentionally...to strand them.

Porter was just starting to recover but he could barely sit up. She fed him some of the dry bread the women had made over the past two days, and little by little she fed him from the canteen of water he wore around his neck.

When he was finally coherent she helped him walk into the shallow wooded area fifty yards from camp to relieve himself and clean up as best he could. When he was finished she sat next to him under the sparse trees. Out of the eye and earshot of the rest of the camp, she encouraged Porter to drink liberally from her canteen as she slowly updated him on what had happened with the wagon master.

"It seems the wagon master has finally shown his true colors to all," Porter said.

"And the rest of them are beginning to show their true colors as well," Zahara replied.

"How bad is it?" Porter asked, his face painted with concern.

"Well everyone worked together to skin and dress the deer but after it was salted and packaged, the stealing started again."

"But it's only been three days," Porter said.

"And every minute that you're sick, it gets more and more precarious for us."

"How so?" Porter asked his eyes burning.

"I overheard Mrs. Norris saying to the Minister's wife that she didn't understand why food and water was being wasted on you, that you obviously weren't getting any better. Understand Porter, they want to leave here tomorrow. I don't trust them. And if they don't think you can travel, I don't know what they'll do."

"Between then and now, we will be vigilant," Porter smiled weakly then closed his eyes.

"Are you all right, Porter?" She asked placing her hand on his forehead. "You're cold. Let's get back to camp and get you near the fire."

"Good idea," he said then graciously accepted her assistance to rise to a standing position and with the help of a gnarled branch he employed as a crutch, they walked together back toward the camp.

"Maybe we should get everyone to wait another two days to leave, or maybe we'll just let them leave without us and we'll follow them when you're better," she said.

"I am feeling better, now," he said, "No matter what, if they decide to leave tomorrow we have to leave with them. It's far too dangerous for us to travel the prairie, alone."

By the time Porter and Zahara returned to camp, the place was in a flurry of activity. Everything was being packed away and tension was in the air.

"We need to break camp…tie up these bedrolls, take what we can carry and head west in the morning," one of the carpenters said.

"*West?*" The Hungarian salesman cried, "We're in the middle of nowhere. Do you have any idea how far it is to San Francisco?"

"Well, it's probably too far to go back to Chicago," Mr. Norris said.

"But maybe there's towns going back east that we missed," the other carpenter said.

"I think there probably were, and I think the wagon master took us out of the way on purpose," Zahara said. "He didn't want us to be able to find our way back."

"What? What are you saying, that the wagon master did this?" Mrs. Norris cried, finally saying what they all were afraid to voice.

"No. It's obvious it was Indians…right?" Mama Weiss said hesitantly, "just like he told us…they must have forced the wagon master to drive the engine for them or maybe he is somewhere injured."

"What Indians? Did you see any Indians? Did you hear any?" The Minister's wife asked, the fear evident in her eyes and her voice.

"They must have come while we were asleep," one of the Norris daughters said.

"Where were their horses? Do you see any horse tracks? Did

you hear any horses?" Zahara asked.

"Are you trying to say that the wagon master did this?" the minister asked.

"Of course the wagon master did this!" Zahara shouted.

"He…he…asked me if we had anyone waiting for us in San Francisco," Porter said as he sat up, still groggy, "Does anyone here have…someone…anyone waiting for them in San Francisco; someone who might miss you if you don't arrive?"

Everyone was silent.

"He asked me if we were leaving anyone behind in the east. I told him, 'no,'" Mr. Norris said.

"Does anyone here have any family…friends, anyone back east that might try to contact you or knew you were taking this wagon train to San Francisco?" Doc Roxbury asked.

Again, everyone was silent.

"You think he left us here." Mama Weiss said, her voice trembling, "No wonder the price of the ticket was so good. He never planned to take us to San Francisco, at all. He has all our money, all our belongings. What kind of person does a thing like that?"

"You don't have to think about that, Mama Weiss," Porter said, "It doesn't matter. We just know we need to be ready to leave here, soon to find water and shelter. If we stick together we can do it."

"So are we all in agreement that we go west?" The first carpenter asked.

The travelers looked around, one to the other and although some looked as if they wanted to turn back, no one raised a voice in opposition.

"Good, then tomorrow we gather everything we can and we'll

leave the following morning," Mr. Norris said.

The next day everyone was busy pulling together whatever supplies they had to make the journey west. The snares were set one last time in hopes of getting something dressed and packaged for the trail before them. In an abundance of caution, Zahara had moved her bedroll near Porter's to keep a close watch. By noon everyone had begun to accept what had happened to them. They were prepared to leave…except Porter.

The exertion from the previous day had proven too much and he was once again listless and non-communicative. Some of the travelers gathered around as Doc Roxbury examined him. He checked Porter's temperature, looked into his mouth, examined his eyes, palpitated his abdomen and smelled his breath.

"He was fine yesterday. Why is he worse, today?" Zahara asked.

He knitted his brow then asked, "Did Porter drink any tonic?"

"Now that I think of it, no. Porter hasn't been drinking lately… not to say your tonic is alcohol, Dr. Roxbury," she quickly added.

"Well, I would be less than honest if I said that there wasn't maybe a touch of bourbon for flavor, but most of it is water, herbs and coneflower. The alcohol is harmless. Even Mrs. Norris and Mama Weiss give all their children two tablespoons of my tonic every day.

"Everyday?" Zahara asked.

"Yes," he said, "Now my tonic may not be good for *everything* that ails you, but it relieves pain. It's good for the stomach, an antidote for some poisons—"

"Do you think we may have been poisoned?" Mama Weiss asked.

"Possibly. Everyone, even me, thought it was the tonic that made everyone sick the other night. But now I'm not so certain. My tonic has persimmon extract. For those who were made sick enough to vomit, the persimmon extract may have kept any poison from entering their system."

"What do you think it could have been," the minister asked,

"It could have been anything...the rabbit, the beans, the bread but this looks like the type of poisoning when a person or an animal unintentionally eats foxglove." He said.

"But wouldn't everyone have gotten sick?" Zahara asked.

"As far as we know, Harry, you are the only one who didn't get sick," Doc Roxbury said, "Did you eat everything?"

"No...I didn't eat the rabbit...I gave mine to Porter," she said.

"So Porter had twice as much of the rabbit as everyone else," the doctor mused, "This can't be good."

"So what you're saying is that the wagon master didn't just leave us here. You're saying that he left us all here for dead. If it wasn't for your tonic everyone would be like Porter or worse."

"If I had any of the tonic now, it might help, but everything was in the wagon. Everything is gone," he said shaking his head sadly.

"What are Porter's chances?" She asked.

"I'll be honest with you. It doesn't look good. If we had more water to flush this thing out of his system that might help, or maybe if you could force feed him some coneflower, it could buy him some time until we get help. Coneflower usually doesn't grow well into September but I saw some growing around the edge of the wood," he said.

"Which ones are they?" She asked as she stood and pulled

herself together to travel.

"They're the yellow ones with the tall thick middle. Bring back all of it, even the root."

Before she headed for the woods, she knelt down beside Porter and whispered, "I'm going back to the edge of the woods to get some coneflower. Doc Roxbury said it should help. You'll be all right. I'll be back, soon."

Zahara headed off quickly to the woods planning to bring back as much coneflower as she could carry. There was a long way to Alliance and she was going make certain that Porter would have more than enough time to get some help.

When she arrived at the edge of the sparse wood she found that the coneflower was not plentiful, and that it took nearly an hour to find a substantial enough amount that she felt Porter would have a fighting chance. But she gathered what she could find then rushed as quickly as she could, back to camp.

As she approached there appeared to be a commotion. Voices were raised and dust was rising around the campsite. She had known there would be trouble. The thefts and fighting were bound to begin when things got scarce. Even with this smaller band of travelers, she didn't see how they would all make it across the prairie together, intact.

But as she got closer she couldn't believe it what she saw. There were arms and legs flying, kicking, pulling and dragging. People were shouting. Everyone was snatching and wrangling so much that no one even noticed her. All her civility fell away.

A crack sounding like a lightning strike split the chorus of angry shouting. The travelers turned to find Zahara: leveling a Colt revolver. This was the item she traded her jewelry for at the pawnbroker and which she'd carried on her person every day of the journey.

She trained the sights from right to left over the group of travelers. They split in half as she approached, some of them tripping backwards, all of them letting her pass. Porter lay on the ground disheveled, more dead than alive, it seemed. His hat and jacket were gone, so was his canteen.

He was spilled over onto the dirt where someone tried to pull his blanket from under him. His boots were gone as well. She ran to where Porter lay, while still leveling the revolver at the rest of the Travelers.

"Move back!" she said, "I don't want to hurt anyone! But I promise I will put a bullet through any man, woman or child that takes another step in his direction!"

She touched Porter's forehead. He wasn't feverish but his water was gone, so was the bag of food she had tied around his neck earlier in anticipation of the journey west, on foot. She looked up at them, her eyes blazing, daring any of them to speak. Mrs. Norris responded to the challenge,

"Doctor Roxbury said that he doesn't have a chance of surviving out here! My daughters are alive and they need food and water!" Mrs. Norris cried.

"Your daughters need water so you think you get to steal it? That was Porter's water. He needed it to survive, Mrs. Norris," Zahara said leveling the pistol at Mrs. Norris with a rage so blinding that she had to use all her discipline and self-control not to pull the trigger, "You've condemned him to death."

"Now hold on there," One of the carpenters said, trying to

bring calm to the situation, "We didn't mean you all any harm, we just thought—"

"—I don't care what you thought! But make no mistake I want his shoes and his jacket and I want you all gone from here!"

"We hadn't planned on leaving until tomorrow," Mr. Norris said.

"You already have your supplies. You have the deer. You've already stolen *our* supplies. What else do you need?!"

She hadn't finished talking when the carpenters began picking up their bedrolls and walking west. They dropped Porter's jacket and left it lying in the dust. The Hungarians shepherded their things together, and dropped Porter's shoes at her feet as they followed the carpenters.

There was no more conversation. Within ten minutes all the travelers had taken their belongings and moved on following the sun as it moved lower in the sky. None of her supplies were returned though her blanket remained laying in the dust.

Zahara was still leveling the pistol westward, when Porter rose and patted her on the shoulder, "We can't stay here. We need to get moving."

"Maybe we should let them get a few more miles in front of us, first," she said, relaxing her arm and bringing the pistol to rest at her side.

"Harry, going west is most probably a death march. I very much doubt that there were any farms or ranches. The wagon master planned this. There's nothing out there. Unless they are very lucky they'll walk west and they'll all die."

"So what should we do? Should we go after them and warn

them?" Zahara asked.

"We have no supplies and I'm not going to be much help to you or anyone else in this condition, so I propose we go north."

"North?" Zahara shouted incredulous, "You must still be sick from the poison! That's going even farther into Indian territory…into their protected lands!"

"I know that. But we need help and out here they're the only help there is. I don't believe what the wagon master has said. The Sioux have never been an enemy of the Republic--"

"A lot has changed since the war, Porter. A lot of the Indians have complained that promises made to them by the government were broken. And you know some of them have become hostile."

"Would you hand me my jacket?" He asked as he reached over and grasped his shoes, "We need to get moving while we still can."

"But shouldn't you get some more rest?" She asked as he moved slowly gathering what little remained of his belongings.

"No. We have to leave, now. It's about two days journey on foot to get to where we need to go. We have no food and I doubt we will find much shelter, so the sooner we travel the more likely it is that we'll survive."

"Don't worry, Porter. I've got enough that if we stretch it, it should be enough for both of us. If not, I've gone a lot longer than two days without food. We'll be fine."

Porter smiled and said, "Okay then pioneer woman, let's get moving."

§§§

The first day they walked almost the entire day without stopping. Zahara talked the entire time but Porter only responded to questions and picked his way along with the use of the makeshift crutch. Even after nightfall they continued to walk until Zahara could no longer feel her feet.

They made camp with no fire. She ate some of the berries and jerky she brought along but Porter would have none of it. He only accepted a few sips of water, and chewed a little of the coneflower; then brought out his compass. By the light of some kindling he made out their plan for the next day's journey.

When it was time to sleep they used Zahara's blanket to stretch out on and both squeezed under Porter's blanket. As she pulled in close to him Porter muttered, "I hope you unloaded that Colt. It would be a shame to arrive in San Francisco with our feet blown off."

"It's unloaded, Porter," she responded dryly, "And you're welcome by the way—for thanking me for saving your life."

"I doubt they were going to kill me Zahara, but thank you nonetheless for your singular act of heroism," he yawned.

She was going to respond but as she settled in, she felt the outline of the Jane Austen book in her pocket and her blood ran cold when she recalled that she still had Porter's journal. For several minutes she stayed awake wondering whether he had noticed it.

Porter didn't appear to have noticed anything and had descended into a fitful sleep. She still had a small amount of water and a little more food. If Porter was right and they made it to help in another day or so, they would be all right.

The second day they rose before sunrise and began walking. She noticed that Porter was having much more difficulty moving than the day before and knew it was because he refused to eat. She could get him to take a few sips of water, and a bit more coneflower; but that was all. They walked in silence until the sun came up, and little by little saw the mountains in the distance move closer and closer.

"At this pace we should make the foothills by sundown," Porter said. Zahara just nodded and kept walking.

By midday their pace had slowed. Porter, even with the aid of the crutch could not keep up with Zahara who had never been able to out walk him before.

Finally, Porter stopped in his tracks looking off toward the mountains.

"What's wrong?" she asked, "Are we going the wrong way?"

"I apologize for bringing you out here, Zahara," he said, with labored breaths. "I thought San Francisco would be a good place for us to make a new start. I wouldn't be your boss. We would just be two people. You wouldn't feel beholden to me. We would just be friends."

"We *are* friends, Porter. I wouldn't let just anyone convince me to spend almost half a year of my life crossing through this godforsaken prairie," she smiled.

Porter with the aid of the crutch bent down then relaxed into a seated position on the ground and said, "I will not be going with you to San Francisco. This is where my journey ends."

"You said we could make it to the foothills by sundown. It's only a few more hours. If we keep going we can still get there," she said.

"I'm dying, Zahara."

"No you're not. You're just tired."

"Zahara, listen…please. I have been poisoned and I will not get better."

"Well, we don't have to make the foothills, today. You can rest up now then we'll try again in the morning," she said as she sat down beside him.

"I will not be alive, tomorrow," Porter said through labored breaths as he finally dropped unceremoniously and lay on the ground. "It was my own greed. I should never have eaten the rabbit you gave me."

"The rabbit," she said finally, realizing that she sealed Porter's fate with the meat she had politely scraped off her plate and onto his. There as twice as much poison coursing through his system and with no tonic or antidote, he was as good as dead. What she thought had been a good deed back-fired.

"I thought if we left immediately we might be able to make it to help in time," he said.

Then Zahara's eyes grew dark with anger, "You're lying. You never thought we would make it, did you?"

"What does it matter? I'm going to die anyway, Zahara. I don't want you to die trying to save me."

"So, I'm supposed to walk onto some Indian outpost and tell them to take me in because my boss got poisoned, and I left him to die in the desert? Are you insane? They'll say that *I* poisoned you."

"I'm sorry Zahara. I'm not thinking very clearly but you have to listen to me. Take my compass" he said and handed her the wooden box that held the brass gyroscopic compass he has used to navigate them to that point, "walk due north until you reach the foot of the mountains. Then, walk due east for about a mile or two and you'll see round ceremonial burial mounds. They'll look like a grouping of round steps carved out of rock."

"Stand near them and find a way to draw attention to yourself. Scream, shout, dance, fire shots into the air. The burial sites are always guarded these days. Just remember to shoot into the air or away from the burial sites. Even stray shots in the direction of the burial sites might be mistaken for hostility and they will respond in kind."

"You know an awful lot of specific information for a man who needs a compass to walk the prairie," she said.

"It's getting late. You need to go, now."

"First, drink this water," she said pulling off her canteen and pressing the opening to his lips.

"Keep the water. You'll need it," Porter said as he tried to push the canteen away.

"No you'll need it to survive until I come back with help," she replied, "And don't argue because I won't leave until you've drunk it."

Porter rose up onto his elbow and drank the water down quickly, spitefully. "Are you happy now, Zahara?"

"No, but I will be when we are both finally off this prairie."

She didn't wait for him to respond. She looked down at the compass and began running due north toward the mountains that rose in the distance.

§§§

Porter had been right about one thing. He *was* slowing her down. Running, then walking and running some more, she made her way to the foot of the mountains and when she could no longer travel north, she began running eastward with the compass in hand. She saw the burial sites long before she arrived at them and willed herself to continue running until she got there.

But unlike Porter said, the site was unguarded. She looked around and there was no one. Panicked thoughts began to whirl around in her head; *Porter had said that he wasn't thinking clearly. Could he have just made this up? No. Impossible. It's all right here just like he said. They've* got *to be here.*

Zahara stood back and fired five shots into the air. The sound reverberated against the hills as the setting sun touched the horizon. She stood and waited. Porter said that they would come, but minutes passed and no one came. She reloaded and shot several more times with the same results.

The sun was sinking lower and still no help had come. If they didn't come soon it would be dark and they would never be able to find their way back to Porter. Suddenly there was a whistle like the sound of a hawk, but no hawk streaked the sky. Then she knew. She was being watched, but no one was coming to help.

She cried out and waved her arms but no one responded. She ran around in circles calling out until her voice was strained, but still no one responded. She thought of Porter lying on the prairie floor maybe breathing his last breaths as these fools played their games. Then she got mad.

She took aim at the top of the burial site and raised her sight to hit just above it, then pulled the trigger. She took a spot just left of the site and let a hail of bullets fly. The sound of hawks calling and responding grew louder and reverberated against the mountains.

By the time she reloaded and again and took aim, from the corner of her eye she saw three Sioux warriors rushing her from her left. Before she could call out to them, the breath was knocked out of her and everything went black.

§§§

When her eyes opened, her ears were simultaneously assailed with whoops and hollers. Her feet were barely scraping the ground as she was pushed and dragged along by the tide of warriors who punched, kicked and battered her as she was propelled through a dark, stone tunnel.

They came to a stop in a fairly large room with a vaulted, conic ceiling and walls made of what looked like crystal. Light poured in from lanterns above which caused he walls to glow. The warriors continued to batter and abuse her. They shouted and poked at her. She was thrown to the ground in the center of the room and the group of young men circled her, taunting. One yanked her hat off her head and put it on his own laughing scornfully.

"INILA!" A masculine voice cut through the shouting, and the noise immediately died down. The group parted and a tall man who could not have been any older than she or Porter, but whose face showed the wear of responsibility, entered the circle.

He was dressed in buckskin with intricate beadwork. His hair was arranged in two long black braids decorated with feathers and bead medallions. His dark piercing eyes focused on her. His disgust was apparent no matter what the language.

"Inánjinyo," he said to her then indicated at two of the young warriors who grabbed her up and dragged her in front of the man who was obviously their leader.

The two warriors yanked off her jacket and rifled through her pockets pulling out the remaining bullets, the gyroscopic compass and the last of her food and throwing everything onto the cold stone floor. Her copy of Jane Austen's compendium…was being torn apart page by page… as was Porter's journal. The individual folios of his painstaking work were crumbled and strewn across the floor.

Instinctively she pulled away from the men and leapt to the floor feverishly attempting to recover the pages grabbing all that she could, braving the kicks and stomps to her hands and the cold laughter.

She thought about Porter laying alone on the prairie, no protection no shelter. He sent her to these people thinking they would help. But there was no charity in them, only anger. She didn't even know why she was trying to save the pages of the journal. It wouldn't be long before the Indians finished her.

Of all things in her life she had no regrets, except that she should never have tried to come without Porter. It was nightfall. Even if they helped her, they would never find him in time…not on the vast prairie in the dark. Her eyes began to tear.

Before the first teardrop could fall the leader of the group pushed through the jeering warriors and dragged her up from the floor. In his right hand he held several pages from Porter's journal.

"He táku hwo? Lécanu hwo?" He demanded, "What is this? Did you create these?"

First, she was stunned. It took her a moment to realize that he had spoken to her in English. She quickly responded, "No."

"Who sent you? You're spies!" He shouted.

"No sir, we're not spies. My friend did these drawings. He is a very well-known engineer. I was a pilot and worked on his engineering crew."

"I don't see any friend," He said.

"He's out on the prairie. He's sick. He's been poisoned. He sent me here to get help."

"So, you left your poisoned friend out on the prairie? You are not much of a friend." The man huffed.

"Please, *please.* I'll take whatever punishment you give me, just please help my friend."

The Leader called out to the warriors and everyone fell silent.

"Do you know where your friend is?" He asked.

"I don't know. I came as fast as I could. I had to have walked about four or five hours.

"North?" the leader asked.

"No. I walked north then at the foothills I walked another mile or two east to get here.

"Glee Mahpiya Maza! Yaye!" He said to the group of men and they immediately all ran from the room. Moments later she heard the sound of horses whinnying and galloping.

"If your friend is there, we will find him. Let us hope that he is alive when we do."

He then motioned at a woman who was standing to his left and she brought a gourd and handed it to Zahara. The gourd contained a cloudy looking liquid…water. If she has been in Baltimore and that water had been offered to her she would have turned up her nose. But she knew that in this area, the minerals in the soil often showed up in the water. So she took what was offered with gratitude. All the while the leader watched her intently.

"This man, your friend…is he your husband?"

Again she looked up startled that he had realized she was a woman. She realized that when she was at the foothills firing toward the burial mound she was still dressed as a male. But of course after her clothes were ripped and torn and her hat removed, it would have been clear to anyone that she was no man.

"No, he is not my husband. He is my friend. He was my boss."

"I will have someone to help you find better clothing and a place to wait while we look for your friend," the man said.

He walked to one of the walls and pulled out a copper hose with what looked to be a funnel on the end. He spoke rapidly into the funnel and not two minutes later, an attractive woman in a buckskin dress walked into the room.

"What is your name?" the man asked, Zahara.

"Zahara," she said

"Matakah, this is Zahara," he said to the woman. She is our guest. She will need clothing, a place to sleep and a bath.

"We will take care of her, Igmutaka Sapa," the woman said.

Zahara was led by the woman called Matakah to an interior garden. The air was cool and flowers that should not have been able to grow there were in full bloom.

"Our medicine man is quite a horticulturalist," the woman said with a smile. Then she turned a nozzle and out of the faces of several tall sunflowers, a shower of hot water sprayed down. Upon closer inspection Zahara realized that three of the tall sunflowers that surrounded the depression at her feet, were made of metal, the large dish-sized heads that looked so much like natural sunflowers were actually enormous shower heads.

"If the water is too hot let us know so that we can reduce the heat." Matakah said, "I will be preparing your room while Wapataka and Wahca (Blackbird and Flower) assist with your shower.

In any other situation Zahara might have been bashful but she was so tired, hungry and filthy that she sat down on one of the boulders that had obviously been carved and sanded for comfortable seating, and stripped down to nothing.

Less than five minutes later she stood under the flow of the water as the two young women attending her handed her soap and a towel. They even offered to help her with her hair, which she politely declined as she washed and braided her hair, herself.

As she stepped into the dress they provided she expressed surprise, "I thought the buckskin would feel rough and heavy."

One of the young women, the one called Wapataka laughed and said, "It is deerskin…much softer."

"It is so smooth inside and no heavier than the clothes I arrived here in. And the boots are so comfortable. They are so much better than those stiff boots I had to wear when we were traveling," Zahara said excitedly, rushing around like a child on Christmas morning.

The two young women laughed and Zahara laughed too. She tried not to think about what was happening with the search for Porter and silently prayed that they would find him in time.

Seemingly out of nowhere, the woman who had escorted her to the garden shower reappeared and said, "Let me show you to your room."

After being cleaned and changed and not being violently beaten, Zahara was able to take in her surroundings. She marveled that the structure she walked through appeared to be a monolithic fort built into the walls of the mountain. The floors were made of the same rough-hewn stone of the mountains, but polished smooth.

The walls of the corridors were almost entirely formed of crystal with alternating pipes made of copper, silver, gold and bronze and everything glittered in the strategically placed light fixtures. Every wall was adorned with Sioux art and artifacts. Colorful wheels, spears, knives, dream-catchers, coup sticks, war bonnets, portraits and quilts gave the fortress a homey yet regal air.

At the top of a winding stairway the woman pushed open a door and Zahara stepped into the one of the loveliest rooms she had ever seen. The room was a conic shape just like the large room she originally entered. The walls, crystal as well, appeared to have a rosy gold tint and the floor was covered with soft animal skins. Shelves encircled the room at three different levels and each shelf, like the walls outside displayed art and artifacts.

The bed, though it stood only about eight inches high, was thick and firm with a soft covering and was over-laid with a beautiful quilt bearing one of the designs she had seen hanging in the main corridor.

The main lighting fixture hung from the center of the ceiling and was comprised of several small oil lamps; which all looked as if they had been crafted by fairies and hung randomly from the main fixture. On a small table next to the bed was her Jane Austen book with the torn and crumpled pages neatly ironed out then stacked back inside the book jacket.

"Did you happen to see the other book," Zahara asked, "the one with the dark cover?"

"No, but I will ask," the woman replied, then pointed toward the opposite side of the bed where a tray of food had been placed, "But now you should eat. I will ask about the book and I will return soon."

Until she began eating the food, she hadn't realized how hungry she was. There was meat and a bulb vegetable that tasted like turnips, and what must have been the greens from the vegetable. She ate all the food, drank the juice made of berries and drank half the gourd filled with water.

She lay down on the bed and reached for the Jane Austen book. It took some maneuvering to read and flip the torn pages but gratefully it took her mind off of the situation with Porter. She didn't know how long she had been reading when a sound like bells sounded and the woman who escorted her to the room peered inside the door and said, "Your friend has been recovered."

"He's alive?" Zahara asked as she leapt from the bed.

"Yes, but he is very, very ill. Our healers are with him and will do all they can. But for now you should sleep. Maybe he will be ready for visitors tomorrow."

"How can I sleep when he is just hanging onto life. I have to see him."

"He has had a difficult time and some of the warriors are helping to wash him down. I am certain he would appreciate your patience and allowing him these moments of privacy to become presentable," she smiled.

"Of course. Of course," Zahara sighed, "Instead of worrying you, I should be thanking you...all of you for your help, your hospitality. Porter would have had no hope without you."

"We are glad to help" the woman said, then after a moment asked, "Where are you from, Zahara?"

"I am from Quincy...from Florida. I am not quite sure where

Porter is from. From his accent, I would say New York. But he is very guarded about his past."

Matakah nodded thoughtfully. "What about you?" Zahara asked. "I don't want to seem presumptuous, but I didn't know so many Indians spoke English. Are you from here?"

"Yes," Matakah smiled, "I was born in these hills."

"Strange," Zahara said with a knit brow, "you sound like Baltimore."

The woman smiled broadly, "Yes, I was taught English in Baltimore many years ago."

"Really? Did you like it...Baltimore, I mean?" Zahara asked.

"Yes, I did."

"So why didn't you stay?"

"I came back to help build this" she said raising her arms indicating at the building around them.

"It is very impressive," Zahara said, "I have never seen anything quite like it."

"Get some rest. Tomorrow morning, I will come by early. I will take you on a tour of the facility and then we can check in on your friend."

"Thank you again," Zahara said. The two embraced as if they had known each other all their lives.

Zahara watched as Matakah took the winding staircase down. If she had known her way around the labyrinth of the fort she would have followed her out and tried to make her way to Porter. But she didn't know her way and it would have been disrespectful to wander around without permission or a guide. So she went back to reading until the words stopped making sense.

She put out all the lights and went to bed hoping that Porter would be lucid enough to speak to her in the morning.

§§§

The next morning Zahara was up bright and early. She had washed and was dressed, long before the door tone sounded and an older woman walked in carrying a tray of warm food. She ate gratefully but quickly in anticipation of the tour and ultimately the opportunity to see Porter.

Almost as soon as she was done eating, the tone sounded again and the man from the previous night, the one called Igmutaka Sapa, entered the room carrying a bundle under his arm.

"I know you were expecting Matakah this morning. But considering your work I have a better tour in mind."

He handed her the bundle which was a set of buckskin shirt and pants, in the design of her normal work clothes.

"You might also want to wear your boots. We will be walking in some rougher areas. He pulled out his pocket watch, glanced at it and said, "I will be back in fifteen minutes, then we can get underway," He left as quickly as he had come.

Zahara shrugged her shoulders, and changed into the outfit provided to her by Eagle. She was dressed and ready long before he returned in exactly fifteen minutes. He escorted her out into the corridor and began the tour.

"This fortress the *He O Uyapi,* our Mountain Settlement, actually had its beginnings hundreds of thousands of years ago as the caves within the mountains we call *Mako Sica,* and that you call the

Badlands expanded to the size where anyone standing upright could walk through comfortably. Long, long years ago before even my grandfather was born, there was a flood on the plains that forced the people off the prairie floor and into the mountains."

"These caves became temporary shelter. Over time whether from weather or war these mountains became a refuge. It didn't take too much imagination to see what this system of caves could become."

They walked past the interior garden Zahara recalled from the previous day and into a large open area with decorated walls, drums and seats lined against the walls. Other musical instruments, some she recognized and others she didn't lay nearby on tables.

"This is where we have our major feasts and gatherings. In the next few days we will be having one with the council of Elders. Maybe you will be in attendance."

"I look forward to it," Zahara said.

They wandered the labyrinth of halls viewing the guest quarters, the bathing facilities and the council room.

Their journey down the halls ended at a closed door. Igmutaka turned the large raw crystal handle and opened the door into a small room. "This is the hoist that will take us down into the main part of the fortress," he said.

"There's more?" Zahara asked incredulous.

"Much more," he said as he turned a crank on the wall, and then moved a lever in the floor forward. She could hear the sound of steam escaping as the hoist descended through a tunnel of crystal and copper; landing with a lurch when Igmutaka pulled the lever backward braking the hoist. When Igmutaka opened the door they stepped out onto what looked a lot like the engineering floor of Cross Continental.

It seemed more than fifty Sioux male and female dressed in work clothes much like the ones she wore were busy moving about maintaining the machinery that presumably ran the entire facility. There were steam generators responsible for almost every energy need in the fortress. There were copper pipes moving along the walls to the upper floors providing water and heat.

All of that was a wonder, but the best was saved for last. Igmutaka handed her a pair of goggles and pulled on a pair himself then motioned to two workers who pulled on a set of large levers. A warning claxon sounded, and the majority of the workers quickly moved away from a large set of bay doors which began to slowly slide open. A blast of heat roared from behind the door.

As they stepped through and after she became accustomed to the heat she saw a huge blast furnace where several workers, covered head to toe wearing safety helmets and air filters, poured molten metal into molds of rods.

Other workers were transporting those rods to another machine which heated and stretched the rods until they were as thin as wire. Then the last section was filled with what looked to be twenty looms where workers were weaving the wire into large sheets of tightly enmeshed cloth.

"See," Igmutaka Sapa said, "We are working with a Beryllium Aluminum alloy. It is stronger and lighter than iron. It is flexible and durable and can withstand very high heat."

"What do you do with it?" She asked.

Igmutaka Sapa smiled and directed her toward the corner where there was another door with a large natural crystal knob. She understood it to be another hoist and headed toward the mechanism.

She was so excited she could barely keep from skipping and when Igmutaka Sapa directed her into the hoist she was surprised that the hoist flew upward. She could see Igmutaka Sapa's crooked smile from the corner of her eye and wondered what he had in store.

After a few moments he pulled the lever slowing the cab to a stop.

"Ready?" He asked.

"Absolutely," she responded.

He pushed the door open and Zahara gasped. She stepped out of the hoist and onto the platform of an Airship launch bay. There were seven ships completely outfitted with a large engineering crew attending them. The names were written in large script letters: *Maia, Electra, Taygete, Alcyone, Celaeno, Sterope* and *Merope.*

"The Pleiades…the 'sailing ones,'" she said.

"Exactly," Igmutaka said with a twinkle in his eye, "The seven sisters are our first fleet. They are fast, can sleep a skeleton crew and carry a ton of cargo. Each of the crafts can easily hold twenty passengers in the gondola."

"Looks like they were constructed for speed," Zahara marveled.

"And comfort," Igmutaka Sapa added. "These are made for mid-range journeys and we hope to begin our own Airfleet in due time."

As Zahara looked upward it became clear as to the purpose of the metallic fabric being woven below in the belly of the mountain. Each ship's framework was covered in an envelope of the fine mesh that was stronger than iron but light as aluminum.

"It's genius," she whispered.

"Yes it is," Igmutaka Sapa replied, "but come on. We are not done, yet."

Zahara's head swam. She couldn't imagine that there could be anything else. But as the two of them walked the length of the launch pad then stopped at its edge and looked downward, she saw the reason for the trip. Rising upward from near the prairie floor was an airship that dwarfed the other six. The gondola alone was larger than any of the other crafts. It rose higher and higher, its beryl aluminum alloy hull and envelope shining in the late midday sun.

"This is the Ironclad bison!" She cried.

Igmutaka Sapa laughed, "No. It's not the Ironclad bison. It is called the 'Iron Cloud' bison named after the designer."

"Well, you learn something new every day," she laughed still transfixed by the enormous Airship initiating its docking sequence. "How long does it take to dock?"

"Hmmm," Igmutaka said while glancing at his watch, "Quite a bit more time than we have. We were expected an hour ago."

"I would *love* to speak with the pilot," she said hoping to get an audience.

"Maybe tomorrow," he said, "But for now, we must hurry to our next appointment.

Igmutaka Sapa led her back through the launch area and into the hoist. As they traveled downward, he called into one of the copper tubes with the funnel shaped opening, presumably their communication device, saying, "We are *en route*."

Once inside the hoist Zahara asked, "This structure is enormous. How long have you all been building this?" She asked.

"We have been in this installation for the past ten years. It began with the Lakota then the remainder of the Sioux were welcomed," he said, "then we made a decision which I am not all too sure was the best. We invited the remainder of the prairie tribes to join us."

"Actually, it sounds like a very good idea…security in numbers."

"This is what we believed, but some were against it. Iron Cloud primarily."

"Why?" She asked.

"He believed that some of the tribes did not have the best interests of the Sioux at heart. He thought it was not coincidental that once others were invited in, that several of our designs with only a few modifications were being marketed on both coasts."

"He leveled accusations at the Pawnee who he believed much allied themselves with the whites. But the Pawnee denied having anything to do with the treachery. The Sioux Council of Elders wanted to promote unity between the tribes. Since Iron Cloud was not Sioux, his warnings were disregarded."

"But, I thought you said that he helped build all this," Zahara said.

"He did, and he accepted the determination of the Council. But no more than a month later another incident occurred and incriminating evidence was found in Iron Cloud's belongings."

"HE was the spy?!" She exclaimed, "Why did he do it?!"

"He swore that he didn't but the evidence was overwhelming. Rather than profess his innocence he packed his belongings and left. Six months later we discovered that one of the Pawnee chiefs was involved in trading many of our designs to a manufacturer in Kansas in return for an agreement to build vehicles to attack the Sioux and other prairie tribes."

"So Iron Cloud wasn't the spy?"

"No, he wasn't. But after the accusations and hard feelings we were all too ashamed to look for him," he sighed, "From time to time we still deal with spies but it is difficult to call anyone out, even if you think they're guilty based on what happened to Iron Cloud."

When they disembarked the hoist she realized that they were again near the garden. From there she actually knew her way back to her room, but they took a sharp turn and headed further down another set of corridors. After what seemed like walking twenty minutes through a maze they stopped in front of a door.

The sound of laughter spilled out from inside as Zahara approached. She was overjoyed and taken aback all at once. "It's Porter!" She cried.

"Go on in. He will be happy to see you," Igmutaka smiled and opened the door.

There Porter sat in the flesh…laughing. He was stripped to the waist and secured under one of the beautifully made quilts. He looked wonderful and his skin looked radiant and he was smiling. Not inches from him sat Matakah, her two hands grasping his.

Something about it, something about their interaction made her quirk her brow. But when he saw her his face lit up and he called out to her, "Well I should never have doubted your resolve, Harry."

"I told you I would get you off of the prairie," she smiled as she walked slowly and stopped in the center of the room a formal distance from where he lay.

"I hear that you did exactly as I told you not to do," he chided.

"Believe me I had no other options. But I'm relieved to see you doing so well."

"Well, while you have been lazing away the day in bed, Zahara and I have been very productive," Igmutaka Sapa said, his imperious tone modified by the mischief in his eye.

She quirked her brow again. Igmutaka Sapa's tone was awfully familiar. Even if he was the person who saved Porter's life, a certain amount of decorum should have been maintained. But Porter didn't seem to mind.

"So, what is it that you have been doing today, Harry?" Porter asked.

"This facility is amazing," she said, "All the major materials are made here on the premises and all the machining as well. And you would not believe how the airships are constructed!" She exclaimed.

"I am happy to see you have been enjoying yourself," Porter said.

"And you would not believe it, but I have seen the bison and it's not called the Ironclad bison. It is actually called the Iron Cloud, named after the designer," she beamed, "in fact from what I've learned, today, a significant portion of the fortress was designed by Igmutaka Sapa and what is it in Lakota Sioux...Mahpiya Maza. It means Iron Cloud. Can you believe how many people get that wrong," she laughed.

Igmutaka chuckled with her then walked past Zahara and dropped down beside Porter embracing him, an embrace which was returned by Porter. Then in clear English Igmutaka said, "Welcome! Welcome home my brother, Mahpiya Maza, Iron Cloud."

Zahara was stunned silent. She didn't move. She didn't shift her eyes. There was Porter sitting between Igmutaka and the woman she knew as Matakah. They were all part of this great achievement the construction of the Iron Bison. They were all family and she was a stranger.

"It is nearly time to eat," Igmutaka said, "I will have your food served here as well, Zahara."

"What a fine idea," Matakah said, "I will take my meal here as well."

"I believe Iron Cloud and Zahara have a bit of catching up to do," Igmutaka replied.

"I am sure they do, but I haven't seen Iron Cloud in years and I am pretty certain that I have more catching up than a few hours worth," Matakah huffed.

"Matakah!" Igmutaka Sapa snapped, "I believe that Iron Cloud and Zahara would like some time to speak, alone."

"Very well," Matakah sighed and rolled her eyes, then said, "Welcome back, Iron Cloud," then kissed him tenderly on the cheek. As she passed by, Zahara could have sworn that Matakah smirked in her direction.

When Matakah and Igmutaka Sapa left the room Zahara remained standing at its center.

"I am not contagious, Zahara," he smiled.

"So now it's Zahara? In front of your friends it was Harry," she said with an edge to her voice.

"What's this now?" He asked, "Is there a problem?"

"No problem, Porter...oh, excuse me, I guess I meant Iron Cloud."

"I guess I should explain," he said.

"You don't have to explain anything."

"Come sit, Zahara," he said at patted the area next to him on the pallet on the floor.

She knew it was childish and wished that she could have controlled herself but she intentionally turned and sat on the opposite side of the pallet from where Makatah had been sitting. He chuckled but was again serious.

"I have been unfair to you. I have asked you to travel across the country with me based upon wishes and hopes. I have asked you to trust me, and you've saved my life. What right do I have to deny you information about the person you have traveled with, the person you have come to trust, the person whose life it is that you have saved?" He continued without allowing her to respond. "For you, my life is an open book. Whatever you would like to know, I will tell."

"Well, where are you from?" She asked.

"I am originally from New York. I am the third of four children."

"Is it true that you worked for the government during the war?"

Porter hesitated then said: "Yes, I did some work for the Army of the Republic."

"Were you a spy?" She asked.

Porter took a deep breath and responded, "Sometimes, but primarily I was an engineer. I helped to create many of the military vehicles—maybe even the dirigible you piloted."

"And all this, you designed?"

"I designed a lot of it. So did Igmutaka Sapa and Matakah. We all studied together at the Benjamin Baneker Institute."

"There's a lot more I want to ask, but I think it is going to take time for me to formulate everything."

"There is no hurry. My life remains an open book," he said as he wrapped his arm around her shoulder. And thank you…for saving my life," he said giving her a hard squeeze and a kiss on her forehead.

"Don't try to cuddle up to me, now Iron Cloud. I saw how you and Matakah were making eyes at each other," she huffed but didn't pull away.

"Matakah and I are friends," he smiled, "just friends."

"Like we are," Zahara replied.

Without fanfare he leaned in and kissed her on the lips. "Not like we are. It is long past time that we admit that we are more than friends, Zahara."

With that she settled into his arms and listened as he told stories of his childhood, his missions during the war and his time working to build the He O Uyapi. She had no idea how late it was when the door tone sounded and Porter called out for the person to enter. An older woman walked in with a tray of food which she deposited near the bed.

"So, what do you prefer to be called," Zahara asked, "Porter or Iron Cloud, or Mahpiya Maza?"

"Whichever you like best is what I like best," he smiled.

The door tone sounded again and before they could respond Igmutaka Sapa entered looking harried, "Iron Cloud…some distressing news."

Iron Cloud sat straight up in the bed and listened as Igmutaka Sapa groaned, "Your journal is missing."

"My journal?" he asked.

"Yes, the journal Zahara brought with her."

Zahara saw the rage brew behind his eyes as he growled, "Why didn't you tell me you had the journal?" He asked.

"I—I didn't mean to have it," she stammered, "I thought I could return it before you knew. Then after the wagon master stole the caravan and you became ill. When I arrived it was taken from me and torn apart. I asked Matakah about it. She said she would find out."

"But you knew it had been taken here?"

"Wait," Igmutaka Sapa said, "Makatah said she didn't know what happened to the journal? I gave her the journal. I gave it to her myself."

"I know what might be going through your mind Igmutaka, but wasn't the accusation of one friend, enough?" Iron Cloud asked.

"No accusation," Iron Cloud, "But Mayakah has just taken the Electra and left here claiming to have an errand to the East which no one recalls her mentioning. I am certain that she has only the best intentions but can you tell me what was included in your journal?"

"Weapons and military vehicles," he said, "I was going through a very difficult time and I created these machines. But they were my private notes—not meant for other's eyes."

"I'm sorry Porter," she cried.

"You have no idea, Zahara, the peril you have placed us all in."

"Peril?" She asked, stunned, "I have done nothing to endanger us or anyone, else."

"It's not her fault Iron Cloud. You never told her. Neither did I," Igmutaka Sapa said. "Zahara, one of the possible perpetrators of the leak of our designs was Matakah. She had access to the journal and has a history that implies that she might be willing to sell."

"What are you talking about?" Zahara asked.

"Matakah has always considered herself somewhat of a War Maiden. Even at the Institute, she was obsessed with the protection of the tribes and making the whites and their supporters among the tribes, pay for what they have done to the tribes," Porter said.

"She even tried to enlist us to help her raise an army," Igmutaka said.

"I know that you two don't want to hear it, but I think I agree with Matakah," Zahara said, "If I had the knowledge and capability that you all have here, I would have done it long ago."

"Zahara, it is not that we disagree with Matakah, but her plans are not realistic," Igmutaka said, "Even if she built a fleet of airships loaded down with every advanced weapon, there would not be enough of us to hold back the whites."

"Certainly we could hurt them and for a while they would feel the devastation that they have forced on our peoples. But in the end Zahara there are entirely too many of them. When they decide to seek revenge it could eliminate all the tribes once and for all, Porter said.

He directed his attention to Igmutaka Sapa. "We'll take the Maia. She's the fastest in the fleet. With a good wind and a lot of luck we may be able to catch her before she does something that cannot be undone."

Still a bit shaky from his bout with the poison, Porter stood up and grabbed his clothes.

"Assemble a crew, we're on the hunt."

Igmutaka immediately spoke into the communication system and Zahara could hear the scramble of boots outside the door.

"At these speeds I am going to need a good pilot. Are you game?" He asked.

Zahara nodded and followed him out the door. She probably should have been afraid. But even under such dire circumstances she shook her head. It seemed that no matter what, she was going to find herself on the path chasing behind Porter and the Iron Cloud Bison.

THE REFUGE

KOCHAVA GREENE

"Mother Angelita, there is a...lady here to see you."

Mother Angelita swept her needlework to the side. She was a tall, large woman, and moved with great elegance. "Thank you, Sister Selina. I will go to her at once."

Mother Angelita walked briskly down the stone and adobe corridor of the convent, her sandals gently tapping and her habit creating a breeze behind her. At the end of the corridor, she turned a large key set into a stone door, moving a series of gears and bars to open the door to the reception room. Once, the convent had been a refuge for escaped slaves, and the sisters found the defenses useful against the desert's unwanted visitors.

The woman waiting in the parlor was plain, wearing a practical traveling dress and brown boots. She held a hat in her hands; her fingers were long, with short nails.

Despite her unadorned appearance, she had an air of grace about her. Was she a minor member of one of Texas's newly resident royal families from Cape Verde or Senegal? The daughter of a rich Ceutan family? The widow of a Tanzanian merchant?

Mother Angelita smiled warmly at her. Opening her hands in a gesture of welcome, she asked: "How may we help you?"

The woman spoke directly."I understand you admit novices of any age," she said. "I want to join the convent."

Mother Angelita took in the woman in front of her more

closely: she appeared to be in her late thirties, with twisted ropes of long hair gathered into a thick coil at the nape of her neck. A small scar stood out near the corner of her mouth, pale and raised against her dark skin.

Her voice had the soft accent of a Carolinian, but Mother Angelita would have sworn the woman was African. Few Carolinian women were so dark-skinned, or had the almost-hidden tribal body markings of many African nations that Mother Angelita could make out just behind the woman's ears.

Then she noticed the woman's thinness, the way she had covered as much of her body as possible, the slightly-tattered edges of the shawl that fell over her shoulders. Still, she was surprised: this woman had the bearing of a noble, not a class usually found in the brothels under any circumstances.

"Are you coming here from …the life…in the city?" Mother Angelita asked delicately.

She knew that St. Laurita's had gained, mostly fairly, a reputation for accepting women from the city's brothels. Currently, there were two former prostitutes from the city's Rose Room, and one who had come all the way from the Rocky Mountain Territory by automated carriage train among the convent's sisters.

She herself had never worked in the life. But her aunt had, becoming a famous courtesan in Culiacán, where men of every race had found her irresistible, despite a general preference there for pale, blond women.

"I've come from Carolina," said the woman. Carolina did not border Texas: the woman had made a significant journey. When Mother Angelita looked at her expectantly, the woman continued. "I

made a vow that when my daughter finished school, when she was
settled, I would....retire here."

Mother Angelita didn't know quite what to make of this new
postulate. Other women usually humbly knelt, or begged admittance,
citing stories of abuse, poverty, or tales of other hardships, often along
with professions of religious fervor.

She fingered the plain stone spiral that hung around her neck:
the holy symbol of the All-Mother. There was no question that the
woman would be accepted: the order never turned away a woman
wishing to join, or, for that matter, held it against a woman who wished
to leave.

She did wonder, though, why a Carolinian woman would have
left that wealthy and civilized Eastern land for the barren desert
surrounding St. Laurita's? Then again, non-white women were not
always as well-treated there as they were in the country of Texas,
where men and women of a variety of social and racial backgrounds
had made alliances almost since the country's founding.

"You realize that our lives here are very difficult," she said
finally. "We live plainly, serving the All-Mother."

"I welcome this," said the Carolinian quietly. She smiled very
slightly."My mother said the All-Mother freed her from her life on a
plantation. And the All-Mother has...saved me more than once. I want
nothing more than to work for her here."

The woman declined to provide her name or that of her
daughter, or the location of her daughter, even in case of an emergency
or death. "She is safe and independent," said the woman, "and we have
said our farewells."

Mother Angelita pressed further, and found that the woman had last lived near the city of San Lazare, located where Carolina territory curved up against Louisiana and situated precariously between the gulf and a large lake. San Lazare was well-known for its dangerous location on the water and its rough ways. Unlike inland Texas, where beautiful cities had risen from the deserts, San Lazare was a place for adventurers, opportunists, criminals, and unsavory elements from across the continent.

Mechanical constructs roamed there, created to clear the marshes and waters of the foul creatures that lived in the depths. Engineers entered the city to repair these Gulfmen and left quickly. While automated carriage trains ran to and from San Lazare twice weekly, and airships could dock at an extravagant facility north of the city (containing a casino, brothel, and sundry other businesses that airmen might never need leave it), few members of the upper or middle classes of Carolina—or anywhere else—ever ventured there, sending proxies for business instead.

Mother Angelita had never known anyone from San Lazare, and tried to suppress her curiosity. She called for Sister Carlita to take the woman to her cell and see her appointed, and settled before afternoon work began.

As the woman rose, Mother Angelita saw that she walked stiffly, as though her knees were affected by severe arthritis. The buckles of the woman's boots gleamed as she passed by the older woman, and she bowed her head in gratitude and respect. Mother Angelita called out to stop her at the edge of the room as Sister Carlita worked the locks on the door to the convent's inner chambers.

"Sister," Mother Angelita said. "Will you choose a new name before you go to be robed?"

The woman paused, her boots clanking slightly. "What is the custom?" she asked.

"Any woman's name," replied Mother Angelita. "Often we take names for Her aspects—Selina, for example—or try to reclaim names taken by followers of the Unnatural Sect, to restore them."

Worshipers of the All-Mother were diametrically opposed to the religions of the non-natural, particularly the sect of the Unnatural Man, who was said to have circumvented the laws of nature and its elements, even death. Its followers were mostly men, who used the myth to oppress natural philosophy and its traditional religion of nature worship.

The new woman thought for a moment, her fingers playing over the buttons on her high collar. "There is a St. Amelia, is there not?" she asked, recalling a Louisiana story of a cunning woman who built silver wings to escape suspicious and ignorant men who were chasing her with dogs raised to hunt humans. When Mother Angelita smiled, inclining her head, the woman said, "If you will, then, I will be Sister Amelia."

The newly named Sister Amelia was assigned a small cell in the interior of the convent. Sparsely furnished with a bed, desk, chair, and washbasin, it had red adobe walls inscribed with the sacred spiral on three walls and the back of the wooden door.

Sister Carlita, a woman near to Sister Amelia's age with the facial features of both indigenous Mexican and black ancestors, showed Sister Amelia the washroom, lined with washbasins, private bathing and toilet chambers; and a feature many would find luxurious for a convent: a steam room.

Sister Carlita explained in a light soprano voice that the steam rooms were an integral part of the convent life: places in which sisters could gather or go individually to inhale herbal steam and pray, heal, or seek visions. Sister Carlita returned the new woman to her cell to dress, saying that the novice mistress would summon her for a full orientation shortly.

On her bed, Sister Ameila unrolled her new uniform—a long green gown with a rust over-apron, the colors symbolizing the elements of the earth; a sleeveless undershirt and loose drawers that came to her knees; and a turban a shade lighter than the gown. She washed her hands and face in the basin and dried them on the cloth provided.

She shook out her hair, running her hands through its thick strands. She didn't miss the constant combing and application of slick potions to make it behave more like that of her white counterparts in San Lazare. She removed her travel tress, unbuttoning the high neck and wrists first. She rolled it down, and then reached to unhook the skirts from where they were attached above her knees with brass snaps.

The snaps were her own invention—small straps of fabric that laced through tiny copper eyes. There were five such sets of snaps and eyes down to her ankles, designed to prevent her skirt from ever accidentally rising.

Her boots had similar tethering devices. Sister Amelia's legs were copper from the thigh down.

Still standing, she removed her shift and utilitarian corset—a far cry from the damask and embroidered silk and satin undergarments of her days displaying herself to the various men—judges, gamblers, rangers, dancers, soldiers—of her now-past life. She rolled the undergarments with her dress, and sat on the bed.

Working with the speed that comes from years of practice, she unfastened her legs from her thighs, removing a small key from the side of each leg and using it to unlock bolts on each side of her legs. She spun sets of gears just above the inside and outside of each knee and released two bayonet-socketed bars, and the legs slid off. She rubbed the ends of her thighs briefly and adjusted the specially-made stocking-silk caps that covered them.

Sister Amelia removed the boots at the ends of her legs and then put on her new sandals on each foot, which had been convincingly painted to give her individual toes and to match her flesh up to about mid-calf. She pulled on her new, loose, soft habit and adjusted the turban to cover her hair, then reattached her legs. She lay back on her bed and had rested a quarter of an hour when the summons from the novice mistress arrived.

The novice mistress was younger than Sister Amelia had expected. Sister Margaret was a petite white woman, barely out of her teens who had joined St. Laurita's when she was only sixteen, and had never left the convent's lands since. Her family had pledged her to the convent after a team of St. Laurita's sisters in Saltillo had saved her older sister, who had married a mine-owner there, from bandits.

Sister Margaret's own trip to the convent had been terrifying. Her family's coach, traveling by itself and not part of a convoy or automated train, and attracted the attention of both bandits and the creatures of a great inland lake to which her driver, foolishly, had passed close by on the way. During an overnight stop, three bandits and two creatures approached the carriage almost at the same time from opposite directions.

Sister Margaret's mother, two younger brothers, and two family retainers lay buried in the nearest town's cemetery. The bandits were last seen being dragged into the lake. Two weeks later, Sister Margaret had taken permanent vows and her father and the surviving bodyguard had returned home by private airship, where her father swiftly drank himself to death and the bodyguard retired to a sanatorium to recover his health.

Sister Margaret told this sad story to Sister Amelia as the toured the convent complex. Sister Margaret issued Sister Amelia her own basic set of keys and a passcode to the cellar's hidden safe cell, a large, well-concealed room designed to protect the sisters in case of a raid or other calamity. Sister Amelia asked about the dangers of the area. She had chosen St. Laurita's in part because she assumed it to be safe in its desert fastness.

Convents of the All-Mother were known to be poor, but well-defended, generally discouraging thieves, rapists, and others with a criminal or violent bent. St. Laurita's was not too far from a lake, but maps indicated it was small and highly unlikely to be a habitat for the creatures that had terrorized many waterside communities before people got smart and started moving inland. The creatures were widely assumed by the sisters to be natural sea animals contaminated by poisons or actions made by men.

Others held different ideas: that the sea creatures were embodiments of the evil nemesis of the Unnatural Man; that they had seeped into the seas through cracks in the ocean floors from an underworld within the earth; that they had come from distant stars; that they were the monstrous reincarnations of executed criminals, "fallen women," and children sacrificed by desert cults.

Sister Amelia and her fellow brothel-workers had once tried to think of themselves as creatures from the deep, and they had laughed over the idea. Now mention of the creatures brought only a firm set to her lips.

Sister Margaret told Sister Amelia that indeed the convent was safe, but that all houses serving the All-Mother were heavily protected and possessed of a small armory in addition to the safe room, just in case of trouble. Indeed, she said, almost embarrassed to mention it, Sister Amelia would need to turn over any weapons she had with her to the communal trove. Sister Amelia yielded up two sets of dueling pistols and a clockwork repeating stiletto, but kept silent about the single-shot pistol and scimitar knife locked into her legs.

Sister Margaret took these and said that they would be kept in the armory, and that Sister Amelia could practice with them any time. She continued, saying that skinwalkers—men and women transformed into animal-like beings—had been once rumored to live in the desert as well, but, she added uncertainly, no one had seen them in a long time. Sister Amelia sighed slightly, and said nothing.

In the following months, Sister Amelia cleaned the convent and learned to cook, particularly delighting in cooking cactus and scorpion, and tended the garden of succulents and lizards. She sometimes felt restless, but the feeling was usually put aside by throwing herself into new work and learning.

Twice a week the women took practice at martial arts; once a week they received messages from the telegraph operator in the nearest town, and once a month they held a service to celebrate the moon. Every several weeks, a traveler or two might stop by to pass the night in St. Laurita's guesthouse, bringing news of Texas and other nearby countries: Louisiana, Carolina, and vast Columbia, now grown to some 32 counties and territories.

Often travelers brought gifts as well—a songbird, tools, books, and, on one occasion, a small gray burro, who was immediately dubbed Sister Brayana. Sister Amelia became fond of the little equine, prettying her up for festivals and growing special grains for her mash. Every once in a while, though, Sister Amelia yearned for the excitement of the city, and fantasized about running off on the little gray donkey.

But remembering her past also brought back memories she was less fond of, and in the end always found herself happily returning her mind to her new life.

After a year at St. Laurita's, Sister Ameila made her own permanent vows and became a full member of the community. As recognition of her new status, she was invited to partake of the steam room for the first time.

Sister Amelia wasn't exactly sure why she had concealed her physical differences from her sisters for so long. She wasn't worried about her body—women of St. Laurita's were in every size and shape imaginable: most were black, like herself, or Latina. And many, again like her, bore scars or marks of some kind—from childbirth, abuse, or, in the case of two elderly Mexican sisters, traditional tattoos.

Everyone had already seen the marks of her homeland—which was Comoros, as she had eventually told Mother Angelita; although her family there had been betrayed by trusted French traders and sold into slavery in Louisiana and Carolina when she was an infant—behind her ears.

But her legs...Perhaps she had hidden them because she had been sold on the basis of her freakishness so often, or because she didn't care to tell the story behind her shining clockwork limbs. Or out of the small fear of Mother Angelita's disapproval. After all, the older woman held the natural in the highest regard. What if she was asked to discard her legs, which she felt necessary to her independence, security, and self?

She would be completely bare in the steam room: no clothes or jewelry, save spiral stone necklaces, were permitted. And so she demurred for some time, but on a bitter February afternoon, she was not asked, but summoned by Mother Angelita to join a handful of other sisters in the steam room. She was the last to enter, hoping, somehow, that the room would be clouded enough to obscure her legs. But it was not.

And so, trying to ignore the others, themselves trying not to stare, she sat near the door, unfastened her legs, and placed them outside of the chamber. She peeled away the sticking-caps and draped them over the tops of the legs. She closed the door, and, back straight and graceful, waited for reactions. After a long moment, Sister Margaret spoke, tremulously. "Creatures?"

"Yes," said Sister Amelia, and, trying to put her sisters at ease, said, "A very long time ago." Remarkably, the rest of the sisters remained silent, some nodding; others meeting her eyes briefly in solidarity over physical difference, and Mother Angelita poured herbed water over hot stones. An enormous cloud went up, and the group fell into meditation.

Sister Amelia had no particular vision she sought, but saw herself on a flying ship, still dressed in her nun's habit. She dismissed it as a silly daydream, and refocused on the All-Mother. Her mind still wandered to Carolina, where she saw herself swimming in a river, and again she dismissed it.

The steam room session ended and Mother Angelita dismissed the group. Sister Amelia reversed her actions of before, drawing on her stocking-caps and legs before leaving the warmth of the steam chamber. After she washed and dressed, she found Mother Angelita waiting for her. To her relief, the Mother Superior said only, "Please let us know when you need any materials for repair." And Sister Amelia realized that she was finally fully part of the sisterhood. She was comfortable, a feeling she'd rarely known before, and her fleeting desires to leave subsided entirely.

The comfort did not last long. In March and April, several elder sisters began to speak of disturbing visions: rotted lilies floating on the nearby lake, men running across the desert, a horse being burnt on a pyre. The All-Mother had never given any of the sisters false visions before, so the community added an extra person to the daily and nightly watches.

Sister Penelope gave everyone extra lessons with the convent's brass-ended quarterstaffs, bows, and guns. Sister Amelia also practiced in her cell, withdrawing and loading her palm-size pistol and knife. They were cleverly hidden within her legs, and while she had never used the gun, the knife had saved her from more than one abduction from the brothel and from certain serious injury at the hands of one very drunk, very strong client.

He was not allowed back in the brothel after that—even if Sister Amelia's fast reflexes had not already relieved him of his reasons for visiting. Sister Amelia also always spoke with visitors about what unnaturalness they might have seen, sharing the information with her sisters about defense in case of an emergency.

Late on a hot summer night, two men on horseback came to the convent. Speaking through the grill in a side door, they pled to be allowed to spend the night inside. Something from the lake area was stalking them, they said, and their horses were exhausted.

Despite some misgivings, Mother Angelita let them in and installed them in the guest quarters. Travelers knew not to get caught in the desert at night. Natural animals were common enough, and, in recent months, engineers had been trying to take advantage of the powers and strange properties of the lake.

Visitors had spoken of all sorts of strange sightings in the recent months, although none had had direct contact with anything previously unknown. The sheriff and his men, who visited St. Laurita's on a regular basis, both to check on the sisters and buy their foodstuffs and medicines, had no reports of new problems. But it paid to be cautious.

Indeed, the men had not been careful at the lake. Hours after their arrival, Sister Pippa, the stable-mistress, came screaming into the convent's inner chambers. Struck wordless, she could only lead Mother Angelita, Sister Amelia, and two other sisters to the stables, where she could finally speak. The travelers' horses had died suddenly, in a matter of moments, bled out from wounds caused by long, limber claws emerging from their ribs.

Sister Penelope, who slept near the stables, had killed the creatures, but the danger was far from over. Alarmed, Mother Angelita woke an auxiliary defense team and sent them first to the armory and then to the guest quarters. Sister Amelia was part of the team, along with several of St. Laurita's best fighters, and women with experience in the outside world.

As the regular night team on duty patrolled the walls of the convent, Sister Amelia and three others made their way to the guest quarters, moving cautiously in the candle- and torch-lit convent compound. If the men had been unknowing enough to let their horses drink from the lake, they may have done so themselves. Sister Amelia found herself tense, her breathing rapid.

As they approached the door to the guest quarters, it was clear her apprehension was warranted. Shadows danced through the windows; and even as the team took up positions on either side of the door and prepared to enter, the door burst open and one of the men, a small, light-skinned fellow with a well-trimmed mustache and beard, ran out, his eyes open with terror.

He screamed as he ran, and Sister Amelia gestured to another woman to follow him. Lowering her six-shot revolver to a shooting position and drawing her old repeating stiletto with her other hand, she and the two remaining team members leapt into the room.

Against the wall, the second man was undergoing the eruption of a lake denizen. His hands flailed uselessly as his throat swelled and chest heaved. The bones of his legs broke with the sound of gunshots, and the man's eyes widened and widened as them became covered with a thick green film.

Sister Amelia took all of the sight in at once. Sister Monica, on her left, asked in a low, urgent voice, "Can he be saved?" Sister Amelia was already lining up her shot, and said, "No. Throat, chest, knees." Her first shot missed the thrashing man, but her second was straight through his throat, and her third took out his left knee.

Sister Monica finished destroying the man's knees, and Sister Cristina put a neat triad of shots over the man's heart. The man fell to the floor, and they approached carefully, waiting for the lake creature to appear. After a long moment in which they could hear the distant sobbing of the first man, a long limb ending in a claw broke through the man's side. Sister Amelia put out her hand to stay her fellow team members.

A second claw, then a third, felt their way out onto the guest house's floor. Within a few moments, a diamond-shaped head with long narrow eyes and a large mouth pushed its way out of the man's mouth. Amelia sighed. She knew this creature all too well. She threw the repeating stiletto solidly into the creature's head, where the clockwork mechanism began to unwind, neatly slicing the head into multiple fragments.

The team waited until the knife had run down, and pulled the limbs away from the head. They carried all of the creature's parts to the infirmary, where they were packed in oil to be sent to scientists and to be made into medicine—ironically, tinctures made of the creatures' bodies mixed with certain herbs hastened healing of wounds, particularly amputations.

Sister Amelia had been treated with a similar mixture when creatures took her legs. It had left the ends of her thighs smooth and healthy, and she had never experienced the phantom limb pain war veterans and others who had not had access to the salve suffered. In a nearby chamber, Mother Angelita was watching over the first man, who was sedated and lay unconscious on a cot.

Outside, Sisters Pippa, Penelope, and two assistants had dragged the horses to the courtyard, where they prepared to take the bodies into the desert to burn them.

Sister Amelia stopped them. "Burn them here," she said, "in the courtyard. The fire will bring others."

Sister Pippa looked at her askance. "We always—well, the other time—we burnt them in the desert."

"And nothing came?" asked Sister Amelia.

Sister Pippa shook her head, confused. "You were very lucky. Burn them here."

She went to find Mother Angelica. Later, the convent's leader would write a report, implore the local lawmen to do more to prevent travelers from accessing the lake; and contact other convents in the desert to warn them about the visions and creatures. But now, she sat stroking the hand of the surviving man.

Sister Amelia sat with her, her clothes covered in blood and ichor. She reached into a pocket for bullets and reloaded her gun, her reflexes quick from her previous life. Mother Angelita looked at her, her eyebrows crowded together with a lack of understanding.

"Mother, you may continue to hold his hand for a moment, but you may...be splattered." She stood, and emptied her gun into the man's head, throat, heart, and knees.

Mother Angelita rocked back on her chair. "Sister Amelia..." she struggled for words. "What..."

"I'm sorry, Mother," said the other woman gently. "I've seen this before. A stronger or older one transforms first, to protect the second. The other man was much bigger. This man...he's small. It only made sense."

And as she spoke, Mother Angelita's eyes opened wider as she stood, pointing at the body. "It's...he's..."

"Yes," said Sister Amelia. She had the repeating stiletto ready again. As it began to work on the creature, she unlocked the single-shot pistol from above her knee, and shot it in the head, as insurance. She replaced the gun, and looked at the Mother Superior. Mother Angelita was too stunned to have completely taken in this additional use of Sister Amelia's prostheses, which satisfied Sister Amelia well enough.

"Sit, Mother Angelita," she said, guiding the woman to a chair. She removed the stiletto from the creature's head and used it to cut the emerging limbs from the man, avoiding the claws. She folded up his small frame, and began to carry him to the pyre already aflame in the courtyard.

Even without the flames from the pyre in the convent's courtyard, it was a bright, with the moon high in the sky and stars shining like sequins in the night.

Sister Penelope approached Sister Amelia with a bucket of water. Sister Amelia thanked her and squatted to wash her hands and the repeating stiletto.

Finally, after much scrubbing, Sister Amelia dried her hands and the knife on her apron and turned to her fellow sister, still holding the stiletto. "Sister Pippa said something like this happened once before."

Sister Penelope shook her head. "What happened before wasn't like this. This fool Ranger broke away from his company and got lost. When he found this place, he'd almost become a skinwalker from eating and drinking all the wrong things in the desert, and being gnawed on."

"He would make this...partial change." She gestured to her upper body. "He was dying anyway. Sister Bonita—she died a few years before you came, an old, old lady—she knew about skinwalkers and nursed him a little while until he passed. He wasn't a creature or whatever those were."

"Creatures," Sister Amelia said, "from the lake. Those are water creatures. Specifically, at least according to the scientists in San Lazare, they are Oaxacan Water Pinchers. But I think most people—" she waved her hands about, indicating the world at large, "call them Wajas."

"Well, what the blazes are they doing in our lake?" Sister Penelope was more angry than frightened. She ground the end of her quarterstaff into a hole in a brick. A rare woman in a Buffalo Soldier regiment, she'd fought things few of her sisters could imagine.

Sister Amelia sighed. "I imagine someone stopping there recently contaminated it; maybe even one of the scientists." She stood and brushed off her skirts, then raised them on one side to return the stiletto to its usual slot in her leg. She looked up at the moon. "There probably won't be any coming tonight, or tomorrow, but I would guess within a few days they'll return."

"They shouldn't be in the lake, though—it's far too small for a colony to survive." She looked thoughtful, her fingers playing over the stone spiral at her throat. She looked at Sister Penelope. "They attach to anyone who drinks from their home lake. When those...hatch...they send out signals that somehow make all the others grow and follow them, usually to a new lake or to the sea."

"When a signal doesn't come, a few mature Wajas are sent to find the hatchlings and take then back to the lake. Then they send out eggs again until hatchlings send a signal."

She felt confident in saying this, having learned much from the scientists and doctors she had come to know when her legs were taken. They had been very forthright, those men and women, even on occasion making Sister Amelia squeamish with their discussions. She hoped to keep some of the worst from her sisters now.

Leaving a new guard on watch, the women returned to their cells. Sister Amelia did not sleep, but thought and wrote until dawn, when she went to find Mother Angelica. The Mother Superior was still in a state of shock. Her red eyes and drooping posture belied her hopeful morning invocation and prayers.

"Mother Angelita," began Sister Amelia. "We have to remove the creatures or cleanse the lake. If we wait for the creatures to move, they could kill us on their way to open water."

Mother Angelita looked at her. She had reports to write, warnings to make, and bones and ash to clear from her courtyard. Cleansing the lake? How could that even be possible? She looked bewildered for a second.

Sister Amelia continued, "Please let me tell you my idea."

Mother Angelita seemed to come back into herself, focusing her eyes, and took Sister Amelia's hand. "Yes," she said, "but first we will eat."

The nuns took their breakfast in the refectory, a warm room on the outside wall of the convent where morning sunlight streamed through a large circular window and several smaller spiral windows filled with stained glass.

In the sun with the scent of morning grains sweetened with the convent's honey, it was hard for Sister Amelia to reconcile the attack of the night before with the sense of comfort the room and its inhabitants offered. She began to think again of leaving the convent, looking for another safe place.

No, she thought, looking at her sisters nervously eating their meals. *I can't leave them to face this.*

After the sisters' communal breakfast, Mother Angelita and Sister Amelia returned to the Mother Superior's office. It was almost as spare as the nuns' cells. A long plank of wood lay across two file cabinets served as her desk; on it she had a typewriter and a blotter for handwritten documents. On each wall, a stone-worker had carved a bas-relief of the scared spiral: the symbol of the All-Mother.

Mother Angelita gestured to a set of chairs on the side of the room. She brushed her own apron nervously and sat. She looked into Sister Amelia's eyes, deliberately not looking at the nun's mechanical legs.

"Sister Amelia, I'll be blunt," she said. "I haven't lived my whole life in a convent, but I've never dealt with the creatures either. I've lived inland all my life, and never thought our lake here would be a threat. The sheriff will be here early this morning; he thinks we will all be fine. But I want to know from you—you said we wouldn't. I want to know why you say that, and what we can do?"

She paused. "But," she said, "I do not think I can be party to doing anything that will hurt the lake or the natural animals that live there. The All-Mother entrusted us with this world, and we cannot harm it."

Sister Amelia wasn't eager to speak. The things she had to say were not going to reassure her Mother Superior. But she did know about the creatures, perhaps more than any of the other nuns; and she could certainly speak about them more calmly than could Sister Margaret.

"Wajas begin the move to a bigger lake by sending out an advance party: two or three egg sacs. They wait until the eggs are ingested, and begin counting the days back in the lake. They aren't dumb animals: they plan. Once someone or something swallows an egg sac; well, you've seen what happens. One egg develops, kills its brothers and sisters, and works its way out. It uses its pincers to grab food, and summons the rest of the colony with a special scent."

"The grown Wajas leave the lake, join the new ones, and eat their way to a larger body of water." She stopped. She swallowed, hard. "They will attack and eat any living thing." She closed her eyes a moment. "Most people do not survive an attack. I was very lucky—you should know that—the All-Mother saved me."

Before Mother Angelita could ask about this last statement, Sister Amelia continued, "They seem to wait about five or seven days, in case the eggs' hosts have traveled far before the eggs hatch. But if the hatchlings don't send out the signal, the grown ones send a search group. They are strange and even more dangerous than the hatchlings, and can live outside of water for a while. I'm not sure how long. But the Wajas will follow the trail of the egg sacs here when they leave the lake."

Then came the worst part.

"We can fight them in the lake, or we can poison it."

Mother Angelita was predictably aghast. It was impossible to imagine, utterly unthinkable, to go against the All-Mother in such a way, to behave in the exact opposite of her vows. "I understand you have special knowledge, Sister," she said, "but there must be another way. Poisoning the lake is just not possible."

Sister Amelia bowed her head. She knew what she said was a heretical suggestion. She could be asked to leave the order immediately. But she had a plan; she just needed to convince Mother Angelita. She raised her head a little, and said, "I do have an idea for fighting them, if you will hear me out. And I will be the one to fight."

Mother Angelita listened. When the bell for lunch rang, she dispatched Sister Amelia to write a telegram (which Sister Amelia had already drafted, anticipating what was needed) to be sent to Texas. She began the mid-day meal with the usual blessing, and spent the rest of the day in the steam chamber, seeking a vision from the All-Mother.

Sister Carlita took the telegram to the closest office. "Make sure not to leave anything out, no matter what the telegraphist says," Sister Amelia told her. "We need Honey to bring everything listed there, and quickly."

It was a long list, with items Sister Carlita had never heard of: a 1/3-size Gaspar steam-engine, an Asclepion breathing machine, and three reels of something called Copper Mold. Sister Amelia also asked for twelve dozen copper rivets, two clockwork band-revolvers, and the Zambian, although who or what that was, Sister Carlita couldn't tell.

Sister Carlita asked, "Who's Honey?"

"She made my legs," replied Sister Amelia. Sister Carlita rode quickly, did not wait for a reply, and returned before nightfall to the convent, where again a larger than usual night watch was on duty.

Two days after Sister Carlita sent the telegram, Honey and the Zambian arrived. They could be seen coming from a long way off, the twin screws of the airship pushing through the hot desert air. Trailing behind the airship was a flag declaring the ship to be The Airship *Yam* of the Royal Navy of Comoros, an old joke between Sister Amelia and Honey.

As the ship approached, the nuns of St. Laurita's could see that she was a decommissioned Texan ship. Yellow and reddish metallic armor plated her sides, and she had three guns front, rear, and sides, as

well as a giant winch and what appeared to be escape gliders hanging
below the ship's main body. Many of the sisters came out into the
garden to watch the arrival of the *Yam*, shading their eyes with their
hands.

Sister Amelia rushed out to help secure the airship to the
convent's Northern wall, and Sister Pippa ran to help her. They
grabbed the ships' long landing lines and brought her down to the edge
of the convent, the ship firing off short blasts of air as it descended. A
few moments later, a door in the armor opened and a stout wooden stair
dropped out.

The woman who emerged from the *Yam* could have been Sister
Amelia's sister. Tall and graceful, with long thick coils of hair falling
around her shoulders. She too had the scars of a woman of Comoros:
intricate patterns that swirled and twisted behind her ears and down her
throat.

She wore a traveling outfit none of the sisters had seen before:
a cutaway skirt that ended at her knees, attached to long, flowing
trousers, a high-necked green-striped blouse with long sleeves and
worn boots in the same dark brown as the "trouskirt" (as she called it)
topped off by a Texas Ranger's hat with a wide, thick band.

She embraced Sister Amelia in a hug that seemed to last an
hour, the two women swaying from side to side. Finally, they let go of
one another, and Sister Amelia remembered her manners. Stepping to
the side, she said, "Sisters, this is Honey Washington, the Machinist.
Honey made my legs for me, and she's going to help me fight the
Wajas in the lake."

The sisters saw little of Honey for the next two days: she was
covered by an enormous welding mask that shielded not only her head

but also her entire torso. She and Sister Amelia worked outside in the courtyard, though, so everyone could see what they were doing. The Zambian, it turned out, was a short metal capsule, with a propeller at the rear and a place for two people inside.

Honey said, "We call it the Zambian because it was first tested there, in Lake Bangweulu. It's not a Hunley-type submarine, just for small bodies of water. It's for exploring, but we're going to use it against the Wajas." She scowled at the name and spit. "*Bastards!*"

They outfitted the Zambian with two more propeller-like circles of blades, connected to handles on the inside. And, with a feverish intensity, they molded and connected metal to the breathing machine using the steam engine. The result was a box with tubing.

"Sister," Sister Penelope asked Sister Amelia, "what does that do?"

Sister Amelia grinned. "It fits over me," she said happily. "I'm hunting Wajas!"

On the third day after Honey had arrived, five days after the deaths of the two travelers, the sheriff rode to the convent around midnight. He got down from his horse and tied her loosely to a post inside the thick outer walls of the courtyard.

His hat in his hand, he entered the visitors' area to speak with Mother Angelita, who flew from her rooms, sweeping down the adobe corridors. He scratched his forehead.

"Mother," he said, dipping his head. "Jasper McJohns says he saw a Waja leaving the lake early this evening and headed this way. I wanted to let you know, I have a handful of men on the way to help protect you all."

"This is the worst timing!" Mother Angelita stared at the

sheriff.

"No, it's perfect," said Sister Amelia, who was on night watch and had followed the sheriff in. "It's absolutely perfect."

Sister Amelia told the Mother Superior and the sheriff to expect several Wajas, guessing that there would be three to five of them.

Then she went to wake Honey and change. In her cell, she removed her apron, dress, and underclothes. She stepped into a large metal box with holes for her legs and secured her legs to it. She tightened the metal box around her, using gears and locks to draw in webbing and strapping that circled her torso.

She drew water-tight covers down over the attachment points on her legs, and slid her arms through long, articulated metal tubes that were capped at the ends with rotors. At the end of each tube she grasped a rotor control to check that the weaponized rotors would spin easily.

Awkwardly, she lifted up round helmet with a piece of glass across the front, and tucked it under one arm. She inserted her other arm tube into a tangle of webbing attached to yet another roughly welded box, and headed for the front of the convent.

Mother Angelita didn't know what to think of the clanking box that emerged from the convent. Sister Amelia was entirely enveloped in metal, save for the glass rectangle in her helmet. Honey connected the breathing device, usually used in hospitals, to a set of pumps and tanks from the *Yam*, and checked all of the socket points on the suit.

Sister Amelia smiled at the Mother Superior who was watching them intently. "Mother," she said. "Will you bless me?"

Mother Angelita was startled, but covered it smoothly. "Of

course," she said.

She cast about the room for a moment, and then asked to borrow one of Honey's screwdrivers. She stepped up to Sister Amelia and carefully, almost hesitantly, scratched the spiral of the All-Mother into the breastplate of the suit.

She bowed her head for a moment, touched the spiral, and stepped back. "Go with the All-Mother," she said. "Save the lake."

§§§

With Sister Selina and three men newly arrived from the sheriff's office, Sister Amelia, Honey, and the Zambian left the convent on a cart pulled by Sister Brayana. The moon was just past half, and the stars lit up the sands of the desert as they made their way to the lake, moving quietly to avoid the Wajas heading in the other direction.

At one point they all stopped, seeing a shadow move past. The group exhaled as one when it had gone, and reached the lake around three in the morning. Honey lifted Sister Amelia down from the cart and connected her helmet to the tanks from the *Yam*. Filled with oxygen, they would keep her alive for an hour underwater.

Honey also attached a balloon full of jelly inside Sister Amelia's helmet and had the sister run her rotor blades one last time. As the moon traveled on its way towards the earth, Sister Amelia slipped into the lake. Honey climbed into the Zambian, and Sister Selina, monitoring both Sister Amelia's oxygen, pushed the tiny submarine into the lake.

§§§

At St. Laurita's, Sister Margaret took up a staff and joined her sisters in the courtyard. Mother Angelita, in a steel box suspended above the courtyard, gave directions. Six Wajas were trying to get up and over the walls—they were largely succeeding. Sisters Pippa, Penelope, and Carlita were ready for them to drop down into the courtyard, where they would be easier to fight. In the infirmary, Sister Monica readied supplies for wounded nuns, and Sister Cristina prepared jars in which to preserve the Wajas' dismembered limbs.

§§§

Sister Amelia sank straight to the bottom of the lake and took several minutes to adjust to the darkness under its waters. Her helmet had a small light attached to the top of it, but the water was murky and thick, a definite sign of Waja presence.

She knew that Wajas usually nested in the center of lakes like this one, and, training her air supply line, began pushing through weeds and the choked water to get there. Honey, in the Zambian, whirred around the edges of the lake, searching for Wajas away from the nest.

§§§

Sister Pippa pinned the first Waja as it came down the wall, its claws reaching out and snapping even as its legs scrambled for a purchase on the adobe. Elated by the easy first defensive kill, the women threw the body to the side as three more creatures breached the courtyard.

§§§

"On your left, Sister Margaret!" yelled Mother Angelita.

Sister Margaret was paralyzed for a long moment, and Mother Angelita stopped breathing; then the young woman swung her iron-pointed staff at the closest creature, solidly hitting it in the head. To her right, Sister Penelope was fending off a second Waja that was soon joined by a third. As a Sheriff's deputy fenced with yet another, a final emissary of the lake slipped unseen over the wall behind them.

§§§

She was getting close, Sister Amelia thought. To her left, she saw the unmistakable outline of a cow's skeleton, ribbons of flesh rising up as she moved the water with her copper legs and thick suit. And there was the nest: at least a dozen grown or mostly grown Wajas and a handful of egg sacs. She breathed deeply from her air line, prayed to the All-Mother, and stomped in, crushing egg sacs with her feet.

The startled Wajas rose up around her as she wound the clockwork gears that made the rotors on her suit begin to spin. Honey found a single Waja near the east side of the lake and chased it down as it tried to maneuver away from her.

As it zigged and zagged across the lake bottom, Honey released the catch on a long spring, and an enormous knife—like Sister Amelia's dagger but much larger—sprang into action. It caught the Waja's back legs and Honey quickly ran over its back, sharp rotors taking apart the creature in seconds.

§§§

In the courtyard of St. Laurita's, Sister Carlita shot a downed and beaten Waja in Sister Amelia's prescribed locations: head, throat, chest, knees. Sister Pippa's staff was grasped by one Waja's set of claws, and it pulled itself up the staff towards her, as another Sheriff's man turned to help her.

On the edges, three nuns grabbed the killed Wajas and dragged them to the convent door, which was sealed tightly from the inside. The Waja on Sister Pippa's staff let go with one claw and, faster than she could see it, closed hard onto her arm. Sister Margaret screamed, driving her staff into the back of the Waja's head.

§§§

Sister Amelia spun, a whirling dervish in the service of the All-Mother, removing unnatural creatures from the lake. She spun, and spun, dizzying whirls in the nest, her eyes almost closed as she sliced through the creatures under the water. On the shore, Sister Selina kept her eyes on the oxygen tank's gauge, and three of the sheriff's men stood ready with guns should more Wajas emerge.

§§§

A big Waja grabbed Sister Penelope at the waist by the from behind her. One of the men grabbed at the Waja's back legs, which kicked him in the stomach. Sister Carlita bashed at the Waja's middle with her staff as both creature and woman fell to the ground. Mother Angelita called for the backup fighters. From the sidelines, Sister Michelle rushed into the fight, joining Sister Carlita in trying to remove the Waja from Sister Penelope, who thrashed and screamed on the ground. Sister Margaret helped Sister Pippa to the doorway of the convent, keeping her staff pointed on the wounded Waja that followed them.

§§§

Honey found two more Wajas on the edges of the lake, and destroyed them almost as easily as the first. Sister Amelia was caught up in the whirling and whirring of her body and the rotors when her right hand failed. The mechanism growled, tangled on pieces of Waja and weedy muck. She stopped spinning, losing her balance briefly in the process.

She reached out with her left arm and swung it at the Wajas still coming at her, circling her from their nest. She looked down quickly, and stepped on the remaining egg sacs. The floor of the lake began to rumble and shudder. Honey felt a faint vibration as well, and headed for the center of the lake.

§§§

Sister Margaret returned to the melee, nearly knocking over one of the sheriff's men in the process. With staves, she and Sister Michelle and Sister Carlita were able to kill the Waja on Sister Penelope. Sister Carlita administered the final shots, and Sister

Margaret put her staff through a last twitching Waja body.

§§§

The nest was moving. The bones and flesh around it were being pushed away by some kind of tide, a tide inside the lake. The floor under Sister Amelia's feet shook and broke, sucking water under the ground and issuing forth a dark shadow. Sister Amelia jumped back, away from the nest, and was jerked down—her legs were caught in weeds and the tangle of the nest.

As she neared the center of the lake, Honey pushed the Zambian faster and faster. She caught a glimpse of copper, and saw Sister Amelia fighting to get free of the nest. She wound up the clockwork knife again.

§§§

Sister Monica applied preserved Waja jelly to Sister Pippa's arm, where the Waja had ripped away muscle and ligaments. Sister Carlita and the sheriff's men were dragging the Waja bodies to the infirmary. And in the courtyard, Sister Penelope's eyes had been closed, and Mother Angelita knelt by her body.

§§§

Wajas hurled themselves at Sister Amelia, claws beating on her suit, legs seeking openings. But as the crevice in the lake floor opened, the last of the Wajas were sucked in by the shadow inside. On the shore, Sister Selina began to look worried: the tanks had hit the halfway point, and there had been no tugs on the lines to indicate that she should pull Sister Amelia up or signal Honey in the submarine. The sheriff's men shifted their weight uneasily, keeping their rifles ready.

Out of the crevice the shadow was growing. Sister Amelia struggled to release her legs from the nest. As the shadow emerged from the crevice, she began banging her arm tubes against the newly modified keyless socket mechanisms that kept the copper legs bolted in place to her natural ones.

She managed to release her right leg when an enormous Waja-like creature lunged at her. It was easily three times as large as a normal Waja, and had a wide mouth, fanged at the corners. Its legs were not the thin, insect-like legs of the smaller Wajas, but sturdy, thick limbs ending with hoof-like feet with sharp spurs on the ankles. Its mouth was open, and Sister Amelia felt it begin to suck her in.

She frantically beat at the socket of her left leg as its jaws closed over her lower body just as she saw the Zambian's flashing knife swoop in at it. The dark water and the giant Waja surrounded her, and she blacked out.

Sister Amelia came to just a second later. She grabbed at the lines supplying her with air, jerking them to signal Sister Selina that she needed to rise. As she felt the lines begin to tighten the webbing around her, she took a huge breath, grabbed the helmet from her head, ripped away the air lines, and shoved the helmet into the giant Waja's mouth.

Surprised, the creature swallowed, and as Sister Amelia rose towards the surface, it began to thrash and claw at her torso, disappearing out of its reach. Honey steered the Zambian directly at the

Waja, slamming into its throat and backing out as fast as she could go.

All Sister Selina could see was blood—blood from Sister Amelia's legs, blood from the Wajas, blood in the eyes of the sheriff's men as the nun broke through the surface, missing her helmet and legs.

The Zambian surfaced just behind her, Honey throwing open the hatch on top and racing out. Honey cradled her friend on the shore of the lake, laying her gently down as Sister Selina tied off Sister Amelia's left leg above the Waja bite.

Sister Amelia gasped and gobbled for air. In the center of the lake, the water rose in huge waves, and the giant Waka broke the surface and sunk again, its claws and legs beating the water. The men shot at it, hitting the body.

Sister Amelia panted, "It's dead already. It's dead."

The others stared at her. How could this behemoth creature be dead when it was flailing around the lake?

"I put the helmet in its mouth," she gasped out. "And I made it swallow," Honey beamed. Sister Amelia nodded weakly.

Sister Selina and the men looked at Honey for an explanation. "There's a jelly packet of poison in the helmet," she said. "It was for the Sister here in case she needed it for herself. It'll easily kill the Waja —you can drag the lake later to remove the body."

Shortly after dawn, Sister Brayana appeared at St. Laurita's main gate, pulling a cart carrying Honey, Sister Amelia, the sheriff's men, and a good deal of battered equipment. Sister Margaret ran from the convent gate to them.

"Sister Margaret," said Sister Amelia gently and with a smile, "what are you doing outside of the walls?" Sister Margaret collapsed onto Sister Amelia's shoulders with relief and sorrow, crying and hugging her.

Inside, Honey and Sister Margaret took Sister Amelia to the infirmary, and Honey went to the *Yam* to retrieve her original plans for her friend's legs. "We'll just need to add more at the top of the left one," she told Sister Monica later. "Plenty of room there for an extra weapon or two...."

As the sisters in the infirmary helped Sister Amelia sleep, she thought, *I might never leave again either.*

But deep in her mind, she knew more than ever that it wasn't true. Her work here had changed things; she would become restless again.

But I don't have to worry about it now, she thought, drifting off into a soft sleep.

§§§

Sister Penelope's ashes were scattered in the desert, returning her to the All-Mother. Not long after, Mother Angelita called Sister Amelia to her office. Sister Amelia arrived in a small wind-up carriage base, a temporary device until her new legs were finished. She bowed to her Mother Superior.

They chatted for a few minutes, about when Sister Amelia's legs would be finished, about Sister Margaret's new desire to travel to work with other victims of the creatures, about St. Laurita's summer crops. Then Mother Angelita picked up an envelope from her desktop.

"This is from a woman from your part of the world," she said. "She wishes to join us, but is being held by a plantation master in

Carolina. He is using some kind of creatures to keep people there. Do you—and Honey, if she will help us again—feel up for a trip?"

THE SWITCH

(EXCERPT FROM THE SWITCH II: CLOCKWORK)

VALJEANNE JEFFERS

Z100 stood on the tube platform waiting for the next car. She was dressed in a one-piece, white jumpsuit and thigh-high boots: standard dress for the upper city. Pods only seated three to a car, and were propelled by compressed air through tunnels that webbed across Tyrol. Access was granted through palm recognition scanners.

On her left, a Latino couple waited for the car. The man was dressed in a derby hat and striped pants with suspenders; the woman wore a bustier, and skirt with petticoats. Their musty smell reached her, and she wrinkled her nose in disgust.

At least these cars are self-cleaning.

An egg-shaped pod slid to a stop in front of her. She pressed her palm against the scanner and then shot an icy glance at the couple.

They looked away. They knew better than to try to ride with her. Under dwellers were not permitted to socialize with city residents, and only ventured above ground to work. They would wait for the next car.

The hatch door lifted and she stepped inside, sitting on a cushion beside the three-inch window. The pod sped off and Z100 gazed out the window: the rounded towers of York were a blur of beige and white. In the distance, she glimpsed the tripod mansion of the supreme leader.

The car reached her platform. Z100 stepped out of the transport tube and climbed into a waiting hover craft.

"Where to, ma'am?" a mechanical voice asked.

"Mulberry 5000." The hover craft zoomed forward.

In minutes, Z100 had climbed out on her porch that stood miles above ground. She stood at the door of her oval-shaped condo, and placed her palm against the flat box beside the door. A laser strip slid down her palm.

There was a brief hum. "Welcome home," her house announced.

The clear hatch lifted and she stepped inside. Z100 walked up the floating staircase to her bedroom, and undressed in front of her mirror, turning to the side so she could admire her implants.

Her honey-brown skin and thick, bobbed hair were natural. But her green eyes and full lips had cost a pretty credit—as had her 38 C breasts. Naked, Z100 twisted again to admire her waist and rounded hips, also natural, then slipped on the kimono lying across the bed.

Adjacent to the king-size bed, was a picture window with a stunning view. She walked over to it and stood for a moment looking out over the city's multicolored lights.

"You look beautiful, Ms. Z100," the house said in a baritone male voice, "as always. What would like for dinner?"

"Broiled fish with sea salt, green salad and white wine."

"No dessert?"

"No."

"Very good."

Z100 walked down the stairs into her living room. Across from the futon and coffee table were three opaque closets. An android stood inside each one, clothed only in white trousers.

She lingered before them, choosing a dinner date. She decided on the third one, Jason, a robot with chocolate skin, exquisitely defined muscles and a nappy cap of hair.

Z100 punched in the definition codes on the curved stand beside the closet: *Dinner in 20 minutes. Dress: casual. Language...*

At this she hesitated. English tapes sounded so flat lately. But other dialects were worse. The tapes were recorded by under dwellers that were paid only a fraction of a credit for each one. So they were stepping on them—using the original track to produce five, even ten, more tapes.

They were given an upgrade today, but it probably won't make any difference. *To hell with it.* She typed in: *Language: English.*

She pushed set and the android stepped jerkily out of the closet, walked past her and up the stairs. From his chip, he knew to pull male clothing from her closet and dress.

Minutes later, Jason came down the stairs and sat in the dining room alcove. Another robot began to set the table. The second one had a head with only the semblance of a nose and mouth. Beneath its pink shoulders were a metal torso and limbs.

At times, Z100 longed for a real man, but she'd never mate.

In the twenty-fifth century doing so was dangerous.

Her line of work made it even more deadly.

Tyrolean law said that women and darker peoples were second-class citizens. Women of color had the lowest rungs on this ladder. Poor whites were also assigned lower class citizenship.

Once a woman married, all of her credits became her husband's. And forced marriages, as well as the murders of newly wedded women, were not uncommon.

Z100 had been a key player in the war that unseated the first rulers, catapulting her to the top class. Because of her role in the coup d'état she, and a handful of other female spies, were immune to these laws.

But if she were to marry this would change. Even taking a lover was risky. She'd heard of wealthy women drugged by men they were sleeping with, waking up to find themselves married. And penniless.

The overthrow of the old regime had created a class of ultra-wealthy Tyroleans. The rest became under dwellers —those who lived under the city and earned only enough for food, shelter and oxygen; like her housekeeper Simone2.

And because Z had helped to overthrow the old world, because she worked as a spy to make sure nothing changed, she was hated. She had enemies everywhere—men and women who'd cheerfully murder her to bring down the society she'd helped create.

Z100 sauntered over to her futon, sat down and pushed a button on the underside of the end table next to the couch. The top of the table flipped over, revealing the keyboard hidden underneath. She twirled the dial of her wristband to release a disc and slid it into the front of the keyboard.

Z100 tapped the play key. A holograph of a thirtyish black man appeared. This was H36, a lawyer suspected of being sympathetic to the rebels. As she looked on, the man stepped from behind his desk to meet with a client.

She sighed. *God, he's boring.* She forced herself to watch for another twenty minutes. *He's clean.*

Z reached over and pushed the next button on her keyboard.

The image vanished and another holograph took its place: this one of an older white man. Like the target before him, T40 was dressed in tunic and slacks. But he wasn't alone.

Z's lips curled up in a tiny smile. *This ought to be good.*

She pushed pause, got up and went into the kitchen, detouring around her android butler to pour a glass of wine, and then made herself comfortable on the futon once more.

As she looked on, the target unzipped his jumpsuit and pushed it down. His blond companion sauntered over to his desk, and slipped off her pants. She straddled him, curling an arm about his neck. With her other hand she unzipped her tunic to bare her plump breasts. Moans of pleasure filled Z100's apartment.

Z100 watched them, arousal spreading down her pelvis. She cut the tape off, got up and poured herself another glass of wine. She'd planted the tiny cameras in the men's offices. They were later retrieved by spies posing as under dweller janitors.

I should send him a holograph thanking him. I bet the rest of the tapes are nowhere near this interesting. He's clean too. Nobody cares about him knocking off a piece of tail in his office.

"Dinner's ready, Ms. Z100," the house announced.

She smirked. *Time for my date.* She pushed the button on the underside of the desk, hiding the console. You couldn't be too careful.

She walked over to the alcove and sat down facing Jason. The robot butler sat the plates in front of them, then two glasses for more wine. The android wouldn't eat of course, but it would spoil the mood to have an empty place sitting in front of him.

Z100 smiled, her teeth flashing against her honey-brown skin. Her smile activated his AI chip, cuing Jason to respond to dinner conversation.

Jason blinked and shifted in his chair. "Good evening, Z100," he said in a rich baritone. "You look lovely tonight."

Boy, he's good! This is one of the best I've heard! She made a mental note to buy from the same shop when his tape wore out.

"How was your day?" she asked.

His lips spread in an amazingly human smile. "I missed you...I thought about you all day."

Her question had stimulated a second response chip. Different questions triggered different menus. But he was still a robot—still chemically treated human skin stretched over plastic limbs.

Gazing at his ebony face, Z100 pushed herself to forget this reality and embrace the fantasy.

"We're finishing up the senators' profiles for the next election," Jason went on. "But it's all for show. They aren't going anywhere. Citizens aren't going to vote—not in this century."

The android was hardwired to "believe" he was a politician. Candidates, including the supreme leader, weren't voted in. They were appointed to lifetime terms.

Very realistic dialogue, thought Z, *I am so loving this tape!* Out loud she said: "You better watch your back— the rebels are waiting for a chance to gun you down."

He flashed his gorgeous smile again. "We got enough snipers on the payroll to handle anything they throw at us. How was your day?"

Z100 gulped her wine. She felt giddy, reckless. And his brown eyes were so intense.

"How about my life story instead?" she blurted, her eyes hard and bright. "Once upon a time there was a little girl working as a courier for the most powerful man in Tyrol. Don3000 the supreme leader."

"She was screwing him too, so she had access to his most private files. She plotted with his enemies to have him and the heads of state killed and replaced with look-a-likes."

Z giggled hysterically. "The imposters pushed through laws to have senators appointed to lifetime terms. Then they shifted credits to a lucky few and the little girl — that would be me — became rich beyond her wildest dreams!"

"I'm still a courier. But now I'm a courier of death. One word from me," she popped her fingers, "and that's it. And because I'm so well liked, at the end of the day I get to eat—and screw—an android. No real man, no real love for me. Not ever. Not if I want to keep my head attached to my shoulders."

"There endth my story." She took another sip of her wine. *What's wrong with me? I must be drunk!*

For an instant, she thought she saw Jason's face tense in anger. *I am drunk. He can't get angry. I probably blew his circuits with all that crap.*

The android's face melted into a smile again. "I can see you had a rough day, baby...You just need daddy to give you a little, tender loving care," He stood and pulled her to him.

Jason cupped her face in his big hands and began to kiss her slowly at first, running his tongue and lips over her mouth and neck. His kisses became greedier, his hands roaming over her body...

By the time he lifted his mouth, her head was spinning. Foreplay and lovemaking were part of his programming, but this—this was beyond anything she'd ever experienced!

She didn't know what chip this was, and she didn't care. All she cared about was the tightness between her legs —the heat, the desire to have him.

"House off!" she gasped.

"Ms. Z100, are you sure —"

"House off, damn-it!"

The circuitry was only another machine. But she couldn't let it listen in on this, and she certainly didn't want it taped.

"As you wish."

Jason picked her up, and carried her up the stairs. When he reached her bed, he tossed her on to it and crawled up beside her. He tore the thin garment from her body—ripping it in his haste to have her —and pushed his pants down.

In the next moment, her legs were on his shoulders and he was thrusting inside her in hard, quick jabs, while she screamed in pleasure and pain.

Z100 passed out.

Dumas2 let her legs down and pulled out of her. He lifted her eyelids with his thumb. Once he was satisfied she was unconscious, he rolled off the bed and went to her closet.

He slid a panel back, and pulled out three sets of under dweller garments: jackets with wide lapels, stovepipe leg trousers, and derbies with feathers.

Dumas dressed in one of the outfits. With the rest of the clothes over his arm, he ran down the steps and over to the closets. He typed in the buttons for release.

The doors slid open, and two men stepped free of the closets.

Dumas handed them their gear. "It's done."

Carlos2, a coconut-colored man with wavy hair, smiled with relief. "Damn, I'm glad to get out of that cage!"

Richard2 grinned; he was paper-sack brown with a shaved head. "You were probably hoping she'd choose you."

"No worries on that score." Carlos smirked. "The lady prefers tall, dark hombres for her stud service. Me and you were just decoration."

Richard laughed. "Simone is gonna kick your butt," he said to Dumas.

Dumas looked nervous. "How about we don't tell her? Where is she anyway?"

"Right behind you," a female voice said.

The men whirled around. A woman stood in the doorway of the kitchen, dressed in a white jumpsuit and boots. An onyx-handled derringer was strapped to her waist.

She was identical to Z100.

Dumas strolled toward her. "Baby! You look just like her!"

"Yeah, I know," she cut him off. "Seems like that's what you prefer."

"Naw, it ain't like that!" Dumas protested. "I was playing a role. What could I do?" Carlos and Richard chuckled at their friend's discomfort.

Simone's green eyes flashed angrily. "How about waiting for the dope to take effect?"

"You mean waiting until she realized she'd been drugged?" he countered. "The woman's not an idiot, Simone! I had a hard enough time convincing her I was a robot!"

"Whatever," Simone2 said dryly. "You guys better rinse the sedative out of her wine bottle. No sense in taking chances." She pushed past her lover and strode to the end table. Once there, she bent over and pressed the side button: revealing the hidden console.

Simone2 clicked the saved file. "Come to Mama!" She grinned. "Addresses for the supreme leader and his two top aides are right here on the hard drive—plus the identities of every phony politician in New York."

She slid a round disc inside the console and pressed copy, then turned to the men. "You got what you need?" asked Simone.

Richard reached inside his breast pocket and held out his palm...to display a square capsule with three pills. "Yep. This is the same formula that'll turn us into their look-a-likes—the same formula I gave you—and the same pills they used to steal our world."

"The upper city dwellers think they're the only ones with nano-medication," Dumas said with a smirk. "Under dwellers helped them develop it."

Carlos smiled. "No worries baby, we got this under control."

"Who the hell are you people?"

The four whirled in unison to find the real Z100 standing on the stairs, holding a sheet around her naked body. In her other hand, she held a laser.

"HOUSE ALARM ON!" she shouted. Z bared her teeth in a predatory smile. "Move and I'll sever your heads from your worthless bodies! You four are about to stand trial for high treason!"

Dumas dropped low and charged at her. Z100 fired— taking a chunk from his arm. In the next instant, Simone drew the pistol from her hip and put a bullet in Z100's forehead.

Z fell to the steps, dead.

"HOUSE ALARM OFF!" Simone2 shouted.

"Ms. Z100, I cannot comply."

"House I gave you a direct order! House alarm *off!*"

The computer hesitated, trying to process the conflicting data. His mistress was lying dead on the floor... and standing in the middle of her living room—very much alive—shouting at him.

House computers operated on pure logic. They weren't wired for moral judgment. And a live Z trumped a dead one.

"As you wish, Ms. Z100."

"Delete surveillance video for the last twenty minutes, and go into sleep mode."

"Ms. Z100 —"

"Do as I command, House!"

"Very good, Ms. Z100." There was a brief hum as the computer went to sleep.

She ran to Dumas, touching his injured arm gently. "You okay, baby?"

"I'm alright." But his face was gray with pain.

Richard was almost dancing with agitation. "They'll be here in minutes! What can we do?!"

"You didn't give her the right dosage!" Carlos agonized.

"Are you kidding?!" Z exclaimed. "She drank enough of that stuff to be dead in twenty-hours—just enough time for me to discredit her and you to move into place!"

"The plan can still work!" Dumas said, hissing with pain. "Put the real androids back in their boxes. We'll hide in the closet." He nodded at Z100. "We'll put her in there with us."

They scurried to hide the evidence—dragging the heavy androids downstairs. Z100 pulled the futon over the drops of blood and blotted the rest from the carpet.

She changed into Z100's kimono and, in a sudden burst of inspiration, activated the real Jason android.

BAM! BAM!

She stood beside the robot. "House video restart, Jason sit on the couch: entertainment mode."

BAM! BAM! BAM!

Simone2 took a deep breath, and strolled to the door. She pushed the button, and it slid upward.

"Officials." She greeted the two men garbed in tan jumpsuits.

"We had a disturbance call?"

She smiled coldly. "Everything is fine here."

"We need to do a sweep!" one of them, a pudgy white man, barked.

"Of course," Simone said in a blasé voice. She moved aside, her heart thumping a drumbeat.

They swept their eyes over the room. "Who else is here?" asked the second official, a tall swarthy man.

"Only me and my male friend. Jason, say hello to the nice officials."

Jason smiled. "Good evening." His voice sounded as if it was underwater.

"What's wrong with him?"

"He's an android—it's a poor quality voice tape," she explained.

The constables glanced at each other, but said nothing. Z100 was a rich, powerful woman. Her toys were her own affair.

They walked into her living room, and stopped before the closets.

Simone willed herself not to sweat, as she spotted the tiny hole left by Z's laser. To her left, there was a bloodstain on the steps.

Steady, steady. Just a little longer.

The first man spotted the hole. He turned to her with gimleted eyes. "What's this?"

"I have no idea. It was here when I moved in."

"And the blood on the stairs?" the other one asked.

"That's not blood that's wine."

"We'll need to see the surveillance video."

Time to turn up the heat, and act like the high class, city drone I'm pretending to be. "Gentlemen, as you can see, I was entertaining."

"What set off the alarm?"

"A malfunction, I suppose. It happens all the time. Now if you'll excuse me—"

Their hands hovered over their lasers. "We need to see that tape!" the thin one demanded.

"Is something wrong honey?" Jason asked.

Simone blew out her breath. "No, Jason, everything's fine. House, play surveillance for the last ten minutes."

Immediately a holograph appeared in mid-air showing Z100 in Dumas's arms. Smoothly without any pause the tape cut to Simone2 standing beside the android Jason as he sat on the couch.

"This tape's been edited! We'll have to search your home!"

"Now you hold *on* one minute!" Simone shouted back. "Do you know who I am? With the push of a button I can have your jobs or your *lives*. I've let you into my home and you've watched my video. If that's not good enough, call your commander and we'll all search the house."

Her green eyes narrowed. "But you'd better find something!" she spat, "or you'll be patrolling the underground before morning!"

They turned red. The pudgy one swallowed. "We're sorry to have bothered you ma'am. You know we patrol for your safety," he babbled. "We have to check out every alarm."

Simone smothered her grin and looked haughty, while the man kissed her behind. "Yes, yes, I know you're only doing your job. Goodnight."

She let them out, nearly weeping with relief. "Surveillance video off," she whispered.

"Very good, Ms. Z100."

She ran upstairs, and pushed aside the panel. The men scrambled out, holding Dumas up between them.

"He's bleeding pretty bad." Richard said, looking worried.

Simone ran into the bathroom, rummaged around and came back with bandages, and one of Z100's pain pills. Carlos packed the wound to stop it from bleeding and then tied up Dumas's arm.

But when Simone offered her lover a pain pill he shook his head. "It might stop the nano-meds from working," he grunted. "Once we get underground, I'll be okay."

"He's right!" said Carlos. "If he can't impersonate the senator, all this will have been for nothing!"

§§§

At the door, Simone pressed one of the discs into Carlos's palm. She'd made a second copy for herself, then took Dumas's face in her hands and kissed him. "I love you, baby."

"I love you too. You gonna be all right? Can you pull this off? Can you be her a little longer?"

Simone's lips thinned into a hard line. "I'm a warrior. I can do this."

But there were tears standing in her eyes. If they failed, they both knew that the next time they met would be at the guillotine.

"I'll go through her tapes, and submit the false reports. She's been tracking our people—like T40. If she'd watched that whole disc, she'd have seen a lot more than him getting laid."

"Yeah, they're going to be real surprised to find just how many city dwellers hate their world," said Richard.

Worry painted Dumas's broad face. "Promise me you won't get too comfortable. Lots of folks hate Z. If her enemies even suspect her—you—of wrong doing it's over."

"I know." She held her lover's gaze. "If we don't all get there…"

"I'll meet you on the other side," Dumas finished softly.

§§§

The three men stepped out on to Z's porch, hoping the night would cover them. They were in the upper city after dark, which made them targets for any gun-ho official. Under dwellers that lived in the homes of their employers, carried papers to show officials. Those who lived underground made it their business to be underground by nightfall.

A vacant pod hovered in front of them. They crawled inside, Dumas struggling not to pass out.

"Underground station," ordered Frederick. The pod zoomed to the multi-rail. At the station, they found an empty car and flew down.

The long tubes that led to ground stank and were heavy with dirt, as was the hover craft they caught to the staircase. But tonight, they were too worried to care.

As soon as they reached ground, they ran into trouble. Four officials were standing across the street from their stairwell.

"Hey!"

They couldn't be stopped and searched. Not tonight.

"HEY YOU! Stop!"

Frederick and Carlos—carrying Dumas between them—rushed down the stairs into the waiting underground.

Going below ground was more than leaving the upper city. It was like entering another world. Skylights were carved into the metal, for natural light, to keep under city dwellers from going blind.

Yet it was always gloomy, and the steam used to power their machinery created a perpetual fog. All refuse was recycled through pipes attached to brick walls along the alleyways that carried the waste farther below. The smell clung to the under dwellers skin and clothing.

Yet for all this, the underground had it charms. Cobblestone lanes adorned by streetlights ran the length of the under city. Wooden shops and flats overlaid with brass lined the avenues. In the distance, a clock tower chimed.

The people were known for their outrageous gear. As part of their rebellion, they refused to dress like those who oppressed them.

As the fugitives reached the street, a steam-powered auto puttered along the stones, its motor clearly visible in front. On the left a couple strolled past, the man dressed in knickers and stockings; the woman in a form-fitting dress with a bustle and pill box hat.

To their right, an old man carrying a walking stick stood before a haberdashery. He had a salt-and-pepper, handlebar mustache; and wore a red jacket with tails, and pants with suspenders.

Behind them came the running steps of the constables.

The old man stepped in front of the fugitives, as if to block their path, and tapped the stones with his stick.

The stones slid back, revealing a steam-powered elevator; it rose to the street. Carlos, Richard and Dumas crowded inside and the elevator slid back down, the stones sliding over it.

The old man stepped back on top of the stones.

The officials reached the street. And the under dwellers faces closed over, hiding the rage boiling inside them. They twisted their faces into passive, happy masks.

"You! Old man!" a burly official hailed him.

"Yes, suh?"

"You see three men run past here?"

"Naw, suh." He grinned. "I ain't seen a thang."

"Don't lie to me, you old buzzard! There's no way you could've missed them!"

"Fact of the matter is, I was in the alley."

"Doing what?"

"Why, catching these…" The old man opened his coat to display three rats hanging from hooks in the lining.

The officials drew back in horror. "What the—!"

The old man winked. "They makes a right tasty stew."

"Come on, let's go!" his partner said. "They're long gone by now." They threw the old man another disgusted look, turned and headed back up the stairs.

"These people are less than animals!" another official spat. "Jeez, I think I'm gonna lose my lunch!"

Daniel chuckled to himself. "Works every time," he whispered.

Beneath his feet, the three men waited. *Tonight,* thought Dumas2, *tonight the revolution begins.*

BENJAMIN'S FREEDOM MAGIC

RONALD T. JONES

The Confederate stars and bars waved high above the mansion belonging to the Jensen family. Five airships descended upon the estate in V formation. The lead airship, larger than the others, landed softly on a patch of gray tarmac, its side-mounted turbines shifting horizontally to cushion its descent. Blasts of steam whooshed out of the craft's side and top vents, as its landing struts touched the surface with an impact lighter than a feather's kiss.

The other airships remained airborne, circling the estate, their pilots scanning for security threats.

A slender, slightly bent man of middle age, wearing a black suit with a matching bow tie and top hat, emerged from an opening near the front of the ship. He stepped onto the protruding gangplank followed by two more men in tweed attire.

Cicero Jensen, Master of the famed Jensen Estate, was on hand with his servants to greet the visitors.

"Ah, Secretary Patterson," said Jensen with an ear-to-ear grin. He extended a beefy hand to the top-hated gentleman.

Patterson's pointed chin and narrow, upturned nose appeared designed to project an imperious disdain, even if their owner never intended it. Ice blue eyes took the measure of the rotund, flamboyantly dressed man before him. Patterson took the other's hand in a firm clasp and allowed himself to be led deeper into the estate. The servants quietly dispersed when their master departed with his guests.

Jenson took no offense at not being introduced to the men in the tweed suits.

From their erect postures and vigilant stares, they were obviously security. The bulges beneath their blazers only confirmed Jensen's speculation. While he would have liked to ask what type of guns they carried, given his love affair with weaponry, Jensen thought it best to keep silent. Patterson exuded an air of impatience as palpable as the afternoon humidity.

The four men walked across the estate's immaculately manicured. Slaves, men and women, tended the grounds. The men doffed their hats, the women curtsied when Jensen and his guests sauntered past.

The patriarch paid no attention.

As they entered an area just beyond the slave quarters, Jensen gestured toward a barn with more enthusiasm than he perhaps intended. "Right in there, gentlemen!"

His florid hue deepening, he cleared his throat. It wouldn't do for him to appear unhinged with excitement in front of a very important Richmond representative. "Yes…if you please."

"You keep this item where the nigras reside?" Patterson queried with a disapproving curl of his lip.

Jensen chuckled lightly. "Not to worry, good sir. My slaves know better than to go into that barn. And if one were foolish enough to do so, he wouldn't have the slightest comprehension of what he was seeing."

Abruptly his smile vanished, replaced by a harsh glare directed at a tall, muscular slave carrying a sack load of cotton. "Boy! Open this door!"

"Suh!" The slave dropped the sack, rushed to the barn door and pulled it open. He slumped his shoulders and hung his head when the white men entered the barn.

A column of light from the opening illuminated the dimly lit interior. A large bench sat in the center of the barn. Surrounded by all manner of tools and machinery for forging metal. An object consisting of five wide, slightly curved blades attached to a circular axis rested on the table. Everything in the barn bore a worn, dusty appearance, save for the object, which had obviously been scrubbed clean for the purpose of presentation.

Jensen struck a match and proceeded to light a pair of lanterns hanging on hooks next to the entrance. He unhooked the lanterns and placed them on the table at opposite ends to cast the object in a better light.

Patterson drew close to the table, peering at the object with a sudden show of interest. "It's quite small." The assessment was observational not critical.

"Small enough to be adaptable to the new engine," said Jensen. "On its mount, this propeller can shift on a dime."

"I'll be looking forward to seeing your claim demonstrated."

Jensen smiled a broad, confident smile. "The prototype is ready to be tested."

§§§

"Boy! Open this door!"

"Suh!" I dropped my load of cotton and made for the barn door with vigor. I pulled it open and Jensen and his guests disappeared inside. I managed the briefest glimpse of a table, surrounded by clutter, before dropping my eyes as was expected of a slave when in the presence of whites.

I wanted desperately to see what it was that Jensen harbored inside this barn. Upon pain of fifty lashes, Jensen forbade slaves from entering the barn. That prohibition extended even to the white overseers.

Whatever the barn held was clearly important enough to attract the Secretary of Military Affairs. I recognized Patterson from photographs and drawings.

Jensen didn't tell me to close the door; neither did he command me to stay. I took the absence of further orders as an indicator to return to my interrupted duties. Reluctantly I picked up my sack, hefted it on my shoulder and headed away from the barn, daring not to let a fleeting rearward glance betray my interest.

§§§

The airship was a Saber Class Bear Tooth, approximately twenty yards long, fifteen wide. It had four side mounted propellers, two on each side, a bottom positioned combustion chamber, two Gatling guns, and swivel cannon perched on the top middle section.

The Bear Tooth was the most heavily armed and maneuverable vehicle in the military of the Grand Confederacy. It was also fast, owing to narrower steam compressors, which gave the craft much greater push than the average engine.

Of course, tactical airships like the Bear Tooth were hardly unusual. The British had them, as did the French, Prussians, Spanish, and other European powers with the know-how and finances to upgrade their militaries. The Ottomans recently completed building a fleet of such airships. The Chinese acquired its first batch after beating back an Anglo-French punitive expedition. The African nations had no air power to speak of, but not from lack of trying. The Africans were doing all they could on the ground to block the rapacious advance of European colonizers.

For black nations outside of Africa, the situation was different. The Kingdom of Haiti possessed thirty tactical airships, based upon a French model that was shot down over Port Au Prince when a French expeditionary force attempted to retake the island.

Rumors abounded of the Republic of Delany attempting to augment its small military with tactical ships, either through purchase or construction. Needless to say the Grand Confederates were keeping a close eye on Delany.

While the United States continued to support the Negro Republic it helped to establish, the idea of blacks possessing a premier weapons system struck a chord of discomfort in its leadership.

Jensen was just as bothered by that nettlesome little patch of the Dark Continent in the midst of a white man's land as any self-respecting Confederate citizen. After the day's test flight, he gleefully anticipated the Grand Confederacy being in a stronger position relative to the United States. He didn't want another war, however. No repeat of a conflict that burned like a hot brand in his memory.

He hoped greater strength would persuade the United States to grant the G.C. certain concessions...such as the overthrow of the former's Abolitionist-backed government and the formation of an alliance to eliminate Delany. The Bear Tooth was the key that would shatter a thirty-year-old stalemate in the Confederacy's favor.

Jensen's eyes gleamed at the thought as he observed a prototype Bear Tooth soaring in the powder blue sky above, performing maneuvers once thought impossible for a ponderous airship.

Of course, while the propeller that made the Bear Tooth's aerial agility so uncanny was a product of his plantation, Jensen bore no illusion that he could in anyway influence Confederate policy regarding its northern rival. Though he had a feeling that the Confederate government was as anxious to avoid war as he was.

The Bear Tooth dove a few hundred feet before executing a tight, fluid turn.

"Remarkable," Patterson commented, his hand above his eyes to shade them from the sun. "The propeller's smaller size lessens the airship's burden of weight, compounding its advantage over opposing craft."

"That is a most astute observation, Mr. Secretary." Jensen struggled to contain his euphoria. "I'm currently exploring ways to make the propeller even smaller. It is my one purpose in life to secure an insurmountable advantage over our foes."

Patterson regarded the plantation master with increased toleration. "I will admit to skepticism upon my arrival here. But it's clear to me that your design has merit."

"Merit enough to go into production?" Jensen boldly ventured.

"It certainly has my endorsement." Patterson raised a brow. "When the president receives my report, he should have no problem advancing this project forward."

§§§

Another grueling day of back breaking labor. So far, I experienced two weeks of what my fellow laborers had experienced since birth. Daily aches and pains besieged me to the point where I often wondered if I could endure another hour under these punishing conditions.

The mental toll was equally fatiguing. Having to bow and scrape before these slave holding, slave driving wretches in a degraded show of feigned servility chafed at the very core of my manhood. The only thing keeping my mind from sinking into a dull rut was the mission.

I stood just inside the slave cabin, generously referred to as a housing unit, staring in the direction of the forbidden barn. My curiosity about what that nondescript edifice housed metastasized to a full-blown obsession. Therein, must lay the reason for this assignment.

Rumors abounded among the slaves in regard to the barn. Most seemed to think that it was used for some ill purpose.

Jed and Red Eye, my roommates, suspected that "Massa Jensen be butcherin' colored folk and puttin' they body parts on ice in that barn."

Mae, one of the house servants, was convinced that there was some "evil doctorin' bein' done on us." Her medical experimentation theory no doubt arose from her having been previously owned by a doctor.

Another slave, Joseph, a stable hand, confided in me that he saw Jensen's valet, Benjamin, entering the barn, in Jensen's company at an hour close to midnight. I refrained from asking how Joseph too came to be outside at night when slaves were supposed to be sequestered in their quarters.

A sustained rumble disrupted my musing. I ducked inside the cabin, reducing my view of the night to what I could glean through the vertical sliver of a partially opened door.

An ungainly mass of metal plates and coiled tubing, resting on wheels that looked like inflated burlap, rolled through the slave quarters. Its immensity nearly encompassed the lane it occupied. Thick black smoke boiled from an exhaust pipe jutting from the rear of the machine.

A man in a wide brimmed hat sat on top of the conveyance, clutching a circular railing, his head swiveling from one end of the quarter to the other.

There was another man somewhere in the guts of that monstrosity piloting it.

I could see why the slaves were frightened out of their wits at the very mention of an escape attempt. Those machines, what the white men called iron dragons, must have appeared as metal monsters to a helpless, downtrodden folk.

I spotted guns of large caliber variety mounted topside, within easy reach of the man. Twin lights shined from the dragon's lower front section like glowing eyes on a malevolent beast.

The hardware was obviously sophisticated. No one knew how many of these dragons Jensen possessed. But if he and his equally wealthy peers could afford to keep their slave patrols equipped with such expensive machines, they could just as easily afford to dispense with slave labor and mechanize their agricultural production.

Yet that kind of rational progression did not accord with the

G.C.'s central philosophy that espoused the superiority of the white man over the black man. What better way to emphasize that twisted notion than through the institution of chattel slavery?

"Sam, that thing gon' see us!" Red Eye whispered in a nervous rasp.

To ease his concern, I closed the door just as the dragon growled past our unit.

"Ain't nothin' ta worry about," I responded in my flawless vernacular. "Them dragons be lookin' for darkies that's outside not inside." I went to the unit's single window to catch a final peek of the dragon.

"I'm sho you right," Red Eye admitted, sitting at an old table next to the far wall, sipping rot gut from a tin can. "Jus' don't wanna take no chances."

Jed was already asleep in the corner.

I decided I should get some sleep as well. A full day's work awaited and getting insufficient rest would have done my weary body no good. Additionally, I calculated that a rested mind would yield me an idea as to how to unlock the mystery of that barn.

§§§

Cicero Jensen was too excited to eat, a rarity to his mildly astonished wife. After picking at his dinner, he rushed to his study, a midsize basement level room that was off limits to everyone...except for a thin, gray haired black man, hunched over a table perusing a large sheet of paper.

"Well Ben?" Jensen asked, anxiously joining the black man at the table.

Ben, Jensen's valet, cast an eye at his master that held none of the subservience routinely emitted from others of his color.

Jensen often cringed at this, each time suppressing an urge to put the nigra in his place.

In light of the day's successful demonstration, Jensen's ire on this occasion was less potent.

"The engine housin' need ta be a few inches deeper into th' hull." Ben lowered, lifting a corner of the paper upon which was drawn a detailed schematic of a Bear Tooth airship. He settled a weathered finger on a section of the drawing. "I can adjust the propeller to match th' change."

"And it'll increase the maneuverability?" Jensen queried with a dollop of skepticism. "What about making the propeller smaller?"

"Don't need ta be smaller," Ben insisted in a tone that briefly raised Jensen's hackles. "All I gotta do is slightly change the engine placement and fine tune the swivelin.' Th' ship will run twice as good as before."

Jensen ran an eye across the schematic before settling a severe gaze upon the propeller's designer. He supposed he should have been gratified that this nigra was going to make him a fortune on top of the one he already possessed, while making the GF stronger at the same time. Instead, a two-pronged loathing poked at his pride and dignity as a white man. Jensen loathed this slave's engineering genius, and he loathed himself for his lack of it.

"So be it. Damn your devilish hide, you had better be right."

"When they starts buildin' these ships, Massa…You'll free me?"

Jensen glanced back at the schematic. "I got your freedom papers drawn up. But don't be distractin' yourself with that matter. I need your undivided focus. You have my word I'll sign those papers the minute your improved design goes into production."

Benjamin gave his master an expressionless gaze before shifting his head in a curt nod.

Not so much as a thank you… Jensen hid his consternation, drew himself up and walked out of the room.

§§§

I seized an opportunity to slip out of our unit while Jed and Red Eye slept. I had spent the previous four nights timing the dragon's movements. The one that passed by our cabin did a round every hour. The machine was not fully out of sight when I darted to the other side of the lane, taking cover behind another shack.

I waited a minute, and then made a dash across an open field toward the overseer's compound. The Jensen mansion loomed nearby, its contours etched in a wan moonlit glow. The barn lay on the other side.

I only had Joseph's report to rely upon concerning Benjamin's presence in the barn. If the valet were not there at this hour, then this risky excursion of mine would have been for naught.

§§§

Benjamin ran a hand across his forehead, wiping away sweat. He took a step back from the worktable and appraised his creation with mixed feelings. The propeller did what it was supposed to do for which he felt his usual craftsman's pride. Who and what it was doing it for soured a good portion of that pride. He examined the object from every angle, searching for areas that needed adjustment. After a few taps here and there with his mallet, he placed the tool on an adjacent rack, grabbed a lantern and headed for the exit.

When he opened the barn door Benjamin was suddenly confronted by an imposing figure doused in shadow. A vice-like grip seized his arm, as the lantern was snatched from his hand. An irresistible force jostled him back into the barn before he could react.

The figure held the lantern up, illuminating both of their faces. "You're Benjamin?"

"Who wanna know and why you bargin' in like this? You mus' be crazy for a lashin'!"

"I've heard things about this place..." the figure swung the door shut. "I was curious. Maybe you could answer some questions."

Benjamin jutted his head forward, his eyes squinting before widening in recognition. "You that new slave...Sam...but you don't talk like no slave."

"Only when I have to," Sam said, his attention drawn to the worktable and what lay on top of it.

And then it dawned on Benjamin, "Wait a minute...you mus' be...my message...it mus' ta got through!"

Sam started for the table but halted and looked back. "Message?"

"A slave escaped from here almos' a year ago...said he was goin' to Delany. I told 'im if he made it, ta tell them Delany folks what I was workin' on. I didn't give 'im no notes in case he got caught. He had ta remember everything thing I told him."

Sam pointed to the object on the table. "About that?"

Benjamin nodded. "It's a new kind 'o airship propeller. It makes them smaller airships faster, quicker."

Sam moved closer to the table, poring over the propeller. "An escaped slave did cross our border bringing word of a new propeller design. What he passed on was so detailed and plausible that my government sent me here to investigate." A flicker of discomfort crept into the spy's voice. "It looks like he was right."

Benjamin reached in his back pocket and pulled out a folded sheet of paper. He handed it to Sam. "That's a drawin' of the propeller in every detail. That's for you. Get it to your leaders. The U.S need ta' know about that, too."

Sam set the lantern on the table, unfolded the paper and studied the drawing under a shimmering light. "Well, I know a little something about engineering and what you've got here looks damn good."

"An' it works. An airship was tested wit' it down in th' valley a few days ago. Once I improve on this, more o' these propellers gonna be put on airships."

Sam looked up, pinning the valet with harsh eyes. "Why are you helping your slave master?"

Benjamin did not look all discomfited by the question. It was almost as if he expected it. "I got a wife an' two girls. We was together at the Montgomery plantation til we got sold. My wife an' girls went to one buyer. I went to another. A year later I heard they escaped. Heard th' railroad helped 'em get to Delany."

Sam's brow rose at this.

" I ain't seen 'em in six years." Benjamin's expression warmed in reflection. "My girls almos' full grown women by now. Anyway I like to tinker with machines, try ta make them better. I was lookin' at airships one day and was thinkin' 'bout how it could move faster, quicker. I came up wit' an idea and told Massa. I tol' 'im I'll make a new propeller if he promise to free me."

"Of course he agreed," Sam said with a cynical sigh.

Benjamin nodded. "I miss my family." He seemed to want to add more, but looked away instead.

Sam folded the paper, shaking his head. "I sympathize, Benjamin, I really do, but this invention of yours hurts us. It hurts Delany and hurts our supporters in the United States."

"That's why I'm givin' you that design. I realized a while back that what I done was wrong…selfish…not what my family would want me ta' do, helpin' these goddamn rebs."

A tiny smile parted Sam's lips. Thirty years after the war, with the South an independent nation and its citizens were still referred to, among other pejorative terms, as "rebels."

"You do know, Jensen will never free you," Sam said bluntly. "He'll see you dead before he allows you to step foot off this plantation armed with the kind of knowledge and expertise that you possess."

"I know." Benjamin leaned forward, lowering his voice a tad. "I can see th' lie in his eyes ever' time he make that promise. That's why I'm workin' on somethin' else…somethin' Massa don't know about. But it's gonna be for Delany only. When y'all get it, Delany will have th' upper hand 'an you won't need th' U.S. or no treaty ta' keep th' rebs offa you."

"What is it?"

"Can't say. Gotta keep it secret for now." Benjamin's

weathered face took on a revitalizing glow. "Massa has a library in his study. He fancies himself a educated gentleman, but he don' do no readin.' I do. I read all his books on science and got a few ideas from 'em."

"I can get you out of here," said Sam. "Whatever it is you're working on, we have the facilities you'll need in Delany…"

"Much obliged, but I can't go nowhere yet. Not until I finish this thing I got brewin'." Benjamin shot a glance at the surrounding tools and machinery to highlight his point. "Now go. You got on this plantation, you know how ta' get off it. When you get back home, see if you can find my family, Mary, Theresa and Polly Montgomery. Mary…she my wife. Tell 'em I'm all right. Tell 'em I'll see 'em soon."

Sam looked at the older man, trying to think of something to sway him. Finally, he ceded a reluctant nod and stalked toward the exit.

He stopped and glanced back. "I'll find them. Good luck."

§§§

I snuck back into my unit, my head swimming with the night's astounding revelation. The Grand Confederacy was about to attain (albeit temporarily) a military advantage. I longed to see what the reactions of its leaders would have been were they to learn that a slave was responsible for that advantage.

The thought tickled me to no end, so much so I convulsed with a laughter that pulled an irate Jed out of his slumber. "What de' hell so damn funny?"

"Nothin'." I curled on my mat, pulling a threadbare blanket up to my shoulders. "Funny dream is all."

I made my escape two nights later. Jed and Red Eye were sound asleep when I slipped out of our unit at the very latest hour. I regretted leaving them behind for they had become like brothers to me during my brief ordeal in bondage. In any other circumstance, I would have included them in my escape plan.

But matters of state made their involvement problematic. My mission was completed and I needed to return to Delany in all due haste. Jed and Red Eye's company would have hindered my journey.

I scurried out of the slave quarters and hid in a grove until a dragon rumbled past. I took flight after the machine, catching up to it and clambering up the rear chassis.

The man behind the turret gun whirled about, but I quickly silenced him with a forearm to the head. I dragged his limp form to the hatch, pulled it open and tossed him inside. His body landed atop the driver and the machine faltered. I jumped through the hatch and seized the driver in a chokehold, incapacitating him.

The driver's cabin barely contained enough room for three. I made the best of the space available and took the dragon's controls. I struggled to right the machine. Its controls were sluggish, making the dragon difficult to pilot in comparison to most Delany vehicles.

I peered through the observation slit. The dragon's twin lights folded back the murk of darkness, enabling me to see my way toward the edge of the Jensen estate. I kept going, embarking down a well-traveled road on a north bound heading.

I passed a slave patrol on horseback, but felt no trepidation at their presence. They had no probable cause to stop me. The idea of a slave hijacking a dragon would have been as implausible to these riders, as a horse sprouting wings and flying.

At some point I would have to abandon the dragon and its unconscious occupants. Until then, I kept going...

§§§

Storm clouds billowed, preparing to usher in a thunderous new war.

The Civil War...or what historians would commonly refer to as the Great Succession War ended in a stalemate. When both sides grew weary of feeding soldiers into a ravenous grinder of a war without seeming end; when both sides could no longer endure their cities being bombed to gravel by gargantuan airships; when famine and disease consumed the lives of soldiers and civilians by the hundreds of thousands, the Union and Confederacy sought desperate solace at the peace table.

But what could they decide on? The Union's reason for resorting to arms was to prevent the South from breaking away. As the war ground on, slavery became a galvanizing issue, with the Union encouraging slaves through proclamation to abandon their masters. The Union hoped that by denying the South its precious black labor, the Confederacy would cave.

But French and British materiel support, along with key military victories, kept the Confederacy afloat. Most importantly, the South, with substantial British aid, had opened up a corridor through which airships loaded with African captives could be transported to Southern plantations, thus replenishing lost labor.

At the end of four years, the South remained as strong as it was at the beginning of the conflict. The Union, having repelled a Southern invasion at Gettysburg, retained the ability to carry the war as deep into enemy territory as their prodigious resources would allow, but at this point, could no longer conjure the will.

The peace talks proved as contentious as the war. The North demanded that the South return to the Union, abolish slavery, and pay reparations.

The South's demands included a withdrawal of Northern troops from Southern territory, recognition of the Grand Confederacy, the return of all slaves who escaped to the North, and of course, payment of reparations for war damage inflicted on the South by the North.

It was clear that neither side would capitulate to the other on either point. But as the combatants no longer had an appetite for war, countless hours of negotiations blossomed into an arrangement. The North agreed to recognize the independence of the Grand Confederacy in exchange for the establishment of an independent black nation.

The Radical wing of the Republican Party, led by John Brown, pushed hard for this proposal. On one hand, the Lincoln administration considered the plan a bitter pill to swallow since it had failed in its goal to preserve the Union. On the other, a black country, carved from a chunk of Southern territory was perceived by many Northerners as a measure of vengeance against the South. The biggest prize, in their racist estimation, was the anticipated migration of Northern blacks to this new nation.

The Confederacy feared an influx of escaped slaves to this land called Delany, named after a famous Northern black activist who agitated for black separation.

Both hopes and fears unfolded as blacks from both sides of the North/South divide settled in Delany.

The Treaty of Appomattox stipulated that the Grand Confederacy would not attack Delany. The Confederacy promised to honor the treaty, all the while biding its time, awaiting that anticipated moment when the United States' protection of the black republic would wither away.

Radical Republican influence over successive administrations, kept the U.S. bound to its treaty obligation. As a result, Delany prospered and grew strong, much to the Confederacy's everlasting ire.

Over the decades, however, United States commitment to Delany waned. While tensions continued to exist between the U.S. and the C. F., the former had demonstrated its lack of interest in Delany when it failed to respond to repeated Confederate incursions into Delany territory.

A sweep of election victories placed Democrats in the White House, the Congress and the Senate. The public had spoken. The average U.S. citizen had no desire to take up arms on behalf of a black nation. Acting upon that widespread sentiment, the new administration withdrew U.S. military support from Delany. The Radical Republicans vehemently protested that sharp policy shift to no avail. Their day was done. A new era beckoned.

Shortly after the election, the G.C. probed boldly along Delany's borders, testing the sincerity of its rival's policy shift. When no U.S. forces mobilized, the Confederates massed their own forces with the enthusiasm of wallowing sharks in blood soaked water.

Delany's days were numbered...

§§§

Samuel Aquinas Tanner stepped into the director's office wearing a dark gray waist coat with matching trousers, black shoes and a gray Homburg hat tucked underneath one arm. It took Samuel quite some time to get reacquainted with proper fashion after almost a year of wearing, dusty ill-fitting rags. Eight months earlier, he was known simply as Sam, the property of one Cicero Jensen, the wealthiest plantation owner in the Grand Confederacy.

Director Hilda Hall of the Special Services Division gave the new arrival a cursory glance as she and two military officers pored over a map laid out across her desk.

"Aerial spotters picked up a train coming out of South Carolina," stated General Marvell Foster. A rich gray froth of a beard covered the lower half of his face. He stroked it contemplatively as he ran a finger along the map's surface. "It was loaded with heavy dragons. The train stopped here, picked up additional dragons and proceeded eastbound."

"That rail line runs all the way to the coast," said General Emory Pickett. He raised his massive cannonball head. He didn't need to look at the map to unravel the enemy's strategy. "They'll start building up on our Southern flank once they get those machines unloaded."

"They're not even bothering to hide their deployments or their equipment from us," ventured General Foster, a scowl cutting deep into his obsidian brow."

"Of course not," Director Hall replied with a sardonic lilt. "Would you hide your boot from the insect you plan to squash?"

In spite of the seriousness of the situation, Samuel and the generals shared subdued chuckles at the grim analogy.

The thin, matronly director occupied the highest position a woman had ever attained in the Delany government. A devoted nationalist, she was old enough to have experienced firsthand the plight of slavery. No one was as thrilled as Hall to have witnessed the birth of a black nation. Now, she awaited the day when the barrier blocking the advancement of capable women like herself was completely torn down.

Hall looked up at Samuel, beckoning the agent forward. She respected the young man immensely in light of his last mission. Few, if any agents, would have actually volunteered to pose as a slave in the Grand Confederacy.

She had lived the experience, and definitely would have turned down the assignment, which made her feel guilty. Hall liked to think that she would never send agents on missions that she herself was unwilling to undertake. She sighed bleakly at her high-minded self-assumption.

"The president has approved my plan to sabotage the G.C.'s essential rail lines," she said to the generals. "It won't cripple the rebs' overall effort, but I'm hoping it will severely dent it."

The generals voiced ascent.

"That's what we're counting on," said General Pickett. "The less of their dragons and artillery our men face, the better."

A minute later, the generals filed out, exchanging nods of greeting with Samuel in passing.

Hall leaned back in her chair, extending a hand to the leather bound cushioned chair in front of her desk. "Sit, Samuel. I have good news for you."

Samuel eased down in the chair, an expectant gaze locked on his superior.

"Benjamin Montgomery is here in Douglassville."

The agent's face lit. "Madame Director, that is good news. I was worried he wouldn't be able to get away." Samuel remembered the stabbing guilt he felt as he relayed news to Ben's wife and daughters of their patriarch's well-being.

Samuel often thought he should have bound, gagged, and carried the man out of bondage, instead of leaving him behind to languish in its wretched bosom. But Ben insisted on staying. His wife knew her husband well enough to understand why he had to stay, and thus held no animus toward Samuel for escaping without him.

"How long as he been here?" Samuel asked.

"Six months."

"Six months…but, I wasn't told…"

"I restricted news of his arrival. I wanted only the most essential persons to know he was here, especially in light of the extremely valuable information he brought with him. Not that you're not essential, just in a different context."

Samuel hid a wounded look. "I understand, Madame Director."

With her hair pulled back and knotted in a bun, and wearing a practical blue dress that frilled at the neck and wrists, Director Hall bore the appearance of a school teacher.

The indulgent glint in her eyes amplified the likeness. "Don't fret, Samuel. Soon, you'll be privy to plenty of secrets. In the meantime, now that we have made use of the information Mr. Montgomery has given us, you can pay him a visit. He's been asking about you."

Samuel could hardly contain his elation. "Thank you, Madame Director."

Hall primly picked up a quill, dipped it in a small jar of ink, and wrote on a blank piece of paper she pulled from her desk's front drawer. "Mr. Montgomery's home address, although at about this time of day you may catch him taking his daily stroll through Tubman Park."

Samuel accepted the paper, glanced at what was written, and rose. "With your leave, Madame Director, I'll head to the park immediately."

Hall nodded her consent.

The agent turned to depart, but paused. "Madame Director, soon our nation will be embroiled in war. I am available as always to do my part."

Director Hall folded her hands, offering a wry smile. "Well, rumor has it that before you joined this distinguished service, you were a fairly competent airship pilot."

Samuel grinned at the understatement. Undoubtedly, his recognition as the highest rated pilot in the Army Air Guard was included in his personnel folder tucked away in a cabinet under lock and key in the corner of Hall's office.

"I was…adequate," he said, playing along.

"That being the case," Hall began. "We're going to need all of our adequate pilots. If you're willing to be loaned out to the Air Guard."

"More than willing, Madame Director."

§§§

Tubman Park was no more than a ten-minute walk from the

National Department building, where SSD headquarters was located.

Entering this oasis of green in the midst of a metropolis, I spared a moment to peruse my surroundings. *Douglassville. Delany's glorious capitol.*

Well, perhaps not as glorious as London or Paris, or the jeweled cities of the East, but in my eyes Douglassville glowed every bit as radiant. Its buildings were mostly low rises. Some were simple, utilitarian designs, others ostentatious. Some copied European architecture. The more ambitious structures were borne of African influences with their conical roofs and surfaces adorned with vibrant colors arranged in a stunning geometry of patterns.

A wave of melancholy suddenly swept over me at the thought that all of those fine buildings, this majestic park, could be extinguished in a flood of war and conquest…that my country could cease to exist.

The imagery that accompanied that grave reflection caused me to squeeze my eyes shut to purge it. When I opened them, I spotted Benjamin Montgomery in the near distance, walking along a pebbled path next to a small pond.

Joy subsumed my fears and I raised my voice enough to gain his attention, but not so loud as to disturb the surrounding tranquility. "Mr. Montgomery."

He turned in my direction and his face instantly broke into a grin of recognition.

I quickened my pace toward him and we embraced. "I just found out you were here." Dapper and distinguished in a gray suit and bowler hat, freedom had done wonders for this once enslaved inventor's appearance.

"You can stop wit' this 'Mr.' nonsense. Call me Benjamin."

I would rather have accorded Benjamin the honorific due his status as a free man, but I respected his wish as a free man to be addressed in the manner he requested.

"Benjamin," I acceded.

"Good ta see you Sam...or should I say Sam U El?"

We both laughed at Benjamin's exaggerated pronunciation of my name.

"Sam will do," I said. "So, how did you escape?"

"I snuck off th' plantation on my own. Th' railroad helped me th' rest o' th' way."

The Underground Railroad. Metaphorical transport arteries leading from the bowls of slavery into the light of freedom for thousands of slaves. In some places, the underground part was literal. Slave owners often called on the aid of airships to help them locate their missing 'property.'

Thus the railroad operators dug tunnels, most of them leading from G.C. border areas into Delany and U.S. territory. Unfortunately, the election of an unsympathetic administration in the United States within the past five months led to the closing of tunnel exit points along its border.

"And what about this thing you were working on?" I asked. "What is it?"

"Still can't say. Your boss tol' me ta keep it under my hat."

I pursed my lips in disappointment. "I'll certainly be happy when she starts entrusting me with more privileged intelligence."

"Don't worry. When th' rebs' make their move, ever'body'll see what I got for 'em."

At that moment three formally dressed men approached us from the opposite direction. I wouldn't have given them a second thought, except the hardened gazes they radiated in our direction set off an alarm bell inside me.

Though crime was non-existent in this section of the capitol, I was certain this trio harbored criminal intent.

"Benjamin," I urged, my voice low. "Let's walk."

Before Benjamin could say a word, the malefactors were upon us.

All three men carried walking canes with bronze handles.

A big, burly fellow at the head of the trio swung at me.

Instead of ducking, I lunged forward, catching his swinging arm by the wrist and forearm and kneeing him in the gut.

The attacker doubled over with an *oof!* Subsequently, I snatched the cane out of his hand and smashed him across the jaw with the handle part.

As the big man sank to the ground, his accomplices were raining blows upon Benjamin with their canes.

I cracked one of the attackers on the back with my appropriated weapon.

The third attacker shifted his attention from Benjamin to myself and charged me, his cane raised high.

I sidestepped him, using the pointed end of my cane to issue a sharp jab to his rib. I followed up with whiplash kick to the same area, knocking him down.

The second attacker recovered quickly from the blow to his back. He spun toward me, reached in his jacket's inside pocket and whipped out a knife. But instead of coming after me, he advanced on

Benjamin, who lay on the ground, writhing in pain.

Well, this certainly changed the dynamic of this contest.

I leapt to intercept the attacker before he could do further harm to my friend.

Bringing the cane up in an underhand slash, I connected to the criminal's wrist. The knife pin wheeled out of his hand.
By this time, the big man was on his feet and he tackled me from the side.

I twisted my body in a way that enabled me to leverage his momentum against him. We both hit the ground hard. I rolled upright and struck the big man on the back of the head with such force that it broke the cane clean in half.

The big man went out like a light.

The attacker I struck on the back took to flight, but the knife wielder stayed behind. Rage burned in his eyes…but there was something else I noticed…something that bore the look of desperation.

He flung himself at me.

I tossed aside the remnant of the broken cane as I eluded a series of wildly delivered blows.

My opponent reared back to hurl a right cross. I caught him in the nose with a jab, followed by a bruising uppercut to the chin that sent him stumbling backwards into the pond.

I rushed to Benjamin, kneeling beside him. Crimson gashes splotched his face. The hair on the back of his head was slick with matted blood. Yet, he focused on me with a steady, coherent gaze.

"Benjamin! Good God…" I took him by the shoulders to help him upright.

"Those men wasn't tryin' to rob us," he managed breathlessly.

Benjamin's suspicions mirrored my own. When I pulled him to his feet, I immediately turned to the villain in the pond, who lay face up, dazed.

I splashed into the water, reached down, gripped the man's lapels, and roughly dragged him onto the pebbled pathway.

"Why did you attack us?" I demanded, pressing a forearm to the man's throat.

His eyes bulged. He gasped for breath and I relinquished the pressure on his throat just enough for him to speak. "We...was...sent... to kill...Montgomery..."

Somehow I was not surprised. "Who sent you?" I hissed.

The man's mouth quivered in seeming hesitation.

Impatient, I clamped down on his throat briefly. "Who sent you?"

"Jen...sen...it was Jensen!"

"Cicero Jansen?"

A deafening clap! I bolted upright at the sound, turning toward a cluster of buildings across a wide busy street dividing the park from the government district.

A column of black smoke poured out of a huge flaming mouth of a hole in the National Department building. A second explosion ripped additional chunks out of the structure, raining stone and glass upon the street below. To my horror, the twin blasts comprised a comparatively minor portion of this destructive event. An entire corner of the ND building collapsed to powdery rubble.

Passersby and vehicles were subsumed in a fiery avalanche and all I could do was stand there, numb, speechless, watching this devil-spawned spectacle unfold in a grisly tapestry of death.

"Director Hall!" I started toward the devastation, but a hand on my shoulder stopped me. Benjamin's hand.

"Sam, ain't nothin' you can do. If she in there, she buried like the rest!"

My madness-induced urge to enter the burning ruin abated, but not my sorrow or my rage.

Two more blasts followed. The third one hit the capitol building; the forth tore through the Congressional House. Up to five hundred persons died, hundreds more injured.

As luck or Divine will would have it, SSD Director Hilda Hall survived the National Department blast. She had just stepped out of the building on her way to a meeting with the president when the first explosion rang out. That she happened to be far from the corner that collapsed compounded her fortune of survival.

The Grand Confederacy government brazenly took responsibility for these clear acts of terror, referring to them as: "The first in a series of initiatives designed to correct a wretched wrong."

In other words, the Grand Confederacy intended to wipe the stain that was Delany off the face of the Earth.

Most of the Confederates who committed these violent acts had been captured. They were disguised as businessmen or dignitaries from European nations.

The Confederates were promptly dealt with. After confessing their crimes, they were publicly hung in executions meant as much to send a message to the G.C. as they were dispensations of justice.

The attempted assassination of Benjamin Montgomery was handled in a different manner. The crime received no attention, at the behest of Director Hall, who wanted to keep Benjamin Montgomery's existence and purpose classified.

The black perpetrators of the attack claimed to be motivated by Cicero Jensen's promise to them to free their families. They were placed in indefinite detention.

A week after the attacks, three divisions of G.C. troops, preceded by tactical and strategic bomber airships moved across Delany's border.

§§§

Cicero Jensen had served in the army in his younger days, reaching the rank of captain. Now he was back in the service as a general, commanding the Army of Northern Virginia. The feel of uniform fabric against his skin was like a caress from a lover whose touch he hadn't felt in decades.

To him and his forces would go the honor of seizing Douglassville. The depredations he inflicted along his route of advance foreshadowed what he intended to do the capitol.

Every single Delanynian structure in his army's path was trampled underfoot. Delanynians who resisted or so much as looked at a Confederate soldier in the wrong way were cut down like dogs.

Jensen stood in front of his tent watching his soldiers drill. Messengers had delivered dispatches to him throughout the day, but the one bit of news he eagerly anticipated was yet to come...if ever. No word on whether that treacherous nigra, Ben, was dead or alive.

When I get to their cesspit of a capitol, I'll kill half the blacks and sell the rest into slavery, Jansen thought with teeth baring relish.

Ben will either turn up among the bodies or on an auction block, I swear by the Almighty!

§§§

The United States did nothing as G.C. forces plowed deeper into Delany.

Many Delanyians had harbored a sliver of hope that the U.S. would see the error of its ways and restore its alliance with the black nation. It was not to be.

A horde of airships darkened Delany's skies like roving storm clouds. Nitro bombs dropped from their holds, carpeting populated areas in oceans of fire. While on the ground, massive, smoke belching heavy dragons maintained an inexorable pace, crushing all in their paths, their smoothbore guns turning idyllic landscapes into crater filled expanses.

Delanyian opposition was vigorous but futile. Delanyian dragons were as large and powerful as those of the enemy. The problem lay in their quantity. There were simply not enough of them to halt the G.C.'s juggernaut momentum. But frontal engagements by Delany forces were selective and meant more to delay than halt. Mostly the Delanyians resorted to guerilla tactics to counter the enemy's enormous advantage in troops and armor.

The United States did mobilize its border forces, but only to ensure that Grand Confederate armies kept their aggression focused on Delany.

§§§

I climbed into the cockpit of my airship, buckled my safety belt, and pulled my helmet goggles over my eyes. Two weeks since the terror attack on the capitol. Two weeks since Benjamin's attempted assassination. Those events clung to my mind with the tenacity of a leech.

As I joined the newly formed Raptor Air Wing and trained night and day to hone aviation skills degraded by my long absence from the Air Guard, I thought of nothing else. A thirst for vengeance burned a seething void in the place where my heart had been.

I flicked switches on my control panel, initiating water flows through tubings leading to my engine's steam compressors. My flanking propellers spun, lifting my ship off the ground.

A different set of vibrations emanating through the floor panel told me that my bottom propellers were folding out. Benjamin's revolutionary propeller design proved as fantastic a benefit to our side as it was to the G.C.

It kept our air force from being blasted from the skies…for the time being. Given an attrition rate favorable to the G.C., it was inevitable that we were going to lose the air war. The G.C. had the resources to replace men and airships. We didn't. All we needed to do was keep the enemy occupied enough to buy time. Time for what? I did not know…but I had a feeling.

§§§

Bullets clanged off my chassis. I pivoted my ship as the opposing Bear Tooth whipped past, its rotary guns spinning out a blazing gusher of rounds. The air ship I piloted was a 224 Steel Fist. Smaller than a Bear Tooth, and nearly as well armed.

I thumbed the control for the surge gun mounted on the nose of my air ship. Large caliber shells thumped from the weapon's black snout, raking the opposing ship's bottom.

The Bear Tooth staggered, sputtered, then plummeted ground ward, smoke streaming from a tangle of damage to its rear.

I had no time to rejoice my kill. I spotted two Bear Tooths on a Steel Fist and promptly flew to my fellow pilot's aid. I dropped behind the nearest Bear Tooth and triggered the surge gun along with a smaller caliber swivel gun mounted up top.

The Bear Tooth's exhaust housings erupted from a spray of bullets, knocking the airship out of the pursuit. I targeted the second ship as it banked to avoid my furious fusillades. Bullets scything from my swivel gun shattered three of its bottom and right side propellers. Another Steel Fist angled in from above me, stitching bullets across the Bear Tooth's top segment from rear to front.

A fan of debris jetted from the back of the second ship. Something erupted inside it, most likely a compressor. A blast of escaping steam fogged my visual.

I swerved left to elude a storm of metal fragments ricocheting off my cockpit glass and hull.

Without its compressor, the enemy ship was so much dead weight in the air. It dropped like a brick. I caught a glimpse of the pilot escaping his doomed craft. He soared from the vehicle on glide wings sewn into the fabric of his uniform.

I thought about riddling his body. It would have violated an unwritten code of air combat: prohibiting ejecting pilots from being targeted by opposing air ships. Of course, I would have only been following precedence, given G.C. pilots' utter lack of regard to that code when our ejected pilots were exposed and vulnerable in the air.

The rapid pinging of the instrument panel clock interrupted my illicit musing. The clock signaled that it was time to withdraw and I hastily joined my pilots in that effort.

The sky heaved with the enemy and despite having acquitted ourselves well; we still lost too many ships.

To this day, I wonder if I would have actually shot that unarmed man out of the sky.

I didn't know how many airships we had left, but adhering to a tactical plan, we embarked on an eastbound heading...toward the Atlantic.

With our ports occupied and a naval blockade in effect by the enemy, I wondered why we were escaping swarms of wasps only to fly into their nest.

Sounds of bullets striking my ship reverberated through my cockpit. An alarm alerted me to a damaged stabilizer. A pair of Bear Tooths pursued me. They barely exceeded the size of my thumbnail in the distance. Steel Fists and Bear Tooths shared similar speeds. While that guaranteed I would not be overtaken, it kept me in perpetual range of much faster bullets.

A spatter of rounds peppered my rear cockpit glass, slamming into a non-essential section of my instrument panel. A bullet lodged in the back of my seat. Were my seat not lined with an iron plate, I would have, God-willing, been entering through those Pearly Gates.

A shimmering blue expanse of the ocean gradually came into my view. A dark pall began forming off the shoreline. A storm was brewing. No…as we drew near enough to the ocean, I realized that I was seeing smoke, not storm clouds. The smoke was issuing from burning naval ships. I counted thirty-three of them. At least a third were sinking into the drink.

More smoke arose from demolished structures on shore. I saw figures on the ground darting about with the frantic aimlessness of scrambling ants.

Before I could even begin to ruminate on what was transpiring below, one of the G.C. airships pursuing me exploded with such clamorous effect that my heart skipped a beat.

I twisted about in my seat, catching sight of my second pursuer's total demise.

Nothing remained of the Bear Tooths but smoky, debris-strewn residue. More G.C. ships exploded, until the sky was dotted with blackened smears.

Lest my eyes deceived me, it appeared that some kind of distortion effect preceded the destruction of those ships— as if a divine hand were ripping reality apart along a set of invisible seam lines! Astonished at the totality of our victory in the sky, even if our vaunted Steel Fists had nothing to do with it, I exhaled a sigh of relief.

This had to be Benjamin's doing, I thought. *It had it to be.*

§§§

On Delany's Eastern front, Grand Confederate ships comprising the blockading task force were converted to so much wreckage by a mysterious weapon.

The Western and Southern fronts witnessed the same stunning

reversal of fortunes for the invaders. Similar weapons destroyed a G.C. Advance, spearheaded by one hundred dragons three miles short of Douglassville. Every dragon was targeted by some kind of fast moving, uncannily accurate projectile and blasted to shards. A thousand Confederates died in a violent deluge of conventional artillery before the rest panicked and fled.

Heavy bomber airships en route to Douglassville were torn apart by more projectiles delivered by a Delanyian super weapon.

The G.C.'s high command reeled from those defeats. The president of the Grand Confederacy immediately ordered a unilateral ceasefire. He was not about to risk losing additional men and machines to whatever satanic weapons resided in the blacks' possession.

§§§

Director Hall and Benjamin emerged from the medium airship. A dozen soldiers met the pair, as they descended the ramp leading from the belly of the bottle shaped craft.

I suspected the guard detail was more for Ben than Hilda. I was sure our government was taking no chances where Ben's safety was concerned. I stood on the edge of the landing field adjacent to the harbor our forces had retaken after the sinking of the enemy's ships.

One of the weapons responsible for our victory loomed beside me. At first glance it appeared to be a standard artillery cannon. Its pitch black thirty foot barrel was pointed in the direction of the sea. Its breech rested on a rounded, solid support, narrow at the top with a flaring bottom. Attached to the support was an open-ended operator's booth, containing a waist high console studded with dials, buttons and gauges.

There existed nothing around the weapon's breech to cushion its recoil...inferring quite plainly to my befuddled eyes that this cannon did not recoil when fired.

Director Hall looked radically different and more than a tad youthful in aviation headgear, long leather jacket, and khaki slacks tucked into a pair of black knee high riding boots.

Ben wore an army uniform with a broad brimmed olive green hat, no doubt to disguise his appearance.

"Director Benjamin," I greeted eagerly, when they approached me. I took Ben's hand and gave it a vigorous shake.

"It's good to see you in one piece, Samuel," said Hall sporting a bright smile.

I threw a gesture at the cannon. "I have Ben's invention to thank for that."

Ben held up a hand in modest denial. "Thank th' ones who know how to use it."

"And used it well they have, from here to Douglassville. So this was your big secret. How does it work?"

"It's a magnet gun," Ben replied, regarding his weapon with a pride he could not completely conceal. "It uses magnets to fire shells."

At my incredulous look, Director Hall elaborated. "There are magnetic coils lined inside the cannon's barrel. A battery at the base of the weapon provides electricity that magnetizes the coils. The force produced by the magnetic energy is such that it can accelerate a projectile to speeds far exceeding conventional propellants."

"So fast you can't even see it..." That explained the linear distortion effects I saw before the enemy airships were destroyed.

"I read about magnetism in one o' Jensen's books," Ben interjected. "I figured I could do somethin' with it. I started experimentin' with applications th' same time I was workin' on the airship propeller. That's why I couldn't go with you that night. I was makin' strides in my research. I was so close to a breakthrough. I needed to keep my focus. Runin' too soon woulda' threw me off."

"Well," I commented, thoroughly impressed. "There's something to be said for maintaining one's focus."

"Ben came to us with a complete blue print of the magnet gun." The director tapped her temple. "In his head. We put our engineers to work building a workable model. It was a flawless design. Complex, elegant, yet easily mass producible. In light of the United States' abrupt change of heart, this is a development I'm glad we didn't share."

I nodded heartfelt agreement. "So now we have a standoff."

The director's expression dimmed. "Yes. Though I'm not satisfied with that outcome and neither is the president. The rebs' advance have halted on all fronts. While some of them have fallen back, they haven't vacated our territory. I've begun running operations behind enemy lines to rectify that problem."

I thought for a few seconds. "Madame Director, seeing that the enemy won't be taking to the skies anytime soon, hopefully never, I wouldn't mind participating in one of your operations."

Director Hall looked at me in consideration…

§§§

"Damn cowards! I'll be goddamned if we withdraw any further than we already have!" General Cicero Jensen pounded a fist into the palm of his other hand for emphasis.

He walked past a dragon, one of twelve machines remaining in the armored element of the Army of Northern Virginia. And the only reason they were still intact, was because they had not been deployed for the main assault on Delany's capitol. Jensen had held them in reserve.

Colonel Justin Philips, commanding officer of this much-reduced armored force, almost broke into a jog to keep pace with the rapid strides of his fuming superior.

"But General…sir, the president's order…"

Jensen whirled on the Colonel, his bulging eyes threatening to pop loose from a rage-reddened face. "I'm well aware of the president's order and I'm willfully disobeying it! We've been holding this position for damn near two weeks! I've grown tired of holding! And now we're to retreat further, lose more ground to these darkies? I say no more! Are you with me, Colonel?"

Philips straightened, his expression hardening with resolve before softening in concern. "Of course I'm with you, General, it's just that…" The colonel grimaced. "Well, the men…they're afraid of these Delanyian weapons…"

"Any weapon can be countered, Colonel."

"I agree with you, sir, but there's…um… been talk of the coloreds using some kind of magic…that African voodoo…hoodoo, whatever it's called. It may be hard convincing the men otherwise, considering that the more backwoods types tend to harbor a strong belief in their own superstitions."

General Jensen scoffed and resumed walking until he stopped in front of his tent.

"Here's what we're going to do. We're going to form raiding parties and bring fire and sword to every town and village in the surrounding area. When the men see blacks runnin' from us like terrified rabbits, all this talk of African magic'll fall by the wayside so fast..."

Jensen seized up, suddenly unable to continue his rant. Gasping for breath he noticed Colonel Philips taking several steps back, his eyes widening, his mouth hanging open in shock.

Jensen lowered his head, discovering, through blurred vision, the reason for his incapacitation.

A blistering hole the size of a fist lay square in the middle of his chest. An agonizing burning sensation swirled through that hole, surging to his back.

Jansen tried to breathe, his blurring world shading to gray and finally, black. He fell to his knees and plopped on his face, dead.

§§§

I saw Cicero Jensen fall, and a ruthless, feral satisfaction brought a knife-edge smile to my face.

A half mile away, concealed in wooded terrain buffeted by high winds, yet my shot was dead on.

I considered taking out the officer standing next to Jensen as a bonus. Instead I plucked several high explosive shells from my ammo belt and inserted them into my weapon's chamber.

I was holding a magnet gun, a prototype, portable version, courtesy of Benjamin.

The mini-magnet as I called it, was meant to be an assault

weapon. I thought it could also perform a long-range function.

I am proud to say that the scope attached to the gun was of my design. Its lens could clarify a grain of dust on the moon. My technical acumen might pale in comparison to the insurmountable inventive genius of a Benjamin Montgomery, but in the area of weaponry, I was certainly no slouch.

I leveled the weapon and peered through the scope, ignoring the pandemonium generated by Jensen's death. Confederates scurried back and forth in a panic, some stopping to take shots at nothing and everything.

Random shots in my direction fell far short of my position.

I twisted a dial on the scope, adjusting the image of my next target: an iron dragon.

I squeezed the trigger, feeling a mild vibration as the magnetic coils inside the barrel powered up. A sharp hiss was the only indicator that the shell had exited the barrel.

No betraying smoke, no muzzle flare, no recoil. Just a deadly, sibilant whisper heralding death and destruction.

The shell penetrated the dragon before my finger lifted from the trigger. Flame and metal spewed out of the machine's side, before an ear-bursting hammer of explosive pressure flipped it bottom over top.

I rapidly targeted the remaining dragons, each one falling victim to a highly combustible shell, delivered by a combination of new technology and the expertise of a trained marksman.

Twelve shots. Twelve seconds. Twelve dragons down.

Quietly, I withdrew from my concealment. I cast a loving gaze upon my mini-magnet, anticipating the additional mayhem I would cause with it.

My smile broadened. *Thank you, Benjamin.*

ONCE A SPIDER

REBECCA MCFARLAND KYLE

A woman's terrified scream forced Nansi to move with her day-to-night transition incomplete. Off-balance, despite the many years of nightly changes from two legs to eight, she raced through the tangle of alleys along the river toward the sound. Somewhere in the city, a big cat stalked, claiming the lives of citizens nearly every night. Nansi's goal was to stop the deaths.

Keep to the shadows, her eight-legged mind, bent on survival, tried to assert itself. *Hurry,* her still-human heart urged. So she sped along on her eight legs, using the smoke from stacks to camouflage her inky form.

If the night sky wasn't so thick with fog, the moon would be eclipsed by beautifully colored pleasure balloons owned by the wealthiest that enjoyed soaring above the city and looking down upon the silver ribbons of rivers and snow-capped mountains. Dirigibles, both great and small, also flew in more clement weather. These more sturdy crafts served for long-distance travel and the city's emergency services, including the police and fire brigades.

So far, none of the denizens of this fog-bound city, where a wide river met the sea, were aware of her dual identity; but that could change any time. The more the cat killed, the more in danger the other shadowy residents of the city were.

Daytime Nansi kept a carpetbag packed in her rooms above her shop. The myth who sired her and given her part of his name was immortal, people of color still told tales of the Trickster to their children. Many, who once lived in slavery, used the spider as a symbol of freedom. Nansi herself lived countless lives longer than any human ought, but she could be hurt—and anything that could be hurt, could be killed.

Her keen senses led her quickly to a factory rooftop above the scene. A dark-skinned girl lay on the ground, sobbing. She was barely old enough to have breasts and hair between her legs. Her attacker, a solidly built blonde sailor reeking of whiskey and desire, loomed over her: unbuttoning his breeches, taunting. No cat, but she'd deal with him, anyway.

"You ain't seen nothin' like—"

"Please, Mister." the girl sobbed, struggling with fear to speak.

Nansi spun a bit of silk into a noose and roughly snared the man, lifting him with ease to her perch. Her tiny kindred could not perform such a feat, but the thin silk spun from her body was nearly strong as the copper wire factories prized.

He shrieked pitifully at the sight of the eight-legged fury above his prone form.

"No, I suppose you haven't seen something like this." The remnants of Nansi's two-legged voice cooed in a half-seductive whisper and half-cat's purr. As the night grew darker, she'd lose her voice until the first light appeared at the East. Winter was the worst time for her because she spent most of the dark season hidden in her arachnid form, yet still aware of her surroundings.

Penance, for my past? she wondered.

Nansi lashed out with her fangs, biting the man once in the belly. She usually struck near the neck; but this one got a slow and cruel death which men such as these who preyed upon innocent children deserved.

"Run, child!" With the ragged remnant of her voice, Nansi called gently down to the youngling who scampered to gather her torn clothes. The girl glanced up, but only saw the factory looming above— not the benefactor who'd plucked away her attacker.

"Thank you!" the girl called up to the rooftops in a trembling soprano.

Please hurry, Nansi thought. She didn't want the girl to be more terrified seeing her departure.

Nansi quickly spun the cocoon that'd serve as his living sarcophagus. The task would be easier if she had a web to hold his body. But as much as her nighttime form craved building webs, some part of her two-legged brain still controlled that instinct. Imagine the city dwellers' panic if they found such a web spreading across their ever-taller skyline when the sun rose?

Good, Nansi thought, as she continued winding up her now-weeping prey; rolling the long form between her legs as she spun the silk to bind him.

Now her reward was simply doing well, but she always appreciated knowing the people she risked so much for were grateful.

When she'd first started using her nighttime form to help those being victimized, she'd been incautious. Too many times, she'd awakened to neighbor's tales of horror about a giant spider. As the men girded themselves for a daytime hunt, she'd packed her bag and departed, regretfully leaving much of the life she built behind.

Nansi's old bones disliked the cold and damp of her present home far North of the warm sunlit country where she was born. She chose the place because the river's fog, nearby forest's mist, and smoke from the numerous factories, riverboats, and train yards cloaked her massive form.

Once the cocoon was complete, Nansi hastened to the forest to offer her gift to the winter-starved wildlife. While the bears slept fat in their caves, the large wolves with human eyes would feast on her offering. Or perhaps the Giant, whose massive footprints were plain in the snow in the darkest, most ancient part of the forest where the factories had yet to sunder the trees to feed their giant furnaces...

Call it courtesy between the oddlings. If anyone wondered what happened to the sailor, his disappearance would most likely be blamed on the big cat.

§§§

Nansi awakened naked and shivering atop her covers as the winter sun's rare golden light poured into her bedroom window. She wanted to turn away from the light and claim the solace of sleep for just a bit longer, but she knew there was work to be done. While having her own shop meant some freedom, she was the only employee. If the shop wasn't open, she would get no trade.

Her customers were a combination of the discerning few who appreciated the skill of a fine weaver, and those poor ones who needed the tattered remains of their garments to last. Each presented differing challenges which made her work rewarding.

Moving quickly, despite the bone-deep ache from the damp river air, she washed her slender body; then clothed herself in a loose woolen caftan of yellow adorned with a spider at the belly and a matching scarf covering her long snow white hair.

The clothing was both comfort and advertisement. While some of the younger women of color eschewed clothing from their native country in favor of the long-sleeved blouses, tight corsets and long skirts were also the fashion.

Nansi sold most of the vibrant loose-fitting outfits to the practical pale-skinned ladies, who wished for garments that didn't bind their bodies while they were with child or lounging. It pleased her to see people from other cultures wearing her homeland's attire. Perhaps this small gesture could spark tolerance.

Nansi's Web, her shop, was in a gray area between the city's affluent pale neighborhoods and the homes of her dark-skinned brothers and sisters who often served them. Merchants were a congenial stew of white, yellow, red, and brown folk offering various wares from shoes to healing herbs.

Her father's blessing followed her wherever she traveled, even halfway around the world. Each time Nansi opened a new shop, word quickly spread both up and down the social ladder that a talented seamstress and weaver was available. Nansi had created garments for all with meticulous care, charging what the customer could afford—or accepting barter when those in need had no money.

Nansi moved downstairs and broke her fast with a cup of hot tisane and a bit of cold lentils from her previous night's meal. The tisane came from a neighboring shop, owned by one of the cat-eyed coolie women, Jinjing, near ancient as Nansi, who worked as a healer for those who could not afford the science of modern medicine. Oddly, her shop was not in the area where her people primarily traded, but like Nansi, Jinjing spread her talent farther than just her own. Strange to walk in and see people sprouting enough thin needles to make them look like hedgehogs, but the treatment worked for those who were brave enough to try it.

Nansi was never that brave. She stuck to the herbs. The taste was bitter, but nowhere near as much so as the pain she felt each morning when she tried to rise from her bed.

A knock at the shop door made her nearly drop the teacup, a delicate pellucid bit of china gifted to her from one of her affluent customers.

Nansi held the cup closer. It was a particular favorite because the thin glass transferred heat from the tisane to her hands: once so beautiful with long, dainty fingers, now her walnut flesh was spread thin almost to a pale pink atop rheumatism-swollen knuckle and wrist-bones. Her hands still served her, but not as efficiently as they once did.

"Come in!" Nansi called, moving from down her sparsely-furnished living quarters on the top floor to the large front room which comprised her shop.

She expected her customer to be one of the early-rising workmen off to a shift at the factory, only to discover a tear in his work clothes.

A wise workman, she thought. *So many realized too late that a stitch in time truly did save nine.* That old cliché was painfully and often true. Nansi had a bit of magic with the cloth, but some rents were too large to repair.

Instead of the expected worker, the young girl attacked the previous night stepped inside. Her dark eyes were still too wide peering out from an often-patched wool cloak, which was just large enough to cover her head and torso, but not long enough to keep the river winds from chilling her.

Nansi's heart stuttered: an occurrence that was happening with alarming frequency of late. She knew the tapestry the gods wove at her birth would soon unravel. She'd lost count of how many years she'd lived, how many people she'd seen grow old and die. To avoid that pain, she seldom remained in any place too long.

This cool green place was to have been her last city. With the girl arriving on her doorstep, the accusations could begin today. She couldn't bring up enough air around the constriction her fears created to summon her voice.

"Missus," the girl entered with her head bowed respectfully, showing neat lines of alternating earthen-brown scalp and expertly woven braids.

When she saw Nansi's hand shaking, the girl gently extended slender hands for the cup and placed it on the counter with especial care, her nut-brow eyes alight with curious wonder at the fine glass and the scented herbs within. She removed a well-patched woolen cloak to reveal the remains of her clothing.

"I was wondering if you would help me repair my dress? It's the only one I have that fits…Mama died with the cough before she could finish teaching me the needle…I can't let Papa see me like this."

Breath whooshed from Nansi's lungs. Winter claimed more than its share this year to various maladies, but the cough was the worst. People's bodies shriveled as they hacked their lifeblood into cloth after cloth making the rag-man the most popular merchant, even among the wealthier homes.

Whole families perished because those tending the sick were not well informed enough to realize they must thoroughly wash their hands and boil the cloths before they re-used them.

She nodded and found her voice.

"Step behind that screen," Nansi heard the sound like a creaking hinge when she spoke and picked up the cup and hurriedly swallowed a bit more of the tisane scalding her throat.

She coughed; hoping air from her lungs would cool the bitter burn on the back of her tongue.

The girl's eyes widened with concern, but she hastened to follow Nansi's order when the older woman gestured toward the screen again. That piece was her pride and joy. She'd traded reweaving a torn silk kimono of Jinjing's for the Asian artifact, which featured a white tiger stalking through bamboo.

"Yes, Missus," the girl said obediently. "Thank you."

The little one moved quickly, removing the tattered remains of her garment, which was, if possible, even more worn than the woman tasked to its repair.

Nansi paused, realizing the mending would last well past the child's next growth spurt come spring.

"I have some clothing donated by my customers that might fit you better. You still have some growing to do," Nansi shuffled to a rack of shelves concealed by curtains near the screen the girl waited behind.

"Missus, I couldn't...."

"Wealthy people throw these clothes away as soon as they have been seen in them once. You might as well use them as anyone."

Nansi's voice gained strength as she glanced at the shelves. At the top were hats, the tall black ones both men and women wore as well as the fur-lined leather caps and goggles for airship travel. Second, were women's clothes: blouses, skirts, corsets. Nansi located an ivory high-necked blouse, brown corset, and long tan divided skirt, leggings of soft wool, underclothes, along with a pair of sturdy buckled boots from a neat pile on the floor that'd keep the child's legs warm, and brought them to the girl.

"Missus?" The girl's eyes widened at the sight of things lovelier than she'd ever imagined wearing. "I can't."

"Should my shelves keep wearing these clothes that would rather keep you warm and protect your coming womanhood?"

Nansi appraised the naked girl carefully. If she grew into her feet, she'd be tall as a warrior. Already, the curves of her mahogany-skinned face showed the beginnings of a graceful beauty. Her smile lit the room far better than the cold light produced by the new science of electricity.

The child lowered her eyes, her skin deepening with her blush. Nansi glanced away, wishing she hadn't just reminded the child of what was probably the most frightening moment of her life.

"Put these on," Nansi spoke softly, and then stepped out from behind the screen to allow the girl some privacy. "Let me see how they will fit."

"I'm Candace," the girl offered the magic of her name as she worked to dress herself the unfamiliar clothing. Nansi stood nearby; anticipating Candace would have questions about the buckles on the boots and fastening the corset.

"Nansi," she answered the girl. "It is a pleasure to meet one so polite."

"Thank you, Missus—"

"Nansi," Nansi corrected. "You know, you are named after an

ancient Queen from our home country?" She heard the rustle of linen, and then the girl spoke.

"No, Missus—I mean, Nansi." Her voice shook with pride and wonderment. "Papa told me Candace was a *Bible* name.

Nansi fought a tear. The masters first stole away her people's language, then their faith and lore. They were doing the same now to the yellow-skinned "coolies" who worked to lay tracks across the land and the red-skinned "Injuns" unafraid of walking the heights to build their factories. What better way to enslave a people than to rip away their ancient customs and magic?

Moments later, Candace emerged from behind the screen wearing her new garments. Her slender face glowed with pleasure.

Nansi clapped her hands at the transformation from a ragged child to a budding young beauty, a simple bit of magic even the non-gifted could do. The clothes definitely made the young woman. Candace carried herself with smiling pride befitting the descendent of an ancient Queen.

"Now," Nansi took Candace's old dress from the screen. "Wash this, cut it up, and use it when your woman's time comes."

Again, Candace blushed furiously, nodding. "Mama told me it'd be soon."

Good, Nansi thought. *Her Mama told her that much before she passed. Even better, she would not have borne the sailor's child had he managed to force her.*

"Did your Mama tell you how babies are made?" Nansi asked.

Candace ducked her head, blushing furiously. A single tear slipped down her cheek.

"There's nothing you should be ashamed about," Nansi spoke

before she realized. "If some man rips your clothing and attacks you, that's on him. He acts like an animal, he deserves to be treated like one."

I've said too much. Nansi watched the girl for signs she recognized her voice, her hand reaching for the knife in her pocket instinctively.

Taking a deep breath, Nansi removed her hand, rejecting the choice that saved her so often in the past. *Why rid the world of such loveliness when I am nearing the end of my days?*

When Candace couldn't meet her studied gaze. Nansi realized she was too shamed by the encounter to be thinking about the timbre of her voice. And how would a decrepit old woman even reach the top of a factory building so tall it blocked the rare sunlight until near midday?

Candace shyly started to hand over a few coins. The child's hands were already rough and careworn, but Nansi saw blue-black staining along the outside of her left hand. Ink. The girl knew how to read and write.

Nansi shook her head. "These were given to me. I give them to you…"

Before she could object, Candace rolled up those ivory sleeves, then picked up Nansi's broom and commenced to carefully sweep out the shop. She then found cleaning wax and rags and polished the oak counter until it gleamed. Then, she went outside with a bucket full of water she'd warmed at the coal stove and washed the exterior shop window.

"Enough!" Nansi felt the sting of grateful tears in the corners of her eyes. "You've more than paid for the clothing! Thank you."

Candace proffered a smile, which warmed Nansi's old bones.

"If you like," Nansi spoke carefully. "You may come here if you ever have questions a woman could help you with."

Candace nodded. "When I'm not in school, may I come here and learn to sew and weave?"

"Of course," Nansi considered the week. She was most busy on Saturdays, but Sunday afternoons were sparse and most people of the city reserved them for family.

She only kept her shop open in case a person working the other six days should need a repair. "Would your father mind if you came Sunday afternoon?"

"Papa would be pleased at any knowledge I could gain," Candace said. "In turn, I'll keep your shop swept and do what other cleaning you need after school lets out."

"You go to school?" Nansi was surprised.

"Our church runs a school," Candace smiled proudly. "It's for the children of factory workers, so we can learn to read and write and hopefully have better positions later."

"We have a bargain," Nansi smiled. She held up a finger and returned with a cloak she'd woven out of many shades of yarn, which was longer than the patched cloak Candace had. "Take this to seal the deal. You'll need to keep warm and the cloak can serve as a blanket on the cold nights."

"Don't cry," Nansi added when the child's eyes gleamed and she could not bring words to her lips. Nansi longed for a bit of her father's magic to pass along to the child. All she could offer was her skill, and she wondered whether that would be pertinent soon.

Clever inventors improved the steam-driven factory looms almost daily. Garments and rugs woven from those looms were clumsy at first like, Candace's novice works would be. As the engineers progressed, the items were near indistinguishable from those Nansi wove. They even created sewing machines that could rival the finest hand-stitching. Factories were full of women seated for hours sewing the same garment over and over. Nansi feared soon she would only find employment operating a machine that did the work many times faster than her skilled hands.

Still, she thought. *The factories could use a smart woman who knew how the machines were supposed to work.*

§§§

Crying brought Nansi back out on the silvery rain swept streets later that night. She ran along rooftops, sheltering her massive form near the warmth of smokestacks, listening for the cry again.

Need had no color, sex, or age. In the rare instances where she had to choose, she'd seek out the poorer parts of town, knowing the city police were scarce and overworked.

This time, she found a babe so new the umbilicus was still attached, lying in a trash heap barely swaddled by old papers and rags. The mother's love she supposed was within every woman, deprived of babes of her own, ached to take the child to her warm hearth and care for her. She carefully dropped to the ground before the child.

A throaty roar erupted from the shadows.

Nansi froze, her eyes focusing on a white tiger; face smeared with blood, still bent over the corpse of a yellow-skinned woman a bit deeper in the shadows.

The cat leapt, forcing Nansi back.

Nansi struck, her fangs digging into the tiger's vulnerable muzzle.

The cat screamed, eyes narrowing.

Claws tore at her right foreleg. Nansi struggled to keep upright, sinking fangs into the beast's paw, then its shoulder. She clawed back at the beast, struggling to sink her talons into flesh beneath the thick black-and-white fur.

This is it. Nansi's eight legs folded.

Her abdomen struck the ground. Her lung chambers quivered. She could smell the stuff that was her nighttime blood pouring from her front leg.

The tiger loomed, a purr of satisfaction becoming a confused cough as the toxin of Nansi's fangs did its work. The big cat stumbled to one side, glared hatefully at Nansi, and fell on its side, paralyzed.

Nansi struggled up, forcing her legs to unfold. She bit the tiger twice more on its paw pads. She quickly spun a web cradle for the babe, and managed with her uninjured legs to scoop the newborn up, ignoring the trail of droplets that seeped from her wounds.

Where to take the babe? Her human brain warred with the spider's instinct to eat the infant like a bug.

Her first thought was the cat-eyed healer, her friend Jinjing, who'd brewed the tisane. But the coolies were poor as her people. Perhaps a family would take the orphaned child in, but more likely they'd all suffer.

Mercy. The name of the physician's wife, a customer who'd been unusually kind, came to her.

She scampered up to the roof and hastened across the rooftops past the gray and into the affluent pale side of town. The wind blew cold, damp air from the river, veiling places where shadow was sparse. She hastened onward on seven legs, fighting the urge to feast on the unprotesting infant.

Light! She recoiled, seeing gas lamps on every corner and often in between. Even the alleyways were wider, offering single lanes sufficient for back-door deliveries to the finer homes and establishments.

Both halves of her questioned every step, but Nansi forced herself to press forward. Too many regrets, for deeds done in youth's impatience and seemingly impervious, cast shadows on her soul.

She knew the route well by day, but it was far different going by stealth. She'd delivered clothing to Missus Mercy on several occasions. Unlike her other wealthy customers, Mercy made certain she had fare for the fancy steam-powered carriages both ways, and paid extra for her time.

Carriage wheels rattled. Nansi ducked behind a three-story home, just in time to hear a black dog in the yard barking furiously at her, loud and deep enough to waken people for blocks.

The dog shambled toward her growling.

She escaped over a stone wall to a vacant yard and contemplated leaving the child in the backyard after a good solid poke that'd waken the child up.

No, Mercy's home was close. Who knows what these strangers would do with the child? The city provided segregated orphanages for all four colors of their denizens, but they were nothing more than workhouses. Children consigned to that fate ended up slaving in the factories with no hope of learning anything more than the basics.

She ducked downstairs windows where an electric light shone

through carelessly drawn drapes. Inside, a silver-haired woman swallowed up in furs slept in a chair in front of a roaring fire.

Nansi huddled against the side of the building within a fragrant cedar hedge when light appeared overhead. A police dirigible passed nearby, hissing steam, casting a light near where the half-crazed dog still barked.

"Come inside, Albert!" A man shouted from the house where the bear-sized canine continued raving. "Stop making so much ruckus."

Silence reigned after a few tense minutes. The dog was inside, the police gone. Nansi straightened her stiffened limbs, continuing on with her burden.

Another pause as she crept to the street to orient herself. Mercy's home was just a block over.

No cover.

Nansi looked in all directions, and then shot across the street and down the block. She dropped the naked babe on the doctor's doorstep and hammered the door quickly with her uninjured left front leg.

She couldn't wait for sounds within the home. Nansi ducked between the doctor's home and the next and fled toward the alleyway.

"What is this?" Mercy's shout was clear enough for her to understand. "Edwin, hurry! There's a newborn on our doorstep!"

Nansi hastened forward and found herself in a pool of light from above. The police dirigible hovered within feet of her. She'd been in such haste to get the babe to Mercy's home she'd forgotten the vessel was still nearby, patrolling the wealthier homes.

Incredulous cries split the night as the dirigible made an abrupt turn, and lost control.

Nansi didn't wait to watch the crash, but she heard the sound and the yelling. She dodged and ran between homes and finally took cover in a park with enough brush to hide her form.

Within a few minutes, she heard fancy steam-powered vehicles and horse-drawn carriages rattling down the streets, hurrying to provide aid to the fallen police crew.

She waited until near dawn before moving again. When she heard nothing but occasional traffic nearby she cautiously ventured forth and managed to keep to the shadows for the rest of her trip home.

She made it through the back door to her shop/home as the first rays of dawn pinked the horizon. The change normally took care of any injuries. This time, she had an ugly set of claw marks that were near as wide as her thin forearm. Nansi applied unguent and a clean linen bandage.

By the time she'd donned her caftan and drank the last cup of her tisane, she could scarcely move. She certainly was not going to attempt the narrow flight of stairs to her living quarters with her human legs feeling near as flimsy as the spider's.

Nansi pulled a cloak around her and took up the bamboo pole Jinjing gave her, to walk the few feet to the woman's store next door. She paused, seeing a line of coolies in dark clothing wailing by the door.

"What's happened? Is something wrong with Jinjing?"

Few of the workers could understand English; they merely shook their heads and raised the volume of their wails. Nansi made her way through the crowd to the shop, her worry growing with each too-deliberate step.

When she finally set foot across the threshold, the interior was far different than her last visit. The statue of Buddha, set in a place of respect where incense could be burned, was covered in red paper. White candles burned everywhere as well as incense.

The shop was much like Nansi's with living quarters above. A white cloth hung at the door to Jinjing's living quarters and a gong stood to the right of that door.

"What's happened?" Nansi inquired of a coolie, who was more middle-aged than the black clad people outside. His hair was a mix of silver and black and he wore all black. Though his features were composed, Nansi noted his eyes were red from weeping. A woman in white and younger children, clad in blue stood protectively around him.

"My mother has passed to the next realm," he answered, bowing his head to weep.

"I—I'm sorry." Nansi stammered, feeling near as fragile as the paper objects people were bringing in and setting upon the counter. Nansi spotted money, one of the fancy brass steam cars, a hot air balloon, and other beautifully painted symbols of wealth. She felt the room spin and a strong hand steer her to a chair near the entrance where Jinjing often set people down to consult.

Good death was a concept Nansi understood from her friend. Nansi knew Jinjing's coffin was already ordered and preparations for her wake had been discussed with her family. One didn't reach such a great age and not think of such things; and custom was important to Jinjing's people.

Jinjing was expecting to have a five blossoms death since she'd married, bore a son, was respected in the community, and had a grandson who loved her. The last blossom, she remembered, was dying in her sleep. While she expected weeping, the air was thick with grief and fear.

"What happened to Jinjing?"

"We found her this morning in the shop," the son answered, choked with tears. "She had been bitten on her nose and feet by some kind of serpent."

The world spun and nearly slipped from her. Nansi shivered.

"You are unwell," the man said. "I wish my mother were here to tend you."

Nansi shook her head, doing her best to protect her injured arm. She swallowed the knot in her throat and rose to depart.

"I just came for the healing tea that Jinjing brews for me," Nansi said. "I'm so sorry to interrupt. If there is anything I can do…"

Jinjing's son nodded and went to the shelf to hand over a jar of the tisane.

"My mother was grateful for your friendship," he said with a bow, declining Nansi's offer of coin. "Take this."

Nansi wobbled out of the shop and back to her own, clutching the jar with her free hand. Part of her wanted to dash the jar to the floor. She did not deserve the family's kindness—and she certainly had earned the pain she'd feel without the tisane. The thought haunted her as she shuffled through her work that day, trying to ignore the pain in her arm—and the worse discomfort in her heart.

I killed Jinjing.

§§§

Nansi couldn't say when she developed a conscience. She killed like the hourglass spider whose image she wore at night. She'd wed a few of her lovers, but none survived. Perhaps it was when her own body aged past its calling for men, and her heart started calling for justice.

Could my divided heart not think of both at once or did the spider always rule?

Nansi shook her head as she set to work at her loom. Her nighttime persona emptied her spinnerets every morning and left her with yards and yards of heavy silk threads that would be perfectly good for yarn. Somehow the spider knew to eject the smooth webbing, not the sticky kind prey would be trapped in.

Nansi supposed the spider had to eject some of the silk periodically to keep her spinnerets functioning properly. For years, she'd balled the stuff up like yarn and carried it along with her. When she saw the silk pouch hot air balloons, she realized there was a market for the heavy silk cloth she could weave from the spider's gifts.

Silk was imported from Jinjing's homeland and it cost a good deal of money. If she could weave the spider-silk into cloth, she could charge what the Asians did for heavy silk.

She kept at her work part as habit, more as penance. Her right arm dealt out pain with every movement. Occasionally, she'd stop to look at the loom and marvel at the beauty and durability of the cloth coming to life beneath her fingers.

By the third glance, she was content enough to tap her foot and sing. Women from her homeland often worked together at the loom and told stories or sang to make the work go smoother. Her old voice was more like crows on a battlefield than the songbirds she grew up listening to.

A knock at the shop door startled her from the near hypnotic trance of music and movement. The door opened, revealing Mercy with the tiny coolie child in her arms.

"Nansi," she said, her plain pale features illuminated with delight. Her chestnut hair tumbled down her back in a rough-tied ponytail. Beneath her cloak, she saw a plain gray nurse's uniform.

"Look who I found on my doorstep last night."

Nansi smiled to see the child settled against Mercy's ample breasts. Of all the wealthy women she'd sewn for, Nansi took the most pleasure in making attractive clothing for those plain women whose beauty was in deeds.

"Edwin's investigated with the police and the Asian community and it appears the child may have belonged to the latest victim of the big cat that's been attacking people by night," Mercy bubbled on. "I'm not sure what Good Samaritan rescued her and brought her to me, but I thank God she's safe and sound now."

Nansi rose unsteadily and wobbled over to Mercy to check on the child.

"Imagine," Mercy breathed. "The umbilicus was just torn. She hadn't even been cleaned yet—it's a miracle she survived."

"Will you keep her?" Nansi's voice sounded more of an unsteady croak than usual.

"You're bleeding," Mercy's doe brown eyes shifted to Nansi's right arm. She quickly settled the babe on my counter and moved to her side.

Nansi glanced down to the right side of her caftan in horror. The right sleeve of her beautiful turquoise robe was covered with a scabrous brown stain. She blinked as her vision narrowed. A warm arm wrapped around her and Mercy sat her down on the chair and hastily unwrapped her sloppily bandaged wound.

Bitter bile rose in Nansi's throat. What wasn't slashed open to the bone was thickly swollen weals.

"What got you?" Mercy's voice, normally a low rational tone, was a high-pitched squeak.

"The white tiger," Nansi husked, her body trembling despite her attempts to force herself to remain still and breathe. She might have considered lying to anyone else, but Mercy could plainly see that claws made those tracks.

"You weren't the one who brought me the child?"

Nansi shook her head, so she wouldn't meet the woman's eyes. It was a partial truth, but merited in case someone actually saw the spider on the doctor's doorstep.

"You sent someone?"

Nansi nodded, not quite meeting the woman's eyes.

"How did this happen?"

"I was somewhere I shouldn't be," Nansi said. "The beast attacked me. I had my bamboo walking stick that Jinjing gave me and I beat it back."

Nansi winced. Lying to Mercy and using the gift of the friend she'd killed felt hypocritical. Jinjing wasn't doing anything Nansi herself hadn't done too many times over the years.

"Come with me, I need to have Edwin look at your arm and we'll get you to the police so you can tell them what happened," Mercy urged.

Nansi shook her head, fear knotting in her stomach. A glance out her shop window told her night was coming soon. She'd lost track of time, left herself out in her shop. What would happen if she'd changed and someone saw her?

"At least, let me stitch up the portions that are open," Mercy offered gently. "You can tell me where you were attacked and I'll pass that along to the police anonymously. They're going to step up patrols in this area seeing as the babe's mother was killed near here. They crashed a ship last night near our home."

"One of the officers aboard saw a large black creature on the ground and thought it was some kind of spider. Imagine that! The only thing they saw to match the size was our neighbor's Newfoundland. Edwin says the officer who claimed to see the spider had whiskey on his breath."

"I don't think the police believed him, but they're anxious about those cat attacks. My goodness, people are in such a panic since the attacks began. The police will be grateful to know the cat is a white tiger, at least. That will give them something to look for. Finally."

Nansi nodded, extending her arm and allowing Mercy to pull out a kit from her traveling bag and carefully wash, then sew and bandage her arm. Patrols meant light—and light meant she was trapped in her home at night as the spider. She'd been in the situation before, mostly due to the spider's incautiousness and her inability to control the beast. It rankled that she'd done a good deed and was trapped by it.

"Now, keep that bandage on and let me see it in the next few days," Mercy said.

Nansi nodded, glancing warily at the windows. Was a storm brewing or was it darkening, already? She still didn't comprehend the weather in this strange, new place.

"I need to purchase some clothing for the babe," Mercy said. "Can you help me?"

"Of course," Nansi answered quickly. She moved to the shelves of new handmade clothing and came away with a couple of simple gowns in pink, which would fit the child now and for a bit longer. She also gathered some soft and sturdy white cotton cloth and brought that back to Mercy.

"This is all I have that will fit her now," Nansi said. Her hand trembled as she passed the items over. She could feel her nails lengthening into claws and tucked them in letting them bite into the palms of her hands. The spider urged her to protect herself. Mercy knew too much. "The cotton you can cup up into squares and make napkins for her."

"What do I owe you?" Mercy reached again for her traveling bag.

Nansi shook her head, hoping to get the woman out quickly. She could feel the quivering in her limbs, which signaled the start of the change.

"I couldn't charge for a foundling, especially since you've cared so kindly for my arm."

"The cloth you're looming is lovely. I've never seen anything so—" Mercy stared between the thread and the child, looking thoughtful.

"I'm making the cloth for a balloon. I had some silk yarn and I thought perhaps they could use it," Nansi answered, quickly, hearing the grate in her voice more akin to the spider.

"I've always wanted to weave," Mercy picked up the child, cooing gently as she slid the girl into one of the pink gowns and smiled approval. Her hopeful glance turned to Nansi. "I just never had anyone to teach me."

"I'm—I'm holding classes this Sunday afternoon—after church," Nansi wasn't sure why she said that, perhaps to get the woman out and away.

"I'll be there," Mercy looked pleased. "If it's acceptable to bring the baby."

Nansi's head shook up and down.

"You be sure to come to me at the free clinic in the next two days so I can look at the wound and make sure it's not infecting," Mercy ordered. "And I expect you at the clinic in two weeks so I can remove the stitches. It's getting dark. I must go—the carriage is waiting and I don't want to be out with the child and a tiger running the street."

Nansi nodded emphatically, "Be safe."

Good thing. She'd barely shut and locked the door and got the shade pulled before the change took her. Nansi shivered into her nighttime form shedding the bandage like discarded clothing.

Go after her, the spider urged, hungrily. *Let me bite her and eat the child!*

§§§

Nansi wouldn't have realized it was Sunday, save for the party through the streets every Saturday night. For most of the workmen in the area, Sunday was their one free day. Long shifts left them tired weekdays. The young and the tempestuous were tired of their workday prison and ready to seek adventure.

Not even the threat of the tiger could keep them off the streets. Nansi's nighttime form watched the merriment from the safety of a small slit in her upstairs window. Years ago, she remembered longing to take part in such festivities, wishing she could dance and make love under the stars like other girls. Now, she was content to watch.

Balloons and dirigibles orbited the night sky like gaudy stars. The sound of horns and drums echoed up and down the busy street. Couples who couldn't afford the entrance fees for the clubs and the party boats steaming down the river danced in the streets despite the mist and chill fall air.

The coolies brought out long dragon kites threading them along the avenue like brightly colored snakes. And everywhere, merchants offered food and drink to the dancers. Delicious scents of food: spicy Asian, roasted nuts, and fried bread from the Indians perfumed the streets.

Nansi allowed herself to rest. Even if someone needed her, it'd be impossible for her to get through the crowd to help undetected. Besides, she had a class tomorrow and she needed all her strength to be ready.

Amidst the music and the sound of the crowd, she never wakened for the screams.

§§§

Nansi awakened feeling more alive than she had in many months. Perhaps the spider should sleep more often.

She opened the new packet of tisane to prepare her morning elixir. She paused, her nose tickling at the smell. The herbs were fresh, but stronger than she recalled when she opened the last batch.

She prepared the tisane as Jinjing instructed and got herself a bit of bread to break her fast. The first sip was too bitter. Nansi added honey to the mix, thinking she might have gotten too much of the herbs.

After three sips, the tisane boiled back up, spewing out of her mouth and onto the floor. Nansi dumped the rest of the mix by her back door and set to work determining to be more careful in her preparation the next morning.

Nansi considered all kinds of projects for Mercy and Candace. In the end, she chose the silk cloth she'd been weaving. Pure white wasn't the easiest weave to see, but some urge drove her to the loom working as fast as her hands would allow. She finished the bolt she'd been working on and set up the loom for her students.

Then, she began work on more baby clothing. Mercy's child would need little dresses and pajamas in bigger sizes soon. Spring and summer always brought more babies. The city certainly needed a bit of joy after having lost so many last winters.

Mercy arrived first, bearing a basket full of near flawless clothing for the poor and the babe in her arms. Nansi knew she'd made the right decision even if it meant risk to her. The girl-child was already filling out and burbling contentedly in the sling Mercy fashioned to carry her.

"How's your arm?" Mercy glanced at the sleeve of Nansi's red caftan. She placed her bundle carefully on the counter one-handed while she still maintained careful hold of the baby girl.

Nansi flushed, realizing she hadn't re-bandaged the nearly healed wound. She rolled up her sleeve and showed Mercy, knowing nothing else was going to stop her from seeing for herself.

"You heal miraculously fast," Mercy extended a gentle hand and felt the weals for heat. "I was afraid the wounds would fester."

Nansi forced a smile and nodded. How could she explain the gifts from a god whose name the kindly pale-skinned woman had never heard of?

"I am fortunate in that way."

Also fortunate was Candace's arrival. The girl stopped, seeing Mercy.

"Oh, Nansi, you have customer—I can come back…"

"No," Mercy and Nansi said as one.

"Please, wait," Mercy added.

"Missus Mercy is learning to weave with you," Nansi said. "Mercy, this is Candace. She's the reason for these classes. I wish I had more than one large loom. The other's a good deal smaller and I think, less suitable for beginners."

"Why don't I tend the baby and watch first?" Mercy suggested.

Candace paused, feeling the silk thread, her eyes wide and thoughtful. Then, she set to work. She learned quickly how to set up the warp, which was the base of the fabric and then weave the weft like a web.

The ghost of Nansi's nighttime persona approved of the girl's obvious desire to learn. Knowledge was a good thing for her people and the old crafts still would stand them in good stead.

"Dear me," Mercy said, smiling. "I do not believe I can manage the craft so well…"

They all paused when the shop door opened. Nansi looked at an Indian girl close to Candace's age. She wore her ink black hair straight down her back and parted in the center, a thin braid holding the front out of her face. Such a natural beauty looked odd in the strict starched black and white uniform their school required. Nansi was most intrigued by the large odd-shaped cloth sack she carried on her back.

"How may I help you?" Nansi asked.

"My name is Rose," the girl spoke in a quiet voice, every syllable of English pronounced with exquisite care. "I came to ask for your help selling some things I have made."

Nansi gestured to the counter and the girl emptied part of the sack. Inside were dyed willow baskets, carefully woven with a multitude of colored designs. Nansi's eyes fell on the black spider against a red ground immediately. She picked up the basket, amazed at the beauty and intricacy of the workmanship.

"I'll buy this one," Nansi said. "And I'd be honored to show your work in my shop."

Rose lowered her eyes, flushing, a grateful smile on her face. Other baskets detailed wolves, white bison, various insects and plants.

"And I want these," Mercy had a couple of baskets with flowers on them. "I can use them for the sewing—and for Lin's things."

They quickly discussed prices and Rose was paid. Rose glanced at the fabric on the loom, her brow quirking curiously.

"Would you like to stay and learn how to loom cloth?" Nansi asked. The spider already knew the answer, but humans must go through formalities.

Rose nodded.

The three women took turns setting up and weaving the cloth. Candace and Rose were both adept at the loom. Mercy struggled, but both girls offered guidance and encouragement.

Nansi stood back. When they weren't talking about their

3203

320320320

320320

320320

lessons, she began telling tales of Anansi, and the other great ones of her people. Candace listened raptly, asking details. Nansi saw her pull out a scrap of paper and take notes. Nansi pulled out the book she used for accounting and tore off several pages, then handed the bound book to Candace.

"Here," she said. "Write them down and tell the other children."

Rose paused as she wove, looking thoughtful. Nansi made a note to have the girl tell some of her tales the next time they met. Perhaps her tribe had stories about a spider.

The best way for people to learn was to help others. She'd been doubtful of Candace's request, but now she was proud of her pupil's accomplishments.

"Why are you selling the baskets, Rose?" Mercy asked when they stopped to take a break. She'd brought tart red apples and white cheese to share as a treat.

Rose paused. "I am not supposed to be making them…"

Mercy flushed and didn't speak. Most knew that the Indian children could not speak their language or participate in their customs. Rose surely was not this girl's name, but Nansi approved of the choice. It fit her.

"My fingers would not permit me to stop," Rose said. "I've hidden these with my grandfather. Then, last night, the cats killed him. We have no money to bury him in accordance with the City's wishes."

Oh no. Nansi's heart did a flip-flop.

A hopeful part of her wondered if she actually had not killed Jinjing and it was indeed a snake, which stung her in her bed. The more practical part knew that was just a fancy. Too much coincidence.

Wolves ran in packs.

Cats had prides.

§§§

Nighttime Nansi emerged from the back door of her shop. Sunday night was a safe enough time. Many residents attended church. Others were recovering from Saturday night physically, financially or both—some even prepared for their work the next morning.

She paused, seeing a dead mouse by the stoop. The creature was right where she'd poured out the tisane.

Poison, her spider-self had better senses than the two-legged part of her and refused to partake of the free meal.

She glanced toward the back door of the next shop, Jinjing's herbery, and quickly ascended the building across the way searching for a vantage point where she could watch the comings-and-goings and not be observed.

The nearby skies were empty of balloons and dirigibles. She heard a whistle from the train coming along the tracks, which served the factories and knew they'd be unloading raw materials and picking up manufactured goods at the nearby depot.

She found a place just as the back door opened and a pair of young white tigers emerged.

How did Jinjing manage this? Nansi wondered, a flicker of jealousy igniting the fire of anger already burning in her. She suspected the poisoning was deliberate retribution for her killing Jinjing?

Did they know?

Nansi stalked the cats from the rooftops. They clung to the

shadows, heading for the darker area of town where Nansi's people lived.

She contemplated her options. Take them on. It'd been difficult enough fighting Jinjing. The two cubs were young yet and possibly foolish, but they were stronger than she was. And they might well know what she was as well.

There could be another reason for Jinjing's son to poison her tonic, but she couldn't think at the moment what that reason might be. They'd existed in peace for at least a year now. Why could that not continue?

Contact the police. That would be Mercy's solution to the problem, but Mercy was one of the pale-skinned elite. If Nansi came to the constabulary with this kind of tale, she would spend the last day of her life in an asylum. The minute they saw her change by night, she knew they'd kill her and probably do their damnedest to forget what they'd seen.

Seek out the wolves? They'd gotten enough food specially wrapped by her to be aware of her existence, but none had contacted her.

Or, had they?

Nansi recalled the baskets Rose brought for sale. Many featured the shape of a wolf. In the back of her mind, Nansi nearly sent those baskets back with Rose when she left to return to the school, because she wasn't sure she could sell an item with an animal so many were fearful and superstitious of. Seeing the girl's need, she hadn't the heart not to try.

She hesitated, considering the stalking cats. So far, they'd only taken one life per night. The city was battened down against them and most were not going outside at night alone if they could help it.

One life, as opposed to how many, would be taken if she didn't try to reach the wolves?

§§§

Ancient forests bordered the city on the three sides, which weren't bounded by the river. The trees hovered on the periphery of civilization waiting for a landowner to be remiss so they could reclaim their space. In the poorer sections, vines and weeds were the foot soldiers, making their incursion unnoticed by people too occupied by day-to-day survival.

Nansi made the journey through the forest quickly keeping to the rooftops and the shadows until she could find a neglected spot where the saplings and vines were thick and the resident were resting in preparation for a day's hard labor.

A sudden light flared and she paused, flattening herself as much as she could on a rooftop groaning against her weight. An older man stumbled out of the house with candle in hand, clad in only his nightshirt, heading for the even more rickety outhouse.

Nansi waited until the door was closed and hastened past the last of the homes. Every neighborhood had its pitfalls for nighttime travel. In the case of the poorer homes, they didn't have the addition of the crapper, which her shop and Mercy's home enjoyed.

Soon, she could barely see the sky for the thick canopy of evergreens above her. The scent of fresh pine was a comfort after the constant smell of industry: coal, wood, oil, everything burning to keep the factories going.

Nansi paused, quivering. The giant stood before her.

She'd never seen anything but his footprints, which were big enough to smash her abdomen easily. Now, he stood above her, more massive than any of the great apes from her homeland, though he was nowhere near as hairy as the stories said. He wore a patched cloak, which was sewn from the hides of black bears and other long-furred animals.

He sang a children's rhyme about spiders in a roar somewhere between a lion's and a rock slide. Nansi quivered on her spindly legs, but remained firmly in place. A few steps and he could overtake her even if she moved at her fastest, which was no longer possible.

"What brings you here, Black Widow?"

"I need the help of the wolves," Nansi answered, realizing her voice was no lovelier than his.

"They wonder why you bring them food instead of eating it yourself," the giant remarked.

Nansi paused. "I bring them people who would do harm to others less strong."

"Is that not the predator's way?"

It had been Nansi's way for generations. Worse, she'd stolen the lives of people who loved and trusted her daytime self because it was her nature. Because she could.

"Is that not the spider's way?" the giant pressed, moving closer to Nansi.

Her nighttime persona considered a strike. His legs were bare and haired little more than the average pale-skinned man. The human part of her spoke from her heart.

"It is," Nansi said. "My kind build webs to trap the

unsuspecting as food. But I'm not a spider all the time. I am a human woman by day. I wish for a better fate for the people of the city: my people, and those of other lands who are willing to live in peace."

"Admirable for one who's armed with poison."

"I've used my weapons enough indiscriminately in my youth," Nansi confessed. "I let the spider rule me and together we killed every man I ever loved. I cannot undo the harm I've done to them and their families."

"I want to at least leave this place better than I have found it. And, if animals threaten the people of the city, they may well go hunting after the wolves as well once they have found the cats. Wouldn't it be better if we delivered the cats to them?"

The giant paused, looking thoughtful. Nansi noted his eyes, older than the forest around them, perhaps even older than the legend that sired her. This wasn't a big dumb beast, but then again, neither were the apes.

She blinked, seeing luminous eyes in a circle around them. She hadn't been aware of the wolves' arrival, but the giant clearly was.

"Welcome," he said, gesturing for the wolves to come forward. "Join me at my fire."

Nansi didn't see the gesture that conjured the fire, but there it was. The wolves weren't frightened as they should have been. Instead, they moved toward the warmth and light to allow their lupine faces to be seen, a gesture of trust.

She fought the urge to hop back, stirred by her nighttime form's panic. So the colossus had magic. That really shouldn't surprise her. Most creatures possessed some native magic and anyone that lived as long as he had, must possess more than most. She stirred her limbs to motion and came just enough forward to let the wolves know she was willing to cooperate, but she could coax no more from her body.

The largest of the wolves bowed and slowly morphed into an Indian, clad only in the skin he'd had at birth. Nansi stared; surprised at the grace of the change from beast to man and the fact that the creatures could summon the change at will, unlike her own imprisonment within the confines of the magic.

While she had a stand mirror in her shop, she'd always changed in a place less likely to have witnesses. Only one man saw her transformation from woman to spider. It killed him.

"My thanks for the food you've brought us," the elder of the group spoke while his companions changed one by one making up an assortment of both Indian and pale-skinned people of both sexes from teenagers to near as old as their leader. "We do not often have such gifts brought to us—particularly by a spider who speaks."

"I'm grateful for your help disposing of them," Nansi tried for what she hoped was humility in her pose. "They were not good men."

"They tasted good enough," the leader chuckled, rubbing his slender belly. "What brings you to us on this night?"

"Why doesn't she change, Grandfather?" Nansi recognized a familiar voice and turned her head to see Rose among the tribe of wolves!

She was older than Nansi originally thought from the nunnish garments the school forced upon her; old enough to have the dark triangle of hair between her legs and full breasts.

"I thought you said your Grandfather was dead." Nansi spoke carefully, not wishing to challenge the girl, but to clarify what she'd been told.

"Most people come with more than one," the elder chuckled. "I am not kin to this girl, but I am proud to call her part of my pack."

"Why doesn't she change?" Another of the wolves asked.

"Daylight turns me back to a woman," Nansi explained.

"You're the weaver," Rose moved closer, surprisingly unafraid of a spider, with a red hourglass on its back, big enough to eat her. "Now I know where the silk you're turning into cloth comes from, Grandmother."

Nansi made a noise of acknowledgment.

"She's a good woman," Rose continued. "She's helping me sell my baskets."

"We will listen to what you propose," the leader said.

Nansi told them of the attacks in the city, and her belief that the white tigers were all Jinjing's family in the shop next door.

"These attacks are stirring up the city," a young man near Rose's age spoke up. "The spider's right to want to be rid of them. The city is lit up bright as day in some places—that would inhibit her ability to travel at night, too."

"I have remained inside more than my nighttime form cares for," Nansi agreed, feeling the tension in her limbs. The spider wanted to run, to feast, and if she didn't find a way to restrain it, she'd be back to her old routine.

"Then, let us rid you of your nighttime form," the giant's rumble startled Nansi. Before she could object, Nansi felt herself tumbling to the soft earth, a wrinkled old body among handsome muscular warriors.

Nansi's arms crossed over a body she'd not been ashamed to flaunt in younger days. A warm pelt slipped around her. She glanced up to the giant in thanks.

Her human eyes saw far more than the spider's could. He was dark, not so much as she, but olive skinned like those close to the Mediterranean with a cap of curls with just a touch of silver at the brows. In the crinkles around his deep brown eyes, the smile-lines around his mouth, she saw amusement.

But those ancient eyes were wise beyond anything she'd known. They'd seen pain—his body bore the marks of it. But he'd shunned the bitterness and sorrow many forged from such scars and chose to accept his life with grace.

It'd been a long time since she was attracted to a man, but she knew it wasn't just the pelt and the fire that warmed her old bones. Nansi felt a girlish flush flowing from her cheeks down her neck when the giant glanced her way, flashing the briefest of smiles.

"A family among the coolies are trying to take over the poorer parts of town," one of the young men standing next to Rose was saying. "They're charging protection for businesses and many who've refused to pay have had employees attacked by the cats."

"Jinjing wouldn't—" Nansi couldn't help but defend the old woman, someone she'd seen much like herself.

"Her own child is among those killed by the tiger," the eldest wolf said. "Rumor has it, she dared to lie with a young man who was not one of her own."

"I took the child to a safe place." Nansi said.

Around the circle, heads shook. The elder sounded sad. "They want the child dead, too. I've heard many inquire about a foundling coolie child. Soon enough, the house that harbors such will be attacked."

"Mercy!" Nansi said the word at the same time Rose did.

Nansi glanced at the young girl, unashamedly naked among her pack. She'd not suspected the girl of being anything but ordinary when they'd first met. Then again, she'd spent entirely too much time hiding her own secrets to pay the attention she should to others'.

The leader turned his face to the sky and howled. Nansi heard the call resounding through the woods, echoed by other beasts toward the city.

"It's the best we can do to protect the family," the leader said. "Perhaps they will not attack tonight. Perhaps they are chasing the dragon instead of taking their form."

Hopeful words. Nansi didn't believe.

"Many have chased the dragon in her shop," the young man answered, gently. "Perhaps you have been too busy trying to cover your own tracks, to see what was going on around you."

Nansi nodded reluctantly. "She was kind to me."

"She was kind to many," Rose said. "But a healer's shop on a respectable street is a good place to provide a shelter for darker deeds. Didn't you ever wonder why the old woman was not in her own part of town? Her's is the only Asian business in your district."

Nansi shook her head.

"She sold to your people, to the whites, and sometimes even to our own—those who'd lost in battle and felt themselves defeated," the young man continued. "Those who wanted to climb mountains instead of high beams on a factory construction site."

Nansi swallowed, she knew too well what broken dreams did to a people. Too many of her own turned away from their native faith or worse, to drink and abuse their women and abandon their children.

And what did I do?

Nansi tried not to dwell on the past, but sometimes the soul deep ache overwhelmed her. She'd left too much hurt, too many lives in disarray in her wake to ever repay it by saving a few people.

Maybe saving the city would be enough, though in her own mind, she could not be certain.

§§§

Nansi rushed back to the city with Rose and a pair of the bigger Indian youths. She'd never seen the night with human eyes and had to force herself to focus on the hike back to civilization.

Once they were there, they hastened to Mercy's home.

Too late.

Nansi knew it the minute they smelled smoke approaching the better part of town. Once they'd cleared the trees, the sky was red with the reflection of the flames. The nose-burning stench of kerosene was near thick as fog in the air. Still, she hurried and hoped she was wrong.

By the time they'd reached Mercy's home, half a dozen balloons and dirigibles as well as the steam-powered carriages surrounded the place. The fire was out, but the home itself was skeletonized with smoke and ash swirling around it. A steam pumper, or kettle, as the Fire Department called it, still doused the home with water but it was evident the place was a total loss.

"My friend lived here," Nansi spoke to a young pale-skinned fireman who was standing off to the side getting a bandage placed on a burnt arm by another of his fellows.

The fireman didn't raise a brow at such a claim. "Mrs. Mercy was a friend to many of us, Ma'am. I'm sorry about her and her husband."

"The baby?" Nansi asked. "They'd taken in a coolie child."

"All dead," the firefighter said. "I don't know who'd want to set fire to the home of some of the kindest people in town."

Dead, Nansi hated that word. Hated herself for being the reason it was used to describe three people she cared for.

And I killed them just as certain as I'd struck the match.

§§§

"You can't go back to your shop," Nansi hadn't been aware of the younger member of her team departing their company and returning. She'd taken a seat on the curb a few houses down from Mercy's home, tears streaming down her face, unable to go any further. The ache in her bones from hiking so far on rough terrain was inconsequential compared to the ache in her heart.

"I gave her that child and that's what got her killed," Nansi's smoke-roughened and tired human voice sounded much like what came from the spider.

"You didn't know." Rose spoke kindly, extending her hand to help Nansi up from the curb.

Even with help, Nansi creaked to a standing position.

"You can't go home. A tiger's waiting at your back door." Rose told her once they were further away from the fire scene and could speak.

Nansi glanced at the sky with the first rose of dawn showing on the horizon. By now, she'd be home—and probably dead.

"Where am I going? Nansi no longer cared so much. All she wanted was some hot tisane. She shook her head. No, even that was poison.

"Back to Magog," Rose answered, gently. "He can keep you safe until we have an idea how to strike."

Nansi glanced at the young woman. "Magog? I've heard the name."

"It's in the *Bible.*" One of the young men whose name Nansi had already forgotten, provided.

"He's that Magog?"

Rose nodded.

"He may well be older than my father." Nansi mused. "He may well be as old as the world."

She hoped the wise-eyed giant could help her find a way to take the weight of her world off her shoulders.

§§§

"A cave?" Nansi glanced between her three companions. She wasn't sure where she'd imagined a man near as tall as the trees living, a man if the name and the rumors were true had been alive near the beginning of the world, and a cave was the last place she'd imagined.

Shouldn't the descendent of angels be living at the top of a mountain? Then again, people strove for the heights. A hidden cave might perhaps be the best way to survive in a world where the strange and different were shot and hung up on the walls of the hunters as trophies.

Nansi recalled with sorrow a mountain of buffalo skulls on the Western plain. Her younger self danced merrily around that pile and made love to the famous hunter who'd killed most of the creatures, a predator like her who'd fallen to her sting. At the time, she'd agreed with the hunter's assessment of the overlarge herd beasts' deaths. Nature didn't have a place in this modern, gear-driven world.

"Come in," Magog croaked, when Nansi reached the entrance to the cave made her want to back right out again.

"Thank you for providing me shelter," Nansi bowed her head to the giant, then blushed when she realized how foolish that must look.

Magog chuckled. The man was still blissfully nude beneath the bearskin garment. Nansi wondered if the thing itched him like it did her. She glanced away, pretending to study a wall made up of rams horn-shaped fossils embedded in the side of the cave. Opal, amber, and other precious stones gleamed from the surface of the ages-old creatures rendering a romantic ambiance in the firelight.

Nansi caught her breath and settled opposite the fire from her host. He passed her a bit of honeycomb and some apples.

"What do we do now?" she asked him.

"We wait for darkness. By that time, my spies will have determined a bit more about the tiger's movements," he dribbled honey down his fingers and licked it off...slow and sensuous as a cat.

"I believe we can find a way to amuse ourselves."

§§§

Nansi volunteered to be the bait for the Tong.

None of her allies liked the idea, but Nansi had a compelling argument. All but Magog were younger than she and they had lives to lead. She was old, creaky, and tired of living, tired of the perpetual conflict she endured with the spider and tired of the battles humans were fighting with each other.

The next night, Nansi took back her nighttime form and approached her shop from the rooftops. When she reached the building next to hers, she jumped down in the alley and started to pull open the door of her shop with the three claws at the end of her forefoot.

If she hadn't been prepared, the tiger pushing the door toward her from the inside would have knocked her over. Nansi stepped aside, slashing the big cat across the muzzle with her claws. The beast roared and another answered from above.

Hurry up, wolves. Nansi thought.

Their ghost-like gray forms filled the alley in seconds. The biggest of the wolves engaged with the tiger who threw the door open. Nansi glanced around the room seeing three others—and Candace.

The girl stood at the back of the room with a gleaming knife pressed against her throat. Two young tigers protected them.

"Run!" Candace screamed at me.

She knew! The realization electrified Nansi. She rushed forward, slashing at the right most of the tigers.

"Surrender," Jinjing's son ordered in a voice far deeper than Nansi ever heard. "Or I'll spill this girl's blood all over your floor."

Candace stood there with tears in her eyes. The weaver, the storyteller, the promise that Nansi's people would know the tales of her father and the other greats, Candace meant more to Nansi than her own life.

Nansi bowed acquiescence as best as her spindly legs would

allow.

Jinjing's son laughed then slashed Candace's throat, throwing
her near on top of Nansi. The spider ignored the hot shower of blood
and rushed the man, intent on killing him for his betrayal.

One of the tigers' jaws closed on Nansi's slender head. She bit
the beast on the tongue, and the creature issued something between a
roar and a retch. Just enough time for Nansi to pull her head from
between its jaws before the poison made the cat clamp down. The
animal struggled, fighting the paroxysms which came fast, then fell on
its side panting and growling.

Jinjing's son's silken kimono ripped as he shifted to tiger and
engaged with the alpha wolf. Nansi ran to Candace's side.

The girl still lived!

"Magog!" Nansi screamed with her ragtag voice. "Help!"

The room filled with the angel. Yes, angel. Up until then, Nansi
have sworn he didn't have wings—she'd seen all there was of him,
after all. But, attached between his shoulder blades were glowing wings
— gray as rain and singed at the tips.

He filled the tiny shop near to bursting. All combat stopped as
the wolves and Tong members struggled just to find a place to stand.
The wolves were calm, but the Tong members were quietly working
their way to the door, probably hoping to flee without losing their lives
now that their leaders were dead.

"Help her," Nansi choked out. "She's a good girl—too young
to go like this."

Magog glanced down at Candace's blood soaked body, his
dark eyes so full of sadness Nansi's eyes blurred with tears. He laid a
hand on Candace's forehead and closed his eyes.

The room went silent as the blood on Candace's clothing disappeared and the girl's eyes opened. She glanced at the angel above her and sobbed.

"You're not dead," Magog's voice wasn't reassuring.

Candace swallowed, a shaking hand reaching to her throat. She nodded thanks and rose, giving a wide berth to Nansi and the animals.

"Get out of my town and never come back," Magog told the Tong members. "Treat your people and all others with respect and perhaps I won't see the need to visit you in the future."

The remaining Tong fled, bowing multiple times.

"Come, little spider," Magog said.

"Candace, Rose," Nansi turned to the two girls who stood together. Rose had just changed back to her human form and was once more naked, but she held her friend without shame. "I leave this place to you. There's enough gold beneath the floorboard in the bedroom to repair what's broken, perhaps even buy the herbery next door—the store is yours to do with as you choose."

"But—" Candace stammered.

Nansi felt the daylight's magic shift her to her human form. Candace moved to pass her a cloak from the shelves of donated clothing. Nansi winced when the soft cloth touched her shoulders and she recognized it'd been Mercy's from last year. It still smelled of the lemony perfume she liked to wear.

"I can't stay here," Nansi told the girls regretfully. "Between the two of you, you can figure out what you need to know—or find older women to help you. Just listen to each other and remember to treat your customers with kindness and respect. And finish those bolts of spider silk cloth. You can sell those for a good deal of money to the balloonists."

She turned to follow Magog out the door, unsure how they were going to get back to the forest in her state of dishabille and his size.

"You have a choice now," Magog touched Nansi and they were back in the forest at the mouth of his hideout. "Renounce your power and I can give you a full human life—or remain what you are for the little time you have left."

Nansi didn't need him to finish the sentence. Each day, she could feel herself fading with the sun.

"What life can I have?"

"Whatever you choose," Magog spoke gently. "You will live like the rest of the flesh creatures. I cannot extend your father's blessing. That's not within my powers. I'm sure he's still around in your country, if you wish to seek him."

"No," Nansi took the giant's massive hand. "Let me have the night with a human form—and with you."

§§§

And so the former spider-woman regained her youth and beauty. She lived in the old forests with the giant for awhile.

But, she always kept her carpetbag packed.

And, one morning while her lover dozed, Nansi placed a kiss on Magog's forehead, never realizing his deep breathing was all a ruse, and spoke a quiet farewell.

While she was fully human, some part of the spider still remained in her and that dark shadowy part had begun to whisper in her ear when the night was still. Just that night, she'd felt her canine teeth and looked longingly at her lover's neck.

His magic could take the change from her, but the instincts still remained. The Black Widow wanted to devour her mate. After all, human flesh was the only meat she ever desired.

Rose and Candace never saw their friend again, but lived long lives, full of happiness, husbands, and children. They took Nansi's advice and found wise women from all four communities to teach them various crafts from weaving to tatting lace.

Their joint venture prospered. Despite the ready availability of factory-made clothing, customers came from all parts of the city to buy hand-made clothing with a distinctive flair.

And they never killed any spider that crossed their paths.

ON WESTERN WINDS

CAROLE MCDONNELL

In The Annals of Beatha Chezuba, Headmistress of the
women's college in the eastern capital,

*The sixth day, the fourth month, the eightieth year in the third
century after the Great Aggression:*

It is reported that several young boys, sons of local fishermen,
found a disturbing object upon our Eastern coast, with Asian
ideographs. Our students, along with the Queen's guards, were
dispatched to see this strange sight.

They found the account true. What is to be made of it, I do not
know, but the superstitious among us contend that it portends some
disaster. I am inclined to believe them. For the superstitions of those
who make their living on the sea are not to be easily discounted.

*The seventh day, the fourth month, the eightieth year in the
third century after the Great Aggression:*

Today, although encumbered with much work I, with my two
assistants here at the college, ventured forth by balloon—for the day
was amenable to flying—to see this great sight the sea.

I found myself fascinated by this occurrence. Indeed, all who
stood at the shore—the young boys, the fishermen, the guards—were
amazed. It is a dock, most certainly—or part of it—and it appears to

have been brought to our land over many great waves. It is made by human hands, of foreign craftsmanship. Worn, sea-weathered, so large that only a great uprising of the earth could have mightily ripped it from its moorings.

However, it has not traveled to Africa's coast alone but was accompanied by much biological debris and mechanical detritus—iron, steel, and such—that could survive the sea-journey. Flotsam and jetsam, barnacles and many ocean species cling to it.

I do believe our local marine species have been nudged into a minor battle, but they, like us, are a hardy species. However specimens must be collected; tests must be performed, quarantines have to be established.

The thirteenth day, the fourth month, the eightieth year in the third century after the Great Aggression:

It has been a most hellish day. The Dean of the male college, who loves to have the preeminence above all others in all things, has inserted himself into our affair. Indeed, he has compounded what was already a complex matter.

For, without asking me or any of my learned colleagues, he ordered the dock bound upon a hydraulic and, with much labor and over the course of six days, he caused the wreckage to be brought to the Queen's Gate. It was not a wise decision.

Perhaps if he had seen the thing with his own eyes, he would not have done so. I have told him that all research and findings concerning this dock must be brought to the Kritai for their final judgment. But he argues against this. Indeed, in his last telegraph, he told me he is traveling by the Queen's very own dirigible and that he should be arriving at our gates within a few hours. Remembering the events of two years ago, I shall try to keep silent. My reputation has only been lately restored to me and I have no intention of tainting it again.

Tomorrow, I shall travel outside the gate to see what he intends to do with this dock that has been dragged across both foreign seas and our native sands.

The fourteenth day, the fourth month, the eightieth year in the third century after the Great Aggression:

The Dean of the male college is profoundly stupid. Unfortunately, he has control of these matters. I have ordered my assistants—former and current students of the college—to collect, measure, and organize the data. Eala, a girl who reminds me very much of myself because she has never been one to stay at her desk, and has never liked poring over papers, is much pleased at the prospect of leading this project.

I have promised her that if she does well, she shall receive a passing grade and all her past misdeeds (taking my balloon for a joyride without asking permission) will be forgotten. I, Beatha, headmistress of the college, have power to do this. So she has begun her work.

In the meantime, I have sent to the western college for a foreign student, one Ji Boong-Do from the Goryeon kingdom, who will help her decipher the strange writing along the side of the dock. Alas, I am no good at languages and the ideographs on the dock are—I have heard—not generally used in the East.

The sixteenth day, the fourth month, the eightieth year in the third century after the Great Aggression:

I am writing these matters now late into the night because I have spent the past two days running hither and thither at the beck and call of those with authority to make me run. Namely, the Queen, May her she forever be honored, and this cursed imperious gloating Dean of the men's college and his male contingents.

How shall I say it? She has decided that the Dean and his colleagues should rule all matters concerning the dock. I had not so much as heard that there was a male contingent until I saw them walking toward us, looking for all intents and purposes as if they were going to put us womenfolk in our place.

When I told the Queen, May she forever be honored, that she had betrayed me and all womankind, she reminded me of my failure in last year's experiments. (It was a terrible explosion, lighting up the sky of the city and causing a three-day-long fire, destroying the financial center of the city, but no deaths occurred.) Apparently, she wants to distance herself from me.

I understand her concern but that she should make the Dean the overseer of this matter, it is a great bother to me. Eala, the dear little thing, approached, dragging that lame left leg of hers, and the scorn on the man's face stirred my ire. She is quite intelligent, Eala, but her appearance is such that others readily assume superiority toward her.

All but one of the scholars treated her with disdain. No one wished to partner with her and even Makna, my other assistant, fled from her side. Fortunately, the Joseon Lord of Doctrines—so these scholars from Goryeo style themselves—walked from the Dean's side to hers. Thus, he has become her partner in this project. The Dean's face was an irritated frown, but he did not rebuke the Joseon Lord. Perhaps this Goryeon scholar is more important than I know.

He must be for he wears those purple and lavender silks as elegantly as the Dean of the male college, a king's son from the Uribe tribe, wears his linen caftans. Boong Do, the Joseon Lord, does cut a sharp figure under all those robes, though. At least, I suspect he does.

The seventeenth day, the fourth month, the eightieth year in the third century after the Great Aggression:

I shall not write the account of the day in detailed conversation. I shall try to summarize the matter. I arrived early to find Eala and Ji Boong Do, the Lord of Doctrines, in a makeshift tent, studying specimens under a microscope.

I hailed them and after they greeted me, they informed me that such specimens contained parasites that were not known to our shores. Ji Boong Do has encountered these specimens before.

I have begun to fear that these microbes will become invasive and who knows what the end of that invasion be? These microbes litter the dock; in addition to other much larger invasive species such as conch, sea urchins, kelps and other such creatures.

I was told by Eala and Boong-Do that they had measured the heat, salinity, acidity of our shores, and the prognosis is not good. These many species will surely multiply. Something, they say, should be done to stop this or our native species will be overrun.

As they spoke, who should appear clothed in his arrogance but the Dean of the male college? I attempted to quickly forestall the conversation, that he would not hear. But my attempt was misguided. Apparently, the dean's own assistants had come to the same conclusion as Eala and Boong-Do; and the Dean is now under the impression that because he was the first to mention the problem...he was the first to discover it.

It was a curious incident. For neither Eala, Boong-Do, nor I seem inclined to challenge his assumption. Perhaps we are merely quietly arrogant and do not wish to argue with those who are obviously proud. Perhaps we are simply guarded. Perhaps we find it unnecessary to claim credit for something so obvious.

The morning continued with the gloating Dean telling us all his discoveries. But then, despite our silence, trouble reared his head. For the Dean is now requiring that we loosen the gates and drag the float within our gates. This, despite the aforementioned problem. I did not agree with him.

Why should our city be contaminated? Although I do not believe contagion or death to be a great possibility, I do consider it best to err on the side of safety. So I spoke my mind. And Eala, and Boong-Do, stood with me. All to no avail. The Dean, it would seem, has great influence with our Queen, May she forever be honored.

And although my voice faded as the day grew longer (it is now completely strained and my voice is nothing more than a harsh whisper) the dock was drawn inside the gates. And now the whole city clambers to see it, is walking atop it and pulling shells and seaweed and other debris from it. It is all quite badly-done.

But I have no say. And Eala and Boong-Do—who, it seems,

have developed quite a friendship—are as distressed as about the Dean's foolishness as I am.

I shall have to speak to Makna. The girl daily disappoints me. For she stood among the Dean's scientists, smiling foolishly as if she believed they were more wise than we. I do not know what I will do with this girl.

The eighteenth day, the fourth month, the eightieth year in the third century after the Great Aggression:

It is a difficult thing to sum up; and so I shall have to write the day's conversations to the best of my ability.

The day rose with drumming and calabash, as is usual for the capital region. Women carried baskets on their backs or their heads. Again, usual matters. The sand blew wildly in the morning wind, covering the huts and the grand houses and even the palace with a thin mask. The Queen's foot soldiers went to the barracks for their morning meal. All quite normal.

But then before sunrise, as I stood upon the rampart of the tower, a spyglass in my hand, I looked out to sea, as is my wont, and saw a sight that made my heart shudder. Out on the waves, rolling toward our shores were multitudinous bodies and body parts. Clothed, unclothed, all pale-skinned.

To my horror, when I looked at the seafront, the sand was covered (Truly, there was no place that was not covered!) with either corpses or birds pecking at them. I immediately telegraphed the Queen, May she forever be honored. I will admit I was at a loss to understand how these bodies could have made it across the sea in relatively good, albeit, non-living shape. Should not the birds of the air and the fish and mammals of the sea have gorged upon them? And when and what, exactly, has happened across the sea to send these bodies to our coast?

§§§

I had not finished telling the Queen my concerns, when she interrupted me to say the Captain of Her Majesty's Sub-mariner has detected a pulse within the depths of our ocean. What this pulse may be, I do not know.

But apparently, no living thing, fish or mammal or bird, can come near it. Apparently, we humans are not affected by it, and the sound not only has prevented fish from eating the bodies, but it has made the waves unusually steadily calm. Though we humans are not immediately affected by this unheard pulse, I had no doubt it would not bode well for us.

I therefore asked the Queen if I should perhaps retrieve my notebook from her, the one confiscated after the explosion. "For," I added, "if such a time existed for my dirigible to be built, it is now."

She informed me that she and the whole city had not yet recovered from my experiments, and had I not heard about the Hindenburg disaster in Europe?"

Try as I could to explain to her that, "I would not be using Hydrogen but another form of gas," she would not hear of it.

While I mused and bewailed my lost notes, I resolved to arrive at the site of the sub-oceanic pulse by balloon. As I prepared myself, and called Eala and Boong Do from their task examining the dock, a telegraph arrived from the Queen, May she forever be honored, stating she had asked the Dean of the male college to join us. He arrived, with three of is adjutants, and Makni (who apparently has no sense) at his side. When I informed them that the balloon was made for no more than four, average-sized women, they proceeded to berate me on my lack of knowledge of the air sciences.

I retorted that perhaps he should have used his own balloon, whereupon he stated that he only used dirigibles, and he had determined that the pulse might harm the instruments of his finely-tuned vehicle.

A balloon being the safest thing, he commanded my balloon to be made ready. We complied but the thing would not rise. Thereupon, Eala, Boong Do, and I were summarily kicked out my own balloon and the journey continued without us.

Now, it appears the Dean and his officers are lost somewhere above the sea, above the dead bodies. I will only say that I miss my balloon, much more than I miss the Dean. But now, all are looking to blame me and Eala. Boong Do and I, are now being joined with the Queen's marines to rescue the Dean's party and to find the source of the pulse.

The nineteenth day, the fourth month, the eightieth year in the third century after the Great Aggression:

Tomorrow, we sail in the sub-mariner Nubia at dawn. The Queen should have spared us a larger vessel but she hearkened to her advisers, men who know nothing at all, who told her the Nubia's small size: "Would make it stealthy."

Make it stealthy. I do not like cramped spaces. I do not like being under water.

True, the sub-mariner is a state of the art machine built by the now disgraced Scientist Prince Cophetua. But it was built for a crew of four, at most six, and was created for oceanographers. I cannot shake a fear. Perhaps it is something one picks up in the ether, or something seen and felt only by the wizened, like ectoplasm. But I sense that Cophetua the mad prince is behind the watery pulses.

Eala and Boong Do have no idea who Cophetua is, or how much our sciences owe to him so I gave them a quick summary of his past actions. To tell of Cophetua's projects, ruses, convictions, and passions would cause my— and their—heads to swim. And my jaws would grow weak with relating all of them.

So I spoke only of his major concerns: how he was a prince from one of the least tribes in our land, a tribe destroyed by the commerce in the Eastern sea; a commerce the Queen winked at because the tribe was not her own, and the international community had paid her well. The Queen, May she forever be honored, is not perfect. She loves travel, good wine, good food, seeming important, and fine shoes. She is not an enlightened woman.

Cophetua, although a recipient of a fine scholarship at the Dean's college, grew to dislike all the evil he saw around him, especially the tribal feuds that decimated his clan. He thought that because he had advanced our country's skill in sonar, radar, electrographs, telegraphs, marine life, and dirigibles, that he would improve the lot of his lowly tribe.

He could not. Some have said he was the Queen's lover. I will admit that after seeing him in the conference in Nairobi, I had hoped to befriend him. With his turban, robes, Grand Bubu, and earrings, he cut quite a dashing figure.

But whether Cophetua was the Queen's lover or not, he was summarily dismissed from the college, where he had become a Master Professor and Scientist Extraordinaire. The last I heard of him, he had left our shores. After I told this to Boong Do and Eala, they glanced at each other, then at me.

"It is he," Boong Do exclaimed.

"I agree," Eala added.

So now they believe as I do. If it is true that Cophetua has done this, the Dean will have much sorrow. For the Dean and Cophetua, to put it plainly, are not friends.

The twentieth day, the fourth month, the eightieth year in the third century after the Great Aggression:

This worse vehicle is than I feared. I have left the wide expanse of the desert and the comfort of my quarters in the Women's College to find myself beset with gears, knobs, tubes: all of them clinking and clunking with disparate rhythms. A relentless cacophony. The passageways are especially trying. In such a cramped space, it is inevitable that embarrassments occur.

We eight passengers walk past each other, our breasts, butts, and faces touching. Only Boong Do and Eala do not seemed to mind it. Indeed, the forced touching of their bodies as they pass each other in this metallic corridor often brings blushes and smiles to their faces. We others simply endure the sweat and bulk of each other and for four days we shall have to endure our collective stink.

I, myself, will have to wear the same kaba until we return. We will arrive at the pulse in two hours, and examine it for three days, rising from the depths and navigating and measuring its circumference. While Professor Balogun does the electrical experiments, Eala and Boong Do will study the effects of the pulse on life forms, Changa and Imaro will examine radiation levels, Valjeanne and I will test for sub-molecular changes, and DjaDja will of course steer. Then, on the fourth day we will return.

As the saying goes, "A Man can plan and plan but the way a thing falls out belongs to the Creator."

We have entered the pulse zone and I find myself, along with Valjeanne and Eala, utterly useless. We have all developed nausea to a most excruciating and disgusting degree.

At first, we surmised that the food had been tainted. But, soon enough, the cause of the nausea became clear. The deeper we entered into the pulse, the greater the nausea grew. Headaches as well. Moreover, the vents and air systems have detected gases tainted with man-made hormones—the kind that are used for fisheries in the Eastern Sea—but at vastly dangerous levels.

I am no fool. Cophetua is behind it.

§§§

I lie here in bed, only slightly comforted by the fact that I am not alone in my distress. The men have decided we women should: "Tough it out til the fourth day and endure all for the sake of science."

I do so dislike enduring.

The twenty-first day, the fourth month, the eightieth year in the third century after the Great Aggression:

I have finally ventured forth out of my bed. I had to. Cophetua
has captured us. I have not yet seen the great man, but his officers —
warriors from his tribe— have declared he will descend within the
hour. In the meantime, they have allowed me the freedom to write my
annals.

I am unsure how this parchment is made but I am more than
half-convinced the ink is octopus ink. Indeed, as I walk about this
vessel—he has given us total freedom—I see much of Cophetua's
ecological inventions, as he calls them.

The external walls of this quite roomy sub-mariner are made of
coral, its tubing of pearlstone, and the glass through which we see the
oceanic world around us of a translucent mother-of-pearl. All here
wander its rooms, mouth agape.

A great table is set before us. Women from Cophetua's tribe
walk back and forth bringing what appears to be foods for his guests. A
large undersea worm, some three meters, long is coiled sizzled on a
large clam shell platter. Kelp and algae abound. I have yet to see the
Dean.

§§§

I lie in bed now. Amazed. (I shall not describe the bed on
which I lie, but I will only say that I am glad to find myself borne by its
whalebone rather than in the whale itself. The mattress itself is made
from down but not the feathers of any bird I have ever seen.)

But on to Cophetua.. What a man! Again, his physique is

worthy of description. I cannot say he is not at all unpleasant. Witty, passionate, handsome, he did much of the talking while we ate. Many of them were answers to questions given by Boong Do and Eala, but most was a kind of manifesto. Cophetua, apparently, wishes to conquer the world.

I am at a lost as to why scientific intelligence and the vengeful desire to conquer worlds often go so hand in hand. But there it is. The prince is not only mad, but…well…mad.

"Chief Cophetua," I said, "I understand your anger against the Queen, and against those who have destroyed your tribe, but you must carefully consider your goals. Already, the governments of Nippon and those in Europa are on your trail. Can you not destroy perhaps only a small bit of the world. When one African nation rises up against another, or experiences internal strife, the western and eastern nations hardly notice. Certainly they rarely interfere. But if you—"

"I am not a child, Beatha," he said. And with that I silenced myself. It seemed futile to go on.

I ate my kelp and worm in silence for the rest of my dinner. The hormonal fluctuations have stopped. At least a certain kind of hormonal fluctuation has stopped. I will admit that, like the Queen, May she always be honored, I have always liked dangerous sociopathic geniuses; and the more Cophetua speaks, the more enthralled I am.

He is a hateful man, however. He does not like Boong Do. And the fact that Boong Do and Eala are apparently in love has not escaped his attention. (How could it? It has not escaped anyone else's?)

The Dean has been alone in something like a little prison, guarded by what appear to be gigantic steam-powered crabs. Whether these are naturally this size or are born from Cophetua's experiments, I cannot say. I only know that now Boong Do and the Dean share a common cell. Boong Do, it appears, will have to bear the sins of all Asia.

Sufficed to say that at the dinner, the Dean did not speak.

The twenty-second day, the fourth month, the eightieth year in the third century after the Great Aggression:

Last night, after I had finished penning my observances, Eala came to my door. She wore a garment of wondrous weave, very like silk but apparently created from the scales and skin of some hitherto unknown underwater fish.

"The great chief came to my door," she said, "I gave him leave to enter and when the door was opened, the great chief stood there, clothed only from the waist down. He held a garment before me." She pointed to her clothing. "This." Then he said to me, "This is reserved for my Queen, and now I have found her."

"Ah," I said, "you have fallen into some trouble."

"That I have."

I do not like the man. Anger is a powerful thing, and Cophetua's rage knows no bound. "It is a strange mix, this passionate love and this desire to destroy one's enemy," I replied.

"But, Mistress, what shall I do? For I fear Boong Do shall not survive Cophetua's ragings."

Oh, prophetic words! For today, I woke to find that Cophetua had set Boong Do and the Dean afloat in the midst of the ocean. It was with much anger that I tried to plead with this angry Chieftain. Poor Eala was beside herself. And, it seemed, the more she wept for her lost lover—for so he apparently is— the more enraged Cophetua became. So all my pleadings were for naught, for Eala would not cease weeping.

So Boong Do and the Dean of the college are no longer with us. We others have been spared. At least for now.

The twenty-third day, the fourth month, the eightieth year in the third century after the Great Aggression:

I am writing this with my head covered under a blanket. I am writing in haste. All about me the echoes of explosions batter us. Indeed, I awakened this morning to a hail of gunfire and mustard gas and was not surprised to hear that we are at war. It is unclear which nation is targeting us—whether it is our own Queen, May her name forever be honored, or the Eastern Empires of Nippon, Ming, or Goryeo; or if they intend to kill us all, disregarding whether some of us are captives or not. But there it is, war:

I have also discovered that while I slept we have moored on some island. The Queen is not as stupid as I had supposed and seemingly has been tracking Cophetua for some time. His lair has been known all this time.

When morning rose, although the sky was gray from explosions, Cophetua ordered that we all decamp from the sub-mariner. Thus, amid all the gunfire, vomiting from mustard gas and other noxious fumes sent down from the Queen's dirigibles, we hastened behind Cophetua while he hurried us toward a large hill.

We ran, not knowing why but because he ordered us to and because gunfire and explosions nipped at our heels. It was then we found that his den was hidden inside the hill. We are somewhat safe but alas, I am now engaged in warfare and am now forced to help my enemy if I am to survive.

The twenty-fourth day, the fourth month, the eightieth year in the third century after the Great Aggression:

I suspect this will be my last jottings. I, who had hoped to leave much more in life than this, must now come to the conclusion that this is the end of my life. Cophetua has notified us that he does not intend to be taken alive, that he will not be hauled in front of the global tribunal for war crimes.

When I told him, calmly, that his crimes are not ours and perhaps he should let us go, he declared he would not. For reasons I know not, perhaps he does not wish to enter the afterlife alone, he is determined that we should die with him. There is no arguing with the man. So I sit here writing or stand pacing, waiting, waiting.

It is a curious thing waiting, not knowing how one will die. Will our captor take us deep into the depth of the hillside? He has, in this place, a conveyance that moves up and down within his lair. One steps inside it at one height and it moves upward or downward through the rock to different heights or depths.

The sea is below us and I have found myself fearing suffocation or drowning in the watery depths. There is another possibility of course. He could bring upon himself and upon us a more merciful death. Who knows? Eala is useless, grieving as she is for Boong Do.

And the others are separated from me, in their own little rooms. I will admit, I would have liked examining this place. I would have liked living the rest of my days as well. But now I am captured by a madman and awaiting the culmination of his insanity.

The twenty-sixth day, the fourth month, the eightieth year in the third century after the Great Aggression:

I have still not died. Although my male colleagues have. It seemed in their manly way they planned an insurrection against Cophetua last night and...it would appear they did not succeed. Cophetua reported this to me with much glee. I am glad we were separated from them because I might have, in my desperation, gone along with their foolish plan.

Cophetua has taken little Eala to his bed. The little thing's shrieks echoed throughout the depths of this hill all night. I wept for her. Yet...I had not thought I would be so glad to have been born as ugly as I am.

This morning, this wretched monster informed us that we are to travel through the shale of the sea mountains across the globe. A strange thought, and one I would not believe possible if I did not believe in the devilish intelligence of my captor. He declares that we will journey to his home in the New World, that on some island in the Western Hemisphere, there is a dead volcano and he has created a home within it.

What terrifying intelligence the mad have! And how indifferent he is to emotions that are not his own!

The twenty-eighth day, the fourth month, the eightieth year in the third century after the Great Aggression:

It is difficult to sleep when one is traveling within a vehicle that pierces through rock. I had managed to fall into an uneasy slumber last night. But this morning, I was rudely pulled from my fitful sleep by Cophetua.

"You must save her," he was shouting.

"Save who?" said I.

"Eala, of course! Last night as I slept, she took a knife to her wrist and even now lies at death's door."

I hastened from my bed to find her lying in a pool of her own blood.

"She is dead," said I. "There is no hope."

The great Captor looked upon me, crestfallen. "No hope?" said he. "Do you think me a man who cannot hope?"

"There is no hope against death," said I.

"Bring her to life again," he ordered.

Such a command coming from any other would be piteous or laughable, but from the mouth of such an insane one, they are terrifying. For what has this man not wrought? What has he not built? For such a one, death is a mean and small thing. I have heard tell of a certain ship's captain who roamed the world in search of a white whale against which he had a grudge. Such a man is this Cophetua.

I sit beside the corpse even now. It has been many hours. I cannot bring her back to life. I have prayed, I have pleaded, I have attempted—as the Englishman Doyle has spoken—to call her soul back into her body. All to no avail.

The twenty-ninth day, the fourth month, the eightieth year in the third century after the Great Aggression:

Cophetua arrived at Eala's room and demanded why she had not returned to life. I told him that he had asked an impossible thing. He lifted my journal and read it while I stood beside the corpse. After reading, he flung it at me. I am to be buried tonight, within the walls of this volcano. I shall be buried alive. I pleaded with Cophetua that he should not kill me. He tells me repeatedly that I will not die, but I will be punished forever for spitefully not returning his beloved to life.

Whither he will take me, I do not know. He said only that I will forever be alone under the sea, with Eala's corpse at my side. "It is a little haven," he said, "a little haven, deep under the sea."

He has declared that I will not need my journal there, and that food is ample although I shall have to venture forth in a sea-suit to gather it for myself. Again, whither he will take me, I do not know.

But he has stated it is deep inside the earth, at the bottom of the mountains of the sea. I will miss the sun over my head and the sand under my feet.

But Cophetua tells me I will get used to it.

THE LION-HUNTERS

JOSH REYNOLDS

The hot wind rolled down the streets of Mombasa, fighting with the cool sea breeze for control of the air. In the stifling alleyways, the tang of spices clung to everything and the cries of the street vendors and sea gulls and stray dogs mingled in an urban roar that made those not used to it cringe.

In the harbor, vessels from a hundred nations rested on the dark waters or drifted lazily above the city, attached to rooftops and specially-provided spires, their props twisting gently in the breeze. Thousands of men—black men and white men and brown men— jostled each other in the streets, looking for gold, ivory and spices. Among those thousands, however, there were eleven who merely waited.

The lion-hunters waited. As if in the tall grasses of home, they waited. Barely breathing, barely thinking. Merely waiting.

"This place smells like oil and shit," one said. "Not clean shit either."

"There is such a thing, Kakuta?" Saitoti Ole Koyati said, as he stroked first the length of the broad-bladed, short-hafted spear resting beside him, then the breech-loading mechanism of the *Answar*-model rifle resting across his bent knees. Lastly, he stroked the scars on his chest, light on dark.

He had a strong heart, beneath those scars, and a better heart than most. It was made of copper and gold, rather than muscle. But every day he was keenly aware that he would have to prove himself worthy of its rhythms.

"Do not get him started," one of the others said, but too late. Kakuta held up a hand.

"Too late Parasayip! Five types of shit, young Saitoti," he began, grinning. "For the education of the uninitiated among us."

Saitoti bristled slightly, and stroked his scars again, thinking calm thoughts. The scars were both a gift and a reminder. If not for a passing Persian doctor, Saitoti would have passed on in childhood, a victim of a weak heart, without the chance to prove himself a man.

After all, that was the reason he was here today. He blinked, pushing the thought aside. "Three. Three at most, surely," he said, egging his companion on.

"No. Five. I have made a study of these things," Kakuta said loftily. "Intensive."

"He is on his knees quite a bit," Mvrudi said. Kakuta shook his spear mock-threateningly.

"Only because your sister begs me, Mvrudi!"

As they bickered, Saitoti smiled and closed his eyes, taking comfort in their voices. The voices of his brothers. Experienced hunters all, tested and blooded in a way that Saitoti had yet to be.

The breeze curled through the alleyway, hot, like he imagined the breath of a lion to be. He swallowed, biting back on the bile that surged up suddenly.

He had never faced a lion before. Seen them, yes. At a distance. But never at the other end of his spear. He touched the weapon, feeling the shape of the blade. Somehow, it didn't feel strong enough to stop the charge of a lion.

The thought didn't sit well. He took a breath, and looked up.

The great shapes of airships wallowed through the blue sky. He could feel the thrum of their great engines, so like the one that rested in his chest, even at this distance.

The rhythms shuddering through his bones comforted him now, as he watched the gas-bag ships block out the sun, and felt suddenly small. He had never been in the city before, and it was overwhelming to a man more used to the wide plains and dense bramble forests of the Wakuafi wilderness.

The others had been to cities, he knew. They displayed none of the nervousness he felt, and he wondered whether or not he would be so brave once he'd made his first kill. Had they been frightened at first, had they felt as nervous as he felt?

He wanted to ask, but he couldn't force the words out. Instead, his hands tightened on his rifle and he checked the ammunition for the third time in as many minutes. He looked up at the mouth of the alleyway they occupied, wondering where their leader was.

Maimai was the most experienced man on this hunt. He was, as far as Saitoti knew, the most experienced man in their tribe. He had killed lions for the Berbers and the Ethiopians, for the Franks and for the Turks.

That was what the Massai did, after all. Kill lions. That was their calling, their gift to other peoples. The Masai killed lions. Four-legged or two-legged, with wings or a scorpion's sting, three-rows of teeth or merely one, it didn't matter. If it was a lion, they would kill it.

That was why they were in Mombasa, crouched in this filthy alleyway, while Kakuta sang a song about shit. Someone, somewhere, wanted them to kill a lion.

It was to be Saitoti's first hunt. He knew he should have felt proud of that fact, but all he felt was worried.

Bare feet scraped across the ground, and as one, the group turned in the direction Saitoti was already looking.

"Stop it," Maimai said, as he entered the alleyway.

"Stop what?" Kakuta said.

"Whatever you were doing."

"Have you found them?" Saitoti said, immediately regretting the eagerness in his voice. He waited for Maimai's rebuke, but the older man didn't so much as look at him.

"We go," Maimai barked.

"Oh good. I was growing bored," Kakuta said, grinning. Saitoti shook his head as the man made an exaggerated gesture. Sometimes he thought Kakuta laughed too much.

They moved through the streets briskly, the citizens of Mombasa knowing enough to step aside. Maimai led them silently through the maze of crowded streets, his face a mask. Saitoti was familiar with the other man's moods, and knew enough to keep his mouth shut, as did the others. Save Kakuta, of course.

"Enough!" Maimai snapped, after yet another of Kakuta's jokes had fallen flat. "There is the Ethiopian." He pointed.

"Safo," Kakuta said, helpfully. Maimai grunted.

"As if it matters."

The man called Safo was waiting for them outside a massive lean-to of Aegyptian silk, his broad body covered in vibrant robes, his thick fingers intertwined on the ivory head of a Frankish walking-stick.

He looked much the same as he had that day in the village, when he had approached the elders on behalf of the Trans-Afriq Railway and its backers.

He had been dressed that day in rich robes and bearing a document with the seal of the *Negusa Nagast* and had come to the home of Saitoti's clan, looking for the best lion-hunters to be had. Eleven men had answered the call, eager to hunt, eager to earn the money the *Negusa Nagast* had promised. Such was how the Masai earned their wealth in the months when the cattle had been sent to market, and the calves were not yet grown.

And Saitoti too had joined, in the end. Maimai had been unwilling at first, but Saitoti's father had convinced him, eager for his son to earn the warrior's marks. No one had asked Saitoti's opinion on such matters. He was not yet blooded, and as such, voiceless.

Why they were meeting here in Mombasa, Saitoti couldn't say. Only Maimai knew, but he hadn't deigned to share the reason with them.

Safo inclined his grizzled head as the men stopped before him, Maimai stepping forward, his hand on the hilt of his sword. Tuareg-made, it did not gleam, but it was no less dangerous for that. A straight length of iron hammered into a wedge and sheathed through a twist of looped leather. Maimai was proud of it, though the elders disapproved. Then, the elders considered any weapon not a spear cheating. Saitoti clutched his rifle and felt that old, slow flush of guilt.

It wasn't his fault that a rifle felt safer than a spear. And a dead lion was a dead lion, wasn't it?

"Well? Where is she?" Maimai said. Saitoti's ears perked up. He glanced at Kakuta, who grinned and winked.

"And a good day to you, mighty hunters," Safo said. Maimai glared at him silently. The Ethiopian sighed and turned, sweeping aside the silk. "Inside," he said. The Masai trooped past him.

The woman was waiting on them within. Seated on a wooden stool, she was dressed in white robes and linen trousers. Her skin was the color of burnt cinnamon; and Saitoti thought that she might be a Berber, or a dark Persian, for he'd never seen a woman quite like her. Her hair was cropped short, Frankish fashion, and wrenched back from her lean face with a comb-clasp of inlaid ivory, and her wrists and ankles were heavy with golden ornaments.

A gun belt hung over the edge of the stool, and the gun itself laid on a prayer rug between her bare feet, disassembled. As they entered, she lifted a smooth ammunition cylinder and carefully cleaned each chamber with a twist of wool. A curved dagger lay nearby, still in its sheath.

"Are these our hunters?" she said, without looking up.

"In the flesh, dear Bahati," Safo said, entering behind them. "The best lion-hunters in Kenia or at least the best the *Negusa Nagast*'s gold can buy."

The woman looked up, her dark eyes flickering over them like a hot breeze. They paused as they came to Saitoti and then moved on. "Are you?"

"We are here," Maimai said, face tight. "That should be answer enough."

"Not quite, but one must make do, one supposes." White teeth flashed between her pale lips. "I am Bahati Mazarin, and there are two lions that I need dead." She sniffed. "But you knew that." She began to re-assemble the pistol. "They are not normal lions, though. Or so they tell me."

"Devils, they say," Maimai said, fingers tapping the hilt of his sword. Saitoti rubbed his chest. His heart seemed to skip its rhythm. No one had said anything about devils to him.

"Maybe. Or maybe something worse." Her eyes caught Saitoti's again, just for a moment. "You may die."

Saitoti wondered if she were speaking directly to him. He had almost died once. He wasn't eager to repeat the experience. His fingers dug instinctively into his chest until they went numb to the knuckle.

"Men die in the hunt," Maimai said curtly. "That is the way of things."

"How stoic," Mazarin said.

Saitoti was only half listening to them. Ten years he'd had his new heart. Ten years it had never done more than hum. Now, it roared like a lion and clawed at him from inside. Was the scar glowing? Was it hot to the touch? Was that what this woman—this Mazarin—was looking at?

Kakuta snapped fingers in front of his face. "Stop listening to that contraption, and start listening to her, young Saitoti," he said, grinning. Saitoti blinked and looked back at the woman. She was sitting on her haunches, a map unrolled on the floor in front of her. Maimai and the others followed suit, sinking down around her.

She tapped the map with a finger. "Here. The attacks are too regular to be motivated by opportunity."

"Lions are greedy," Maimai said thoughtfully. He brushed his fingers across the map, and glanced at Saitoti. "What does your heart say?"

"It says they are denning nearby," he said. It was the obvious answer. Maimai and the others chuckled, and Saitoti felt heat on his cheeks. Kakuta slapped his chest.

"It is wise, your heart."

Saitoti slapped his hand away and rubbed his chest. Mazarin rolled up the map. "Find the lions. Kill them."

"And if they are not lions?" Maimai said. She looked at him. "If they are *Martyaxwar* or *Gryphus*," he clarified.

"Kill them anyway. Especially if they are not lions," she said.

"We would have done that already, if you had not insisted on seeing us," Maimai said sourly. "This was a waste of our time and your money."

"No. Complaining is a waste of time," Mazarin said. "Besides, if we are to take the train out there, you needed to be here, yes?"

"We?" Saitoti blinked, suddenly realizing that he'd spoken. The woman looked at him and smiled.

"Oh yes. I am coming with you, of course."

They left Mombasa that day, on the train. Safo did not accompany them, though he did confer with Mazarin on the steps of the train. Maimai glared at them suspiciously, but said nothing.

The train itself was designed in the Frankish pattern, an iron worm that chugged along steel lines. Another of Emperor Menelik's innovations, the railway was an iron road cutting from Alexandria to Mombasa; a joint effort funded by Aegyptian and Ethiopian concerns.

Too, it was an intentional thumb of the nose to the masters of the Iberian Rail-line slithering its way southward through Dyazer. Saitoti's people appreciated such gestures, especially from kings, and the *Negusa Nagast* of Ethiopia was fond of making them, especially where the Spanish were concerned.

Maimai had not argued with the woman, surprisingly, about riding the train. Saitoti said as much, sitting on the roof of the train with Kakuta.

"He knows better. Most would, I think," Kakuta said, leaning back on his elbows. He was not so much older than Saitoti, but old enough. "She is not only the *Negusa Nagast*'s woman, you know." He said it slyly.

Saitoti frowned. "No?"

"Heh. No. She was at Gonder, when we fought the Franks—" The Spanish, Saitoti knew. Kakuta and Maimai had been among the warriors whom the Ethiopians had hired as scouts. "Working for the English."

"The English?"

"They live thataway," Kakuta said, gesturing lazily. "They hate the Franks as much as we do. Or, rather, as much as the Ethiopians do."

"More, if anything," Mazarin said. The woman had joined them on silent feet. Her gun belt was low on the swell of her hip, and the curved dagger was thrust through a colorful scarf slung around her waist. Kakuta fell quiet as she sank into a crouch beside them. "I do not serve the English, though."

"Then who?" Saitoti said. She smiled at him.

"Myself. As ever. The *Negusa Nagast*, at the moment." She watched the scenery move past. "Your heart. I can hear it."

Kakuta laughed, and Saitoti forced his hands to remain at his sides. She looked at him. "It is artificial, yes?" He wasn't surprised she knew. Artifice was becoming more common, especially in the south. There was a man in Ulundi who had a spine made of sheathed brass, he'd heard.

"A lion's heart," Saitoti said, so quietly the wind almost took his words away. He didn't know why he'd said it. She didn't seem the type to be impressed.

§§§

And in truth, it wasn't that impressive a story. As a boy, his head shaved save for its nape to brow baby strip, Saitoti had pitched forward at play, his heart splitting in his chest.

The Persian, a jolly man, heavy and hook-nosed with delicate fingers, had been passing through the lands of his clan, coming from the kraals of Zululand to the Barbary Coast, studying the medicines and mechanisms of Afriq. Or so he'd claimed.

When Saitoti's heart had burst, the Persian had scooped him up from the dust and brought him indoors. Had, according to those who had seen it, cut his tiny chest open and spread his thin ribs with those graceful fingers, all the while running a current from a tiny battery he carried with him in his pack into Saitoti's body.

And then he had scooped out Saitoti's heart and replaced it with a new one: one that was copper and iron and had a red eye in its center and was warm to the touch, even through flesh and hard bone. A lion's heart, the Persian had called it, seeming surprised, they said, that it had worked.

You must be worthy of its rhythm, the Persian had said, in awe of his own craft, *you must be worthy of its gift.*

§§§

"Curious phrase," Mazarin said. "I knew a man—a Persian, named Nadir—who built beautiful things, mostly toy lions." She looked at Saitoti through narrowed eyes. "He works for the Spanish now."

"Making toys?" Saitoti said and remembered the clockwork toys the Persian had crafted for the village children, things of wood and wire that moved in expanding circles. Mostly, they looked like lions.

"You are famous you know."

"What?" Saitoti blinked. She nodded.

"Oh yes. Your heart, rather; it was one of the first such operations."

He looked down at his chest and touched it wonderingly.

"It is something to think about, yes?" She stood gracefully and sauntered back towards the ladder that led between the train cars. Saitoti watched her go.

Kakuta whistled and said, "I heard she was looking for us, you know? She sent that fat Ethiopian to our tribe especially. That is what Maimai thinks."

Saitoti looked at his friend. "Why would she do that?"

Kakuta was silent for a minute, then, he said, "Well, we are the best, are we not? Our people capture the *Gryphus* for the Turkish zoos regularly; and Maimai once killed a *Martyaxwar* in order to sell its cubs to the English. A great hunt that one, I must admit."

Saitoti thought of the simian-faced, scorpion-tailed lion of the deserts and shuddered. He had never seen one in the flesh, but he had heard the stories. He wondered if that was what they were hunting. If anything, it sounded less likely to be stopped by a spear than a regular lion.

"And you are famous. Saitoti Lion-Heart, eh? Eh?" Kakuta continued.

Saitoti had no reply, though he did wonder. He couldn't help it.

He hadn't been on a hunt before. He was neither blooded nor experienced in the ways of the hunt.

Why had the woman come? She was no hunter either, was she? Which begged the question, if she was no hunter, what, exactly was she?

"Why can't the Ethiopians kill their own lions," he said, without thinking.

Kakuta looked at him. "Be glad they don't. It is our place to hunt, as it is theirs to ply the seas and connive and pay us our just due."

"They are just lions!" Saitoti said, with more heat than he'd intended. "Why must we do this?"

"Because they want it done properly," Maimai said. Saitoti started. Maimai crouched nearby, watching the scenery roll past. "I saw the woman come up here. What did she say?"

"Nothing of interest," Kakuta said, silencing Saitoti with a look.

Maimai looked at them, his eyes narrowed. He grunted. "Good. Do not listen to her."

"Why?" Saitoti said.

"She sent men into death at Gonder," Maimai said. He stared hard at Saitoti. "She spent them as Kakuta spends bullets. She is a witch, and such women shorten your life."

"I am hardly that terrible a shot," Kakuta protested.

"You are," Maimai said. He looked at Saitoti. "Remember boy, all that matters is the hunt. Think of nothing else and you will see a second one."

"What if I do not want to see even the first one?" Saitoti murmured. Maimai grunted, but gave no sign he had heard. Saitoti looked at him. He had never noticed quite how many scars the older man carried. Each one was the legacy of a hunt long gone.

Would his body look the same, in the years to come? Would he even live long enough to reach that point?

The remainder of the journey to Tsavo was uneventful, and for that Saitoti was grateful. The train pulled into a tumble-down station, greeted by Ethiopians in military dress. Mazarin spoke to them quietly as Maimai gathered the others.

Saitoti looked around. The engineering camp was a lazy sprawl of tent and lean-to's. There were a few clapboard buildings, flying the flag of Ethiopia and the silk banners of the assorted Aegyptian Princedoms. It was supposed to be a monument to the powers of those kingdoms.

But the Trans-Afriq seemed doomed to failure now, stalled on a simple stretch of the Tsavo River, caught in a trap as old and as wild as the land.

They came at night: stinking of deep places and sour meat, padding through the grass, two low, lean shapes, tawny and hungry. They navigated the *bomas* and vaulted the fences. Fire did not deter them and bullets did not stop them. Every night, men died, dragged out through the thorn-barriers and into the wide black of Kenia, with only the stars to witness what came next.

Saitoti thought it an appropriate enough occurrence for Tsavo. It was a place of slaughter. His ancestors had killed the Kamba people there, down to the last boy, or so his mother had said. The powder of their bones mingled with the sand of the river banks and fed the soil.

When the Arabs had run their human cattle to the coast, they had come through Tsavo. Bodies had fallen, walked to death, and were left for the beasts by the hundreds or perhaps thousands. Thus, the inhabitants of Tsavo had come to enjoy the taste of men. Or so it was said.

Looking at the place, it wasn't hard to see the truth in the name. The men Saitoti could see had a hunted, nervous look to them. Every creak of wood or clatter of the bramble fences provoked abrupt reactions.

"Can you smell it?" Kakuta murmured.

"What?" Saitoti said.

"Fear," Maimai said, fingers wrapping around the hilt of his sword. Mazarin turned towards the group.

"They've attacked again." Her face was grim. "Last night." Saitoti looked at the soldiers, who stood clustered together. Only one night since men had been dragged screaming into the tall grass, leaving only a trail of hot red memory to mark their passage. One day since the devils of Tsavo had last fed.

"A fresh trail, then," Maimai said.

"A fresh trail," the woman replied. And it was. The trail proved easy to follow.

Ridiculously easy, even. The lions did not hide their presence, did not slink. They charged like trains through the night, bellowing and tearing the earth. Their tracks crossed and re-crossed, marking the story of their nights.

The Aegyptians were convinced the beasts were twin *afrits*, come to plague them for their assorted sins. Twice now, the workers had almost given up entirely. Twice now, they had lain traps and been given over to wailings when the lions had burst through, unharmed and ever-hungry.

A child could have read the trail of their rampage. The lions moved in circles, re-crossing their own path, wider and wider from the central point, never deviating, never changing, as regular as the rhythm in Saitoti's chest.

The bodies of the dead were ruins of cracked bone and rotting meat. Mangled, but otherwise untouched, rended unto death, but no further. Maimai's face was stiff as they followed the streaks of red into the tall grass. Saitoti wanted to ask if this were normal, but he didn't.

He didn't honestly want to know the answer. He rubbed his chest in annoyance. It was beginning to hurt. A flash of brilliant pain that hummed along the lengths of him, making lights dance behind his eyelids and glisten beneath his skin. He could taste the tang of scorched metal, just at the base of his tongue.

It hurt, but that just let him know that he still lived. He smiled slightly, but only for a moment.

The lions did not eat what they killed, and that alone set the hunters' souls a-quiver in ways that the rumored brutality and so-called invincibility of their prey had not. Devils were less than frightening at a distance, and what did men like these know about lions anyway?

But this was something else. This wasn't a story. Saitoti caught Kakuta whispering a prayer as they examined the path of crushed grass and bloated flies.

"Normally, they take their prey with them," Mazarin said. Saitoti swallowed, thinking of what that meant. He did not want to be here.

"Why do you think they left them this time?" he heard himself say.

"Lazy?" Kakuta said, running his fingers across his scalp.

"Lazy lions always turn man-eater."

"The den will not be far from here," Maimai said. He looked at the woman, who was standing off a little way. "We travel swiftly."

"I can keep up," Mazarin said.

"If you cannot, we will not stop." Maimai rose. The group spread out and then began to run with the easy, ground-eating lope that had made the Masai feared as hunters and soldiers. Mazarin followed at a slower pace, but did not lag behind despite the weight of the Frankish-style pack she carried.

As they moved, Saitoti closed his eyes, listening to the thrum of his heart. It seemed to speed up as they moved farther from the *bomas* and the bodies. He thought of Mazarin's words on the train. He thought of the Persian doctor and his toy lions.

He thought again of the spear in his hand, and how now, even the rifle he carried in his other seemed not at all comforting. He thought of the bodies and of the awful, terrible power on display there.

Devils were mockers, his mother had said. He pushed the thought aside and concentrated on running.

As hunts went, Saitoti was finding his first to be uneventful. They followed the trail until it became less obvious. It carried them through scrub grottos and blade-sharp grass. For three days and three nights, they moved. They heard no roars, no shrieks. The savannah was silent, almost oppressively so. The others grew nervous, whispering among themselves. Kakuta made more and more jokes, and they all fell flat. And Mazarin watched Saitoti.

He could feel her eyes on him. Boring into him, as if she were trying to pull apart his heart and see what made it work. She watched him every night, without fail.

Or maybe it wasn't his heart at all that interested her. He began to wonder if she could see his fear, as it coiled and crawled through him, growing stronger with every silent dawn. He was so careful to hide it from the others, but her eyes were as keen as the edge of Maimai's sword.

By the third night, he had grown sick of it. "Why do you watch me?" he said, louder than he had intended. Kakuta made a filthy joke, and several of the others laughed.

"Do you want to know why I came?" she replied, ignoring his question.

"It is the only way he will learn," Kakuta said, clapping his hands. Saitoti glared at him, and the other man subsided, laughing. Mazarin ignored the laughter and pulled her dagger from her sash.

Using the tip, she carved a crude map into the dirt. "Here we are. And here is the railway. And here up, here are the Spanish."

"What's that?" Saitoti said.

"That is a rock," Mazarin said, plucking the offending object up and tossing it aside. "This is the Iberian line. And this is the Tsavo River. You see?"

"The lines cross." Saitoti rocked forward on his heels. Mazarin smiled.

"Yes. There are certain interests that want to see Menelik's grand undertaking to fail. They want to see the iron road controlled not by Africans, but by Franks." She sat back and shoved her dagger back into its sheath. "And so we come to the lions which are not lions."

"Ridiculous," Maimai said, not looking at her. "We saw the bodies."

"Maybe they are or maybe they are something else. Who

knows?" She shrugged. Saitoti peered at her, realizing that she had not yet answered his question.

"The Franks control the lions?" he said.

"Perhaps they do or perhaps not." Mazarin spread her fingers like claws and drew them through the soil, obliterating the map. "A friend of mine, a very smart woman, says that once is coincidence. Twice is bad luck. Three times, however, is enemy action." She stood. "And the *Negusa Nagast* has many enemies."

On the fourth day, Saitoti's heart stuttered and he almost fell, though no one seemed to have noticed. They were all too busy looking at the cave. It was a stinking slope, bored into the red rock of the hills, a winding bowel-length of passages.

Maimai and the woman were first up, he with his rifle, and she with her pistol. When Saitoti got to the top of the slope, she stopped him with her palm on his chest.

"How do you feel?" she said.

"I am fine."

"Are you sure?" Her fingertips dug into his chest, and he stepped back.

"Yes." He said it, despite the way his heart was rattling behind its cage of bone. "Yes, I am fine."

"It is your first hunt, I hear," she said softly.

"Yes." Saitoti felt a rush of bile and choked it down.

She smiled at him, but said nothing more.

The breeze entered the tunnel mouth with them and became a shriek as they descended with their spears and rifles ready. Maimai, as was his right as leader of the hunt, was first, sword in hand.

They found the first bodies not far from the entrance, scattered about, left to the mercies of the maggots. Limbs wrenched free and strewn about, ribs gaped wide and skulls sunk into themselves like crushed eggs. The stench was heavy on the close air of the caves.

"No shit," Kakuta said softly. "No dung, no scent of piss." Saitoti nodded. There was only the odor of blood and something else. Something none of them were able to place.

In the guts of the tunnel was the cave. It stank worse than any other place, and there were things on the walls that hurt the eye to see. Signs cut into the rock.

"Those are newly made," Mazarin murmured.

Maimai spat. "Witchcraft," he said. The others began to murmur among themselves. Saitoti saw filthy stains on the rocks, old blood, older even than the ravages the lions were undertaking. He swallowed.

Mazarin moved around the cave, not touching the walls, but looking at them closely nonetheless. "Alchemy, maybe," she said, her voice startling Saitoti. "The Franks and the Arabs think calling magic a science makes it easier to control."

"Same thing," Kakuta muttered.

Mazarin leaned towards the wall and then straightened. "A spear, please."

One of the others stepped forward, his spear extended. The woman took it and thrust the blade into the wall. Canvas tore and she swung the spear aside, yanking down a camouflaged curtain. She handed the spear back as she examined what had been revealed.

The two men had been dead for months, and in the hot, dry cave they had withered to brown sticks. Despite this, Saitoti could tell from their clothes what, if not who, they had been while alive.

"Franks," he said quietly. Maimai spat again.

"Definitely witchcraft," he said.

"Spanish," Mazarin said. She turned, looking at the ugly symbols on the walls with renewed interest. "A spirit-cage," she muttered.

"Look at this," Kakuta said, using his spear to dislodge another tarp—one Saitoti had mistaken for a rock at first glance. Kakuta flipped it aside, and stepped back with a curse.

The lion was dead, or, at the very least, not alive. It was a skeleton of brass and steel, with crimson eyes that glared out blindly at them.

"Is that—?" Saitoti said. He'd seen such things before, on a trading trip to Adua; then, a few years later, to Gonder, driving cattle. White men's toys, dressed like men, but not. Steam and gear powered click-men. Like the trains, only shaped not like worms, but men and animals. Kakuta had sworn that the Ethiopian nobles hunted clockwork animals for sport.

"*Corpus mechanicum,*" Mazarin murmured.

"What did she say?" Kakuta said. He found another tarp, and beneath it, a roll of bedding and other signs of residence. "Someone has been living here!"

"It doesn't matter. We need to get outside," Maimai, ever prudent, said. Saitoti agreed. The caves were not a place to face such beasts as these were proving to be. "We camp outside," he continued.

"No. They are here, or they soon will be," Mazarin said. She was looking at Saitoti as she said it. "I know what they are." She gestured to the lion. "What that is. There are things that must be done. We must stay."

"And if they are here?" Maimai grunted. "I would rather face them out there than in here!"

"Why? So they can pick you off? We—"

Saitoti's heart had begun to thunder then as the two argued. It roared and that roar was answered, echoing from wall to wall— a hideous sound, amplified to demonic proportions in that tight space. He thought of the train, and the sound it had made, and then his brothers were screaming.

Maimai's head vanished in a burst of red, popped like a ripe fruit. His sword fell from nerveless fingers. The woman scrambled aside, her pistol barking. Sparks popped and whined as her bullets struck their target.

Rifles thundered as something dark and terrible surged forward, twisting with un-feline agility. There was a screech of metal on metal, a smell of ozone and sparks crested in a flaring trail as claws slammed down on the next man, breaking him and tossing him among them. Spears crashed against an impossibly hard hide, shivering to splinters.

The second lion was already behind them, then. Saitoti whirled, firing blind as the shape loped towards him. It was wrong, that shape. The angles and contours that every hunter learned to recognize were not there. More sparks, and his rifle was broken and ripped from his hands. He fell, borne under in its rush, forgotten.

Kakuta bore the brunt of its charge, his body disintegrating as if struck by a cannon ball. Laughing Kakuta, laughing no more. Saitoti could only watch, paralyzed by a cold weight wrapped around his limbs.

He wanted to run, needed to run, but he couldn't move. Not

even to close his eyes.

Two lions slaughtered eleven men in twelve minutes, reaching and ripping and roaring through them, ignoring bullets and blades. The only hesitation came when a spear had glanced across a wide chest, tearing through the hide, revealing—what?

Saitoti had an impression of crimson light, dripping from that wound. It was a hot glow that reminded him of forge-light or the boiler of a train. The lions moved towards him, jaws wide, their eyes bright-too bright-and their voices like the growl of wild water.

He stood, shakily, spear extended, waiting. It was not going to be enough. Not this flimsy thing of wood and steel.

They stopped, growls rumbling deep in their throats. The darkness of the cave seemed to cling to them, hiding all but their outlines from him. They shuddered, their growls changing pitch. His heart lurched and burned.

And then, after a moment, they were gone. He sank to his knees quietly, his heart pounding in his ears. Something cold pressed to the back of his skull, and he choked on his own sigh of relief.

"Well, that was interesting." The voice had a Barbary accent. "Drop the spear."

Saitoti tossed the spear to the floor. "On your feet." He rose slowly and turned. The man holding the pistol was a Moor, lighter-skinned than Saitoti, with an Arabic cast to his features. He wore light robes over a khaki uniform, and had a saber belted at his waist.

"They hesitated. They never hesitate. Why?" the Moor said. Saitoti swallowed.

"I don't know."

"How did you find this place?"

"We tracked the beasts."

"A shame," the Moor said.

"What?" Saitoti said, looking at the dead. Why had they left him alive? He looked at the withered bodies in the alcove. And the other lion, laying where it had been hidden, silent and stiff, like stone, skinless and gleaming.

"It is a shame, because that means I must move camp. The Ethiopians hired you, of course. Or maybe it was the British?"

"You work for the Franks," Saitoti said, resenting the accusation. The Moor grinned.

"I work for he who pays me, boy. My skills are valuable. I have worked for caliphs and kings alike. The Franks pay better than most, I admit."

"Why do this? Was the railroad so important?" Saitoti said, his eyes locked on the black maw of the pistol.

"Who is to say? They wanted it stopped, but not in such a way as to seem as if they had wanted such." The Moor shook his head. "They think in circles, these Franks. It is all politics, boy, and of no importance to either of us—you least of all." He raised the pistol, but hesitated. "Still, why?"

The Moor cocked his head. He slid forward with serpentine grace and shoved the barrel of his pistol beneath Saitoti's chin. The Moor pressed his ear to Saitoti's chest.

"Quiet, please," he said. Saitoti said nothing. His eyes widened slightly as he caught sight of something moving beneath the carnage that littered the cave.

"Irregular rhythms indeed," the Moor said as he stepped back, frowning. "Your heart is artificial, yes?"

Saitoti said nothing.

The pistol whipped across his face, staggering him. The Moor clucked his tongue. "I can simply pry the answer from your entrails, boy. Why not make it easier on both of us?"

Saitoti glared at him, mentally daring the man to shoot. Better a bullet than the claws of those things.

"Ha," the Moor said, softly. His eyes sparkled. "You see that?" he said, gesturing to the insensate lion. "I bought three, for my purposes. But my employers only gave me two to fill them." He swept a hand towards the alcove, and the mummified bodies. "Of course, those two didn't realize what I intended, but so far their masters don't seem to mind." He chuckled. "Neither do they for that matter."

"Witch," Saitoti said. He packed as much hatred into the word as he could hope to keep the man's attentions on him, and away from the growing movement behind him.

"No, I am a scholar." The Moor frowned. "And what I do is art. Years," he said. "It took me years to perfect the process of transference. Combining the alchemy of the western *Nahaul* with the sciences of the lost *Seljuks* was no simple thing—to tie a mind and soul to a carcass of iron." He gestured sharply and snapped, "as if a hedge-witch or skin-wearing shaman could do that!"

He looked at Saitoti with a keen eye. "And you will be my next experiment." He took aim with the pistol. "I wonder what effect your heart will have on the transference, eh? Will it serve you better-"

The shot was loud, in the quiet of the cavern. Saitoti fell to the floor as the Moor toppled forward, half of his skull gone. Then, Mazarin was standing over him, covered in blood and viscera, her smoking pistol dangling from her hand.

"Damn," she said hoarsely.

"You live," he said, rising slowly. It came out as an accusation.

"I pulled a dead man over me." She shrugged. "That's my explanation. What's yours?"

"What?"

"Why didn't they kill you?" She eyed him shrewdly. The pistol rose slightly.

His fingers rubbed his scars. He looked down at the Moor.

"Yes," she said, and he wondered, for a moment, whether she was talking to him. "Exactly," she said as she gestured with the pistol. "It's good to know that I'm not a complete idiot, unlike your leader

The thought of Maimai made him feel slightly ill. He looked around, then squatted and pried the sword from his friend's hand, ignoring Mazarin. It was heavier than he'd expected, and hadn't done Maimai much good, but he felt better with it.

"The *hidalgos* are tricky," she murmured, "Very tricky." She looked at him sadly. "I thought you would protect them. I had hoped…" She shook her head. "But obviously not, and now there's nothing for it but to do it ourselves."

"Do what?" Saitoti asked. He turned the sword, examining it. Maimai had not even gotten to swing it. Saitoti closed his eyes.

"Why, finish the hunt, of course."

His eyes shot wide. "What?"

"They are heading back to the camp, to kill more. Or maybe to kill everyone, now that we've found their hidey-hole. I cannot allow that."

"Two of us, against *them?*" Saitoti said, his fingers tightening on the sword hilt. He thought of running. Of returning to his clan. Of telling them...what?

There was nothing to tell. Men had died at the claws of lions before. The hunt continued, regardless. Until one or the other was dead.

But these weren't lions. And he wasn't a man. Not yet. "You knew," he said, gesturing with the sword. "You *knew!*"

"I knew nothing. I suspected." Her face twisted. "A man in Cairo mentioned that a merchant in Morocco had purchased three artificial lions from a well-known *deghan*." She kicked the Moor's body. "Not toys, but something else."

Saitoti's hand found his scars. "No."

"It is the nature of the Game to war through proxy. Sometimes those proxies are men. Other times..."

"You used us!" he said.

"Of course." She shrugged and flipped open the cylinder of her pistol. "I told you that you were famous, Saitoti. And now you will be more famous still."

"We could not stop them," he said.

"No. We couldn't. *You* can," she said, briskly reloading her pistol. Spent brass shells pattered to the floor. "Do you know why they hesitated?"

"I..." He looked down at the Moor. Then up, his face set. She nodded.

"It happens with such things. They are listening, in their way, to our blood and flesh. But you confuse them. And that which confuses them, they ignore. They hesitate." She flicked her wrist, popping the cylinder back in place. "That means you have a chance."

"And you?" he said, after a moment.

"I stay here." She glanced over her shoulder at the withered corpses which were glaring at them from their alcove. She looked down at the Moor and spat on the body. "There are things that must be done."

"What things?"

"I can remove their souls. Or set them free, if you prefer that terminology. Break the cages that this filth," she kicked the body, "created."

"You are a witch?" he said. "Like him?"

"No, merely well-traveled. It takes time though, days, perhaps. If you can stop them first..." She met his eyes. "How fast can you run?"

"I don't want to die," he said hoarsely. He closed his eyes and clutched the sword so tightly that his nails pricked the meat of his palm. "I don't."

"No one does." Mazarin looked at him steadily. "But it's a rare man who can choose the time and place." She placed a hand to his chest. "You have a lion's heart, Saitoti. That's what they said. And I never once saw a lion afraid to hunt."

He opened his eyes. And his heart roared.

§§§

He ran through the heat of the day and the chill of the night without stopping. In his chest, his heart was as hot as it had ever been. It was a spinning engine, spitting sparks into his veins, pushing him faster, and faster. The ghosts of his friends ran with him, though he tried not to look at them.

Fear still clung to him, weighing him down, making him slow, but he ignored it. He had not chosen this hunt, but then, no man chose his first hunt.

It took him three days to return to the river and the camp, and when he arrived, there was no sign that any attacks had occurred in the interval. As if the beasts were waiting to see if there were any more hunters, perhaps.

The thought chilled him, as he squatted in the grass, listening to his heart, as Mazarin had bid him. Those rhythms comforted him now, easing the fatigue that tested the edges of his endurance. Saitoti waited, and watched.

He watched men—Ethiopians and Aegyptians and Sudanese—lay track and fell trees in the distance, crafting yet another link in the road that would connect the world, as in Menelik's great vision.

His hand brushed the scars that covered his heart instinctively, taking comfort. He knew no fear, because his heart could not bear it. He had not died because his heart would not let him. It pulsed beneath his touch, comforting him.

The grass rustled in a warm breeze. He shifted his weight, ignoring the flies that swarmed him, ignoring the distant ache of cramping muscles. None of the workers knew he was there. As far as they knew, he and his fellows were out hunting the lions, confronting them in their bloody den.

Kakuta's face drifted across the surface of his mind. He could hear their voices in his ears, carried on the breeze. Their ghosts crowded at the edge of his vision, warning him.

He shook himself. The sky overhead was purple. The savannah grass made a sound like spears being shaken. His hand was pressed to his chest. His heart hummed beneath his palm. The scar tissue felt flushed and warm.

He wondered what Mazarin was doing in the caves. She had been dragging the mummies from their makeshift crypt as he left. Then he pushed the thought away. It didn't matter. All that mattered was the here and now.

All that mattered was the hunt.

Saitoti hefted the rifle, one of the few undamaged ones he'd managed to scavenge, and sighted down the barrel. The sounds of hammers ringing on rail spikes reached his ears. The sun was setting, but the work continued.

Good.

His people were herders as well as hunters. One fed into the other. Lions liked nothing more than herds of complacent cattle. And cattle, for their part, relied on the instincts of the herdsman to stay out of the jaws of the lion.

To lose a cow, after the hunt had begun…well, that was unacceptable by all the laws of his people. Hunters could be replaced. But a cow was too valuable to lose.

What was it Maimai had said? *"Men die in hunts. That is the way of things."*

His heart was roaring now, rattling his ribs. They were close. He did not want to die. Not the way Maimai and Kakuta and the others had died. He sank back down, lowering the rifle. No, he did not want to die, but neither did he want to live with the shame of his fear.

It had been growing in him, all this time, stalking him, even as the lions had stalked their prey. Maybe they were the same. The Moor had created the lions to cause fear, after all.

The stink of blood crept through the grass. The horn of the railway foreman called out, summoning the workers from their tasks.

He turned slowly, head barely raised, scanning the top of the grass, looking for a telltale flash of movement.

They had moved so fast in the caves. So fast. Faster than any lion should move. Reflexively, he checked the rifle. Blood had dried on the barrel. Whose blood?

His heart screamed a warning and he saw the first of them, the bolder of the two, skinning low through the grass. He could hear it, like the rumble of a train in the distance.

Saitoti fired without thinking, the rifle bucking in his hands. He worked the slide with practiced speed, expelling the spent brass, summoning another from the boxy clip, firing again. With a shriek like metal scraping metal, the lion turned, curling, darting for him.

He fired once more as it curved over him, knocking him off his feet. The rifle spun away as he hit the crushed grass, the breath slapped clean out of his lungs. He groped blindly, his fingers touching the haft of the spear as he rolled onto his belly and pushed himself up.

The lion was watching him. Its head hung low, tail lashing. Its eyes were wrong, too bright. It did not move, did not twitch, beyond the tail.

And then, it was on him in the blink of an eye, its weight driving him backwards. His spear scored a black wound up its belly and across the haunch but it didn't show any sign of pain.

Its eyes were bright and empty of all save light and the reflection of his face. Its breath was hot but not foul, beyond taint of the dried blood etched on its fangs and muzzle. Deep, down deep at the bottom of its maw, something glowed red.

Saitoti grunted as the weight of the lion settled on him and something cracked in his shoulder. The fur had parted where his spear had scraped it, fraying like an old robe. The lion watched him, jaws parted, as if listening.

Saitoti tightened his grip on the spear. His collarbone creaked and a hiss of pain escaped him as he jerked himself to the side, sliding one shoulder out from under the lion's claws, tearing his arm to the bone in the process. He slammed the spear home into the space between the lion's ribs. There was a sound like cloth tearing and then the spear point caught on something metal, something that moved. A burst of compressed heat washed over his hand, raising blisters across his thumb and forearm.

The lion jerked up, roaring in hollow agony. Saitoti's heart spasmed in sympathy and he jammed the spear in, forcing it until the haft cracked in his hands and snapped free of the head.

Bucking and spinning, the lion tumbled away from him, its roars descending into muffled echoes. It spun in a widening circle and then staggered, toppling over. A sound like steam escaping a cooking pot rose up and its limbs jerked mindlessly.

Clutching his scalded hand to his chest, Saitoti climbed to his feet and reached awkwardly behind him to unsheathe Maimai's sword from the makeshift scabbard. It slid free silently and he lurched forward, still unused to its weight.

His heart. It had been listening to his heart, just as Mazarin said. The lion's twitches slowed. Whatever drove it was winding down. The end of the spear blade protruded slightly and it wriggled as if it were being struck repeatedly.

There was no time to wait for Mazarin's magic. No time for fear. No time for anything but the hunt.

Saitoti brought the sword down on the lion's neck. Once, twice.

Again and again, metal ringing on metal, the lion skin flapping and curling away as he swung the sword up and down until sparks flew and the sword's edge was notched beyond redemption.

The head finally rolled free on the tenth swing. It revealed a cage of metal, and inside, a heart. A raw, red lump of gristle, trapped in a sphere of rings, whose perpetual motion slowed as Saitoti watched, then, stopped.

Sweat rolled down Saitoti's face and his hand throbbed. He turned as the grass snapped and cracked in the direction of the rail-camp. The second lion had continued on its mission. His heart burned, and he felt as if his insides were aflame.

One lion was all that was required to make a boy a man, to make a herder into a hunter. What did two lions make you?

Dead, Kakuta's ghost whispered, and Saitoti felt a frenzied grin split his face.

He began to run, sword held extended and low, his wounded hand pressed to his heart. His heart began to snarl as the *bomas* came into sight. He spun, pain shooting through him, and the lion was there, only a few feet from the thorns, crouched and ready to leap.

Saitoti staggered and planted the sword, leaning against it. The lion rose from its crouch. Saitoti stepped back, raising the blade. He could hear nothing but his heart. The hum had risen to a howl, and his skin felt tight. The fire had burned all fear from him, and the ghosts of his friends drifted on the wind. Free.

This lion, like its brother, seemed confused by his presence, as if his heart spoke to its own.

Maybe, as such things went, it did. The rhythm of the lions was not so different from his. They had been created to hunt, even as

Saitoti's people had been.

It paced towards him, unhurried, but implacable. Things moved inside him, and he knew that if it leapt first, he would not survive, heart or no.

Past the thorns, men wandered. They had yet to notice the danger, like cattle in a pen. Secure in the knowledge that the herdsman was there, somewhere.

Saitoti lunged, driving the sword forward, digging the notched tip for the red-lit space behind the forest of teeth that opened as if in welcome. The lion sprang to meet him, paws spread. His shoulder connected with its belly as the sword slid between its teeth, the tips of the steel fangs gashing open his knuckles.

He jerked his hand back as it bit down.

He released the sword and fell as the lion leapt over him, skidding and turning, tail lashing. Red eyes blazed as it tore the ground in its hurry.

It made a coughing sound, the hilt of the sword jutting between its jaws. Red eyes blazed crazily as it stumbled towards him, shaking its head.

He spread his arms. He felt neither fear, nor regret. Kakuta and Maimai had been right. This was what the Masai did. And it was not such a terrible thing after all.

The lion gave a squawking roar and charged. Saitoti flung himself at it, his fingers reaching for the hilt. Catching it, he forced himself against it, even as the lion crashed down on top of him.

He tasted blood and bile, and the heat of the lion burned the skin of his arms and belly as it settled on him, eyes dimming. It seemed to shudder as whatever life-force had driven it fled.

Would their ghosts wander, as his people said the spirits of failed hunters often did? Or would Mazarin's magic free them?

Voices rose from within the camp and a horn was sounded. The cattle grew restless. Saitoti wondered, as he collapsed back, unable to move the beast off of him, whether Mazarin was right, and he would be famous for this.

He laid in the grass, bleeding from his wounds, his broken bones rubbing against one another, waiting for the men of the railway to find him. Not thinking of anything-of his heart, or of the Persian, or of the secrets of the killers of Tsavo. His eyes closed.

When he awoke, Mazarin was there.

"You are in the field hospital," she said, uncurling from her seat. Saitoti tried to sit up, but pain flared through him and he fell back. Outside, he could hear the sound of the Ethiopian Empire's expansion, rail by rail. It did not make him feel better.

"Did you—"

"Yes." Mazarin smiled, "Though it was unnecessary, thanks to you."

"How?" he croaked

"As I said, I am well-traveled, Saitoti of the Masai. And playing the Game has taught me many things. Things which you do not need to know." She stood. "They will see to your care here. When you are recovered—"

"This was never our hunt, was it?" Saitoti said. "Not even mine."

"As much yours as mine," Mazarin said. "And what a hunt it was, as first hunts go, eh?"

Saitoti bowed his head. "Yes."

"You did well," she said, pressing her fingers to his chest. His heart thrummed steadily. "The Persian was right, you know."

He said nothing.

She chuckled and said, "Lion-heart indeed." She turned and walked for the door. "But now, the hunt has ended."

"And you?"

"There are always more lions, hunter." Mazarin smiled. "And always more hunts."

"Do you need...?" He paused, tongue-tied. He gestured with a bandaged hand. "I mean..."

Mazarin's smile grew. "Rest easy," she said. "And we'll talk."

She left then, and Saitoti lay back in his bed, eyes shut. Listening to his heart, and thinking of the hunts to come.

THE SHARP KNIFE OF A SHORT LIFE

HANNIBAL TABU

The dark sky was just beginning to brighten as they began, down by the chilly riverbank. A light frosting of snow, the first of the season, descended upon the funeral attendees like it was filmed in slow motion, a crowd of about fifty stood silently as the glass casket was brought forth and set on the platform.

Inside the casket, as pretty as if it was her first day of school, was Jenny Taylor. Her long blonde hair was a cascade of unruly, curly strands, arranged with purple and white talicynth flowers on her right temple; the same as the bunch clasped in her delicate hands, a green-gold ring on one finger.

A white satin gown, simple and strapless, lay across her whisper-thin form so serenely it was as if she was merely napping, moments away from sitting up and setting daylight on fire with that smile of hers. A bed of multicolored roses held her tiny frame in place.

Hiram Gutierrez ran towards her still body and fell down, his hands grasping the shiny brass bar that encircled her clear oval resting place. Racked with sobs, his brother Sam, an oak of a man who looked so sad in his rich purple collarless suit, put a tan leather duster over Hiram's slight shoulders and helped him back to where everyone was standing.

I shouldn't be here, thought Clara Perry, standing next to the spot where Sam returned.

Unprepared with clothes in such a shade of purple as most of the mourners, she wore her dark brown thigh-length duster with all its buttons closed and shined, a borrowed ankle-length black skirt beneath, her spherical Afro pressed into a black top hat. *This poor child would be alive if I'd have had the common decency to die.*

Abernathy McCall ascended to the makeshift podium, a barrel of a man with long dreadlocks, full dark cheeks, wearing a shiny brass monocle, a dark purple top hat and a matching purple tunic with a golden sash that illustrated his role as a man of scriptures.

Odd, given the sort of stuff he gets into, Clara thought to herself, *but I barely get half of what these people are doing.*

"Family, I stand before you weighed down with deep and profound melancholy," Abernathy began, "much as this hallowed glass chamber soon shall be weighed down with the river itself. In accordance with tradition, handed down from the days of Muhsinah, we gather at sunrise to bid farewell to our beloved daughter Jenny Taylor, to celebrate her, and release our sadness as we release her empty form to the dusky bosom of Iya'a."

"We thank the Mother for her love," the crowd said in unison, as Clara struggled to look normal. She kept glancing over at Sam, not just because of the impossible-to-suppress attraction she felt for him, but also trying to fit in.

Abernathy continued, "Will our daughter find Avshalom, off in the unknowable night of the universe, finding new horizons? Will we meet her, somewhere out there, dancing along the light of day?"

"We thank the Father for the spark of life," the crowd intoned.

"Muhsinah tells us yes," Abernathy boomed, getting warmed up now and shaking the snow off the brim of his hat with his emphasis, "The Surrender insists that we will all get our chance to rejoin that holy family in the embrace of divine love! Muhsinah taught that we live in a world of constant change, one where we must be as fluid as this river behind me, adapting to whatever obstacles or challenges may stand in our path, even the loss of one so dear, so young, so loved ..."

"We thank the Surrender for showing us the way," the crowd responded.

Abernathy gripped the wooden podium with both hands, as if he was struggling with something. "Dearly beloved, I'm here to tell you...we can't know the pain of Tasha Taylor today, losing her only baby girl, this bright star in our dim sky. We can't step into the shoes of Hiram Gutierrez there, on the brink of forever; so harshly reminded of the long, long fall just a little past that precipice. We can't even know what it's like for Jenny's teachers, her friends, her relatives."

"What we *can* know is what the scripture says," Abernathy paused to pull out a worn leather bound book, holding his head over the thin paper pages to keep the snow from falling on them. "In the book of Judith, chapter fifteen, verse seven hundred and nine, it says, 'in your day you shall find your head bowed, your eyes filled with sting and water. In your time, you shall know the weight of absence. In your life you will receive the blessings of the gods, and you will be healed in due time.'"

"These words are cold comfort, I know," Abernathy said, plopping the book closed, sliding it into a satchel on the podium and then removing his monocle, "colder than this very morning. But as sure as the light breaks over that horizon, we stand at the beginning of a new day, one day closer to being all right again, one day nearer to seeing Jenny again. She's waiting for us to take those steps, to keep going, to find her on the edge of the break of day. Here we bid her farewell, and here we shall meet her again."

"Ash'a'men," the crowd intoned solemnly.

That's weird, Clara noted; but remembered that her "mission" left her little time for researching anthropological oddities.

Abernathy quietly said, "We now observe a moment of silent reflection, where we will each lay our thoughts and prayers on this cask, weighing it down as surely as the cold, cold waters will when we set our daughter free."

Almost every head dropped in unison, and Clara grimaced as she hastened to follow suit. After a moment of snow falling almost silently and the roar of the river, Abernathy tapped the podium four times in rapid succession, with some kind of conductor's baton, that emerged from apparently nowhere.

The crowd leapt into song, shocking the heck out of Clara, who tried quickly to play along...

> "What could I do
> without you?
> Who would I be
> without your name?
> Where would I go
> you shine through,
> No matter what
> I'll feel the same
>
> When will I once
> again find you?
> Who can I ask?
> who knows you well?

When will I see

divine you?

Without you I

have lost and fell..."

As the mourners repeated this refrain, Hiram and Jenny's mother Tasha stepped forward and sang...well, mostly. They wailed at each other, in key and with gusto, holding one another and bawling— but singing all the same, wordless runs and trills, a lament and a plea.

As they did, Abernathy reached for something in the podium and Jenny's transparent trappings slowly descended into the water. The lower two thirds, separated from Jenny by roses and glass, filled with water. She was taken into the river's flow as she sank, gone forever.

The assembled observers held the final note of the first refrain as Abernathy held his baton aloft; Hiram and Tasha already sitting on the ground, hugging and crying, unable to sing anymore. Abernathy swung the baton downwards and the singing stopped, and everyone started to mill around; some looking where the casket had descended beneath the water, some walking away, some going to comfort Hiram and Tasha.

Clara chose this time to make her way up the riverbank, trying to get back to her mechani-bike and make some sense of what she'd seen. She made it about twenty feet before she heard his voice.

"Clara," he called; and she knew it was Sam, knew that rich timber from her dreams, from the many nights she'd wished she could hear him calling it right next to her in bed.

She turned slowly and regarded him, his pant legs splashed by river water, a single white talicynth bud attached to the right side of his jacket.

"It was a beautiful service ..." she began.

"You've never been to a funeral before," he said. "You had no idea what to do, or when—to not even own any purple clothes...you're not just from somewhere else, to not know the basics of a funeral under the trinity...you have to be from somewhere very far away..."

If the stupid star charts would line up, I could figure out exactly how far, she thought absently. "It's not like that," she protested, "I just..."

"Clara, I don't care about any of that," Sam interrupted, drawing closer. "Hiram doesn't care either, because you were the second most important thing in Jenny's life. None of us care. We accept you...I accept you, whoever you are." Finally in front of her, he took her hands. "Whatever you're running from, you're safe here."

Clara looked into his impossibly deep brown eyes, and wished everything in her life was different. She shook her head, and remembered the body crushed underneath the cryogenic chamber she emerged from in a desert seventy miles from here; and remembered, *He's not really human...*

"Are any of us safe, Sam?" she asked, pulling her hands back. "Doesn't Muhsinah teach that the only constant is change—that we must adapt our behaviors while never abandoning our true selves?" She started moving for her bike.

The right corner of his mouth turned up in a smirk that made Clara's knees buckle as he followed. "Something like that," he admitted, "but she also said: 'We are stronger together than we are apart.'"

Clara nodded, getting on the mechani-bike: a ramshackle

collection of metal and smoke and hope itself. "I'll have to study my scriptures more, then," she said, cranking the engine with a kick. Yelling over the engine's roar, she pulled huge brass goggles on and said: "Please give your brother my condolences again!"

Without giving him a chance to reply, Clara twisted the throttle and the huge forty inch tires kicked gravel behind her as she took off. She reached up and made sure the pins were holding her hat in place... as tears slipped through an opening between the goggles bright brass and her own dark skin.

§§§

One week earlier, Clara was at a back table in 'Dam Scarlett's Diversion Emporium, wolfing down a sandwich-like creation locals called an orkney: several slices of local livestock with a spicy spread between two slices of bread.

Since waking up on this world the natives knew as Pless nine months before, she'd been forced to get used to strange food and unusual terminology despite the fact they (for the most part) seemed to be speaking what she knew as English and were mostly normal-looking bipedal humanoids.

The meat—almost fluid, but filling—was from a bjekk: twelve-legged creatures that was as much mammal as insect and were abundant in both domesticated and wild incarnations. The bread was made with a kind of wheat that grew blue, instead of the sandy shade Clara was used to when she was known as Dr. Erin Jackson. Likewise, the people here...were not exactly people.

On the outside they looked human enough, but she'd been able to examine the remains of one and do some observations of others. Inside, their blood was a rich, vibrant shade of purple.

They had a duplicate, almost backup liver, which made drinking with them an unsafe habit. In addition to the normal skin shades she knew, there were a number of people whose skin was a light shade of slate metal gray. They were universally bald, but considered totally normal by everyone in the very racially diverse society. The appendix of these people, who had been calling themselves "renzings" the way inhabitants of Earth called themselves "human beings," was nowhere to be found.

Also, instead of solid waste they seemed to excrete far, far more carbon dioxide than humans, through every inch of their bodies. In an ill-considered liaison (undertaken in the name of science, of course), Clara discovered that at least they did use a fairly safe kind of prophylactic; and operated largely as she would have hoped, even though while engaged in coitus things could get a little breezy. Hiding and sanitizing her own feces was her largest annoyance. She desperate to avoid detection.

In any case, Clara had largely accepted that she—and her "mission"—had to proceed in this town of Tarndale until she dreamed up a better idea. So she was eating a robust lunch—complete with what appeared to be a kind of elderberry lemonade and bread sticks with a sweet sauce for dipping—in preparations for a meeting with the regional governor to propose technological advances.

Since arriving, Clara had found the greatest minds on Pless and shared some of her knowledge with them surreptitiously, fast forwarding what some of the periodicals called "an age of wonders;" and this had made the largely steam-powered world marginally less annoying.

Clara watched with some amusement as the regular business of a restaurant took place around her alongside a kind of penny arcade with rudimentary distractions: a fully stocked bar that could have laid out a college fraternity with alcohol poisoning from what was on tap, and a brothel so busy a small line waited near the bar.

The proprietor 'Dam Scarlett would be considered Asian on Earth, but her long, bouncy curls of naturally red hair, porcelain-like skin and robust curves were less familiar. She walked to and fro in a huge red hoop skirt and a clinched bustier ringed with brass accents, chatting up customers and spreading bonhomie.

Looks painful, Clara thought to herself as she ate, again noticing her functional, simple clothing also set her apart from the very frilly feminine populace she ran across most of the time.

Screams accompanied a large *WHOOMPH* sound from the rear of the establishment and quickly people started running everywhere. Clara sighed as people began to be evacuated by the burly green-suited security staff, and from what she could piece together, the giant frying vat in back had exploded and was threatening to turn the kindling-formed building into a memory.

Clara sighed, wiped her mouth and grabbed the beaten brown leather satchel she kept at her side wherever she went. She grabbed a man shooing red-clothed cooks out of the kitchen and spun him around.

"Where do you keep the sodium bicarbonate?" she asked testily.

"What...huh?" the man wondered at her. *Not hired for his reasoning abilities, apparently,* Clara sighed to herself.

"Powder," she clarified. "Used to bake breads or stuff like that to make it rise and be softer. Where is it?"

He furrowed his brow and said, "We've gotta get you out of here...!"

"Shut up and answer the question before this whole place burns down, you *idiot!*" she spat out. *I really need to work on my patience with these people,* she pondered. *That's why they said I never made more of myself at NASA...*

"P-pantry is behind you, left turn," he managed. "But I don't see..."

"You will," she said, spinning and running off for the room. After a few quick moments, she figured out which of the bags (*fluffener,* it was labeled) had what she needed and dragged two huge thirty pound ones out with her. She moved towards the smoke and fire and stopped, dropping the bags and knocking her forehead with the heel of her hand.

She rushed back to her table, poured her drink on her cloth napkin and tied it around her face like a mask. She was able to move through the fleeing patrons and employees—some in various stages of undress—back to the bags and then back towards the kitchen.

Pulling her hunting knife from her satchel, she sunk it into a bag and then tore a hole that seemed controllable. She then stashed the knife again and grabbed the bag of *fluffener,* starting to fling the baking soda around, quashing flames wherever it fell. After about ten minutes, she switched to the second bag and was able to get the entire conflagration put out.

Smudged in smoke and exhausted, she looked around, opening windows and doors wherever she could to help ventilate the room. Satisfied that things were under control, she walked out towards the front past one of the businesses' large front columns holding a wanted poster for a horde of outlaws called the Khalditru Gang, still dragging one of the *fluffener* bags.

When she emerged into the bright daylight, bracketed by smoke, a huge percentage of the Tarndale population was milling about, looking at the building: confused. In the midst of them, 'Dam Scarlett was shaking a lean finger at local dandy and bon vivant Abernathy McCall, himself brushing dust off of his rich velvety yellow longcoat with his top hat, despite having no pants on.

"You had something to do with this catastrophe to make me buy your piddling fire protection insurance," Scarlett yelled at the man, "and undercut my support for your proletarian rivals at the Vanity Pomp!"

"As I've already explained, my dear lady," Abernathy said pompously, never even looking at her as his monocle fell from his eye, jiggling at the end of its chain as if it were dancing, "I have no interest in terminating the existence of my most favored intoxicant supplier, let alone the place where I assiduously warm at least one bed per day with my affections. Such baseless allegations on your part do—"

"Fire's out," Clara said simply as she walked up to them, dropping the bag between them.

They both stopped and looked at her with puzzlement.

"I beg your pardon, dear girl?" Abernathy asked.

Scarlett managed, "Honey, wha—?"

"Grease fire from the fryer," Clara explained tiredly. "Your *fluffener* is perfect for putting it out, even though I had to use two bags." She breathed heavily as she looked at them. "Closest place to my photo shop to get something decent to eat, I had to do something."

"Oh my word!" Scarlett exclaimed, taking Clara into a brisk hug before holding her by the shoulders to examine her. "You're that widow Clara Perry, who opened the place with all the real life pictures? You saved my livelihood! You'll never pay to eat here as long as you live!"

"Great," Clara sighed, looking at the damage done. "My meeting with the governor in an hour's gonna go great with me looking like this..."

"Nonsense! I know my own quarters are far enough from this foolishness to have all my clothes intact. You'll come shower in my home, wear some of my very own business attire and I'll convey you to the governor in my personal carriage! It's the least I can do!"

Clara raised an eyebrow, wondering what "business attire" would mean, but shrugged and said: "Thank you."

"Don't think I'm done with you in this matter, Abernathy McCall!" Scarlett growled, jutting her finger back out at the man again.

"I wouldn't dare to imagine such a preposterous state of affairs, madam," he replied with a foppish little bow, sweeping his arm out in an arc with his hat at one end, an odd gesture for such a burly man. "Perhaps you, yourself can serve as the vendor for my next... horizontal purchase in your esteemed establishment!"

Scarlett scoffed at him and rushed Clara off towards a side building, yelling orders for her employees to get the place back in order. Within moments, Clara was rushed into a shower chamber (rare in these parts, Clara had discovered) and told to get cleaned up while Scarlett got clothes and ran to check on repairs.

The water—pleasantly warm, but a far cry from the pressure and temperatures Clara preferred, a lifetime ago—trickled across her snuff-colored skin and she let her head hang low to take it all in. She wished she had time to enjoy this, but she had already pushed it stopping for lunch. She glanced up at the edge of the shower curtain rod where she'd hung her satchel, making sure it was unmolested, and sighed. She turned off the water and reached for a towel.

Moments later, she regarded herself in one of Scarlett's many full length mirrors. The double breasted black suit coat was cut for a woman, and clinched perfectly at Clara's slim waist. A white blouse, much more conservative than Clara would have expected from Scarlett, neatly cinched up to her short neck.

A simple black skirt went essentially straight down, even compensating for the raise her backside provided to be perfectly parallel to the floor all the way around. Scarlett had left a riding crop there; "For effect," she'd said, and Clara figured she could use it to cover her nervousness over making a presentation.

She looked in the mirror, her piercing black pupils focused, her mouth set and flat, her full nose still and not twitching. *I guess I'll do...*

Scarlett came in as Clara was regarding herself, and clasped her hands together at her chin. "Why, darlin' you're just about perfect!" the woman gushed, coming up to check Clara out. "I haven't been able to fit that since I filed for my permit to open this place, but it's literally perfect for you. I insist you keep it as a gift and a gesture of friendship."

Clara raised an eyebrow. "Okay. Thank you."

"No thanks needed, sweetie. Can I call you Clara?" Scarlett asked, and Clara nodded. "The boys have my carriage all ready to go and two of my best mechani-horses to pull it. Let's get you over to see the governor!"

They swept through town quickly, the clip-clop of the mechani-horses hooves perfectly timed with the grinding of their clockwork gears underneath horse blankets showing Scarlett's sigil. The noise of the metal beasts and the clamor of the city didn't stop Scarlett from talking pretty much the entire way.

"...And when the Vanity Pomp swings by *my place* later today," Scarlett insisted, "with its floats and ceremony and splendor, I'll just be *mortified* to not have the place fully ready. Do you know those louts from the Tarndale Fire Service arrived while you were showering? Better late than never, as much as they're in Abernathy McCall's pocket. They said they'll investigate the fire for signs of foul play."

"The embarrassment! Still, my boys insist the front face will at least be presentable. You're...where are you from? Have you ever seen a Vanity Pomp? Oh, it's such a *thing,* Clara—one time every year when the whole town steps away from our drudgery and embraces splendor! It's a great competition, and we've got that loathsome man Abernathy McCall representing the landed gentry."

"They always put forth some gaudy and wonderful flotilla of marching bands and floats and technological wonders—I'm sure you know all about that, as I'm told they contracted you to help with some secret surprise."

"Then when the town's common folk—laborers and ostlers, seamstresses and whores—do their presentation. It's rarely more than one float and a band, but the symbolism and nuance...always something thought provoking. My, but how I go on...oh, here we are, I can't wait to hear all about your meeting with Governor Brodie. I'll have the kitchen back up to at least serve dinner for two, come by and enjoy a meal and we'll talk all about it, you're *so* much fun to gossip with ... ta ta!"

Shaking her head at never even getting a word in edgewise, Clara stepped out of the spherical, pearlescent carriage, looking like it escaped from a fairy tale and landed in a western. Clara took a deep breath and stepped confidently up the stairs, silently thanking herself for not taking the uncomfortable looking high heels Scarlett suggested. Instead, she'd stuck with boots.

Clara found her way to what passed for a conference room in the modest city hall. She examined the dome-like ceiling and saw the rooms seemed to revolve around a large central column, so that was likely where somebody like a governor would be. When she arrived, the man was sitting aside a woman so polished and primped that she made Scarlett look like a dung shoveler.

"My apologies for my tardiness," Clara said as she confidently strode down the aisle, being careful to not trip on the unfamiliar skirt. "My name is Clara Perry and—"

"And you, young lady, are something of a puzzle to the people I've talked to," the man said as he stood, his companion standing shortly after. "I am, of course, Regional Governor Myron Kavanaugh Brodie, and it is proper to address me as 'your honor.'" He held out his hand, and Clara took it, nodding as he bowed slightly and shook.

"I say that not because I feel you lack social graces," he continued, sitting down, "but because in my experience people with minds brimming with numbers and science often forget societal niceties. Understandable, of course. Speaking of niceties, this is my wonderful and long suffering wife Abigail, who will serve as grand marshal of today's Vanity Pomp very shortly."

Abigail snorted derisively. "That's why I should be overseeing last minute preparations and not sitting here discussing flights of fantasy."

Clara raised an eyebrow and Myron chuckled, patting her hand. "You'll have to forgive my Abigail, as she heard that I was meeting with a woman and her suspicions were immediately raised. She's rather traditional in her beliefs regarding the roles of women, so I apologize for any derision she might heap upon you." Brushing off his thighs as he sat back in the broad backed wooden chair, he insisted, "I am certainly here to listen."

Abigail reached over into his vest pocket, pulling his pocket watch out and clicking it open. "For...at least twenty more minutes."

Clara nodded, and quickly clicked through the combination lock on her satchel. "I understand, and my delay was unavoidable..."

"Ah, yes, I did hear about that," Myron nodded, fitting the pocket watch back in its perch and knitting his fingers together across his wide belly. "You beat the first responders to the scene and saved a local...establishment from a fiery fate? Impressive!"

"The work of commoners," Abigail sneered, pulling out the local periodical to open it noisily.

"Thank you, sir...er, your honor," Clara said as she pulled out some papers. "In any case, we shouldn't need long. You are familiar with electricity and the research being done by scientists across the land?"

Myron reached into his suit pocket and brought forth finely crafted spectacles, setting them on his nose as he reached for the papers. "I have done some reading, yes," he said, looking at the papers. "The work around those monstrously large dynamos I've seen at the universities. What of it?"

Clara smiled. *Good, he's not a moron.* "The core of my presentation today, your honor, is that using the power of the river nearby, enough electricity can be safely generated and transmitted to provide electrical power for this entire town, as a pilot program, and eventually for places like the capitol as well."

Another snort from Abigail. "You're more likely to set the entire town alight with such foolishness!"

"Good thing she knows how to put fires out, then," Myron said absently, looking over the papers. "This says that we'd need to build a ... turbine, you call it? A small facility and a turbine to collect the power of the river rushing by and use it to...make electricity? Is that right?"

"Yes, sir ... yes, your honor," Clara corrected herself. "Using plain copper wire at first, we can then take energy from this and transmit it over distance to—at first— provide street lighting at night, which will immediately increase public safety over the effect of existing gas lamps."

"Second, it can be used to transmit power directly into homes and businesses, allowing stores and restaurants to stay open longer and generate more taxable income. Third, it will become a centerpiece of scientific development and serve as quite a feather in your cap, when all is said and done."

Myron looked up from the papers at her. "I don't have a cap," he said, puzzled. "Moreover, why would I want to put a feather in one?"

Different culture, dope! Clara thought to herself. "I'm sorry; it's just something my family used to say. It means it would be an accomplishment to put on your record that would distinguish you and help cement your legacy."

"I'll have you know, young lady," Abigail jumped in, "that my Myron helped establish the first rail transportation across this desolate land. Without him this dung heap of a town wouldn't have two sticks to rub together!"

Myron rolled his eyes and patted Abigail's knee. "Thank you, dear...but I'm sure Ms. Perry spoke of my numerous campaigns on modernity and civilizing the land."

"Now I think about it," Abigail said angrily, "what exactly qualifies you to even talk about these things? For all we know, you stole all these 'ideas' from some unsuspecting man in a basement, toiling away for you!"

Clara smiled and bit back her thoughts. *Doctorates from UCLA and MIT, a master's degree from Northwestern and three bachelor's degrees from Columbia, Yale and Stanford, not that you'd know what any of that means.* "Ma'am, I'm largely self-taught, but..."

"No need to recite your resume," Myron interrupted. "My advisers speak of you as if you were a miracle dropped from heaven based on what you've done in medical fields alone. You got this meeting based on merit, but despite the cultural and scientific benefits, I'm not so sure this is worth the fairly considerable investment it seems this would take..."

"Could you please refer to the last page of my package?" Clara asked. "It outlines the savings to the region in terms of expenditures as well as estimates of increases in taxes paid to the government."

Myron flipped through the pages, examined the material in question and jumped. "My word!" he exclaimed. "If even half of this were true...we'd be able to practically float a third of the entire region's budget off of Tarndale alone."

"I made fairly conservative estimates," Clara said demurely, "based on research I did with your office of budget management, the local chamber of commerce and interviews with business owners."

Myron took off the glasses and put them in his pocket. "I'm going to have my staff look over this, but unless they tell me this will blow up the world, you're going to be a very happy undersecretary of the interior!" Holding out his hand, he said, "We will absolutely forge ahead with your plans!"

She shook his in return, and said, "If it's all the same to you, public office isn't exactly...suited for my temperament. I'm elated to help lead the effort as a consultant, but I'd much rather stay here in Tarndale."

He grinned widely—clearly seeing he wouldn't have to share the credit and nodded. "Done. You'll have a generous stipend and everything you need. Now, I must get Abigail to her preparations before she has us both dipped in stinger bushes and dragged through town!" He stood, took Abigail's hand and bowed again, reaching for his hat.

Clara stood and tried to do the kind of curtsey she'd seen women do now and then, which produced another eye roll from Abigail. The governor and his wife left, and Clara stood there a moment, satisfied. *That part's in process, at least, Now to get back to the shop and wait out this Vanity Pomp idiocy, so I can see about getting these people to have a half-decent industrial revolution...*

Walking out of the town hall, Clara was stuffing her things back into her satchel when she bumped into someone. *Freaking bumpkins in this idiotic place need to...*

She looked up into the soulful brown eyes of Sam Gutierrez. A full foot taller than Clara, his rugged frame would have fit right in one of the Playgirl magazines she sincerely hoped no one discovered at her old apartment.

He wore a loose fitting shirt that would have been called chambray back home, and work pants the shade of sea foam. His brother Hiram—a smaller, teenaged version of Sam—stood nearby, smirking and holding a stack of papers.

"Sorry about that," Sam said, "we were just getting some permits renewed and...well, I guess we ran into you!"

"Uh...yeah...looks like it," Clara said, blushing. "I..."

"Hello, 'Dam Perry," Hiram said shyly. "Is Jenny Taylor still working with you over at your photo shop? Could ... could you say 'hello' for me?"

Clara kept her eyes low, worried about looking up into Sam's gaze and never getting out of those eyes. "Sure, um, Hiram," she said, looking for an escape. "I can do that..."

"Clara!" Scarlett's voice rang out as she came towards them. "Child, did you...oh, my! I do declare, is that Sam Gutierrez, you attractive hunk of masculinity? Is this gorgeous shopkeeper gonna monopolize you all day, Clara?" Scarlett winked at Sam and continued, "She told me she had things to do back at her shop!"

Sam just stared at her, a lock of his unruly curly brown hair almost hanging over his right eye. "Well, if you have something to do ... we were just saying 'hi.' Maybe we'll ... run into each other later. C'mon, Hiram."

Both did a shallow bow and walked off, with Sam looking back just before walking out of sight.

"Mercy," Scarlett said, hand to her chest. "You looked like you were ready to fall out of that skirt. Should I have let you?"

Clara took a deep breath. "No, you did the right thing. Can you give me a ride back to the shop? I know you're worried about this Vanity Pomp thing, but I'd rather just lay low."

"I guess that means stay out of the way," Scarlett said. "Come on, child, I'll run you back over there in two shakes of a targ's backside."

§§§

Clara walked back into the shop and closed the door behind her with a sigh. *I can't let myself get tied up with that Sam guy,* she thought to herself. *Even though it seems our physiologies are roughly compatible, I don't have time to get involved with ...*

"Clara! Clara! You're back!" an excited voice chimed out from the back of the shop. Jenny ran out, holding a drill and letting a pair of brass goggles hang from her neck, the rubbery strap pulling her cloud of curly blonde hair close to her shoulders.

"Oh, thank the mother! I have *so* many questions for you! Okay, so, I'm confused about the ratio of ...what did you call it, carbon dioxide to oxy-whatever? I wanna finish this open compressor you started, but I don't really know the math for this part. I can't figure out what size the bleed off valve should be so the tank can have proper leakage either...oh, and why do we use carbon dioxide, are there any other kinds of gases we could use?"

"Oh, and I spilled some of the liquid carbon dioxide and it ate right through my orkney, why is it..."

"Jenny, Jenny...JENNY!" Clara said, holding her hands up, trying to get a second to speak. "I just got back from town hall and..."

"Did Governor Brodie approve your plan?" Jenny asked excitedly, clasping the drill in both hands and jumping up and down, her elfin features alight with excitement. "Are we gonna wire the whole town?"

Clara chuckled. "We're not going to do it, but he did approve the plan, so we'll be pretty much in charge. But we can talk about that after I check a few things...anything I need to know?"

"A nice family came in and I took their picture, there's a copy on your desk like you asked," Jenny noted, her eyes looking up and to the right while twirling her hair. "They said they were heading on a trip across the plains and wanted to leave something for their family in case the Khalditrus got 'em."

"I cleaned all the lenses and put all the chemicals in the places marked for them. Also, there's a stack of correspondence from your science friends, which I left in the box next to your door."

"Sounds good," Clara nodded. "Okay, lemme check on some things back in my office and I'll come out to help you with your compressor."

Jenny pouted. "You never let me into your office, what have you got hidden back there?"

"You've been an amazing apprentice, Jenny," Clara smirked, walking past the younger girl, "and one day, we're gonna have a long talk about just about anything. But today, I was sure you'd be checking out this Vanity Pomp thing..."

Jenny shrugged as she went back to her work. "As soon as I

finish this project, maybe..." Quickly getting engrossed in the machinery again, she practically forgot Clara was there.

Clara smirked and went back to key in the twenty digit password that gave access to her office in back. Moving in quickly, she let the door close behind her before starting to type in the twenty-six digit password to the second door: finally entering her sanctorum.

The mess in this back room, every surface covered with wires and doo-dads, gauges and instruments, was a symphony of disorder and Clara couldn't suppress a smile as she walked in. *My one corner of sanity in a world gone ...heck, I don't know what it's gone.*

She walked over to tap on the corner of her iPad 13, a heavily hacked and modified version of the consumer tablet, with two adapters sticking out of it leading to a USB 5 hub and even more gadgetry. She tapped the screen and considered what she saw.

"Hm," she said aloud, finally feeling comfortable. "Still no luck matching the night sky with existing star charts, so there's still no idea where the heck I am, and the history books don't explain anything that connects with anything I know...well, there's that..."

She clicked a few more times and regarded the screen. Sighing, she cued up a video, and hit play, sitting back to watch it for what was easily the hundredth time since she'd gotten to Pless.

The video began with a dark skinned man in a wide brimmed fedora, his eyes hidden from the camera. He raised his head to reveal sunglasses over his eyes, and his Van Dyke face broke into a wide smile.

"Hello, Doctor Jackson," the grinning face said. "Who I am is unimportant, as unimportant as how this video got on your tablet. You were chosen because of your unique combination of skills and preparation. When you view this, you'll likely be very confused to not be waking up in the cryo-center in Reno, Nevada, where you placed yourself into suspended animation in the year 2022. Sorry about that."

"You've been placed on the planet Pless to help them kick start their industrial revolution. Your collection of basic medical texts, engineering texts and 'how it's made' basics was pretty comprehensive, and we've only added a few rudimentary maps to help you find your way to relative safety, as well as some general milestones this society needs to reach."

"Don't worry about your seed packages—those were deemed pointless, as you have bigger issues to handle. You're mostly congruent with the local population in terms of dietary requirements and general physiology; so don't worry about getting poisoned or whatever. If they can eat it, you can eat it.

"You're likely asking why you would bother doing what you're being asked; why not ignore these instructions? The reason is that the people of the planet Pless are heading towards an extinction level event, that they cannot survive without being considerably more advanced than they are now."

"Don't you worry about what that event is—it won't be here until you would have been dead for some time. Probably. However, if you do enough towards these ends, you will be taken back home, back to earth, and have all your questions answered. If you don't, well, you'll live out the rest of your natural days on a planet you don't grasp, stuck amongst people who are, comparatively, barely sentient compared to you.

"Take some time to go over the documents left on your tablet and best of luck...unless, of course, you don't think you're smart enough to kick start a planet's industrial revolution all by yourself. Good luck...we'll be seeing you."

The nondescript figure bowed his head into the same position he'd started from and the video stopped. "I'm going to find you, Mister Hat," Clara said through gritted teeth, "and I'm going to shove that hat up your ass sideways!"

She went over her notes. *No background noises or visuals behind him that would indicate anything about his identity or location,*

No record on the tablet of an unauthorized access, which is really weird...the best way to beat this guy is to take the battle to him, but I don't even know where he is...dammit...if only I could get a bead on that weird energy I detected around the cryo-chamber before it self-destructed ... but the archaic tools of this stupid planet ... aaaagh!

The lights in the room blinked and dimmed and Clara muttered a curse under her breath. "Time to start the dynamo again, I guess..." she noted.

She walked over and checked the indicator on the side of a large rectangle of metal and nodded, flipping a toggle switch. It began humming as something deep within spun, beginning a charging process for the devices in the room.

"That'll take an hour or two," she muttered. Just then, a warning chime sounded and Clara asked, "What now? Bah, that's the intruder alert, somebody's outside..."

Clara rushed through the inner door to hear Jenny banging on the outer one. The inner door secured, Clara walked outside.

"'Dam Perry!" Jenny said excitedly, "Reverend Samson is outside with a bunch of people! They're..."

Clara sighed. "Please stay inside; I'll get rid of these...people."

Making sure Jenny was tucked away safely behind the counter; Clara pulled her jacket back on and walked outside.

In front of her shop was a group of perhaps twenty people, holding hastily scrawled signs and walking around in a circle. In the center, a white haired Black man with glasses and a long handlebar mustache pointed his black gloved hand in the sky as he yelled through an improvised megaphone.

"TECH-NO HAS GOT TO GO!" the crowd chanted repeatedly, "TECH-NO HAS GOT TO GO!"

I'm more of a fan of dance-hall myself, Clara considered, *but that is catchy...*

"Excuse me!" she said loudly, trying to get someone's attention. "Pardon me, hey, can I help you guys? Why are you outside of my shop?"

"I'll tell you why, young lady!" the white haired man yelled, walking her way. His long silky white hair flowed down to the middle of his back, and his smartly tailored yellow suit reminded her of the nehru jackets her dad used to love wearing when he was feeling fancy. "You and your technology are at the root of our people's spiritual downfall!"

Getting closer, he ranted with spittle flying from his facial hair-cloaked mouth. "Your mechanical filth has to be eliminated before it tries to lure more innocents away from their faith!"

Clara rolled her eyes. "If you mean my apprentice, she goes to services every week with her mother— just like she did long before she started working with me. Don't try and pin that one on me, or on technology!"

In the distance, the horns of marching bands could be heard,

signaling the approach of the Vanity Pomp. Clara rubbed her face.
"Look ... don't you wanna, I dunno, go protest the crass ostentation and
consumerism of the huge parade stomping its way through town?"

A few of the protesters looked to each other, as if that did
sound like a good idea.

"We'll get to that in due time," Reverend Samson said, stroking
his white beard, as Clara could see her reflection in his glasses.
"You're the vanguard of new technology, and right now we're..."

From the opposite direction, warning bells rang. The protesters
scattered, knowing that meant some kind of invader was heading for
town.

"I'd bet every tommy in my pocket that this is your doing!"
Samson yelled at her, pointing an accusatory finger. "If we had more
pureness of spirit and less of your shiny materialism, the marauders
wouldn't want to come take from us!" Running off, he turned to yell,
"We're not finished, 'Dam Perry!"

Clara sighed. The sound from the Vanity Pomp was so loud,
she was sure nobody along the parade route could hear the warning
bells. *A lot of people could get hurt, crap ... I've gotta go help!*

Clara rushed back in to check on Jenny, but couldn't find the
girl anywhere. Frowning, she shrugged and made her way back into
the office, coming out with a duffel bag she'd been saving for a while.
She walked out and glared at her mechani-bike, its inadequate air filter
hopelessly clogged with the jagged dust motes that made the desert so
potentially lethal.

Frowning, she glanced around and remembered that the bank
had a high roof and a ladder up on side like a fire escape. She started
jogging in that direction to try and do something to help.

The Vanity Pomp was a comprehensive display of gaudy extremism. The parade route followed Tarndale's wide main street, and virtually the entire population was there, sitting and standing in thick throngs along the side of the road. At the head of the parade was The Gaudy Exhibit, the first and most grandiose of the floats, as things got less about pomp and more about substance through the parade's narrative.

This year's theme, "The Future Is Now," was encapsulated in the float, overseen by Abernathy McCall himself. The float stood some forty feet tall. And there stood Abernathy on a platform with a brass steering wheel like you'd see on an ocean liner, a brand new orange plaid top hat and matching long coat, his ever-present monocle fitted with a shiny brass extension and a power cord linking it to a device on his belt.

His flared tan jodhpurs fit snugly into black leather boots wrapped in decorative brass chains, a continually spinning clockwork belt buckle shone in the bright sun, and he held a walking stick almost as tall as he was which had a kind of tuning fork at its top that kept a sizzling current of visible electricity between its tines.

The governor's wife stood at Abernathy's side, waving down at the crowd. She wore a platinum white dress so pristine it shone in the sunlight, with what looked like hundreds upon hundreds of pearls woven into its fabric in intricate patterns; and a perfectly matched wide brim sun visor covering the front and right of her face, so her crown of blazing red hair could cascade out everywhere.

The Gaudy Exhibit itself was kind of a monstrosity, which was almost its purpose. Sixty feet long, it was shaped like a wedge angling up to McCall's "captain's perch," and below him you could see all the proposed advancements of the future.

Right below to his left and right were huge glass rectangles, illuminated by gaslight, where people walked around inside pantomiming great stories—sword-fights, romances, and so on. Just above that, bigger versions of the box-shaped motion engines that would have been called "locomotives" on Earth, chugged in place endlessly at an angle over empty space instead of their normal three-railed track.

A little farther back on the Gaudy Exhibit, a faux megalopolis of spires and towers, with parapets and flaring balconies and steely flourished rose up, ten thousand clockwork vehicles and blimps and tiny people surged through the falsified streets.

As the tiny city receded into its smaller buildings, a huge open space was held behind glass walls, showing an actual formal ball, with people dressed up in finery with gadgets and pockets and attachments on every part of their body. They danced to the music played by a hundred piece marching band, marching ten across behind the float. The marching band was bedecked in white and with shiny gold trimmings on their huge cylindrical hats and military-styled uniforms.

Between the band, the faux "shows" on the rectangular screens and the clanking of the clockwork city, the noise from the Gaudy Exhibit alone was so loud that the insistent strains of the warning bells were completely washed out in the wave of sound, let alone the six bands playing farther behind them.

Like everyone else in and around Tarndale, the Khalditru Gang knew what the day the Vanity Pomp took place, knew that Governor Brodie and his famously rich wife would be there, and knew that the largest part of the local constabulary would be moving in intricate and involved formations about half way back in the parade: illustrating "the cyclical futility of crime."

What the Khalditru Gang knew, that no one else did, was that the normal signal flares of smoke and fireworks attached to the warning bells, had been disconnected the night before. The Vanity Pomp's overwhelming cacophony of noise was part of their plan.

Like every other member of his gang, Micajah Fitzharris Khalditru wore the exact same thing, in order to sow confusion: a wide-brimmed, dark brown hat, over a tight-fitting leather jacket with a V-neck cut to the collarbone, multiple ammo belts, a holster at each hip for a long-barreled handgun, black denim pants and boots with four brass buckles.

Many of the gang were gray skinned and bald as well, although several riders of other shades and even genders counted themselves as Klalditrus. But unlike every other, a smeared handprint of purple blood streaked from Micajah's left shoulder to his right hip, a sign of pride from when he murdered his father and took control of the gang. A bald, gray-skinned behemoth, he rode at the front of the charge, turning on to Tarndale's main street at the forefront of a wedge of a hundred mechani-horse riders, charging full speed.

"Take everything!" Micajah yelled emotionlessly, "No mercy!"

The crowd noticed the motion far more quickly than the people in the parade, and began scattering and fleeing inside of buildings. Many weren't fast enough as children were trampled under mechanical hooves, purses and satchels were snatched and glass was broken.

Atop the float, Abernathy finally stopped bathing in his own presence and noted the marauders as they approached, slamming his staff repeatedly so the spark from it grew brighter and brighter, trying to get the attention of everyone behind him.

Abigail Brodie swooned and fell into the burly man, who managed to catch her even as he continued to swing his staff wildly, trying to signal that something was awry.

The Khalditrus reached the Gaudy Exhibit and started stripping the very brass and metal from its surface. Several smashed the rectangular screens and leapt in, snatching jewels and valuables from the actors cowering within.

By now, Clara had made her way to the top of the bank and was just in time to see two Khalditrus toss a fancily-dressed woman into the street, her bosoms busting forth from her bodice. Clara unzipped the duffel and brought out one of the first things she "invented" when she arrived: a weapon to "settle things" that might be seen as normal.

Sure, she had a fully automatic Ruger 10/22 with thousands of rounds of ammunition stashed inside her workbench. But seeing the relative scale of technological development, she figured this might be a good intermediate step. A flat sheet of steel held the single rotating set of metal tubes, each lined up with a different slot of loaded metal slugs and compressed air, and a handle and trigger mechanism was set up at the rear.

The ammo belt in the bag fed the two foot long weapon with flat topped metal cylinders. She'd even found a way to boost compressed air output with some clockwork gears and tubing from an additional CO_2 tank underneath.

When in Rome, kill like the Romans do... she thought absently as she prepped the weapon. Clara pulled her goggles down—modified tactical wear from her own world and time, aimed over the ledge and began firing.

The laughing Khalditru who'd thrown the woman out—a man with skin as pale and white as schoolroom chalk, and a second who appeared to be of Arabic descent—laughed for a moment until the pale one's chest exploded backwards and he fell, slumping, under the wheels of the Gaudy Exhibit, still rolling inexorably forward. His olive-skinned friend wondered at it before his own head exploded into a fine mist, his hat drifting aimlessly down to the freshly laid cobblestone streets.

Maybe a little less kick, Clara thought to herself, forcibly not looking at the purple blood and viscera. She adjusted the compressed air on her improvised Gatling gun and kept shooting.

Now, at street level, the band had stopped playing (many of its members beaten and stripped of their finery) and the noise was more screams than music. The Khalditru started noticing they were in trouble when more and more mechani-horses fell with shattered legs and heads, the remaining limbs vainly struggling to keep up the pace of their last orders, clawing at air. No one could see or hear the sounds of shots, so it was impossible to determine what the problem was.

Three Klanditru were trying to force their way past Sam into the front door of his general store, and Clara gritted her teeth. She adjusted the compressed air again and fired, detonating all three and bathing Sam in blood. Shuddering, he ran inside and barred the door after himself.

At least you're safe, she thought as she kept looking for targets.

"Sniper!" Micajah yelled before a blast from Clara caught him in the knee. He was thrown to the ground, his mount veering through the window of the furniture store before coming to rest across a tacky pink plaid couch. Another Khalditru rode by and reached down, grabbing his hand and pulling Micajah on behind the saddle. The bandit leader yelled, "Sniper! Retreat! Take what we have!"

As quickly as they came, the surviving riders grabbed as many of their cohort as they could and fled, rounding the same corner they'd come from and disappearing.

Clara climbed down from the bank and lifted her goggles. Abernathy was by now helping the sobbing governor's wife down from her perch and comforting her as Myron rushed over to her. Myron turned to see Clara, holding her weapon.

"Did ... did you drive them off?" Myron asked, Abigail shaking in his embrace.

"I don't know," Clara glanced around. "I shot a lot of them with this thing I invented. I was just trying to help."

Abigail looked up and ran over to Clara, hugging the latter awkwardly. "Oh, *thank you*, 'Dam Perry!" she sobbed into Clara's shoulder, "They would have *violated* me!"

Abernathy brushed off his pants and said, "It seems our 'Dam Perry is the hero of the day."

Just then, a loud scream of concern was heard from the general store. Sam burst through the front door screaming: "HELP!"

Clara rushed in with Abernathy, Myron, Abigail and several other onlookers. In the back they found Hiram crying over the form of Jenny, who lay near the back door next to the body of a Khalditru. The bandit had a hole through the front of his face the size of a drinking glass. Jenny lay there with a foot-long metal tube, just a little wider, lodged through her mid-section, the shattered remains of some kind of pistol off to one side.

"Jenny, no!" Clara cried, falling to her side.

"I'm...sorry, 'Dam Perry," Jenny coughed, blood dripping down her pale skin. "Tried...making something for...Hiram so he could... protect his shop. Guess I...didn't get the ratios right...huh?"

"Oh, *Jenny!*" Clara sighed, holding the girl's hand as Hiram did the same, crying.

"Jenny, don't leave me!" Hiram pleaded, "Don't leave me—I love you!"

"It feels...nice, holding your hand...Hiram," Jenny smiled. "I love...you too...sorry we...won't have that forever you promised ... maybe...I had...just enough time..."

Jenny's body went limp and Hiram screamed, falling on her chest. Clara held a finger to the teen's wrist, hoping that was the same way you took a pulse, and felt nothing.

Just then, another scream came from someone coming in as Tasha Taylor. Jenny's mother rushed in, tossing aside her welder's mask from the brass works. Clara stepped aside as Tasha sat down, her blonde hair just like her daughter's, shaking with her sobs of wordless desperation.

§§§

An hour after leaving the funeral, Clara sat silently in her shop, holding both hands together, thinking. She was still dressed as she had been; her hat still perched atop her head. A sudden rap at the door shook her from her reverie and she listlessly stood to open it.

She opened the door and Tasha Taylor stood there, fingers knitted, looking sullen.

"'Dam Taylor, I..." Clara began.

"We missed you at the funerary meal," Tasha said quietly. "We all grieve in our own way...may I come in?"

"Certainly," Clara said, wiping her eyes and standing aside.

Tasha walked in, rubbing her purple gloved hand across the countertop. "Jenny talked so much about this place, I feel like I've been here before," she said absently. "I should have come to visit..."

Clara, a little out of her depth, frowned. "'Dam Taylor, I'm sorry that..."

"Stop," Tasha said, not even looking at Clara. "I suspected that you might be blaming yourself, because Jenny took things from your shop and made the thing that saved Hiram but killed her. Nothing could be further from the truth."

Tasha turned her green eyes to regard Clara. "Ever since her daddy died, she's been trying to follow me down to the brass works. Did you know that? She's always loved tinkering...When she was nine, while her aunt was sleeping, she used my stove to melt half of the good brass in the house and forge a sword. She's loved science and learning ever since she was a baby."

Tasha walked over to Clara and took both of her hands. "Jenny's death is not your fault, unless you want to say it's mine too. She was smarter than I could ever be, and I couldn't keep up with her. She found another woman who knew how to work with her hands and latched on, and I was honestly glad."

"Her schoolmarms even improved, because she was getting a chance to do something she loved. She wanted to grow up and be just like me at first; then, she decided she wanted to be just like you, 'Dam Perry. You gave her a glimpse of something she wanted, a better life than a renzing girl ever even imagined. When she worked here, she was alive, and you have to know that such a gift, such a chance, in a backwoods town like Tarndale ... it meant everything to her, so it meant everything to me."

"I ... I don't know what to say," Clara said, tears streaming down her face.

"Say 'you're welcome,' because I came here to thank you," Tasha smiled through her own tears. "Thank you for being patient with my little girl. Thank you for being something for her that I wasn't able to be, working double shifts at the brass works."

"You'll always be welcome at my table; and you'll always have a place to sleep if you need it. I heard you're a widow, and I buried my only kin...so we can be each other's family, 'Dam Perry. I'm sorry I've never said it before... such sorrowful circumstances."

Tasha let Clara's hands go and walked over to the door. "We'll be eating at the temple until mid-afternoon, and we'd love to share our meal with you," Tasha said with the bitterest smile. "You're a good woman, 'Dam Perry...Clara, and our community owes you a huge debt."

"Jenny told me about what you are working on with the governor. I sincerely hope you keep doing...all of this, because neither of us knows how many other little girls see a future like the one you offer. May the Mother keep you, fare well."

Tasha walked out of the door and closed it gently behind herself. Clara sighed and another few moments passed before a quick rap at the door made her think Tasha had forgotten to say something. She walked to the door and found no one there, but a single square envelope had been left on the doorstep.

Clara frowned and picked it up, opening it and pulling out the simple white piece of paper inside.

She unfolded it and read: *She's right, your work is important for more reasons than you know. Please don't let these events stop you from doing what you have to do.*

Instead of a signature, there was a small square...with a drawing of the man in her video, his head bowed as he was when it began.

Clara's eyes bulged with anger as she ran into the street. She glared around, looking to see who left this, but no one was nearby, save a drunk sleeping against a building at the end of the block. Clara cursed and started to crumple the paper...then realized she could examine it and straightened it out as she went back inside.

Down the street, the drunk stood up and shoved the bottle in the pocket of his threadbare coat. He walked down an alley and stood behind a huge trash receptacle, the air shimmering around him as his appearance changed into that of the man in Clara's video. Looking to the sky, he held his right wrist to his mouth and said: "All is proceeding as we have foreseen. Maintaining surveillance."

He dropped his arm and light flashed again, now leaving him looking like a constable. He walked out of the alley whistling aimlessly.

THE TUNNEL AT THE END OF THE LIGHT

GEOFFREY THORNE

Ol' Moby spun slowly in the airtides, creaking and groaning as the pressure pushed it this way and that, giving the false but persistent impression that it was alive.

The giant spokes, interlocking like spider webs, the great corroded drum squatting at the hub, even the enormous bolts protruding from the thing like huge dead eyes, somehow implied the presence of some great beast or skeeter.

Of course it was neither of these things. The nearest anybody had been able to tell was that *Ol' Moby,* one of the bigger wrecks floating in the misty aether a few leagues from Breaktown, was that it had been home to some manner of elseworldly persons many, many turns ago.

Those persons were all gone to dust now, leaving no clue about themselves or how they'd found their way into the Other Country.

Nowatimes only the homesteaders and the damned Morikans had any real presence and, of the two, only the homesteaders had been of a mind to take the place for what it was and put down roots.

Damned Morikans, thought Bannecker Jinks, not for the first time. *Just a pestilence on two legs.*

Waiting quiet in his shadow, Bannecker let his jacket suck in some fuel from the surrounding aether, husbanding the embers for later use. He took pleasure in the familiar tingle as it ran like lightning across his flesh. He loved that feeling. It was like bathing in a spark shower without the burning and dying. It made him feel alive.

If there was a better reason to be out here, hot-gunned and gloved, navigating the wrecks, instead of inching around the town square setting up for the jubilee with the rest, he didn't know it.

"Mos jacks is partial to the open spaces," Thaniel Turner had said to him on more than one occasion. It's something questing in the blood."

Bannecker never gave much creed to that sort of talk. It was enough that he'd won his jacket and thereby excused himself from the more mundane duties of working the dirt or keeping Breaktown's ginery going.

"Somebody needs to get a Krewe jacket on that boy, right quick like," his old granny used to say. "Lord knows he ain't good for nothing having to do with sitting still." As if she knew the first thing about rimjacking. As if she had any notion that the only way to catch a fangcat or spy out a push from the damned Morikan hunters, was to sit quiet in the lee of some giant hunk of spinning rust and wait.

Just as I'm a'doing right now, he thought. *All over Kally and her jackanapes.*

Little Kally Freeman was out there somewhere, acting the fool like always. Senior Turner had told Bannecker to take her out with him, help her get the hang of her own newly-won gear so she'd have an easier time when she pledged her first Krewe.

She sported one of the new jackets, smaller than Bannecker's, yet with more space to store sparks and more hidden ginery inside.

While Bannecker had to carry a satchel for his tools and a strap for his hotgun, Kally's jacket did away with the need for both. All she had to do was point her gloves, spark up, think a bit, fire, and all manner of grapples, spikes and other stuff would come into being and stay until she let them fade.

It all had to do with the aether that surrounded them and the little points of light you sometimes saw dancing inside.

"We's all made of motes like that," Tinker Handy was always saying. "Folks, things, even the light. The ginery just helps us move the motes around a bit."

The smiths and the tinkers spent many a long aftersupper gassing back and fro on the nature of the motes.

What were they? Where did they come from and where did they go? How come something so useful, was also so plentiful in a place as unhelpful to folks as the Other Country often was?

They never came close to an answer for any of these and Bannecker had no head for that kind of mind work anyway. He was a "point-and-shoot" kind of fellow, but he respected what the smiths knew and he did what they directed as much as possible.

The length and the breadth of it was, once Kally did get the hang of her gear, it would easily outwork the ones worn by Bannecker and the other longtime jacks.

But that was yet to come. Just now, she was playing seek-n-find and spending the last of Bannecker's patience.

"Come on out, Kally," he said, touching his finger to the speaker patch on his neck, hoping his exasperation showed through. "You mind me now, gal. We ain't got time for this."

The only response was a muffled stream of giggles, broken by the faintest bits of static as it emanated from his speaker.

"All right, Cat Bait," he said. "I'll come after you. But don't you squawk none when I take you to the shed."

"You ain't taking me no place, ruster," she said sharply. Even

through the chaff he could hear the irritation in her voice. *"And don't you call me Cat Bait nomo."*

"Calls as I sees," said Bannecker. "Way you playing now, you lucky if cat's bait's all you end up."

"You just a big bag of talk, Bannecker Jinks," said Kally's voice. *"I heard Senior Turner tell you to bring me here so's I could get a safe feel of the rim. There ain't nothing out this way to hurt neither one of us."*

Well. That was just as true as it wasn't. The rim was the furthest reach of what the people of Breaktown called the Other Country.

"Other than what?" Bannecker had asked over and over as a child; and never got an answer he liked.

By the time he was grown and jacking with the rest of his krewe, he no longer cared. By then all the rim was, to any of them, was the place where the air got scant and cold and where the mists hid all manner of danger unless you knew the lay.

Fangcats made a habit of nesting there, scavenging off the wrecks and any living matter that might come before them. True, they had mostly moved to other pastures by this turn of the season, but that didn't mean there couldn't be stragglers lurking about for a quick bite.

The cats weren't the worst to be feared neither. There were all manner of skeeters, mites, snakeheads and wells peppered throughout the aether, any one of which would spell the end of the careless, no matter how fresh their gear might be.

L'il Kally Freeman needed a lesson in respect for the dangers of the Other Country and Bannecker meant to be her teacher.

Without even using his jacket's seeker, he spotted her,

crouched down on one of the slips of loose rock that drifted in and out of *Ol' Moby's* lee.

He always marveled at the sheer size of the wreck when he got this close. *Ol' Moby,* being one of the oldest, had been picked clean by both the damned Morikans and the homesteaders long since. All that was left of it was the chalk-white bones.

Some were of a mind that it was some kind of ark, like the one writ down in the Good Book, and that it had come into the Other Country by a different route than the homesteaders.

Some speculated that *Ol' Moby* had once been the home to the first fangcats and briar pigs, to name but a few, and that maybe Noah himself had been the pilot.

Sometimes, when the airtides pushed it close enough, *Ol' Moby's* shadow would fall on Breaktown like a sudden sheet of night.

Bannecker hated those times, as they forced everyone to realize how close to the edge their existence really was. A sudden shift of the tide and *Ol' Moby* could come crashing down on the town like God's own Wrath.

Thank Jeho, the wreck mostly kept its place out near the rim, casting its inky blanket over the thousands of smaller rocks that drifted into its sway.

Kally clung to the back of a largish one of those pebbles floating just where *Ol' Moby's* shadow cut first across the light. He had to give her credit for her choice of hiding place. The rock was just small enough to be missed among all the larger ones floating around, but just large enough to hide her body from most eyes.

If Bannecker didn't know how to spot the very faint blue halo coming off her jacket or, if Kally had chosen a rock with a little cave to hide in instead of one with an exposed back, he wouldn't have pegged her at all.

That's you, all in the open, he thought, looking down from his own hidden bit of floating boulder. *And here comes me, with the taking you to school.*

The girl still had her back to him, bless her. She was expecting him to follow the path she'd taken—down under *Ol' Moby* and up the back side—but he was more canny than that.

He powered down nearly all of the ginery in his own jacket, allowing the airtides to take him, pulling him slowly over the wreck's upper edge until Kally was below him. The aether might be breathable and warm and full of the Tinkers's helpful *motes,* but it also had a flow.

It took most new jacks about twenty trips to get the feel of the Up and Down swells but, once they did, that invisible current was as much a friend to them as any of the more obvious tools of their trade.

Out near the rim, the flow pulled mostly down so, unless you set up on one of the wrecks or boulders, you'd spend a goodly amount of your jacket's spark just keeping afloat. Or you could do what every seasoned rimjack eventually did: learn to ride the flow.

Bannecker had even got to like the almost liquid feel of the aether towing him gently this away and that. It was like being wrapped in an infinite yet comforting bed sheet.

He knew better than to let it lull him too much though. More than once some soul had made that mistake, and been lost to the swirling many-colored depths or flung out past the Rim.

He let the current shift him down, more quiet than using his rim gear would allow, until he was no more than two oar lengths away from Kally's hiding place.

"Boo!" he said with more dramatic flair than anyone who knew him would have expected. All he meant to do was scare her a little–give her a start to remind her to keep her wits about her when she was out this far.

At first it seemed he'd got his wish.

Letting out a comical little squeak as the tremor of surprise ran through her, Kally spun to face what she obviously thought was something killing coming her way.

Unlike Bannecker's old style jacket, Kally's held considerable more spark and was wired up straight to points on her flesh. It was supposed to cut down the time it took a jack to fire off something—bolts or sparknets—that could save their lives in a pinch. What it did for Bannecker was give him a face full of sparkfire and send him spinning backwards and down into the abyss below.

"Bann!" Kally screamed as she realized what her jacket had done.

Bannecker watched the girl and her rock dwindle to nothing as the distance between him and them grew.

Stupid, he thought as he fell. *Should'a spected something like that. That gal ain't had that jacket long enough to keep a rein on all its works.*

Still, he hadn't been hurt by the sparkfire so much as surprised. Even as he plummeted, tasting the aether growing thin and bitter around him, watching the normally vibrant swirls of color go flat and gray, he reached for his hotgun and a load of grapples.

"Bann," came Kally's voice over the speaker. She sounded terrible distressed. *"What's your state?"*

"Nothing a bath and some liniment won't fix," he said, trying to put as much calm in his tone as possible. Last thing he needed was that gal coming all unstuck. Truth told, he was a little unstuck himself. He had only a few ticks before he'd be too stiff from the cold to save himself.

"*Say again, Bann,*" she said, still with that growing desperation. "*Your line's all chopped up.*"

Curse it. The sparkfire must have jumbled up his speaker somehow. The panic he had worried about was already taking over the gal's heart and mind. The aether had got too thin for him to waste breath on more talking. Funny how the light went dimmer the further out you went.

There had always been talk of finding some means of going past the Rim, finding out what, if anything, lay beyond, but the Tinkerers frowned on wasting the homesteaders' resources that way.

Now Bannecker was close to finding for himself what lay there. The Under Flow was pulling him out to the edge of the Rim where the light was murky and the chill would kill a body faster than the lack of air.

Big Horace Merse had been lost this way, tumbling over and away into the cold darkness beyond the Rim. So had Bannecker's aunt Pearly. They was both better jacks than he could hope to be.

In spite of the protection given by his gloves, his hands fumbled some as he loaded the grapples into his hotgun.

Cold means dead, he told himself and forced the last little cylinder into the magazine. *Don't let it get to you.*

"*Bann!*" said Kally, now obviously hysterical with watching him fall and fall and fall. "*Be easy! I'm gon' shoot you a tether.*"

He wanted to tell her that was a mistake but he couldn't waste the breath. With her jacket so sparkful as it was, any tether she shot him was as like to cleave him in half as pull him back to the right side of the Rim. He just had to hope that she wasn't yet skilled enough a marksman to hit where she aimed.

"*Be easy, Bann,*" she said again. "*I can work this.*" He could just barely make out her jacket's halo blazing in the distance above.

Now or nothing, he thought.

He brought up his hotgun, taking aim even as the ice crystals formed webs across his spectacles. There was a bright flash of blue from overhead—Kally firing her rescue tether, he guessed—as he pulled gently back on his own trigger.

The recoil shoved him further down into the growing dark as the grapple, glowing red with its own halo of spark, went flying up.

With so many rocks and wrecks about, not to mention *Ol' Moby* itself, Bannecker knew his grapple was sure to hit something and, in fact, hit something it did, but not before passing through the beam of charged motes that Kally had fired down.

He felt a little jolt of pain as the two tether-lines crossed—some kind of spark backlash whipfiring down from his grapple—but it passed quickly through him and was gone. The panic he felt after he realized what had happened lingered.

He wasn't sure, what with the almost blacking out, but he thought he heard Kally screaming. He had scant seconds to recognize the sound for what it was before his grapple hit something solid and dug in. The tether-line retracted instantly, just like it was made to do, drawing him up and away from the icy depths.

His breath returned in great shuddering gulps as he sucked as much aether as he could manage into his lunges.

"Bann!" Now he was dead sure Kally was screaming. He was also certain, now that his eyes and goggles were clear, that there was some kind of haze of sparks storming around the rock she was set on. *"Bann, som**ing's wrong! **mething's hap***ing to my ***ket!"*

The rest was lost to the crackle and hiss of her chopped signal.

"Be easy, gal," he said into his speaker. "I'm almost back to you now."

"***hurts, Bann," her voice went on, in obvious pain and distress. *"Jeho, it****rts so***ad!"*

The rest was her screaming and sobbing, while Bannecker cursed the slowness of his ascent. Whatever it was that was happening up there, it put on one hell of a show.

As he moved upward, Bannecker saw bright bolts of sparkfire radiating out from Kally's rock like purple lightning. It was the very image of the fireworks the tinkers set off every Jubilation Day, though he had a suspicion there'd be no celebration waiting for him when he got back to the top.

"Hold on, Kally," he said as his line pulled him to within a few oar-lengths of her rock. "Hold on, gal. I'm almost there."

Almost' don't count, said Thaniel Turner's voice in his memory. *Only one way to get a thing done, and that's to do it.*

Hand over hand, Bannecker pulled himself up the side of the floating bit of stone his grapple had yoked him to, unmindful of the terrible clattering show of lights above.

All he could hold in his mind from one moment to the next was how Kally Freeman was his cousin, how she was under his charge out here and the awful look he'd see on Than Turner's face should he come home with a report of her loss.

Her cries stopped abruptly and Bannecker allowed himself the hope that it meant she was out of whatever straight she'd found herself.

He murmured encouragements into his speaker as he climbed, jokes about times they'd had as children, bedeviling the teachers and the old folks with pranks and pratfalls. His hope was to put her more at ease until he could get close enough to help. Truth was, all it did was make him more jittery about whatever had stopped her from answering back.

He talked and climbed, talked and climbed until he was standing atop a stone that was close below the one where Kally had been.

She wasn't there now and what she'd left behind put a chill in his bones worse than any he'd yet felt. The storm of light and sound that raged up there during his climb had settled itself into a pulsing glow that Bannecker knew all too well.

"It's a rip," he said, in what was nothing more than the shadow of his voice. "Jeho's Cross. We done gone and opened a rip."

§§§

Thaniel Turner listened, quiet as one of the stones floating around *Ol' Moby*, as Bannecker told him the awful tale. He didn't say one word to blame the younger man for what happened which, in a way, was worse than if he had.

All Bannecker could cull from the few sparse sentences Thaniel spared him was the mirror for his own absolute desolation at L'il Kally's loss, and the growing concern over a rip that size being opened so close to Breaktown.

"So, what you want me to do, Than?" said Bannecker. It was like listening to someone else talk, watching somebody else sitting there in the lee of *Ol' Moby* with the stones spinning all around. All he had in his mind was Kally Freeman's screams and the rip's open maw gaping before him.

How many times had they drummed into the rim krewes not to mix the sparks from their jackets? How many times had the rimjacks been schooled on the dangers that could befall if they chanced to open even the smallest rip?

It was a rip that brought the First's into the Other Country, after all. It was the very same one that had let the damned Morikans follow through right after. Didn't nobody want to chance something worse coming out of even the smallest rip if they could help it.

Bannecker knew all that like he knew the scars on his own skin; but Kally was still gone and the guilt for it weighed heavier on him with each tick of the clock.

"Best you come on back to town now, Bann," said Than after he'd chewed Bannecker's tale some. *"Ain't nomo you can do out there on your lone."*

"What about this here rip?" said Bannecker, staring into it like a man on the edge of cliff, weighing his options. "We can't just leave it to grow."

He fooled himself into thinking he could almost see Kally's figure tumbling and twisting as it fell deeper into the rip. He fancied he could still hear her screaming, but it was only a shadowplay inside his mind, his guilt talking.

"Krewe Onyx is setting up to come seal it right now," said Than, jarring him away from his thoughts. *"You just get on home."*

He almost did as he was told. Than knew best most times and Bannecker had spent his life trying to make the man proud. Only, how proud would Than, or anyone, be of him if he just left L'il Kally to her fate? How proud could he be of himself?

Mirrors could be a cruelty to those with enough regret in their eyes.

"No use lashing yourself over this, Bannecker," said Than softly. *"Come on back, now."*

"Don't think I can, Than," said the younger man at last. "Don't think I could live with it."

He didn't take much note of Than's asking him what he expected to do then, because he was already about doing it.

§§§

Rips are like tunnels, Tinker Handy told them once, between sessions in the practice ring. But they got no rhyme, no reason. They can flush you out right near where you started or they can shoot you off into who knows where, where can't nobody find you. If y'all little piggies know what's good for you, you'll be sure to steer clear."

Bannecker never had much use for Tinker Handy. She was a snotty ol' rail of a thing, full of spite and venom, always talking like she knew best about most, always finding a way to look down her nose on the other homesteaders and the rimjacks too.

A lot of the tinkerers were like that—thinking they was above everybody else 'cause they was partial to working with the ginery. Just let one of them step foot outside Breaktown though, and watch the fearful quaking commence.

Bannecker would've given his best pair of gloves to get Tinker Handy out on the rim for ten minutes. It was one thing to know from books and word streams and quite another to know from living. Tinkerers sometimes forgot that.

So it was especially galling for Bannecker to learn that everything Tinker Handy had said about the rips was dead straight true.

Stepping into the pulsing bright eddy was like getting caught in a whirlwind from out of the bedtime stories, the kind that whisked you away to where giants kept hoards of gold and ate the legs off little boys who came questing.

Near around and far, the motes twinkled and grew, swelling like the bellies of sapflies in Spring. There was a sort of wind swirling around him, spinning him this way and that. There was howling, great long low caterwauls like the shrieks of a thousand-thousand fangcats in heat. There was an awful burning on every bit of him not covered by cloth, glass or leather.

If this was even a part of what Kally had felt, no wonder she'd been screaming.

He fell and spun. He tumbled and turned and, soon, his own voice was added to the wail of the banshee winds.

Then, when the scramble of light and noise got too much to bear, he happily lost his consciousness.

§§§

Bannecker's foot came down on something hard and he realized the first part of his journey was done.

Behind him the rip, its halo become somehow at once larger

and less distinct, continued its gentle pulse. He knew it would vanish completely once Krewe Onyx—the blackjacks—showed up to seal the far end. So he had to track Kally, and get the two of them back home before they could start.

By his watch he figured he had a little more than a quarter-hour. Then they would both be stuck wherever it was they were.

The rip's halo might be faint on this side but it still gave off glare enough to keep him from getting a clean look at the lay of the nearby country.

What he could see of it didn't fill him with happiness. There were high dark peaks out in the distance with smaller hills and valleys between. There was smoke, bubbly and black as tar, rising up from somewhere below—somewhere far below—if the noises that billowed up with it were any sign.

The gravity there held him more squarely in place than any pull he'd felt in the Other Country. The air stank of something like sulfur, actually burning as it filled his lungs. Were he not wearing his specs, he was certain, his eyes would be smarting just as bad.

Kally Freeman was somewhere out in all that.

He had hoped to find her, whatever her condition, somewhere near to this end of the rip but, as with every other time he trusted to luck, his hopes were dashed.

Time and space were funny in the rips. Kally could have got there hours before him or might not yet have arrived. Either way, he had the same dwindling span of minutes to get the both of them home.

He moved away from the rip's brilliance, feeling his heart sink further with each step.

Whatever those huge black shapes were in the distance, they

sure weren't like no mountains he'd ever seen, not even in the Other Country. They were too square-ish and laid too straight and even for anything made by Jeho's Will. But what other hand than Jeho's could create anything so massive? Even the big wrecks like *Ol' Moby* were just pebbles compared to these things.

As he got further and further from the rip, Bannecker's jitters over where he'd ended up grew.

There were stories he'd been told as a boy of the place Old Mr. Scratch hung his hat. Kicked out of Jeho's Heaven, Old Scratch had scuttled off to some ugly dark pesthole and set himself up there as the King of Every Awful Thing.

Thing was, being partial only to what he could see and touch for himself, Bannecker just couldn't give much crede to them kind of tales.

There weren't really no Old Mr. Scratch waiting to snatch up wicked souls no more than there was really a Jeho sitting up there on his golden throne, looking down in Judgement over all Creation.

Now, looking around, fighting the bile rising in his throat from the terrible smells that assailed him, fighting the trepidation put in him by the sight of that impossible black sky—now he wasn't so certain.

It sure felt like he was standing on the very edge of the Pit of Torment. Those sure sounded like the screams of the damned wafting up from below. If Kally Freeman had been cast down amongst that lot–

His feet were moving fast away from the rip before he finished the thought.

"Scratch!" he swore as he skidded to a halt just shy of the lip. *Better keep your wits, Bann,* he told himself. *Whatever the place is, it ain't normal and it sho' ain't friendly.*

Whatever the thing was that supported him it was itself as high as the mountainous black cubes and rectangles that grew at regular intervals between him and the horizon. The ground, if ground it was, felt like a mass of tiny pebbles spread over something wide and flat.

It was too even to be natural but, like those hideous distant shadows, Bannecker couldn't fathom the hand that could have constructed such things.

The noise below, the clatter of horns and howls, grew louder as he moved forward. He was so lost in trying to make sense of the jumble of sounds that he almost threw himself over the edge of what was suddenly a deep yawning chasm.

At the bottom of the gap, a distance nearly the length of *Ol' Moby,* he could see more strange shapes. Some, like the gigantic blocks, were just black silhouettes. Unlike them, these shadows moved. It was if he was looking down on a flowing river of arms and heads and even legs, all writhing and moving in a million different directions.

At spots within the undulating mass were what seemed, to Bannecker, like pillbugs. Only these were as big as cattle with giant glowing eyes and strange motley colors on their shells. They slid around in the black mass like enormous snails and Bannecker was hard-pressed to keep the bile from rising in his throat at the sight.

There was just one word for what he was seeing but his mind rebelled each time it tried to form.

Was he really looking at the demons Preacher was always saying awaited the wicked beyond the grave?

Again he strained his ears, hoping to separate the racket into bits he could understand. Were they really screams or just the sounds of animal baying? Was that the low of some new kind of oxen or was it the noise of fallen angels scouring the world for their unwholesome prey?

He couldn't fathom all that magical stuff, so, with effort, he shoved the unhelpful notions aside. There was only one sound he wanted to hear and one sight he needed to see.

"Seek," he said into the speaker and watched as the tiny dot of light appeared in his spectacles. "Seek Kally."

While he waited for his jacket's ginery to target the spark from Kally's own, Bannecker did what he could to put his mind on other things.

A lot of what Preacher said was bunk to his mind. All that talk of the Pearly Side and the Pit of Torment; it just seemed like so much gas. There were other stories told at Son-day Church, though, stories that carried much more weight.

As a boy his favorite had been the tale of how the First's first crossed over into the Other Country. It was the one he used to keep the long hours when he was out hunting the rim for game.

Tormented by the damned Morikans the Firsts had somehow stumbled on the original rip, just opened up in space before them, like Jeho's Divine Smile.

Seeing the death that was behind them and only swirling light ahead, the Firsts had given themselves over to chance and gone through. Sure, the damned Morikans had followed right on their heels but not before the Firsts came stumbling onto the island floating in the aether at the far side of the rip. And not before they found the crashed and broken vessel that lay there as well.

There were weapons inside the ship, hotguns and sparkwhips. These the Firsts used to fight off the damned Morikans, taking dark ironic pleasure as each lash sent another of their former tormentors scattering off into the Other Country's scarlet and orange aether.

Time and again the damned Morikans tried to take the island from the Firsts. Time and again they got sent running from the rain of sparks and hot metal shot from the Firsts' amazing weapons.

Soon enough they gleaned what was what—not to step foot nowhere near the Firsts unless they meant to get themselves dropped quickly in a shallow grave, and that in smoking bits.

Then, with nothing to do but learn from the strange gines and word streamers found inside the broken vessel, the Firsts set to building themselves a new life.

They found trees like the ones they knew from home growing on the islands floating nearby. They found game they could eat and other plants they could grow. Soon they made themselves a little fort around the broken ship. Soon after that they made a church.

After that it was houses, and a smithy and even a school and soon Breakwood Township was born. Once they'd settled a bit and learned some of the Other Country's strange ways, the first of the Seconds came squalling into the world. Her name was Jewel Freeman and she was as brown and perfect as the bread-nuts that grew on the trees all over the Other Country's many floating stones.

After Jewel was Early White and Frederick Douglass Turner and a slew of other Seconds that proved to the people of Breakwood Township that they really could make a go in their adopted domain.

The Seconds begat Thirds and they Fourths and, by then, the people had picked up so much from the leftover ginery they started building their own.

Sluices and sailcraft, hotguns and grapples, woven metal

strings for carrying spark from house to house and even a means of
sending pictures and sounds straight through the invisible air- all of
these they learned to make while more and more calling the Other
Country not so much Sanctuary as Home.

By the time Bannecker's set started getting born, Breakwood
Township was just Breaktown and they weren't counting generations in
Seconds or Thirds. They were just people now– families and Krewes,
Rimjacks and Homesteaders, Tinkerers and Smiths.

It always bolstered Bannecker to think about Breaktown's past
and how the Firsts had made him and his krewe, hell, his whole family,
possible.

The light in his spectacles turned into a little red arrow with
some numbers right beside.

She's here, he thought, already reckoning the best way down
the side of his impossibly high black square.

The ground rushed up at him with terrible swiftness and he
wondered briefly if he'd figured right on how much spark was left in
his jacket. Before it got too windy for breath, the coat billowed out
behind him, charging the local motes, making a break against his fall.

He slowed to speeds he could control and lit, soft-as-you-
please, on the one patch of ground not occupied by some part of the
writhing shadows.

The space was the narrow stretch between two of the towering
structures. The far end was blocked by more of the stone, or whatever,
the towers were made of. The closer end opened out on the screaming
river of barely lit limbs and heads.

Somewhere beyond that torrent, according to the little blinking
arrow in his eye, lay Kally Freeman. Hoping it wasn't his last,

Bannecker took a breath and plunged in.

The black river was made not just of disconnected limbs but whole bodies, pushing against each other, jockeying for space. They were people—well—of a *sort* anyway, with arms and legs and heads alike. They stank like a slaughterhouse, like the whole rest of this ugly world; they chattered like the four-handed climbing things Bannecker sometimes spied scavenging off the Other Country's bigger stones.

Something slapped hard into his face—an elbow.

"Aymin chok wergwin," said a voice on breath like year old beer. The face was something from his nightmares, pale as a corpse, covered with a thin liquid sheen, with strings of something like hair, black like the sky, plastered to it.

He pushed past it, grateful. But there were other faces, other limbs and other screeching voices, all seemingly bent on taking his wits away.

"*Back,* curse you!" he yelled, still bulling his way forward as the little arrow wobbled in the glass. Did that motion mean Kally herself was moving? He hoped so. The thought of her still on two legs, still awake and mostly well, gave him strength.

The crush of stinking bodies pressed on him, tight, but he hardly felt them. He shoved back when they barred his way and slipped between when they didn't.

Soon he pegged the banks on the other side of the flailing dark mass and, beyond that, another break between the black towers that loomed over all. Beyond *that* there was something his mind couldn't put into words—a wide sparkling something, black as the sky, but shimmering too in a way that Bannecker found oddly familiar.

There was a lot of this place, awful and foreign as it was, that touched him so; but he put that up to all the Good Book tales he'd sat through his whole life. You didn't have to believe for the pictures to stick in your mind.

"Y'rok'n sumtye t'gyryo," said another ugly chattering face, pulling Bannecker back from his thoughts. It had two eyes and a mouth with something like a nose between but, instead of hair, some kind of shiny dark covering its head, like the shell of a beetle.

It was close to a man but not close enough.

It was also big and blocking his way. Without thinking, Bannecker pressed a stud in his palm, letting some of the spark from his jacket flow down into his glove.

The thing screamed as Bannecker's fist, fairly aglow with spark, crashed hard into its chest. Its cry terrified him, not because it was the unnatural shriek of a tormented soul but because it was far too much like a real live human being.

The creature's hollering brought the attention of some of the nearby others. In a moment Bannecker was surrounded not by the indifferent flow of bodies crushing past, but by a ring of the ugly shadowed things bent entirely on him.

They fell on him before he could react, fists and other things pounding into his face and neck, forcing him slowly down. He saw the glint of something like a blade in one of their claws and knew, unless he did something quick, his day was done.

Suddenly both his gloves were full of spark and he was swinging. He didn't take the time to target his blows, only flailed wildly, keeping his ground at first and then, at last, driving the monsters off. Dancing away from one of his glowing fists, one of the creatures fell backwards, opening a way to the narrow gap beyond.

Bannecker was over the thing's head, down again, and dashing away before they knew he'd gone. Then he was running blind, not knowing, or caring for the moment, where he ended as long as it was away from those stinking screeching things and their brutal pummeling hands.

The red arrow had begun to flicker but still pointed steady toward wherever Kally was. The mile marker held steady at TWO but, from where he was, he couldn't gauge the intervening ground.

Bannecker continued to crouch at the bottom of some hard rocky stairs he'd found. The steps led down away from the tumult but stopped at what seemed to be a solid wall.

A few feet up he could still hear the weird cries of his pursuers and the other noises too, the ones he couldn't fathom.

The moment his wits returned he cursed himself for a coward. He knew better than this. He'd brought down ten fangcats all on his on, and helped to harvest sixty more. He'd fought the damned Morikans more times than he could count without so much as jump in his heartbeat yet somehow these ugly things had put Jeho's Fright in him?

No.

No.

Think of Kally, he told himself. *She ain't never seen none of this neither and she's out there on her lone. Who gonna save her if not you?*

Something thundered and screeched above him as one of the giant insect things rumbled past. The harsh unnatural glow from its eyes hit the stone just over his head and, for those few seconds, Bannecker was stone as well.

Fear will do that to a body, he remembered someone saying.

But you can't let it settle in the bones.

Steeling himself, Bannecker checked his spark levels—about half left. The journey through the rip and all that scrapping had taken more out of his jacket than he'd thought. Not the best news. He'd have to be careful if he hoped to get both himself and Kally home.

Bekahm, said a loud, unnatural voice from everywhere at once. *S'jussa** ormal **wer **tage. **ll git th* gri***ackup *une.*

Bannecker felt he was on the verge of making sense of the strange reverberating chatter. The cadence put him suddenly in mind of the prattle he sometimes heard during a feast when too many of the families was all talking at once, not hearing a cursed thing and not caring a jot.

Being on the rim so much, and not as partial to crowds as some, the noise of all those folks would make his head smart something awful.

Stop it, he told his screeching thoughts, forcing them down into the same iron jar he'd shoved the others. He had no time for all this fearful musing. Kally was out there somewhere, dead ahead, and their minutes were steady ticking down.

It took him a few moments to realize that the wide expanse of shimmering liquid was just plain water. It tasted like somebody had dumped a world's worth of bitterfruit into it, and it was a little too green for his liking but it was water all right. He'd never seen so much of it stretched out so far and wide in all his days. All the way out into that immeasurable twinkling black that seemed to vault over and around everything in this place.

Of course he'd heard the words *sea* and *ocean* in the tales the preacher told in Son Day services; but his mind had never really believed that anything like this could actually exist.

Big as a million catchpools, he thought, marveling at it. But, out there in it, was something he found familiar.

Yes, there was some kind of giant figure sticking up out of it and the thing itself seemed strangely anchored to that one place in the water instead of floating free like the ones he was used to, but Bannecker still knew an island when he saw one.

He wondered briefly at the giant figure, its one arm outstretched to the heavens and holding—well, he wasn't sure what that was. All he knew was what the arrow and other symbols in his spectacles told him: that's where Kally was and she wasn't moving so much no more.

It wasn't hard getting out to the strange unmoving hunk of land in spite of that impossible plane of water. Just running a little spark through his boots gave them a halo that let him skate fast across the waves like they was a giant field of ice.

He was happy to leave the noise and tumult of the dark canyons behind him and even happier to see the back of the strange gibbering almost-people that had put such a fright in his soul.

Out on the water, beneath the impenetrable black canopy with that island getting steadily closer, he felt just a little bit like himself again.

His only cares were the time slipping away and little Kally's condition. If she'd made it out this far on her own spark, well, that was one thing. But woe betide if one of them man creatures had drug her out there for some mischief.

He lit on the grim rocky shore of the strange island and checked his spark level. About a quarter left—just bare enough for the return trip and that only if they didn't run afoul of no more of them man-creatures. If Kally's jacket had a charge left after her own little trip, well, so much the better.

The giant figure, monument or temple or whatever it was, loomed over him, dark and impassive as Jeho's own judgment. It was meant to be a person, he thought. But why make something of such a size? Was this how the man-creatures saw Mr. Scratch? If so, why had they contrived to deck him out more like a woman than the pale-skinned, fork-tailed, sickle-horned creature of the stories?

He put that and all his other questions out of his mind. Kally. Kally was all. He had to find her and get them both back through the rip before it got sealed up by his brothers and sisters on the far side.

The great rocks of the beach turned to small pebbles, then to sand and finally to a sort of stone pathway laid through a stretch of what looked like a lawn of low cut witchgrass, green-instead-of-orange.

The little arrow in his specs told him she was near, maybe just over the rise ahead. The voices he heard on the slight breeze told him to get steeled for trouble.

There were more of the man-things here as well—six of them, by his count—all clustered around a figure his seeker told him was Kally.

He'd found her! Finally! And, if the news his jacket's ginery told was true, she was none the worse for her trip. A little scorched maybe, the symbols in his specs read, but otherwise intact.

He fought the urge to rush right in on them. They weren't much to look at and their brothers hadn't been much in a fight so far but, those last little scraps had been with him burning as much spark as needed to get through.

Scattering these creatures would burn up more than was safe. At least until he found out how much spark Kally's jacket still had.

Anyway, they weren't doing too much, were they? No. Just standing there in their little cluster, gibbering softly back and forth in that ugly strange language of theirs.

He couldn't make them out too well in the dark, only their number and their relative sizes. None were overly large and none seemed to sport weapons of any kind. Best, none of them had laid eyes on him yet and, as long as he kept low on his little rise, none of them would. If he held his peace, maybe they'd wander away, back across the water to the canyons and the rest of their kind.

Suddenly one of the creatures made a move towards Kally but was immediately blocked by another. This was followed by a storm of that shrieking language between them, and murmurs from the rest that Bannecker didn't like one bit.

He set his seeker to take the measure of Kally's spark levels. If she had enough left, he could safely burn his off routing this last pack of monsters. If not? Well, he'd still give them a story to tell before they took him down. In any case, there was no way these brutes would lay another finger on her.

The argument between the creatures escalated into rapid angry chattering and low, ominous growls coming from all sides. In the end it seemed the aggressive one had the most pull with its fellows.

With a gesture from their leader, the creatures swarmed over Kally's protector and, in short order, forced it to the ground. It struggled against its brethren, barking out what sounded to Bannecker too much like pleas.

There was a storm of fists and talons rising and falling. The protector fell silent and the others formed a small circle of menace around Kally's prone body.

Bannecker's hotgun was instantly in his hands, a line of stingers sliding into the magazine. *Easy, boy,* he heard Than's voice in his mind as he drew his bead. *Squeeze, don't pull.*

He was a dead shot under normal conditions but here, in the perpetual dark, with them all shuffling back and forth like that...

The first stinger hit one of them hard in what Bannecker thought was its neck. It bellowed and fell forward, sending ripples of sudden panic through its fellows.

The second stinger caught another other of them square in the chest and, from the way the thing lit up in a flickery red halo, Bannecker guessed it must have had some kind of steel on its person. The others, still unsure what was happening or where it was coming from, broke out of their little cluster, sweeping their gazes in all directions for their hidden enemy.

Bannecker's third and fourth shots were enough to drop the two largest remaining brutes and send the rest of them screeching off into the shadows.

A heartbeat passed. Two. Three.

When Bannecker was sure the creatures were gone and not just out gathering reinforcements, he rose from his hiding place and went straight for the girl.

She was indeed scorched, as he'd feared, the skin of her jacket burnt black in places with tiny bits flaking off at his touch. Her flesh was in only slightly better condition but, strangely, showed signs that some earlier grime had been wiped away. Her spectacles were nowhere to be seen.

"Bann?" Kally's eyes flittered open, revealing her familiar golden pupils staring up, wide and happy.

"It's me, gal," he said softly, cradling her, trying to help her rise.

"I lost my specs," she said, still not quite back to herself.

"Lucky that's all you lost," he said, gently.

Her hand found its way to his cheek and she smiled. "You found me."

"Think I wouldn't?" he smiled back. "You know your mammie would skin me alive, I left you somewhere's like this."

She laughed a broken little laugh at that. Bannecker could tell from the sound that she was busted up inside. He told her to be still while he checked her jacket's spark level.

She had plenty as it turned out but her ginery was too broken up for her to make use of it. He'd have to siphon what he could into his own gear and hope it was enough.

As he worked, frantic but skillful for all that, he listened to her tale.

The rip had deposited her at the edge of the canyon of black towers. The noise of her broken gear and the pain of coming through the rip's weird tunnel addled her and she'd stumbled around blind for a time until she found the great expanse of water.

"Y'ever seen the like?" she said, still in awe of it all. It was while lingering at the water's edge that Kally ran afoul of some of them weird half man creatures that seemed to be in abundance.

"They hurt you?" he said, still fretting over the herky-jerky way the spark from her jacket fed his.

"Some of them," she said weakly. "Some of them meant to, I

'spect. But there was this one that kept 'em off me."

"Prolly just wanted you for supper his own self," said Bannecker darkly. Inside, he wasn't sure. The rest of her story was even more baffling.

She hadn't been lucid enough to make sense of it; but seemed her benefactor had taken her off away from the crowds and secreted her in some kind of structure that had been built to move on this water. That part of her journey put her in mind of times she'd gone out in their Uncle Twist's sailcraft to spear rim eels.

A boat? thought Bannecker, allowing himself to relax a bit as his jacket's spark level finally topped off. *A boat for traveling on water?*

"Then, I fainted away, I guess," she said. She was obviously feeling a little stronger, starting to sit up on her own. "Oh, Bann. I thought I was done for."

"Never, while I'm living, gal," he said, stroking her forehead. "Now let's get on home before the blackjacks seal that rip."

Something groaned and moved on their periphery. Even as he turned to face it, Bannecker placed himself between Kally and whatever it was.

"Ezzzimun," said one of the man-creatures, awake again and pushing itself up onto unsteady feet. "Dowannoz tatig."

"You keep away, hear," said Bannecker through his teeth. "We headin' back where we come from. It'll go ill with you if y'try to bar the way."

The thing reached out one trembling hand, palm forward, fingers splayed, as if to show it had no weapon. "Shillmun," it said. "Shezors. Taiker."

The creature seemed to mean no harm but Bannecker wasn't one for chance-taking. Keeping Kally at his back and his hotgun leveled square on the man-thing's chest, he edged the two of them away from it and its fallen pack.

The creature never moved, only watched them drift away, down to the edge of the water. When he felt the first little waves lapping at his heels he told Kally to hug his neck tight. Then he tapped the commands into his gloves that fired up his own halo.

"Ay!" said a voice as Bannecker turned to face the water and the way back to the black canyons. "Aywate!"

The creature, the same one that had protected Kally from the rest was now bounding down the turf towards them, unmindful of the weapon that was drawing down on it.

Just as the shadowy figure grew near, something happened that Bannecker would chew over for the rest of his days. Above them, in that unnatural twinkling blackness, the strangest of all the bizarre apparitions they'd seen thus far began to slowly appear.

It was wide and flat but speckled too, as if it had been picked at by enormous fingers. It was round as any of the dishes in his mother's pantry but as big around as Breaktown itself. Maybe bigger. Maybe bigger even than *Ol' Moby*. It glowed with a kind of soft whiteness, as if projecting its light from behind a thin sheet of gauze or, Bannecker suddenly thought, perhaps from very far off.

"Bann?" said Kally, her voice small and fearful. He felt her grip on him tighten. "What is that?"

Bannecker stammered something under his breath that she couldn't possibly have cottoned on and then stood rooted there, one foot in the rippling waters and the other on the turf.

"Zhamuun," said the man-thing, all but forgotten by the two travelers. "Juzhamuun." It sounded almost amused.

As if in a dream the cousins pulled their gazes slowly away from the strange sight and back to the creature. Only it wasn't a creature anymore. Not an unfamiliar one at any rate.

In the bright cool glow of that orb hanging above them, Bannecker and Kally could now see that what they had both taken to be a monster or even perhaps one of Mr. Scratch's imps or devils, was nothing more than one more of their lifelong enemies.

"Morikan," said Bannecker, scarcely crediting what his eyes were showing him. "Damned Morikan."

There was no mistaking it. It didn't have the strangely painted colors on its face and it wasn't holding a flash spear. Its clothes, if clothes they were, were of different textures and colors than anything seen in the Other Country.

It didn't snarl and, for now, it wasn't trying to kill them but, for all that, it was still a Damned Morikan. Young. Male. Hair the color of witchgrass and skin as pink as the underbelly of a rock grub. His nose was still bloody from the beating he'd taken. One of his eyes was in the process of swelling shut.

Bannecker's gun was up and cocked, the stingers poised to spread the Morikan's face across twenty paces of land if he so much as winked his good eye.

He didn't. Instead he slowly raised his arms. Kally gasped. Her lost spectacles were wrapped in the fingers of his right hand.

"Zheezr'ers," he said.

Unsure what to do, whether to just kill the Morikan and bolt for home or just bolt with no killing, Bannecker watched as, ever-so-slowly, the hand moved forward.

He felt Kally shift a bit on his back and then her own hand, brown and charred, reached past his face.

Before he could tell her to stop, their fingers met and she had her specs again.

"Thanks, kindly," she said softly, drawing them back. Clearly, she was as muddled about this as her cousin. Morikans didn't help. They killed. They raped. They burned. Mostly, when they ran into a rimjack, they died.

They certainly didn't smile.

§§§

Bannecker stole away from the Morikan boy as quick as he'd ever fled from anything. Across the shimmering black expanse of water, his jacket glowing faintly crimson with spark, he cradled Kally in his arms and thought of nothing but getting as far from this place as he could as fast as he could manage.

The Morikan watched them go, standing in place like a sculpture of surprise, his pale bloody face half shadowed by the glow of the strange floating orb. Bannecker carried Kally in his arms for as long as he could and then, when they lit again on dry ground, stood her up and let her lend him most of her weight.

The crowd of shadow figures still packed the spaces between the high black towers, still seethed and groaned like something out of the Son Day tales of flame and brimstone.

It was strange passing among them, now that he knew what they were. All those faces that had seemed so strange before, so sinister and inhuman were transformed into something his mind could chew.

He was happy he'd let the spark in his jacket die a bit. With no red halo to draw their eyes, the crowd paid no more mind to him and Kally than they did to each other. They still jostled and chattered away and still smelled as foul as any carcass you might find rotting in the hot mists of the Other Country, but there was no malice in them anymore. Maybe there never had been. Still, he would have liked for there to be fewer of them.

"So many," said Kally, echoing his own thoughts as they threaded through the mass. "Where you think they all come from?"

It was the same sort of question he'd asked his old mammie so many times. If the damned Morikans followed the Firsts into the Other Country, they had to follow from somewhere, didn't they? So where was that place?

His mammie didn't know the answer, or maybe she just wouldn't say. Seeing the dark world below and the people it held, Bannecker felt he might know why.

"Here," he said. "I 'spect they come from right here."

He was beginning to think something else too. There were other kinds of faces among the familiar, some distorted by the strange head coverings and some just plain strange. The shape of the new eyes, the new lips, the odd, almost golden tint of the new flesh, all these were disconcerting enough.

They meant that there were other sorts of folks out there that weren't like his people or like the damned Morikans neither. Except they *were* like them; no getting by that now. He could see it in the faces, now that he wasn't so crazed with the fear of never finding Kally again. Like all the other bits of this awful world, these folk were something familiar.

Yet, even that notion wasn't the thing that set the walls of his mind to crumbling.

The Other Country was chock full of odd sights and, as a rimjack, he'd seen his fair share. What shook him, shook him the way old Joshua's trumpet shook Jericho's walls, was the sight of all the brown faces peppered amongst the pale.

§§§

The extra spark he'd got from her made their rise up the great black tower as quick as it was easy. Nobody marked them going up or, if they did, they made no signal of it. Even Kally's added weight, pressed into his side like a sack of sweetmash, was nothing in the soft glow of his jacket's halo.

Soon enough the black canyon was spread out beneath them again and they stood before the rip, its open mouth still bending and bowing like the petals of some enormous flower.

Kally faltered a bit before heading in, perhaps remembering the pain of her first time through.

"Go on, gal," said Bannecker, gently. "I'm right behind you."

He watched as she plunged into the swirling mass, saw her seem to fall and bend and scatter all at the same time. He watched until he was sure she was gone.

Where did they come from, he heard his own younger self asking over and over. *Where did we?*

Now he understood that sad eye in his mammie's normally cheery face. Now he understood Thaniel Turner's falling into quiet sometimes for no outward reason. They knew. All the Seniors knew.

And all those tales they told about Mr. Scratch and the Hot Place, all them stories about fleeing the lash and the fire of their enemies, all that was just smoke to keep the youngins in line to keep them from looking too far behind them and longing to maybe find their way back.

He shook his head, a rueful smile playing about his lips—a gallows grin. There was nothing here for his people and any trip through this place with its stench and awful noises would teach that lesson right quick.

As he stepped through the rip, feeling the slight twinge of pain that went through him as its strange energies swept him away home, Bannecker knew that he would find his way back here one day. He also knew that, when he did, he would bring others along.

Every 'jack knew that secrets were death on the Rim. Only the straight truth, painful as it often was, had any value at all.

After all, as Thaniel Turner himself always said, *You can't truly 'preciate Heaven, 'less you done took a walk through Hell.*

RITE OF PASSAGE: BLOOD & IRON

BALOGUN OJETADE

John Henry opened and closed his massive fists, giving relief to his wrists, which ached from the rusty, iron cuffs clamped around them.

He shuffled up the long hallway, his feet unable to move more than a half foot at a time due to the shackles on his ankles.

His four escorts—all clad in navy blue jackets, trousers and constabulary hats and spit-shined, black boots—were in stark contrast to his black and white striped prison uniform. All five men walked in silence toward the double doors at the end of the hall.

Upon reaching the doors, the escort at the head of the detail knocked.

"Enter," a rich, tenor voice commanded.

The escort pushed the door open and then they all sauntered in.

John perused his surroundings. The gaslight chandelier cast dancing shadows upon the light green walls. A mahogany chest sat against the wall in the west corner. Atop the chest were several trophies featuring brass casts of pugilists or wrestlers standing on bases of cherry oak.

In the center of the room was a desk, which matched the chest. Behind the desk sat Victor Clemmons, Warden of Virginia's James River State Penitentiary, smoking a meerschaum pipe carved in the image of a snarling hound.

"Prisoner number four-nine-seven to see you, sir!" The lead escort bellowed.

"Prisoner number four-ninety-seven...John William Henry, correct?" Warden Clemmons inquired.

"Yes, suh," John Henry replied.

"Take a seat, son," the Warden said, pointing toward the chair opposite his.

"Much obliged, suh," John said, taking a seat.

The Warden smiled broadly. "How would you like to get out of here, John Henry...to feel the breeze on your face and to smell that Virginia dirt once more?"

"I'd like that very much, suh," John said, his heart racing with excitement. "My appeal come through?"

"Your appeal?" Warden Clemmons said, tilting his head and squinting. "You're still insisting that you didn't rob that bank, boy?"

"I didn't, suh," John replied. "It was..."

"Sylvester Roper," the Warden said, rolling his eyes.

"That's right, suh," John said.

"The inventor of the—what was it—the steam-powered pony?" Warden Clemmons asked.

Snickers escaped the lips of the escorts.

"He call it a *motorcycle*, suh," John replied. "Mr. Roper robbed that bank, 'cause he needed money to build a motorcycle from steel instead of wood like the first one he built. I was Mr. Roper's driver *and* I did all his heavy liftin', too. When the law come callin', he put the blame on me."

"Well, no appeal has come through for you, John," the Warden said. "However, I *can* offer you a freedom of sorts."

"Suh?" John inquired, leaning forward in his chair.

"The C and O Railway needs some boys with muscle to lay

tracks and drive steel," Warden Clemmons replied. "You've got more muscle on you than a prize bull, and you're stronger than any two of those other boys out there put together."

The Warden took a long draw from his pipe and then blew the smoke toward the ceiling. "If you want, I can release you into the custody of the C and O. They'll feed you, clothe you and even pay you two bits a week. So, what you say, John? You *in*, boy?"

John flexed his thick forearms. His fingers had gone numb and the tips of his toes were just as dead. "Yes, suh...I'm in."

§§§

John Henry's hammer beat a sullen rhythm as it pounded rail spike after rail spike. Rivers of sweat rolled down his broad back as he toiled ceaselessly in the scorching Virginia sun.

"Water break!" A ruddy-faced man shouted from atop his quarter horse.

All of the men working the rails dropped their picks and their shovels and lined up at the water queue.

John Henry, however, kept on driving steel.

"I said water break, John," the ruddy-faced man said, riding slowly toward John Henry.

John kept hammering away.

"Did you hear me, boy? The ruddy-faced man hissed, drawing closer.

John increased his pace.

"Boy!" The ruddy-faced man spat, bringing his horse within an inch of John Henry's flank.

John torqued his hips toward the horse as he raised his hammer, swinging it in a wide arc.

The hammer slammed into the ruddy-faced man's side.

A sickening crunch followed the blow. The ruddy-faced man let loose a choked grunt as he fell from his horse.

John leapt onto the horse's back and snapped its reins. The horse exploded forward, running over the track and galloping toward the trees in the distance.

The five other guards—all on foot—gave chase.

One of the guards drew his Colt Dragoon revolver and fired a shot.

A second later, John felt something hot tear through his back, just below his left shoulder blade.

As the bullet burrowed through his flesh, John's vision blurred and a maelstrom of nausea whirled in his gut. His hammer fell from his fingers and he could no longer hear the wind whipping past his ears. He beat back the encroaching darkness with his iron will, however, and rode on.

After what felt like miles, John spotted a large opening in the side of a hill. He pulled the horse's reins and the beast stopped. He slid from the horse's back and staggered into the opening.

Inside was a pathway that descended into darkness.

A good place to die, I reckon, John thought as he shambled down the path.

Far ahead of him, a light flickered on and off. John continued forward.

The darkness engulfed him; smothered him. John felt the dank darkness coil around his chest and squeeze the air from his lungs. He collapsed onto his haunches and then fell onto his side.

A flame appeared above him. Standing beneath the flame was a naked woman, whose pitch-black skin seemed to be one with the darkness of the cave.

The angels done come for me, John thought, smiling weakly.

And then he succumbed to the dark.

§§§

John Henry sat bolt upright.

He snapped his head from left to right as he studied his surroundings, half expecting to find that he had awakened from a dream and was, in fact, locked in his cell back in James River.

The flowstones, stalactites and stalagmites told him that he was, indeed, elsewhere.

The light cast by the large fire a few yards from told him that he was not alone.

John became aware of something soft beneath him. He looked down. Under him was a bed of grass, leaves and aromatic flowers. He inhaled deeply, focusing past the scent of pine, wheatgrass and jasmine upon which he sat and picked up the delicious aroma of garlic, onion, red pepper and lemon.

He swallowed the saliva building in his mouth as he became painfully aware of how hungry he was.

"You up just in time for lunch."

John turned his gaze toward the source of the soothing alto voice. Standing before him, with a steaming bowl balanced on her palms, was the beautiful, black-as-pitch woman he had earlier mistaken as an angel. She was clothed now, her wiry frame covered in denim trousers, a man's cotton shirt and worn black work boots. Her short, curly hair was only a half-shade darker than her skin and her brilliant smile seemed blinding in contrast to her face.

"You wearin' men's clothes," John gasped, shaking his head.

"I live in a *cave*, the woman said, shrugging her shoulders. "What you think, I'm gon' be walkin' round here in a hoopskirt and a corset?"

"A woman dressed in men's clothes...talkin' tough to a man twice her size in a cave? Only thing I'm thinkin' is—*you crazy*," John replied. But, it look like you saved my life, so I guess you *good* crazy."

The woman thrust the bowl toward John's chest.

He reached for the bowl and gasped as white-hot pain shot across his chest.

"Hurt, huh?" The woman said. "That bullet nicked your lung and just missed your heart. I dug it out...put some Ogun medicine in and closed you up. It gon' hurt fo' a spell. Now, drink; it'll ease the pain."

John sipped the hot soup and, indeed, the pain subsided. The soup was delicious and John quickly devoured it as the woman watched him in silence.

"I'm John," John said, wiping the corners of his mouth with the back of his hand. "John Henry."

"I know," the woman said. "I'm Lana – *Ogun*lana, really – but folks call me Lana, for short."

"Pleased to meet you, Lana," John said. "I would...wait...you *know*? How you know me and we ain't never laid eyes on one another befo'?"

"Ogun told me," Lana replied.

"Who this Ogun you keep talkin' 'bout?"

"The Spirit of Iron and War. He come here from Africa, on them ships, with yo' ancestors."

"Yo' ancestors, too," John said.

"Naw," Lana replied, shaking her head. "I come here long time ago, from Africa...from a city called Onire. I ain't never been no slave; my ancestors neither."

"You from Africa?" John gasped.

"Didn't I just say that? Lana said, shaking her head. "Baba Ogun, why you send me *this* one? He 'bout slow as a dead snail."

"You awful bold, Miss Lady," John said. "You don't know what might happen to you, pushin' a big buck like me. I might jump up and..."

"Die, where you stand," Lana said, interrupting him. "Look, I been waitin' for you in this cave for three years. I gotta train you up fast, 'cause somethin' real bad is comin' and Ogun say you the one to stop it. So, I ain't got time to sugarcoat...I ain't got time to pussyfoot, or tiptoe through no tulips. You gon' learn or you gon' die."

"Ogun said that?" john asked.

"Naw, *I* said it," Lana replied. "Get some rest. Tomorrow mornin', you start yo' trainin'.

§§§

A stinging blow to the thigh snatched John from the peaceful realm of slumber back to his bed of grass, leaves and flowers.

Lana stood before him, brandishing a cutlass.

"What you hit me fo'?" John asked, rubbing the welt on his thigh.

"Get up," Lana replied, ignoring his question. "Time to go to work."

John rose from his bed. The pain in his chest made him wince.

"Follow me," Lana said, walking toward a large, circular hole in the wall before her.

John followed.

Lana crawled into the hole. John followed suit, lying on his belly and low-crawling down the duct just beyond the hole.

The duct opened into a capacious chamber, illuminated by torches that lined the walls.

John looked upward. Embedded in the ceiling was a huge copper disc. Hanging from the disc were scores of thick, iron chains of various lengths. At the end of each chain hung a cannonball.

A loud crack echoed throughout the chamber as the flat side of Lana's cutlass smacked him across the cheek.

John stumbled sideways, massaging his face with his palm.

"Strike me again, woman and I'll tan your hide," John shouted.

"Aw, the big man 'bout to cry," Lana said, feigning tears. "You want me to take you to yo' mama, so she can kiss it and make it all better?"

John searched the chamber for Lana, who seemed to vanish after slapping him. He spotted her on the far side of the chamber. The chains stood between them. "That ain't funny. My mama dead."

"Then, I guess you should have kissed *her* and made it all better, huh?" Lana chuckled.

"What?" John shouted angrily.

He stepped forward.

A hissing noise came from behind the disc in the ceiling. The great disc began to rotate, causing the cannonballs to swing.

"Come and get me, John," Lana snickered.

John darted forward; a cannonball whizzed past his face. He shifted to his left, then to his right, avoiding two heavy, iron balls.

A fourth ball hit its mark, however, slamming into his gut. John collapsed onto one knee as the air fled his lungs.

Another ball collided with the side of his head. John fell onto his back. He struggled to maintain consciousness as he stared up at the ceiling, watching cannonballs fly by, just inches above his face.

"Ogun gon' toughen you up, John Henry," Lana shouted. "He gon' make you as hard and as strong as the iron that put that knot on yo' noggin'. Now, get up and try again!"

§§§

The cannonballs whizzed by him faster than he had seen in his six months of training. John knew that if one of those balls struck him in the head this time, the blow would be fatal.

John exploded forward.

A cannonball crashed into his side.

John shook off the pain and pressed on.

A cannonball sped toward his face. John raised his massive forearms. The ball bounced off of them, leaving only a minor bruise.

John moved through the deadly obstacle course—blocking, parrying and dodging cannonballs with incredible speed and power.

He smiled as he came face-to-face with Lana on the other side of the chains for the first time.

Lana tossed him her cutlass; the cutlass that had rudely awakened him every morning for the past six months.

"Do your worst," Lana said.

John raised the cutlass high above his head and then brought the flat side down hard on her bottom.

Lana barely seemed to notice.

"Why you usin' the flat side?" Lana asked. "I just sharpened her this mornin'; don't make sense to let all that hard work go to waste."

John's eyes widened to the size of a baby's fist and his chin dropped to his chest. "You want me to..."

"Cut me," Lana ordered.

"I...I can't," John sighed.

"Cut me, or I'll send you on your way home," Lana said. "And I ain't talkin' bout that old shack yo' mama raised you in, neither."

John swung the blade at Lana's arm. Sparks flew as the razor sharp edge slid across her ebon flesh.

Lana was unharmed. The blade had not even left a scratch.

"How?" John gasped. The cutlass fell from his hand.

"Ogun live in all of us," Lana replied. "He live in our blood... in our bones. He the heart that beat in our breast, and he the heart at the center of the earth that keep this world spinnin.' I'm Ogun; you Ogun...and iron don't cut iron."

"You say things I ain't never heard befo'," John said. "But, somehow, I understand."

"That's 'cause you a child of Ogun," Lana said. "You was born to understand. Now, come on."

John followed Lana into a smaller chamber, which was empty, save for a long stone table, upon which sat a wooden bowl and something large, which was covered by a red quilt. The room was illuminated by a single torch in the far wall.

Lana pointed toward the bowl. "Drink."

John picked up the bowl. Inside it was a thick, viscous dark brown liquid. John pressed his lips to the rim of the bowl and devoured its contents. The liquid tasted bittersweet and somewhat metallic.

"What was that?" John asked.

"Should have asked that *befo'* you drank it, John," Lana said, shaking her head. "It's blackstrap molasses, with the bullet that I pulled outta you ground up in it. Also, a little bit of this and a little bit of that thrown in fo' good measure."

John's heart pounded so hard, he thought it would rip through his chest. His muscles tensed involuntarily and he began to sweat profusely.

Lana smiled. "Yeah, you ready now."

She snatched the quilt from the table, revealing a pair of large, cast-iron sledgehammers. "Pick 'em up."

John grabbed the hammers and raised them from the table. They felt nearly weightless and fit his hands perfectly.

The heads of the hammers began to glow a bright red, as if they had just left a blacksmith's forge.

"These hammers was created by Ogun hisself," Lana said. "They been waitin' on you in this cave for over a hundred years."

"Waitin' on me?" John inquired.

"Ain't that what I just said?" Lana replied. "Lawd...anyhow, you was born to bring justice to our people and to teach 'em 'bout

Ogun, 'cause they done forgot...and if you say 'Who me?', or anything like that, I'm gon' kill you!"

Lana turned and headed back toward the chamber of chains. She paused and peered at John Henry over her shoulder. "Behind you is a path that leads out of this cave; take it...one mo' thing...four times a year, them hammers got to be fed human blood. Don't really matter whose, long as it ain't yours."

John twirled the hammers in a figure-eight pattern in front of his chest. He could feel the hammers increasing his strength with each passing moment. "Then, I reckon I'll see if they like the taste of Mister Sylvester Howard Roper."

John tossed the hammers over his shoulders and stepped onto the path. He disappeared as he sauntered down the trail, his hammers carving a path through the darkness.

§§§

A powerful hunger clawed at John Henry's gut. His eyes darted left and right, perusing his surroundings. He extended his arms, holding the hammers before him as he slowly rotated on his heels.

The heads of the hammers glowed intensely as their handles pulsed in his fists. John peered down the length of the weapons and gazed at their target—a massive oak tree a few yards ahead of him.

John trotted toward the tree. He raised the twin hammers high above his head and then slammed the mauls onto the earth at the base of the tree.

Soft, brown soil erupted past his face.

A moment later, three dead squirrels—and a cloud of leaves—

cascaded to the forest floor.

John set his hammers on the ground and then busily gathered dry leaves and twigs, dumping them into a large pile. He picked up his hammers and slammed their heads together. A metallic din shook the night sky as white sparks from the hammers rained upon the pile of dry flora.

The pile burst into flames. John shoved the heads of the hammers into the fire. He then picked up a plump squirrel. John pinched the flesh of the squirrel's head and—with a tremendous yank — snatched off the squirrel's fur and skin.

Once he was done skinning the squirrels, he skewered them on a long branch and then rotated them over the red-hot heads of his hammers.

In a short while, John's belly was full. He lay near the fire, resting his head on the hafts of his hammers. The mauls throbbed gently against the back of his neck, massaging him into a deep sleep.

§§§

The cracking din of broken twigs and crushed leaves awakened him.

John leapt to his feet, holding his hammers at the ready. A lean figure darted out of the shadows. John's hammers glowed an intense red, revealing a tall, shirtless teen, whose smooth skin appeared a deep indigo under the crimson glow.

John stepped into the young man's path, pointing the hammers toward the teen's chest. "Who is you and what you doin' here, boy?"

My name's Simi, sir," the young man whispered. "And I gotta

keep movin' before they catch me!"

"Relax," John said. "I ain't gonna let nobody hurt you...unless you deserve it. What you do to have folks after you?"

"Nothin', sir," Simi replied.

"Nothin'?" John inquired, pursing his lips as he shook his head. "You don't get chased fo' nothin'. Try again, boy."

"I was a slave working on *The Alhambra*—a merchant ship, captained by John T. James—when the ship was boarded by Captain Pan," Simi replied. "Captain Pan offered all us young slaves freedom if we came and worked for him."

"Slavery been over fo' twelve...thirteen years now," John Henry said. "What, you was a pirate at three or fo' years old?"

"I was fourteen," Simi answered. "Captain Pan give us a...gift that allow us to age slow...but we age, just the same. When we turn sixteen, though, he ain't got no mo use fo' us."

"When you turn sixteen?" John asked.

"This mornin'." Simi sighed.

"What kind of man is this Captain Pan?" John inquired.

Simi looked over his shoulder and then inched closer to John. "Peter Pan ain't no man; he a..."

"You've been a bad boy, Mr. Smee," a nasal voice echoed throughout the forest.

Simi scurried to ward a tree and then crouched behind it.

John held his hammers out to his sides at the height of his shoulders, bathing the forest around him in crimson light.

All around him were boys—no older than twelve or thirteen—perched high on penny-farthings. Dangling from the handlebars of each bicycle were the skulls of other boys in various stages of decay.

And standing a few yards before John was a Caucasian boy, who looked to be no older than ten years old. The boy was dressed in what appeared to be black leather armor under the light of the hammers, so John figured the armor to actually be a rich forest green. The boy's disheveled hair fell to his shoulders and his wide grin revealed a mouth full of needle-like teeth.

"Trying to steal my Lost Boy, eh, Captain Crook?" The boy hissed.

"The name's John Henry, li'l fella," John said.

"Oh, so you're a Captain *Henry* Crook," the boy giggled. "A Captain H...H...Hook!"

John raised an eyebrow. "O...kay."

The boy drew a cutlass from the sheath that hung from his belt. He raised the thin blade above his head. "Captain Hook, allow me to introduce myself...I am Peter Pan." Peter bowed deeply.

John shrugged.

Peter craned his chin upward and let loose a loud crow like a bantam rooster. The Lost Boys lurched forward, their penny-farthings rolling silently across the dry ground.

John brought his hammers up to the level of his chest.

One boy—a lanky teen with dark, curly hair—sped toward the ebon giant.

John hurled the hammer he held in his right hand.

The maul rocketed toward the boy.

A loud crack erupted from the boy's chest as the hammer struck home.

Simi's jaw dropped as he watched the curly-haired boy shrink into a pinhead-sized dot in the distant, pre-dawn sky—like a pupil in the eye of the moon.

John bent his knees, coiled his back and leapt upward, plucking his hammer out of the air. He then hurled it downward, toward another Lost Boy's penny-farthing.

The bicycle folded upon itself as the hammer crashed into its cast-iron frame. The boy sitting upon it was sent crashing head first to the ground. He convulsed erratically and then went forever limp.

John landed with a loud thud. He raised his hammers high and then slammed them to the ground.

The penny-farthings—and the boys riding them—were sent flying in all directions as a massive wave of earth erupted from the ground beneath them.

Peter Pan flew into the air. He hovered above John, his face twisted into a scowl. "You're strong, codfish, I give you that. But, I wager Tic-Toc is stronger."

"Tic-Toc?" John inquired.

"Run, Mr. Henry," Simi shouted from behind the tree. "Run!"

"Run?" John said, shrugging his shoulders.

White-hot pain shot through John's legs as he felt himself being hoisted high into the air. He looked down. His legs were caught in the jaws of a monstrous, bronze crocodile.

Gray smoke billowed from the metallic beast's nostrils as the huge, brass clock in its chest struck six o'clock.

John spotted a clear, glass dome atop Tic-Toc's skull. Inside the dome sat a stout woman, with pale skin and silky blonde hair atop her huge, square-shaped head, busily pulling levers and pressing pedals with her shrunken, twisted appendages.

The crocodile snapped its head downward, slamming John's

thick frame to the ground.

The air whooshed from his lungs as Tic-Toc whipped the earth with his body over and over again.

John pounded the crocodile's maw with his hammers, dislodging the iron teeth buried in his calves enough for him to free one ragged and bloody leg. John pressed his foot against the crocodile's upper lip and pushed with all the strength he could muster.

Tic-Toc's mouth snapped open. Gears and springs spewed from the creature's throat as its head fell limp.

John slid out of the crocodile's mouth and then leapt up to its skull.

He brought a hammer down upon the thick glass dome, shattering it.

A blow from his other hammer came down upon the shoulder of the woman in the creature's head.

The woman collapsed to the floor, screaming as she clutched at her pulverized shoulder and collarbone.

"Tinker Bell!" Peter screamed as he sped across the sky toward the wrecked crocodile.

John Henry whirled toward the voice, but Peter was already upon him. The boy thrust forward with his cutlass.

The blade bent as the tip of the blade made contact with John's hard flesh.

John smiled. "Iron don't cut iron, boy."

John swung his hammer, striking Peter in the side of the head.

The boy tumbled through the air, landing with a dull thud on the ground.

Peter struggled to his feet. One eye flopped wildly upon his cheek and spittle dripped from his mouth, which now sat askew on his chin. Black ichor poured from his temple down the side of his face.

"Good form, codfish!" Peter gurgled.

John leapt from the crocodile toward Peter Pan.

Peter exploded across the sky toward John Henry.

A sliver of sunlight cut through the dense treetop and touched Peter's neck.

The boy recoiled from the light, screaming in agony as a puff of smoke rose from his charred flesh.

"Uh-oh," Peter said with a twisted smile. "The sun's coming up. I'll have to kill you later, codfish."

John landed on the ground far below, leaving deep footprints in the soil. He perused his surroundings. The Lost Boys lay unconscious and Peter was gone.

Simi sprinted from his hiding place and continued to run deep into the forest.

A rhythmic popping sound—like someone clapping their hands —came from behind John.

He spun toward the sound, hurling a hammer with a powerful wave of his arm. The hammer shot toward a petite silhouette near an old, oak tree.

The silhouette exploded upward, evading the hammer.

The hammer struck the tree, impaling it. The hammer's haft protruded from the tree's thick trunk.

The silhouette landed—without making a sound—inches from the ebon giant.

Standing before him, illuminated by the light of his raised hammer, was a familiar face.

"M-Moses?" John gasped.

The aged woman smiled. "Got a job for you, John Henry."

"Anything for *you*, Ms. Tubman." John said.

"A boy, who go by the name o' Holmes, is chasin' a monster he call the Ripper," Harriet said. "He done hired me to recruit some help; help that the Lawd done blessed with special...gifts. An old friend told me 'bout you."

"'Bout me?" John asked.

Harriet shook her head and chuckled. "She told me you'd say that. You in?"

"I'm in," John replied.

"Then, grab that hammer, John Henry," Harriet said, pointing toward the old oak. "We got some huntin' to do."